The Last Crusade of the Templars

by Lefki Sarantinou

TRANSLATED BY
Villy Meachim
edited by
Leonard G. Meachim

Erebus Society

Erebus Society

First published in Greece in 2012

Published in Great Britain in 2025
Erebus Society

First English Edition

Copyright © Lefki Sarantinou 2025
Book Design Copyright © Erebus Society 2025
Cover Copyright © Ars Corvinus 2025

ISBN: 978-1-912461-78-3

www.ErebusSociety.com

Table of Contens

1 - Templar Commandery Coulommiers, Ile-de-France February 15, 1271 1
2 - Krak des Chevaliers, Syria, February 23, 1271 8
3 - Templar Commandery Coulommiers, Ile-de-France, March 2, 1271 13
4 - Krak des Chevaliers, Syria,March 3, 1271 19
5 - Benedictine Monastery, Soumpiako, March 12, 1271 24
6 - Krak des Chevaliers, March 16, 1271 30
7 - Knights Templar Commandery, Coulommiers, April 15, 1277 39
8 - Hospitaller commandery, Tripoli July 3rd 1277 46
9 - Acre, November 22 1281 55
10 - Hospitaller Commandery, Tripoli, November 22, 1281 66
11 - Alexandria, November 25, 1281 69
12 - Fort Marqab of the Hospitaller knights, May 23, 1285 98
13 - Acre, October 29, 1287 102
14 - Tripoli, February 28 1289 124
15 - Acre, April 30, 1289 139
16 - Acre, August 10, 1290 151
17 - Cairo, November 4, 1290 159
18 - Acre, March 26, 1291 162
19 - Acre, April 5, 1291 170
20 - Acre, May 18, 1291 185
21 - Knights Templar fortress, Isle of Ruad, January 15, 1303 192
22 - Limassol, Cyprus, Templar Headquarters, January 16, 1303 196
23 - Hospitaller Castle Kolossi, Limassol, March 8, 1306 202
24 - Paris, March 18, 1306 206
25 - Poitiers, December 28, 1306 214
26 - Paris, February 18, 1307 219
27 - Poitiers, September 14, 1307 223
28 - Paris, October 11, 1307 226
29 - Paris, October 13, 1307 233
30 - Paris, November 24, 1307 239
31 - Rhodes, February 28, 1308 243
32 - Rhodes, December 28, 1314 247

Historical Notes 252
Endnotes 254

Biography

Lefki (Eleftheria) Sarantinou was born in Rethymno in 1984. She has studied history and music. Today she lives in Komotini and she is engaged in writing, teaching music, history and creative writing and writing book reviews. She has published until now 15 books, including historical novels, collection of short stories, historical books and tales for children, history books and educational books. "The last crusade of the Templars" was the first book she wrote and has been published in Greece in 2012. It is the first volume of her trilogy for Knights and the late Crusades.

1

Templar Commandery Coulommiers, Ile-de-France February 15, 1271

oung Philippe de Ridefort was sitting, in silence, on the simple, wooden bench. A wooden bowl with bread and some cheese lay in front of him, but they remained untouched. Philippe was already too anxious to take even a bite. At last, in a few moments, he would know. Would he be accepted into the order? On the one hand, the hard ascetic life the knights led intimidated him. On the other, the promise he had made to his mother, before she closed her eyes forever, had not left him much choice. Firstly, he had to carry on the family tradition. Two of his uncles had been Knights Templar. One of them, a distant uncle of his, had even served as a Grand Master the previous century. Secondly, he was burning with desire to see his father, his real father, in the Holy Land.

The situation in the Middle East had been very difficult for the Christians since the Mamluk Sultan Baybars[1] had started gaining ground in Frankish territory. The Christians were losing battles and fortresses one after the other. Philippe's father, Jocelyn de Ridefort, had taken part in the crusade that Louis IX, also known as Louis the Saint, had declared in 1248 and which had turned out to be, just as every other crusade in the 13th century had, a fiasco. The Christians were soundly beaten by Baybars in 1250 at al-Mansurah. Of the two hundred and ninety Knights Templar who had taken part in the battle, including Philippe's father, only five had survived. However, not all the knights' corpses had been found and many had been taken prisoner. Philippe hoped that, somehow, his father had survived and that he could, someday and in some way, find him. That is what his instinct told him at least…

At the same time, behind the firmly closed door, anything but unanimity prevailed among the council of knights on the subject of Philippe's admission to the order. The council was made up of the senior knights from each commandery and they, together with the Grand Master, made decisions about the most important issues. If the current Grand Master was not present, the commander of the fortress would chair. Second in command was the seneschal, the steward. His place was important as he managed the land and took care of the commandery accounts and ledgers. He made sure the commandery had the largest possible surplus so that it could be sent to the forts in the Holy Land, which were , in truth, eating up the order's funds. The knights' equipment and the maintenance of the walls were proving to be particularly costly. The seneschal in the Coulommiers commandery was Brother Erich. Third in command was the mareschal, the military commander. Brother Michel served as mareschal here. All the knights were standing around a table. Humbert di Perrault, the commander of the fort, a tall man with a long, white beard and shiny hazel eyes that did not give away his now advanced age, stood in the middle. His head was shaved, as were all the knights' heads, according to the Rule[2] of the order.

Humbert started talking. "Brothers, the time has come for us to decide whether Philippe de Ridefort is to become a member of our order. Most of us have already voted in support of this. He himself longs to become one of us. His age, sixteen years, is the most appropriate one and his identity is known to all, as he is not the first of the de Ridefort family who asks to offer his services to our order. Two of his relatives were members of our brotherhood. One even served as a Lord Master.[3]"

"That is exactly why I am expressing my objections, my lord," said elderly Erich, the seneschal. "Gerard de Ridefort was Lord Master but whether his services were of benefit to the order is questionable."

"I agree with you dear Brother," said another elderly knight, Brother Michel, the mareschal." Gerald succumbed to the sins of arrogance and avarice, which resulted in the tragic events of which we are all aware[4]."

"But it's completely unreasonable to blame a deceased Lord Master for the loss of Jerusalem to Saladin! Could it ever be possible that our Lord Master would wish to allow our sacred city to pass into the hands of the infidels?" argued the youngest of the council, Brother Jean, forcefully.

"I did not say that dear Brother," answered Brother Erich. "Of course no Lord Master wishes to deliberately harm the order or Christendom. But Gerald's behaviour, deliberate or not, together with the behaviour of the overweening Guy de Lusignan and that of the self-serving Raynald, contributed to the loss of our sacred city. If it hadn't been for these men, the peace with Saladin would not have been violated and disaster could have been avoided. Have you forgotten, Brother, who urged Raynald de Chatillon to break the peace?"

"We should not, however, forget what Jocelyn de Ridefort did for the order!" argued Brother Jean again. "He was so brave against the infidels that he was eventually lost in battle and we never found out what became of him! We are not in a position to judge the actions of the past, only God can. In any case, does not the fact that we already have a significant lack in numbers mean that obstacles such as these should not be put in place?"

"Exactly Brother Jean," said Humbert, who was clearly upset by the turn the debate had taken. "Our Brothers who are constantly engaged in battle down there would find our discussions on the topic of the candidate's ancestors completely absurd," he added curtly. "I am of the opinion that we should allow him to prove his worth.

Therefore, apart from the objections about the boy's origin, has anyone anything negative to say about the candidate? I remind you that, according to our Rule, it is better to say something now, whatever that may be, than when de Ridefort is here."

Absolute silence fell in the room. Michel and Erich gave each other a sidelong look, but remained silent.

"Very well then," said the Grand Master, ending the conversation. "Let Brothers Michel and Erich go to the candidate to ask him the preliminary questions, as usual. If everything goes well notify me so that we can go to the chapel for the admission ceremony. You know where to find me." And with those words Humbert left the room.

The chapel was bathed in the half-light of the glow of candles and the reflection of light on the stained glass gave the room a mysterious, almost magical, air. Humbert stood with a chaplain of the order next to the altar. The rest of the knights in the commandery stood in a circle to one side, with Philippe in the middle, on his knees and raised palms together. Everyone was praying for the new member, so that he could, from now on, do God's will and receive divine enlightenment when he made decisions. Humbert took the Book of the four Gospels and gave it to Philippe who, still on his knees, took it and waited.

"Dear Brother," said Humbert, "you previously stated that you will endure all the hardships that your admission to our order entails with faith and love in God and that you will, from now on and as long as you live, be a servant and a slave of our order. You must not, however, seek honour while under the protection of our order. You desire it so that you can leave the sins of this world, be poor and repent during your life on earth, so that the salvation of your soul will come. I shall ask you some questions which you must answer with absolute honesty. If you hide anything or tell lies that may harm the Order there is the chance you may lose everything, God forbid[5]! I therefore expect complete honesty from you. Philippe remained silent as the Brothers had advised him to do before."

"We ask you, therefore, firstly, if you have a wife or fiancée who could demand that you leave the Order according to the law of our Holy Church. Because if you have lied to us and this wife of yours comes to claim you, then we would strip you of your habit, we would make you a servant, we would shame you and put you in irons. And, after you had endured all this, we would give you back to your wife and you would be expelled from the Order. So, dear Brother, have you a wife or fiancée?"

"No, my lord."

"Are you a member of another monastic order? Because if that were the case, after shaming you we would deliver you to the other order and you would be expelled from the Order."

"No, my lord."

"Have you, perhaps, a debt which you aim to pay with the help of the Order? Because your admission to the Order will not protect you from the creditor, to whom we shall deliver you if something like this is proved, without the Order being responsible for this debt."

"No, my lord."

"Are you of sound health? Do you have any physical disabilities? If you lied or concealed anything about your health you would be expelled from the Order, God forbid!"

"No, my lord."

"Have you bribed a Brother or member of the laity in order to enter our order? Because such an action would lead to your expulsion from the Order as punishment, and the Brothers who were bribed would also be punished."

"No, my lord."

"Are you the issue of a family of knights and a legal marriage?"

"Yes, my lord."

"Are you a deacon or sub-deacon? Because you would be expelled from the Order if you concealed something like that from us."

"No, my lord."

"Are you excommunicated?"

"No, my lord."

Humbert then turned to the other brothers. "Are there any other questions from you?"

"No, my lord," they all replied.

"Dear brother, we hope you have answered our questions in all honesty. Even the smallest lie and you will be expelled from the Order, God forbid! Do you, therefore, promise God and the Virgin Mary that, from now on, and for the rest of your life, you will obey the Master or your commander?

"Yes, my lord, God willing."

"Do you also promise God and the Virgin Mary, that you shall, from now on, refrain from all pleasures of the flesh?"

"Yes, my lord, God willing."

"Do you also promise God and the Virgin Mary, that you, from now on, will live in absolute poverty?"

"Yes, my lord, God willing."

"Do you also promise God and the Virgin Mary that you will help, doing everything in your power, to take the Holy City of Jerusalem?"

"Yes, my lord, God willing."

"Do you also promise that you will never abandon our order for as long as you live? Unless of course you are expelled from it because of misconduct, something that no one wishes."

"Yes, my lord, God willing."

"Finally, do you promise God and the Virgin Mary that you will never contribute to the loss of a Christian's life or property unnecessarily?"

"Yes, my lord, God willing."

Then Humbert remained silent and prayed. Philippe felt his heart pound and he shyly looked up from the floor, while he could hear, once again, Humbert's warm voice in his ears:

"We, therefore, through the power of God, the holy Virgin Mary and St. Peter, Bishop of Rome, make you participant in all the benefits conferred upon our order. And you, in turn, make us participant in all the benefits that you have conferred and will confer. We welcome you, therefore, Brother, to our order and we promise you bread, water and clothing, but also a great deal of toil and pain."

Then Humbert took a white robe with a red cross on it that a sergeant[6] handed him and placed it on Philippe's shoulders. The chaplain brother intoned a psalm to welcome the new brother to the order and then they all said the prayer of the Holy Spirit and the Lord's Prayer. Finally, Humbert called upon Philippe to rise and kissed him on the mouth[7]. Philippe's heart then filled with emotion and satisfaction, but, at the same time, his mind was full of doubt that cast a shadow over the joy he felt now that he had finally achieved his goal: "Yes, I am now a monk-knight, as I promised my mother, undoubtedly this is a sacred oath, but have I done the right thing? What awaits me from this time forth?"

***

It was already getting dark and the time for vespers was drawing near when young Philippe, together with the knights, came out of the chapel. Humbert instructed the Keeper of the Wardrobe to attend to the new knight's clothing and equipment for battle. The groom Josephin was also at Philippe's disposal, in charge of his horse's care. Philippe was permitted to keep his favourite horse, Calpurnia, after she was examined right after the ceremony and was considered appropriate for the new life that Philippe would lead as a knight.

"So, dear Brother," said Humbert who was walking next to Philippe, "we should now introduce you to your new life, which is truly hard and austere. Philippe as an individual no longer exists, now there is only Brother Philippe, a member of the Order. The good of the Order is always more important than the good of the individual. There are sins that might cause you to be expelled from the Order or face severe punishment. Firstly, contact with women is prohibited. You shall not embrace your sister or your mother from now on. You must never swear in the name of our Lord Jesus Christ or the Most Holy Virgin, Our Lady. It is forbidden to strike and, of course, kill a Christian. It is forbidden to buy other clothes for yourself; you can only use the ones that we provide you. Cowardice and flight in a battle are severely punished. Silence is a virtue. You should avoid talking a lot and you should never shout or insult anyone."

At that moment, a young knight appeared and addressed Humbert: "My lord, forgive me for interrupting but there is a pressing issue that cannot be left for later. A wagon with wine from our estates is ready to depart for Paris and Brother Accomptant would like you to inspect it before it leaves. I think that you will have just enough time until vespers."

"Alright Brother," Humbert nodded in agreement. "Let me introduce our new knight, Brother Philippe. Brother Francois is our standard-bearer, the person responsible for the grooms that are not members of our order[8]. If we were in the East he would be holding our banner in battle, but we don't have infidels here so we don't have battles either." Then, turning to the knight who had just joined them, he added: "Brother Francois, will you inform our new knight of his monastic duties? I have not had the chance to tell him myself."

"As you order, my lord," Francois responded willingly.

"Brother Philippe, I shall see you at Mass," Humbert said to Philippe while saluting him. "May God shine his light on that which you do."

"Thank you, my lord," replied Philippe, bowing slightly.

As soon as Humbert had left, Francois turned to Philippe. Unlike Philippe, who had brown hair and skin and was of average height, Francois was tall, with fair skin and beard. His face was well-proportioned with bright green eyes that sparkled. "The ideal knight," thought Philippe. "It's a pity he is a Templar. I imagine he was the dream of every lady before he entered the Order."

"Welcome, Brother," said Francois interrupting his thoughts. "I have just enough time to explain the basics. You have much to learn, of course, but this will happen slowly and over time. You can ask older knights about what is prohibited, what is permitted and about the correct behaviour expected of you as a knight. I will briefly enlighten you as to your monastic duties. Don't ever forget that you are also a monk, not only a knight. At two o'clock in the summer and at four in the winter the bell summons us to Matins so we all dress and attend. After that we lie down again until the bell of the first hour[9] summons us, when we silently eat our breakfast and, as we do after every meal, go to the chapel again to pray in thanks for the food. The next services are at the third, sixth and ninth hours[10]. After vespers we have dinner and then it's bedtime. Only chaplains are present at the Service at midnight on Feast Days. You must attend all the Services unless you have urgent military duties or you are sick. You can only be absent if the commander permits it. You must, of course, say thirty Our Fathers if you do not attend the Service. You must fast, unless you are ill, and confessions are only made to chaplains of our order. These are the basics for now. Have I given you a headache Brother?"

"I must say you have a bit, Brother. Have you been serving the Order for long?" Philippe asked, to lighten the conversation a little.

"Three years. I believe that in one or two years they will let me leave for Outremer[11]. It's been my life's dream to go to that world that is so very different from our own! Those who have returned have many great stories to tell about life there."

"So why don't you ask to go, Brother? They are in such need of men there!"

"I suppose you are unaware that the elders of the Order must put your name forward you if you are to be able to go to fight there. That usually requires at least three years here, years during which you have to prove your worth. Only if you are considered worthy can you go. Things in the East are going from bad to worse and the commanders there need young people that have proved themselves, have strong faith and will not deny Christ when they are in captivity for the first time. I have disappointed you, or so it seems." Francois added, seeing the sad expression on Philippe's face.

"It's just that that is my reason for joining the Order, too. To go there. And now you're telling me that this may never happen."

"Do not despair, Brother. Will, effort and good faith and we may be lucky enough to travel down there together," added Francois, to give courage to the young knight who he had begun, in the meantime, to grow fond of.

The sound of the bell for vespers did not leave time for more talk. Philippe was glad that he would be given the chance to relax a little. Francois had made a very good impression on him but after so much tension and so much information given at the same time, the only thing he wanted now was to be alone for a while. This was impossible at that moment but, at least, for as long as vespers went on, no one would address him.

"The bell, we must hurry!" said Francois and he quickened his step at once. At the entrance of the chapel, the two young knights almost bumped into a middle-aged knight. His eyes met those of Philippe and chilled the young man from head to toe. There was something strange about those ice-cold eyes, colder than the deepest sea, as if something was hiding behind that great light blue. He whispered to Francois at once:

"Brother, who is that knight? Has he been here long?"

"Ah, it's Brother Luigi you're talking about," Francois answered, while drawing close to Philippe and placing his hand by his mouth at the same time. We joined the Order at about the same time. I think he is from Lombardy but I don't know why he came to Ile-de-France. He is miserable and lonely but he strictly adheres to the Rule and that is why the elders regard him well. I don't know him well, he is difficult to talk to. Anyway, he is our Brother," said the knight, finishing the conversation and giving a nonchalant shrug of his shoulders. The knights made themselves comfortable on the wooden pews and put their hands together in prayer.

Warrior monks did not attend services standing, as did ordinary monks, in order to save their energy for their military operations. Humbert, who entered in a hurry, sat in front of them. All the sergeants who were not performing any tasks sat behind them. Even like this, there were three times as many of them as the knights and, unlike them, their robe was black – but it did have the distinctive red cross embroidered on it, just as the knights' white robe did. Despite the crowd that had gathered, there was absolute silence in the chapel, which was broken by the chaplain's voice. The vespers began and reverent piety filled all those present.

2

Krak des Chevaliers, Syria, February 23, 1271

he Krak of the Knights of Saint John, otherwise known as the Knights Hospitaller, stood on a tall rock, in the middle of the Syrian Desert and, at first sight, looked impregnable. Called by the Arabs "Hisn al Akrad", which means Castle of the Kurds, it had been built by the emir Homs in 1031. In 1110 it came into the hands of Tancred, Prince of Galilee, and since 1042 it had belonged to the order of the Knights of Saint John. Raymond, the Count of Tripoli, donated it to the order so that he could help them in their task of protecting Frankish settlements in Outremer. This was, however, but one of their duties – as the Knights never forgot the original purpose for their formation – the establishment, that is to say, of hospitals for the care of pilgrims, which was why they were called Hospitallers. Since it had come into their hands, the strong walls of the fortress had withstood many earthquakes, as well as the unfortunate siege of Saladin in 1188.

That morning there was turmoil in the fort. There were rumours that Sultan Baybars would soon come with the intention of achieving what Saladin had failed to do. The knights were saving as many supplies as they could find and were preparing for the forthcoming siege. Two young Aragonese sergeants were patrolling the walls.[12] They were among the few Spanish people in Outremer. The majority of knights and settlers were French. Both appeared to be seriously worried. The younger, Jose, asked the other, Thomas:

"Are you afraid Brother?"

"I admit that I am, Brother, although I shouldn't be telling you this. Baybars has been unstoppable. I think that there are far too few of us to carry this off."

"Since we are expecting reinforcements why are you worried? I've heard that the Lord Master himself is coming! Doesn't that make you feel a little better?"

Thomas stopped walking and, after looking Jose straight in the eye, looked at the sky: "Let's wait until he comes first…because we've been waiting for him for days, but all we see is vultures!" he said, pointing above their heads. "Horrible birds! It's as if they know that there is going to be a massacre here and they are waiting to eat our corpses!"

Jose involuntarily shivered, although he was certain that Thomas was being overly pessimistic. "Aren't you exaggerating a bit?" He asked Thomas, leaning on his shield. "Look at the walls! The fortress is truly impregnable. Saladin himself was defeated here!"

Thomas made a negative gesture with his hand: "You weren't in Antioch three years ago. That's why you say this! Newcomers here think everything is easy. They believe that the Infidels will be defeated at once. In Antioch the walls were stronger than these and there were more of us, but still too few for the defence of such a huge city. There are never enough of us. What was the result? Terrible slaughter and thousands taken prisoner! Baybars does not possess the nobility of Saladin. He is incredibly cruel and will not rest until he drives us all away from here. As soon as he seized Antioch he closed the gates so that no one could leave! So many prisoners were taken that, because the supply was so great, the price of a boy in the slave markets of the East dropped to twelve dirham and that of a girl to five dirham! Can you imagine that? And you talk about reinforcements."

Jose unconsciously bit his lower lips and started walking again at a fast pace, trying, in vain, to stop the dark thoughts that were swirling around in his head. He couldn't find anything to say. Next to him Thomas was also walking despondently. They reached the corner of the fortress. Jose then thought he heard something. It sounded like the hoof-beat of horses. He lifted his eyes from the ground and then saw them: about a hundred horsemen quickly approaching the fortress. Some infantry were following behind. Thomas also lifted his eyes from the ground. They looked at each other anxiously. They could make out a banner but the horsemen were still far away. Was it a Christian banner or was it the banner of the 'Infidels'?

"Yes, they are ours! They have come!" Jose shouted as soon as he saw the Christian banner and the armour glinting in the sun. Instantly forgetting the conversation that he had had with Thomas, his optimism returned and he began to ring the bell on the walls like a madman to signal the arrival of the reinforcements.

Straight away a tall well-built man came up onto the walls and stood beside them. He was the commander of Krak, Guillaume de Boulon. He shaded his eyes with his hand and, after he had observed the horsemen, who had now been very close to the walls for some time, said in a deep voice: "We must all assemble to welcome them. The Lord Master has come too, after all. Brother Jose, ring the bell to signal assembly. Everyone, knights and sergeants, in the forecourt now! Open the gates!"

The commander then left hurriedly to put on his armour to welcome the new arrivals. Before they came down from the walls, Jose took one last look at the troops that were drawing near. They weren't as many as he had hoped for but they were reinforcements at least. With God's help they would drive the 'Infidels' away…

****

The war council that had been convened as soon as the Grand Master had arrived with reinforcements was over. Guillaume de Boulon had officially handed over command of the fortress to his superior, Hugo de Revel, Grand Master of the order since 1258. The knights that had just arrived had been given some time before dinner to put the few possessions they had with them in order.

Foulques de Villaret, having settled in, was in the stables, stroking his horse, while the groom was combing the horse's glossy, pitch black hair.

"Is everything all right my dear?" he whispered looking into her big, watery eyes. "The long journey is finally over! Now you have time to rest until the worst begins!"

Foulques was one of the many promising young members of the order. He had reached the East accompanying his uncle, the mareschal Guillaume de Villaret, and - and this was something very rare – only having served the order for just one year. In France, straight after his admission to the order, he had served as an accountant due to his excellent skills in reading and writings. His behaviour had been impeccable and whenever he had accompanied carts with documents or supplies and had chanced upon robbers, he had forced them to flee with his bravery and his fighting skills. Apart from all this, something else that had played a role in his early departure for the East was his knowledge of the Arabic language, something very rare among the Franks. His uncle had, of course, played his part too. So, despite his youth, at the age of only fifteen, Foulques had found himself in the Holy Land.

"I hope, Lightning, that you get used to the battles here quickly. They are completely different from those we fought at home," Foulques went on talking to the horse, unaware that his uncle was coming up behind him, smiling.

Guillaume was a stocky man with dark skin and rugged features. His beard had just started turning grey, making a strong contrast with his big jet-black eyes. His tough looks were softened somewhat by his broad, bright smile.

"So, young man, what are your first impressions?" said Guillaume, patting Foulques affectionately on the back.

"Oh, uncle, I hadn't realized you were here," said Foulques, turning towards him in surprise.

"How could you have?" said Guillaume, nodding to the groom to leave. "When you are with your Lightning, no one else exists!" He continued, teasing him. "Everyone loves their horses but you…"

"Well, uncle, we have been inseparable for five years! Since these are the only contacts allowed with women, let's say that she is the woman of my life!"

Then, growing suddenly serious and, changing the subject, Foulques left the horse and asked his uncle: "Uncle, you have been here before and taken part in other battles. How do you see things? I see that everybody here at the fort is somewhat pessimistic, not just about the impending siege but about all our possessions in the East in general."

After sighing deeply Guillaume answered his nephew: "My nephew, if we were united everything would be easier. If at some time you go to Acre or to Tripoli, which are cities, you will see that the balance between peace and war is very unsteady. The Italians are constantly quarrelling among themselves about who will get more out of the trade with the Infidels. Peace is good for trade and our revenue here, which is always limited; on the other hand, can we make peace with the Infidels?"

"Of course not! Italians are greedy, the Venetians even ignore the Church. They only make things difficult for us when we are at war!"

"Don't jump to conclusions, nephew," said Guillaume, wagging the index finger of his right hand. "Yes, they are greedy and they are not always loyal allies – but we need their ships and the duties they pay from the trade with Muslims. You will understand this after you have been here for a while. Then, there is the struggle for the throne. You know that, sadly, King Louis died during the crusade last year and, since then, his brother, Charles d' Anjou, has been laying claim to the throne of Acre and is in dispute with Henry of Cyprus.[13] And we, the orders, do anything but contribute to harmony between us!"

"What do you mean uncle?" Foulques burst out, turning red from head to toe and waving his arms about. "And what are we supposed to do? Let these arrogant Knights Templar control everything around here? Those greedy so-and-so's?"

"We've all made our mistakes, nephew, during our long stay here, both we ourselves and the Knights Templar," Guillaume replied softly, making calming gestures towards his nephew. "And the biggest mistake of all is our internal disputes, which give the Infidels the opportunity to beat us. Two orders which were established for the good of Christianity should not quarrel all the time. Because you are young, you see things this way - but it's not right! I don't blame you, before I came here, I too thought in the same way. But, believe me, I've seen so many strange things these seven years I've spent here, that my opinion has changed when it comes to many matters. However, it is not bad to be passionate. It's just that, as one matures, prudence and wisdom come too."

Suddenly, a strong wind blew up. The dust of the desert went into Foulques's eyes. "Damn!" he complained, rubbing them and coughing. "What wind is this!"

"I don't think it will stop soon," said Guillaume dusting off his robe. "There's no wind like this in our country. It's a Hamsin, a southern, humid wind, full of dust. The dust and humidity are not good for the lungs but you will get used to it." At that moment, the bell sounded, calling the Brothers to the refectory.

"Let's go, nephew," said Guillaume. "I know that our Rule counsels abstinence but since it's not a fasting Sunday, and you are in the East, enjoy the Eastern dishes for as long as you can!"

The two knights started walking quickly towards the refectory, the wind causing them to stumble and showing no signs of abating. Brothers, sergeants and servants all gathered in the large Gothic dining hall. It was so majestic and with such a high ceiling that on entering it Foulques could not help opening his mouth wide in astonishment. Such detail and elegance did not exist in western fortresses.

They all sat on the stools at the great wooden tables in order and in silence. Foulques sat next to his uncle. The Grand Master made the sign of the cross, blessing the bread before he started to share it out. "God bless our bread and our wine today," he said, and sat down.

A sergeant was sitting on the floor and had a wooden bowl in front of him. He had been punished and so would eat on the floor. This was a very common punishment in monastic-military orders, which lasted from a few days to a month, depending on the offence. The warrior monks' diet included meat more often than that of other monks as they needed to have strength and stamina for the constant war with 'the Infidel'. There wasn't a great deal of food but it was delicious, and a new experience for Foulques and those who had just arrived from the West. This was because of the many spices that Arab cuisine used. Despite trade, Europe never had such large quantities of spices that they could be used in such quantities. The servants served lamb with white and black pepper, cardamom and cumin, accompanied by vegetables. It was drizzled with lemon juice, something unknown in Europe at the time. Even the wine had had herbs added to it. Hugh raised his glass. Next to him sat Guillaume de Boulon.

"I officially salute our Brothers here. May God give us strength for the difficult days to come," proposed Hugh in his toast and everyone raised their glasses and drank in response. Every one of their faces grew grim at the Grand Master's words. A melancholic silence again filled the room ...

3

Templar Commandery Coulommiers, Ile-de-France, March 2, 1271

hilippe pulled hard on Calpurnia's reins and dismounted. Then the commandery opened and the cart that he was accompanying entered the fort. It was wine from the Knights Templar's estates, and, after the bottles had been checked and counted, it would once again leave, to be sold in the nearest town.

"Is everything in order, Brother?" The seneschal, Brother Erich, who had just appeared to check the cart, asked Philippe. "Anything unexpected on the way?"

"The usual, Brother. One or two appeared and tried to challenge me, but I did not need to fight. As soon as I pulled out my sword they ran like rabbits."

"Yes, yes! Brother Philippe is great, seneschal," the driver agreed, getting off the cart.

It was a sunny day, something quite rare in Provence, especially at the beginning of March. Philippe stroked Calpurnia and looked up at the sky, pondering the last two weeks of his life. He had become a knight but his life was a little monotonous. From the time he had been a young boy, he had been very skilled in the use of the sword very well, but here he had not had many opportunities to show it. His everyday life in France was more that of a monk than that of a knight and he spent most of his time in church services and on various errands. "And according to Francois I have many days like these ahead of me," he thought, shaking his head.

During the two weeks that had followed Philippe's admission to the order, he and Philippe had grown very close. Philippe had realized that he enjoyed the company of this handsome and likeable knight a great deal. They had set a common goal: to provide others with as few opportunities for criticism as possible and to show good conduct so that they could leave for the Holy Land as soon as possible. Trying to behave impeccably in an environment with so many prohibitions and close supervision is something extremely hard. Up until that moment, however, they had not done badly.

"Hey, Brother, wake up! Go and take off your armour. Right after Mass on Tuesday we have our weekly meeting," said Erich to Philippe, looking at him disapprovingly while counting the bottles.

"I'll go immediately, seneschal. I was lost in thought for a moment. Are you sure you don't need help to put the bottles back in the cart?"

"No, Brother, thank you. The commander has to check them anyway. This is an errand for those who have been punished so the Brother who helped me unload will also help me now. You can rest until Mass," Erich replied, looking at him inquisitively. "That boy is strange", he thought. "While there's nothing about him you can complain about, and he always does what's expected of him, he often seems to be daydreaming. It's as if something were on his mind…"

Philippe groaned slightly and headed towards the dormitory. He, as well as most of the knights without a rank, feared these meetings, as did the sergeants. Once a week knights and sergeants would lock themselves in the council chamber and each one would confess their misdeeds and ask for forgiveness. Baseless accusations were often made, but it took little for the commander to impose the corresponding punishment. Without these assemblies the enforcement of the very strict rule of the order could not be ensured. Secrecy was very important so that the servants and the people who worked for the Knights Templar would not learn of their misdeeds. Philippe headed straight towards his dormitory. He then took off his armour with the help of two servants, and put on one of the two pairs of breeches and shirts that he had and his winter robe with its lambswool lining on top of them. Then he sat on his mattress. He had some time to rest until the service and he was alone in the dormitory. Both were very rare events. So he let himself sink into his memories and enjoy his solitude…

***

A cold winter's night ten years before in Philippe's parents' house, and Philippe was only six years old, still a child. Philippe's father, Jacques, was on a trip to the north, to check on their estates. Despite the rain and the strong wind, Philippe's two older sisters had been asleep for some time. Philippe, on the other hand, could not sleep. He decided to get out of bed. He headed for the kitchen. If he was lucky he might find the cook awake and she could make him a hot drink. Then he might be able to sleep more easily. As he was crossing the dark corridor, however, he saw light coming through the half open door of his mother's room. "Maybe she's fallen asleep with the candle lit?" he thought. "If that's the case maybe I should blow it out so that we don't start a fire." His hand was ready to push the door that was half open, but he stopped it still in mid-air. He heard a man's voice coming from the room:

"My love, you're going to drive me crazy with the things you do! Come here!"

Philippe hovered. He allowed his hand to drop and stepped back. "That voice. Maybe Father's back? But that voice sounds like…"

Then he heard loud laughter – Margaret's, Philippe's mother's laughter. "I can't get enough of you! I love you!" Philippe heard the man's voice again and now he was certain – that voice was Jocelyn's, Philippe's father's brother…

Philippe bent down to look through the opening in the door and saw two silhouettes embracing in the half-light. "My uncle with my mother? It can't be!" he thought, bringing his hand to his mouth so he wouldn't yell out in surprise.

"I love you too, my sweet, but where will all this lead us?" said Philippe's mother, sounding very serious all of a sudden. I shiver only to think of what would happen if your brother caught us. Imagine if he knew that his only son is not even his child but yours... God would punish us hard for sinning in this way."

It was as if lightning had struck Philippe. He was Jocelyn's child? A bastard in other words? If his father knew he would certainly divorce his mother and disinherit him! Jacques was a sullen and cruel man, always distant from his children. He was always away working, while the few times he was with his family, he never tired of issuing reprimands and criticism to the boy and his sisters. His uncle, however, was so cheerful! Exactly the opposite of his brother! How many things he had taught Philippe and how much Philippe loved him! That was why he had always liked Philippe better! His uncle had not yet married, despite his brother's exhortations. Jocelyn's voice interrupted Philippe's thoughts, who had squeezed up against the wooden wall so as to remain unnoticed.

"I know, Margaret, I too feel guilty towards my brother," Jocelyn said, sighing. "I have, therefore, made a decision. Are you ready to hear it?"

"You are frightening me, my sweet!" Philippe's mother said, worried. "What is it about?"

"Margaret, you know I adore you. You are the best thing that has ever happened to me. But I am a man, responsible and accountable to God. To redeem myself I have decided to enter the Order of the Knights Templar. I think it is the only solution. I have no wish to marry another woman while my heart belongs to you. But in this way I won't leave anything to my son, whatever I have will go to the Order."

A few minutes of silence followed. Evidently Margaret was trying to digest this unexpected news.

"To the Temple then…" she finally said, in a voice that could barely be heard. "Don't worry about Philippe's property. My son has property from his legal father, which Jacques will leave to him if he finds out nothing. It is hard but you have made the right decision. If we were found out the consequences would be disastrous for all of us."

"I agree. It is precisely because I love our son that I don't want to put him at risk of losing everything and growing up with the stigma of being illegitimate."

"You will come and see us, won't you?" Margaret interrupted him, her voice breaking and the first tears that she could no longer hold back flowing from her eyes. "Let this goodbye be only that of two lovers, at least..." she said hiding her face in her hands. This man was her only solace in the life of misery she led with Jacques, who her family had forced her to marry, and she truly loved him.

"Of course I will come, as often as I'm permitted to do so. Don't cry my love.." Jocelyn hugged her and their passion carried them away for one last time.. Philippe went back to bed, on tiptoe, ignoring the groans and sighs that were getting stronger and stronger behind the slightly opened door. He had heard and he had seen enough to keep him awake the rest of the night! Deep down inside he was glad he had this man that he so much admired for a father and for whom had feelings, unlike his legal father who always seemed to him as if he were made of stone, never having touched him. Talking to anyone about this was, of course, out of the question. He wouldn't even tell his mother that he knew. It would no doubt cause her shame and discomfort, so what reason was there to do so? So let there be a third person to share their secret, without them knowing.

And with those thoughts he sweetly fell asleep in the arms of Morpheus, as outside the sun had started to rise.

***

So that's how it had happened. And the fact that Philippe was now a Knight Templar was also because of that night. When his real father would visit, after he had entered the order, he would tell them war stories and events in the life of the Knights Templar that made Philippe want to become a knight himself one day... He wanted to be close to his real father. His legal father, of course, would hear nothing of the sort. His only son and heir to his fortune becoming a Knight Templar and his fortune a gift to the order? The salvation of the soul and the remission of sins were fine but someone needed to carry on the line. Those had been Jacques' thoughts on the matter and that is why Philippe had not done anything until his father had suddenly died from a heart attack. His sisters had married, taking their share of their father's fortune and, as if by design – to take away all of his responsibilities in the world - God had also taken his mother away. She, without revealing the truth to him, aware, however, of her son's desire to become a knight, made him swear to her that he would look for his "uncle" who, leaving for the East, had never returned. Philippe, without revealing all he knew so as not to cause her any discomfort in her last moments, had sworn this to her. And he was certain that his mother had died from a broken heart, not of course at the loss of her legal husband, but from her distress at the fate of the man she loved, so suddenly lost to her in foreign lands.

A gentle knock on the door interrupted his thoughts. Francois appeared at the entrance to the room. "Here you are! I've been looking everywhere. Anything unexpected on the trip?"

"No, same as always. You?"

"I'm thinking of my sins so I can confess to them now!" said the golden-haired knight happily. "Shall we?"

"Let's go!" replied Philippe and followed Francois to the church.

***

"My Brothers, rise and pray to our Lord Jesus Christ and to the Holy Spirit to send us God's Divine Grace and help us make the right judgments." Those were the words with which Humbert di Perrault opened the meeting of the Council. After they had all said the Pater Noster they sat on their stools. With a nod from Humbert, the first knight on the right stood up, saluted the commander and, after several genuflections, remained on his knees and, with his eyes on the floor, started to talk. He was a young sergeant, impressively tall and well-built.

"My Lord," he began, I ask for mercy from God and the Virgin Mary, and from you and the Brothers, for swearing at Brother Erich and becoming very angry with him because I thought that he was giving me too many chores in comparison to the other Brothers. I ask for your forgiveness and grace, thank you."

"Is this all you have to confess, Brother? Is there something you might have forgotten?" Humbert asked the Brother.

"Only this, my Lord."

"Very well, now you may leave." With these words the Brother stood up and left the room, closing it again behind him. Then, Humbert said: "Well, Brothers, you heard the misdoings that Brother George has committed. His behaviour has been impeccable until now, so I suggest two days of simple punishment.[14] I would like to hear your opinions too, starting with you Brother Erich, as your name was mentioned by Brother George."

"Perhaps Brother George was right. Maybe I wasn't completely fair in the sharing out of chores and, when the time comes, I shall include it in my misdoings. So I agree with you, my Lord," Erich said, obviously sorry for his behaviour towards George. Then everyone spoke, starting with the eldest. Most of them agreed with this punishment, some wanted a lighter one as everyone liked Brother George. However, the punishment was decided by the majority. So when Brother George was called in Humbert announced:

"Your mistakes, Brother, are not very serious ones. This doesn't mean, of course, that you should repeat them. You are to be given, therefore, two days of simple punishment. Ask for forgiveness and we will move on."

After that the assembly continued smoothly, without any accusations from one Brother to another. Brother Luigi, with those cold blue eyes, did not accuse anyone this time, as he usually did. Of course, he always accused himself too and even more severely than he accused others, which was why the elderly Knights Templar respected him as "The guardian of justice and discipline in the Order".

Francois and Philippe were sentenced to extra prayers and Lord's Prayers because their minds had wandered during Mass and were pleased to have come out of another meeting virtually unscathed. It was not uncommon for someone to be unjustly accused due to a personal dislike and then it was difficult for a Brother to prove his innocence.

When the assembly was over, Brother Luigi approached Humbert and said: "My Lord, I humbly ask for your permission to leave for some weeks. I have received notice that my father is dying and I would like to get to him in time to say goodbye. I swear to God and the Virgin Mary that, during my absence, I will not drink and I will be consistent with my prayers. I would like my absence to be shorter but the journey to Lombardy,[15] which is, as you know, where I come from, is a long one."

"All right, Brother, you have my permission to leave – even today – since it is an emergency. Just promise me that you will be as quick as you can. You know that Brothers are rarely away for so long but because of the long distance and your excellent behaviour, we allow you this," replied Humbert, signalling with a gesture that the conversation was over. After all, Brother Luigi was very conscientious and Humbert had plenty of other things to think about.

Thus, he failed to notice the gleam of triumph in Luigi's eyes when he got permission to leave. Philippe was the only one to see this, standing nearby and thinking: "He is a strange man, that's true. I don't know why but something tells me to stay away from him. I have the feeling that he is hiding something."

And with these thoughts he ran behind Francois who was walking with the other Knights Templar towards the Church.

4

Krak des Chevaliers, Syria, March 3, 1271

here was great agitation in the fortress. The bells were ringing like crazy and everyone was running up and down in panic. Sultan Baybars had just appeared under the walls with a large army. He hadn't wasted any time. The 'infidels' immediately began erecting the huge siege engines they had brought with them. An emergency war council was called immediately by the knights in the big Gothic dining room. Foulques was also present, and of course, his uncle who, as mareschal, was second in command after the Grand Master, since the fortress was being besieged.

"Al-Mansur of Hama is with them," noted Pierre de Moulin, the seneschal.

This knight, who Foulques, but also all those who had just arrived, liked immensely, was relatively young for such an office. However, he carried out his duties with great success.

"It was natural that the Emir of Hama would follow Baybars," said Guillaume de Villaret. "What worries and surprises me, however, is that Hashashin[16] have also come. I did not expect that Baybars would have achieved such unity that even heretics would follow him!"

"That should be no surprise to you Brother, but, because of your absence from the East, you have an excuse for being ignorant of the facts," said the Grand Master, Hugh of Revel, unfolding a map of the fortress. "I must, therefore, inform the newcomers that the Masyaf fortress of the Hashasin of Syria was invaded by Baybars last year, so the survivors apparently had no other choice but to follow Baybars on his campaign. The truth is that since Hassan-i-Sabbah[17] died, the Hashasin of Syria have lost their vitality and we have lost a counterbalance in power to the Sunni. You all know that, in the past, not only ourselves but also the Knights Templar to a greater extent, were allies with the Hashasin. However, now, the unification of the Muslim world by Baybars causes us new problems. The more divided the Infidels were, the weaker our enemies. So, for the present, do not expect an ally other than those who share our Faith."

At that moment, a flash of lightning rent the sky. A loud rumble followed.

"Can you hear that? We are lucky! For the time being, the weather is on our side. As long as it rains they will not be able to set up their siege engines," said Hugh.

All this time Foulques listened, thoughtfully. Finally, with an evident anxiety about the answer he would get, he finally got up the courage to ask the question: "I'm sorry to interrupt my Lord but could you tell us which sector of defence each of us will be in charge of?"

"Your first battle, eh?" a middle-aged knight asked him, with a smile.

Foulques's uncle answered in Foulques's place: "The truth is that he has never taken part in a battle like this but he is a fast learner and very brave. That is why," he added, turning to Hugh," I ask you to place him on the walls, next to me."

"Of course, Brother," answered the Grand Master. "He will be a valuable replacement while you are supervising the other sectors too, as the supreme military commander. Therefore I assign to you the defence of the southern ramparts. Brother Pierre and myself will be on the eastern walls, opposite Baybar's tent.

Then, turning to the Spaniards, who hadn't taken part in the conversation, he said:"You, the Spaniards, since there are few of you, will be assigned the defence of the northern sector, which is thought to be the least dangerous, under the leadership of Guillaume de Boulogne. The rocks are very steep and sharp from that side. When the other sectors need backup you will offer it." Finally, he said, turning to the middle-aged knight who had spoken before: " You, Brother Geoffroy will be in charge of the western sector. Our forces will thus be deployed so that the strongest defence is in the southern and the eastern sectors, which are the most dangerous. Our stores are, thank God, full, we have enough water and our hospital is ready. May God's grace give us the power to beat the Infidel. The council is finished for the time being so everybody take your positions."

***

A little while later, in the driving rain and thunder, knights, sergeants and servants were all at their posts. The last of these would give the combatants water and ammunition. In the southern sector, Guillaume de Villaret, soaked to the bone, was observing the enemy's positions. The 'Infidels' were, with difficulty, collecting huge rocks so that they could launch them against the walls with their catapults when the rain had stopped. Occasionally the ropes with which they were holding them would slip through their hands and then the rock would crush some poor slave who did not have the time to run away. There were also Christians among those slaves, who had been captured in other exchanges with the enemy. Foulques was also looking at them with sorrow. Guillaume, who understood his nephew's feelings, placed his hand on his nephew's shoulder and shook his head. "Nephew, you haven't seen anything yet. You should hear how they scream when we throw boiling water and pitch on them."

Foulques sneezed loudly and turned to his uncle: "I'm prepared for the worst uncle. I'm just thinking of those of us who have been taken prisoner. I wish we could set them free."

"However much ransom we give, we will never free them all. There is no point, my boy. You should always remember that, always, whatever happens in battle, it is better to die than to be caught and become a prisoner. You see how we treat their men that are our prisoners."

He wiped the water off his face and went on. "It's good we don't have civilians. They are usually only mouths that need to be fed and a source of uncontrollable panic."

He turned to the sky lit up by the lightening and continued. "This rain is truly a blessing. I don't see it stopping for the time being. Should it abate, however, they will probably attack us. See them? They are positioned for attack. They do not have much chance of success, and they know this, but they want to test their powers. The Sultan is cunning. With one attack, even if unsuccessful, he hopes to find our weak spot. He knows there are few of us."

Foulques did not reply. He was quite anxious. However, Guillaume was right. After many excruciating hours of waiting and endless prayers, sometime in the afternoon, the rain grew less. Then the attack began. In hordes, the 'infidels' rushed shouting towards the walls on every side of the fortress, and they began to climb the slope and the slippery stones. They were holding swords in their hands and wearing a kind of metal armour, too. But it was much smaller and lighter than the armour of the Franks. Some were also holding ladders that they hoped to place on the walls so that they could climb more easily.

Foulques, after recovering from the initial surprise, started to furiously hurl onto them the rocks that the servants had gathered onto the walls in the previous days. Next to him everyone was doing the same and some were pouring down boiling water. Foulques could not see the heads he was crushing, he could only hear the cries of the Muslims in pain and his uncle continuously shouting orders. The rain continued as drizzle but it was enough to make it even more difficult for the Muslims, who were slipping on the stones, to climb. "Careful! Take cover quickly, all of you!" They heard Guillaume's voice, tinged with a hint of fear.

Foulques raised his eyes to the sky and saw countless arrows coming towards them. He barely managed to stick, like a leech, to the wall so that he could take cover as much as he could. A sergeant next to him was not as lucky. An arrow pierced his neck and his hot blood gushed everywhere. The poor sergeant died after crying out and falling backwards. His eyes remained wide open, looking at the sky, full of fear and his blood kept running at Foulques's feet. "Have a nice journey, my friend," thought Foulques, knowing full well that he could just as easily be in his place. After this necessary pause, Foulques continued to throw rocks. The 'infidels' hadn't managed to place, not even for a short while, the ladders that they could use to scale the walls anywhere on the castle up until now. The Krak was built on such a steep slope that the knights feared the underground tunnels that the enemy might build more than an invasion from the walls. It was, however, too early to worry about tunnels.

Despite their failures and losses, the wave of those attacking did not seem to lose its momentum and new forces kept arriving at the walls. Then, suddenly, the rain got stronger and began to pour down. Foulques could not see anything. "At least they won't be able to fire any more arrows at us," he thought.

It had started to get dark and because of the rain the darkness fell faster. The rain was so strong and so loud that the battle had practically stopped, since neither those attacking the castle could see so as to climb its walls, nor could those defending take aim at them. That's when the sound of the trumpet signalling retreat was heard from the Muslim camp. Cries of joy and thanks to God were heard everywhere on the fortress. God had given victory to the Christians in this first battle. Everything seemed to be on their side until now.

Guillaume placed his hand on his nephew's shoulder. He looked exhausted. His face was covered in mud. Blood flowed from a narrow cut to his forehead, but there was no serious injury. Foulques smiled at him, tired: "So, uncle," he said, "we taught them a lesson, didn't we?"

"Yes, nephew, well done! That was fine for your first time. We should not rest, though. If it hadn't been for the rain we would have found it much more difficult to keep them back."

The sound of sobbing made them turn around. A young sergeant was crying loudly over the corpse of one of his Brothers who had been killed by an arrow to his chest. But there was quite a lot of blood running from the young man's shoulder too and Guillaume saw the tip of an arrow protruding. He went up to him, closed the eyes of the dead man and, in a compassionate voice said to the young sergeant: "Go to the hospital boy, this arrow needs to be taken out. Be brave, these things are part of life. Well done for being able to stand the pain of such a serious injury, though. May God protect you."

"Thank you sir," the sergeant replied in a failing voice, wiping his face with his good arm at the same time. He then set off for the hospital. At the same time, the Grand Master was climbing the walls. He met the injured sergeant and ordered him to go straight to the hospital after congratulating him on his bravery. Foulques watched sadly as the sergeant walked away. He felt sympathy for him. He knew what it was like to lose a friend. He too had lost a friend when he was little, Armand, who had been killed falling from his horse. Foulques had not found such a close friend since.

The rain had turned into a drizzle. Fog had started to fall and was making visibility difficult again. The Grand Master addressed Guillaume. He too was dirty and covered in dust, as were all the defenders of the fortress. "Everything went as planned, mareschal. Do you have any dead and injured in your sector?"

"One dead," answered Foulques softly, pointing at the corpse of the sergeant, and only one injured, my Lord. The rain helped us a great deal by limiting the flight of arrows. Do you have any dead elsewhere?"

"One more," said Hugh, looking at the unfortunate sergeant who was lying on the ground. "And three were injured, including your man, fortunately not seriously. The Infidels certainly suffered greater losses but they can cover them more easily – there are many of them, you see. God's grace gave us victory but we must regroup and plan what we are going to do when the storm passes. As we saw today, there are few of us against the Infidels. We do, however, have a strong fortress but we always fear the possible undermining of the walls. For the time being, and luckily for us, the weather is showing no signs of improvement."

Listening to them, Foulques sighed. Really, what were they going to do when the weather got better?

5

Benedictine Monastery, Soumpiako, March 12, 1271

rother Luigi was galloping fast along the narrow dirt road. Around him nature had started waking up from its winter's sleep. Greenery covered the surrounding hills and lilies were timidly growing at the side of the road. It was almost noon and all nature was celebrating this generous sunshine. "Oh, my home land, how much I've missed you!" Luigi thought taking a deep breath of the Mediterranean air! "Here it is even prettier than my birth place, Lombardy. Such nature!"

Luigi had, in fact, gone down to central Italy, going past Lombardy, which he had told the commander he would visit. Near to this small town, around 494, Saint Benedict had lived as a monk in a cave called Sacro Speco, or "Holy Cave" and had founded twelve monasteries. Luigi was a member of one of them.

Without him realizing it, the heavy oak door of the monastery appeared in front of him. Luigi got off his horse and knocked hard on the door. Almost at once, the small window at the top of it opened and two dark brown eyes stared out at the visitor.

"Brother Luigi is that you? I'm so glad to see you again!" said the monk to whom the brown eyes belonged, while opening the door wide.

"I'm glad too Brother" said Luigi, hugging him. "So, tell me your news. How are things here?"

"I should assume that you have all the news. Everything here is as you left it. Our abbot is perfectly healthy and we haven't had any new candidates during the time that you were away. Have you obtained any interesting information?" the monk asked in interest, locking the door and walking next to Luigi through the narrow stone tunnel entrance.

"Brother Mario, I'm afraid I haven't managed to get any useful information from the Knights Templar," Luigi, quietly replied, with obvious disappointment on his face. "The rooms that are of interest to us are guarded well, and, despite the fact that I have won their full trust, I found no way to gain access to them."

"I'm afraid that our abbot won't be very happy," answered Mario, shaking his head in disappointment and looking intently at Luigi. "He hoped that you would have found out something and will be bitterly disappointed. Would you like to rest or shall I present you to him straight away?"

"Straight away. Whatever happens, let it be now," said Luigi, feeling nervous about the upcoming meeting and the strict abbot getting angry. "I shall rest later. I can't stay here for many days. I have to be back in Coulommiers by the end of the month."

"I understand Brother. Let's go then. The abbot is, as you know, always in his office at this time."

They started walking, treading softly between the monks' cells, making small talk about the other brothers of the monastery, who Luigi hadn't seen for a long time. Every so often they would stop to have a few words with some other monk they met on their way and who would welcome Luigi.

Finally they arrived outside the abbot's office. They both suddenly became serious and, after they had straightened their habits, Mario knocked on the door. A hoarse voice that belonged to an old man answered them, saying that they could enter and, wasting no time, Mario hurriedly drew the latch. At once they found themselves inside the abbot's office.

Abbot Giovanni was a very tall man for his time. He was almost two meters tall, when most men then were a little over a meter and a half. This feature gave him a grandeur which, combined with his severe character, inspired the awe of anyone in his presence. Despite his seventy years and the deep wrinkles on his face, he looked much younger and only his voice gave his real age away. He directed the monastery with remarkable vigour but also with strict adherence to the Rule and monastic standards. A deeply religious man and very conservative, he rejected anything new that jeopardized ideas that had been entrenched in the Church for years, such as, for example, the study of Ancient Greek philosophers, which some enlightened monks had warily begun as Europe acquired those first pieces of knowledge from the Arabs that would enable her to move from darkness into light.

When he saw Luigi, a faint smile lit up his face for a brief moment and he stood up to welcome him: "Welcome my son! May God shine his light upon you. After so much time had passed with no sign of life from you, I thought that those heretics had discovered you. I did not expect you to come back to us, and your coming brings me great pleasure."

Luigi knelt and kissed the Abbot's hand. Brother Mario did the same. Then, the Abbot nodding to him to do so, he sat on the wooden stool next to the desk while Mario, also following the Abbot's orders, left the room, quietly closing the door behind him.

Luigi crossed his arms and looked the Abbot straight in the eye. "Father, it has been three years since you gave me my mission and I left the monastery."

The Abbot interrupted him sharply: "Tell me, my son, what happened? Did you trick them easily? And, above all, tell me what is most important: have you found out anything that could in any way help our plans?"

Luigi pretended not to understand the Abbot's expression, full of impatience and expectation, and decided to take things from the beginning so that he could gain some time. "The truth is, Father Abbot, that it was not very difficult for me to hide my true identity – firstly because I have known how to fight since I was a child and secondly because I was far from my homeland, thus excluding the possibility of anyone recognizing me. However, in the beginning, as I wanted to gain their full trust so that I could, in the future, act without suspicion, I avoided eavesdropping on conversations, going out at night or doing whatever could, in any way, make me look suspicious in their eyes."

At this point Luigi cleared his throat with a dry cough. The Abbot then got up and filled a glass with water from a wooden jug that was placed on his desk and offered it to Luigi. He thanked the Abbot and, after gulping it down in one, continued his account. The Abbot sat down and listened silently. No muscle in his face moved and it was impossible to tell what he was feeling or if he agreed with what his envoy was saying.

"When I was sure that enough time had passed and that the elders of the Church respected me enough, I felt ready to go into action. So I waited in secret for some nights and then, without anybody noticing me, managed to enter the accounts room of the commandery. Alas I was not to know that the steward of the Temple, the seneschal, uses two offices – one in the basement where he receives people, and another where all the confidential documents relevant to what interests us, that is details about the exact amount of fortune the Temple has and what exactly it includes, are kept. I looked at the papers that were left on the desk with the help of a small candle for many nights in secret, but they always concerned deliveries and receipts of goods or rents from land and stores that the Knights Templar have. As for the office in the basement, however, entrance is forbidden to everyone, except for the Commander and the seneschal himself. I tried to get in there in secret, at night, but the stair that led there was constantly guarded by two trusted sergeants of the seneschal himself. The only way I could have entered would have been to kill them both, something that, if done, would have forced me to leave or revealed my true identity. I therefore I believe it is impossible for anyone to collect the information you asked for, unless he himself becomes a seneschal or a Lord Master of the Temple!"

"Then go back immediately and make sure you become one! Why have you come since you have nothing important to tell me?" shouted the Abbot, beside himself, and stood up, bringing the palm of his hand hard down on the desk. As he had heard Luigi talking, he had felt the blood rising to his head. He had turned purple with rage. He could not accept failure after waiting three whole years.

"But, Father Abbot, it is very difficult to be voted seneschal, let alone Lord Master! Those positions are usually taken by French or elderly knights. I can, however, give you information about the shops and lands they own everywhere on the Ile de France," said Luigi, frightened and trying to explain himself, as he had never seen Abbot Giovanni so angry. He understood that he could not hide the failure of his mission from Abbot Giovanni so easily.

"These things are not hidden, they are known to us, so this information is totally useless to me. My brother," the Abbot continued in a somewhat calmer voice, "do you know why all those in the ecclesiastical world, except the Pope, hate the military orders, especially that of those vipers, the Knights Templar?"

Luigi thought that the Abbot himself would answer his own question but seeing that he remained silent and looked at him in a way that revealed his hatred of such orders, he realized that he was expected to answer himself:

"Of course. Because these orders have become a state within a state and, above all, because they have their own churches with their own priests, so that many of the faithful attend them and indeed prefer them to others."

"Because of this? You are gravely uninformed my son, if you think it is just that. We do, of course, lose some income in this way, but there is something else that is worst. Have you ever heard of the Papal Bull Omne Datum Optimum?"[18] Luigi shrugged his shoulders in ignorance.

"No, Reverend Abbot, never."

"This damn Bull was issued by Pope Innocent II, acting far from wisely, over a century ago, in 1139 Anno Domini,[19] or 6647 years from the creation of the world, if you wish.[20] Thanks to this Bull the Knights Templar have the right to build their own chapels with their own priests officiating, who answer only to the Lord Master, something that you also know. The Bull, however, also gave them the right to not pay tithes on the lands they own, a privilege that, up to now, only our Cistercian brother monks had! And as if that weren't enough, it established their right to collect taxes from their lands!"

Luigi opened his eyes wide in surprise. It was the first time he had heard all this. "That explains, in a way, why the Abbot is so angry," he thought.

The Abbot sat down again and continued: "You realize, therefore, that all this, plus the fact that many go to church in their chapels, has substantially reduced our Church's income. Moreover, no one can touch them as they are accountable only to the Pope."

"And the Hospitallers, Father Abbot, enjoy the same privileges as far as I know. So don't they deprive us of some income too?" Luigi dared to ask.

"Certainly. They too have exemptions and are accountable only to the Pope. They do not, however, have the huge fortune the Knights Templar have, nor do they grant loans to such a great extent, as the Knights Templar do. And then, the Hospitallers are not so arrogant and money-loving nor are there rumours of them being heretics, like the Knights Templar. Have you heard of the incident that took place around twenty years ago in Ascalon?"[21]

"I'm afraid not, Father Abbot."

"I thought you were better informed in this matter," said the Abbot, folding his arms on his desk. If I had known you were unaware of all this I would have made sure to tell you before you left. Anyway, better late than never. So, when Baldwin III, the King of Jerusalem, besieged Ascalon eighteen years ago, if I remember correctly, the Knights Templar also participated in this difficult undertaking, under the leadership of Lord Master Bernard de Tramelay. When at last there was a breach in the walls, the Knights Templar rushed to get in first, leaving some of their men outside to stop their allies from entering so that they could gain all the glory of victory and a larger share of the loot! In the end, of course, they were punished for their greed because the Saracens saw how few of them there were and slaughtered them all. The rest of the Christians, of course, managed to take the rest of Ascalon later on. The incident, however, shows how greedy they are.[22] You should also know that both orders are always reluctant to pay ransom for the release of Christian slaves from Muslims."

"I understand, Father Abbot," said Luigi out loud. "As if the Church does not have a huge fortune or is neither ambitious! You don't say! Whatever the case, I too despise those overweening knights." He chose, however, wisely, not to share these thoughts with the Abbot.

Then, suddenly, something came into his mind and his eyes brightened. After that he addressed the Abbot again in a triumphant tone. "Reverend Abbot, I have just remembered something that might interest you that concerns the rumours that hold the Knights Templar to be heretics."

The Abbots eyes immediately lit up with hatred and sudden interest. "Of course," he said, looking at Luigi with obvious impatience. "Anything that might harm those two-faced vipers interests me a great deal. Go on then."

"There was this one time, while Vespers were coming to a close," began Luigi, clearing his throat, "I was walking behind two knights, the commander of Coulommiers, Humbert and Brother Jean. They hadn't realized I was behind them as they thought that they were the last to leave the church."

"Well?" the Abbot asked impatiently, playing irritatedly with the knotted belt of his habit and showing much greater interest now.

"So," Luigi continued, "I heard something about an organization in Outremer which was referred to as Fede Santa.[23] I couldn't hear what they were saying very clearly because the wind was blowing hard and I didn't want to get any closer in case they became aware of my presence. From what the wind carried to me, I understood that it was a secret organization. I also heard something about a Hermes Trismegistus and a Kabbalah, though I do not know what they mean."

"Never mind! They mean a great deal to me," said the Abbot with a broad smile. "I knew they had heretical beliefs! Can you remember anything else?" The Abbot seemed very happy now and was rubbing his hands happily.

Seeing him like this, Luigi closed his eyes and tried to remember whatever he could: "I think that I also heard them talk about spiritual transformation and purification of the soul."

After remaining silent for a little he added: "I'm sorry Father, I can't remember anything else because many of those things I had heard for the first time. I remember the words I told you because they made an impression on me. But what are they?"

The old man leaned forward with a conspiratorial tone. "Is it enough for you if I tell you that Kabbalah is Jewish and that Hermes Trismegistus was an idolater?"

"An idolater? Impossible!" shouted Luigi, surprised.

"Unfortunately yes, my son. Don't you know that, even amongst us, there are monks that study idolaters like Plato, Aristotle and others of their like?"

"I heard this from you when you became Abbot – you advised us to stay away from such things."

The Abbot stood up and went up to Luigi, taking on a very serious expression as if he was about to announce something very important. He touched Luigi's shoulders with his calloused hands and said: "Well, my Brother, you might have failed in that I assigned to you, but the information you have given me puts the matter onto a new footing. Your mission must continue and grow harder for the good of our Holy Church. We must protect it from those heretics. So you shall go back, you will continue to pretend and do everything necessary to make them send you to the Holy Land and become a member of this Fede Santa."

"But, Reverend Father, what you are asking from me is exceptionally difficult! The young monk objected, again overcome by a new concern. I might never achieve this, however much they trust me!"

"It doesn't matter, you will try. Even if you fail to do this, you can obtain more information and you will have saved your soul by serving our Lord Jesus Christ and the Church that he founded. You would like to do that my son, wouldn't you?" the Abbot asked the young man, absolute authority in his voice and looking him straight in the eye.

"All right Father, I'll do whatever I can," Luigi said in resignation, realising there was no room to refuse. "But should I be discovered..."

"With God's help you will not be, because you are serving a noble cause. You must find a way to send me a letter every time you find anything out, at least until you leave for Outremer. What do you think? Will you able to go there soon?"

"I don't know, Reverend Father. They do trust me but to achieve something like that would require further effort."

"Anyway, you should stay close to the commander and this Jean. They might try to initiate you into the heresy- perhaps even before you leave."

"I can't promise anything Father Abbott, only that I will try," murmured Luigi, disappointedly, turning towards the door at the same time. "Now would you allow me to rest a little? I came straight to you, you see..."

"Of course, my son. Get some rest and tomorrow you shall return. You have my permission to be absent from today's services. Pray alone and gather strength for your journey and the new mission and, most of all, give some good thought to as to how you can achieve the goals we have set. Before you leave, come here again."

With these words the Abbot nodded to Luigi, indicating to him that he could leave. Luigi kissed the Abbot's hand and went out of the office with mixed feelings. "What will happen if I am discovered?" he thought, while praying to God to help him. The next morning he saddled his horse and, after receiving the Abbot's blessing and final instructions about his mission, and saying goodbye to the monks and to Mario, who he had seen so little of in the end, set off for the Ile de France again, hoping that everything would go well and that he would sometime return to his beloved homeland.

6

Krak des Chevaliers, March 16, 1271

 o, never! We will not surrender simply because the infidels have seized a tower! Will you give up so easily? It hasn't even been three days since the rain stopped and we've started fighting hard now. Anyway, we are expecting reinforcements and have an advantage. Therefore, until we find ourselves in a desperate situation I will hear no talk of surrender!" This enraged voice belonged to Hugo de Revel, Grand Master of the Hospitallers. He finished his speech, banged his hand on the table and lowered his head. Inside he was boiling with rage at the expressions of faint-heartiness by some of his men. Guillaume de Villaret, equally enraged, agreed with the Grand Master. He, however, spoke in a somewhat more calm and dispassionate voice.

"My Brothers, our situation is difficult but not hopeless. We shall try to drive the enemy out of the tower they have taken. Even if we fail in this I believe that we can hold the rest of the fortress until reinforcements arrive from Tripoli. For this reason I ask you to be brave. Personally, I have experienced far worse situations."

Hugo lifted his head and addressed everyone around in a way that showed that he would not take no for an answer. "I completely agree with the mareschal. Everybody take your positions. The council is over!" At once, the knights, in silence, began to return to their posts. Foulques had not taken part in the council. He had stayed on the walls, replacing his uncle, who he was waiting for very anxiously to be given news. During the two weeks or so since the beginning of the siege he felt that he had grown ten years older. He had already killed a significant number of 'infidels', the first in his life. Until then, in Europe, he had only killed robbers and various criminals. Moreover, his constant attempts to carry out his duties to perfection under such circumstances meant that he had become a great deal more mature. His uncle constantly praised him and thanked God that he had his nephew to help him at such a difficult time. In the beginning, as the rain had continued, the siege had brought no victories to the Muslims. They could not set up their siege engines and so limited themselves to small scale attacks, usually during storms, trying to find the 'Achilles heel' of the castle. The Christians however had easily resisted those attacks, and indeed, with few losses, unlike the Muslims for whom these attacks had cost a significant number of men.

However, when the rain stopped, the scales began to automatically tilt in favour of the Muslims. The previous day, the first one without any rain, under the spring sun and on ground muddy from all the rain, the Muslims had unleashed a large scale attack and, despite stubborn defence on the part of the Christians, had managed to seize a tower of the outer ward of the castle from those defending it. "At least, up until now, all their efforts to get past the walls with tunnels have failed, the rock on which the fortress is built probably continues under the ground," Foulques thought, seeing his uncle approaching him.

"Nephew, we just had the first expressions of faint-heartiness from some of our Brothers," he said in a grave voice.

"Impossible! So easily?" said Foulques, amazement clear on his face.

"I found that surprising too. I'm afraid nephew that few new members are joining our order any more, so our Brothers in the West do not have knights as fearless as they used to have to send us. The bad thing is that if the moral of the defenders of a fortress weakens and the enemy has many more men, it is almost certain that it will not withstand the siege. May God, therefore, give us strength and courage so that we do not despair until reinforcements arrive from Tripoli." Guillaume put on his helmet and said to Foulques, "You go to Vespers to pray, I will stay here."

Foulques took off his helmet in silence, wiped the sweat off his shaved head and walked towards the chapel. He truly felt the need to pray, finding peace and tranquillity only when at prayer. "I'll go and see how my Lightning is doing afterwards," he thought. "If only I could take her and gallop with her just for a little while! The poor thing, she has almost gone mad from not moving at all!"

***

Another two weeks passed by in this way – stalemate. The situation would not change. Neither could the Christians drive the Muslims from the tower in which they were now well ensconced, nor could the Muslims seize more ground from the fortress. Disappointment and frustration reigned in the Muslim camp, as it did in the Christians'. A council was held in the white tent of Sultan Baybars. His most trusted general, Al-Mansur of Hama, was sitting next to him together with the rest of the generals, who were disagreeing intensely on what should happen next. They were all sitting on carpets covering the ground. Many slaves were around them, serving them dates and citrus fruit and constantly filling their glasses with a local non-alcoholic beverage. "We must change our strategy. We have made no progress in the last two weeks," said a man with a long pitch-black beard.

"At least we have minimised our losses," said Al-Mansur.

"Our siege engines, though, have caused no great damage to the walls and the tunnels we have attempted to build have all collapsed!" added an older general, clearly disappointed.

The Sultan remained silent. His tanned face and the scars on his hands proved that he was a man who had fought many battles in his life. He appeared to be listening to his generals very carefully, but, in fact, his mind was elsewhere. None of his generals seemed to have noticed when, suddenly, he raised his hand and said in a deep voice that showed that he was a man with self-confidence, "These conversations won't lead us anywhere. It's always the same old thing. I, on the other hand, have a plan to finally drive these infidel invaders from our lands. Listen to me carefully. I do however demand absolute secrecy in this." With a nod from him the slaves left. The Sultan stroked his beard and began to expound on his plan. "As long as these heretic poly-theists[24] hope that reinforcements will arrive they will not surrender and continue to cause us unnecessary losses. Correct?"

"Correct. May Allah prolong your life, my Lord," replied Al-Mansur on behalf of those present.

"My plan is simple. We shall send a forged letter, supposedly from Bohemund of Tripoli, saying that he will not be able to send soldiers to Krak. So, their morale will fall and we will either manage to beat them or they will surrender. I personally believe that they will surrender."

"The forgery must, however, be a successful one. May Allah prolong your life! Who will write it and, most important of all, sign it?" objected the man with the pitch-black beard.

Rather than replying the Sultan whistled. On this signal, a middle aged man wearing western style armour entered the tent. After greeting the Sultan in Arabic and bowing before him, he folded his arms and remained standing, silent. "Here is our man, gentlemen. I shall not introduce him to you for his own safety, as we have agreed. Only I know his identity. All you need to know is that he is a Christian who has his own reasons to hate the Hospitallers and wants to take revenge on them. I introduce him, therefore, with his Arabic name, which we will use – Ali. He spent many years close to the Count of Tripoli and knows his seal very well, so he will help us with the forgery and will pretend to be the messenger who will deliver the letter to Hisn al Akrad.[25] He will stay in the fortress until he can get away and come back to us or, if he cannot, he will stay with those dogs until they surrender or we seize the castle. I assure you that we can fully trust him. He has already proved his commitment to us."

"Clearly you have planned everything perfectly. May Allah prolong your life!" said Al-Mansur. "But are you sure that none of the infidels will recognize… Ali?"

"Absolutely certain," Ali himself replied. "I wouldn't risk losing my head like that for any reason. In Tripoli probably no one knows about my conversion, while I never had too much to do with the Hospitallers. I came across Guillaume De Boulogne, the commander of Hisn al Akrad when I was with Bohemund, but I was still a Christian then. Even if he remembers me I'm in no danger from him because he does not know about my conversion. It has been no more than a year since I embraced the right path of Allah."

"If that's true, I, at least, am in full agreement," said Al-Mansur taking an orange from the dish in front of him.

"Me too," agreed the man with the black beard, followed by the rest of the generals who were in the tent.

"Let's get to work then," said the Sultan.

The Sultan clapped his hands and a black slave appeared, to whom he said: "Quickly! Paper and ink pen!"

The black man bowed and rushed to do what his master had ordered.

****

It was a moonless night. The last night of March. The silhouettes of those defenders dozing off on the walls could barely be seen. Only a faint light from two torches could be seen in the Muslim camp. The Christians only lit one outside the large Gothic dinning room – they had to economize. Those who were not dozing off had their full attention on the Muslim camp. They feared a sudden attack, despite the thick darkness that covered the fortress like an ebony veil. The tower occupied by the infidels in particular came under close scrutiny from the inner ward of the fortress. But the Muslims were also on the alert as they were afraid that a very small group of defenders would try to get out and sabotage one of their siege engines or something else. Nothing, however, was going to happen. Neither of the sides wished to risk losses, each of them for its own reasons.

And yet, in the almost total darkness and silence that was broken every now and then by the call of some bird, a figure crawled along the walls near the entrance of the castle. The man knocked on the door and said, clearly out of breath: "Open the door please, quickly! I bring a message from the Count of Tripoli!", and he continued to knock hard on the door.

The Spaniards, Jose and Thomas, who happened to be guarding the gate and the walls next to it at that time, just managed to see a horse running away. It had rags tied to its shoes so as not to make a noise. "Open the door to him!" shouted Thomas from the walls to Jose who was behind the door. "He must be telling the truth. The horse I could see coming all that time just ran away with no rider."

"So why didn't you say anything all this time?" Jose replied angrily while he was unlatching the door.

"I didn't want to worry you for no reason, Brother!" Thomas said apologetically. "Anyway, it didn't turn out badly in the end!"

A middle-aged man with black hair and green eyes who wore a pitch-black cape that made it hard for anyone to see him in the night, quickly entered as soon as the guard opened the door. He then hurriedly closed it straight away as the man said, out of breath: "Thank you young man. I am Stephan de Perpignan, an envoy of the Count of Tripoli. I have a letter to deliver to the Lord Master. Would you kindly take me straight to him?"

"All right. Have some water and rest first," said Jose, giving him a flask. Stephan drank thirstily and then motioned to Jose that they should set off together, Thomas remaining at his post.

When they reached the Grand Master's office they heard people talking. The door was half open and Jose tentatively pushed it open saying: "My Lord, forgive me for disturbing you at such a time, but an urgent matter requires your attention. A messenger from the Count of Tripoli has arrived with a letter for you." Jose opened the door wide and Stephan entered and bowed in respect. Two other men apart from the Grand Master stood in front of him. Jose turned around and set off back to the walls. He knew he could not stay, even though he was anxious to know what was in the letter.

"Welcome, my friend," said Hugo. "You must have had a tiring journey. Don't stand." He pointed to a wooden chair.

Stephan, after handing the letter to the Grand Master, sat down saying: "It is from my Lord Bohemund, the Count of Tripoli."

"Your name?" Hugo asked the envoy while removing wax from the letter.

"Oh forgive me, I forgot. Stephan. Stephan from Perpignan."

"And this is the deputy Commander of Krak, Guillaume de Boulogne and our mareschal Guillaume de Villaret." Hugo looked at the wax seal and the signature on the letter for a little and, after making sure it was genuine, began to read. Silence reigned in the room. Stephan tapped his foot nervously, knowing how bad, for the knights, the contents of the letter were, and carefully hiding the joy he felt as both Guillaume almost literally hung on Hugo's words. As Hugo read the letter his expression grew worse and worse. Finally, with shaking hands he handed it to Foulques's uncle, saying angrily: "There you have it. Claiming he doesn't have enough men, Bohemund refuses us any help. We are alone."

"This can't be!" Guillaume shouted while the other Guillaume read the letter in his turn. "He promised to help us!"

"He says he is under pressure from the Seljuk Turks and fears their attack – so he cannot give us troops which he might need," he said, gesticulating wildly with his hands. "Here! You read it too!" said Guillaume de Villaret, handing the letter to the other Guillaume.

"Were you aware of the contents of this letter you were carrying? Tell us about what's going on in Tripoli. What were they saying about us there?" Hugo addressed Stephan, who began to sweat and was lost for words, as he had not expected to have to answer questions like these.

"My Lord, I…" he began to say but hadn't finished his sentence when the sound of the bell ringing like mad broke the deathly silence of the night. Within seconds Thomas rushed into the room and interrupted him.

"The alarm," he cried in horror. "We are under heavy attack from all sides! They are attacking us with all their might! What shall we do my Lord?"

"Wake them all up! Everybody to their positions! We shall defend to the death!" said Hugo, and he nodded to his Brothers and Stephan to come near him and whispered: "And don't say a word about the letter! If they find out about it now there will be panic and the Brothers will have second thoughts. When the battle is over we'll see what we'll do!"

"You are right my Lord, our men losing courage at a moment like this would be the worst thing that could happen to us," Guillaume de Villaret agreed, looking at Stephan severely to ensure that he would obey the order. Straight after that he shouted: "Sergeants! My armour! Straight away! Give Stephan some too." Turning to him, while putting on his helmet at the same time, he said: "You won't sit and watch us will you? We are in need of any one who can fight."

"Of course not!" said Stephan, feeling his throat dry and swearing silently to himself. "It would be an honour to fight with you!" While he was helping the sergeants put on the armour on him, he thought: "Damn! How did I get into this? They attacked too hastily! Now I have to kill some of them otherwise I'll be exposed. May Allah give them victory and help so that I am not discovered! No side ever shows mercy to apostates."

At that moment, a loud hollow sound could be heard and the fortress shook as if there were an earthquake. "Damn!" shouted Hugo, running outside with the Guillaumes and Stephan at his side. "That rock must have caused damage." The sun was beginning to rise and, reaching the walls, they were able to see the 'infidels', placing ladders so they could climb them. It was clear that there were not enough defenders to control the whole length of the walls to stop the hoard of attackers from climbing up them. Guillaume could see his nephew who, together with two sergeants, was throwing down a ladder full of Muslims holding scimitars. The ladder finally collapsed with a clatter on top of other unfortunate warriors.

"Come with me," said Guillaume de Villaret to Stephan, who followed him obediently. They came up beside Foulques, who was, at that very moment, cutting down two attackers who had managed to climb up. Foulques had swiftly pierced the chest of one of them and slit the throat of the other without him even realizing after he had tried to help his unfortunate comrade, who was still moaning because of the deep cut Foulques had made to his chest with his sword. Another three had just scaled the walls a little further along.

"Nephew I'll take care of those. You and Stephan throw this ladder down so no others can climb up." Foulques looked at Stephan and they moved on to do what they were ordered to. Yet the 'infidels' climbing up were growing more and more in number, and soon the Christians were no longer throwing down ladders but fighting one on one with the Muslims, as a rain of arrows descended upon them, and they were shaken by the vibrations caused by the rocks falling on the walls. Foulques was so tired he could hardly see and the sweat running into his eyes did not help. He could, with difficulty, see the figure of a man with a beard who was drawing near him, holding a rock. It looked as if they had taken his sword from him and he was trying to fight with whatever he found in front of him. Foulques raised his sword to strike him but he did not have enough time. The man with the beard proved to be quicker and struck Foulques on the head with the rock. The knight felt intense pain and then nothing. Everything went black and Foulques fell to the ground with a thump and stayed there. The sun of the 1st of April was already shining on the hapless defenders with its first rays.

****

Foulques slowly opened his eyes. He could make out the stone ceiling above him. He brought his hand to his aching head with difficulty. He felt dizzy. He finally managed to force himself up from the waist and sit up. He was trying to figure out where he was. Next to him lay other injured people, on the floor. Many were seriously injured and were moaning from the pain. Nurses and doctors were constantly going up and down in this makeshift hospital, helping the injured as much as they could. "May all your sins be forgiven, my son. And rest in pastures green…"

Foulques turned next to him, towards the source of the voice. He saw a priest of the order closing the eyes of an unfortunate sergeant who had just taken his last breath. A deep wound lay where his heart was.

Foulques's hair stood on end as the priest continued. He crossed himself. "The priest could be saying these words for me. Thank you Lord. Great is your Grace."

"Mareschal, your nephew just woke up a few seconds ago. Except for a slight concussion, he doesn't seem to have any other injuries. He was lucky." Foulques turned his head to the other side and saw his uncle, who was talking with the nurse. Their eyes met for a moment. Guillaume's face instantly lit up with joy. He hugged Foulques, thanking God for saving his beloved nephew.

"Thank God you are alive! I myself carried you here, not knowing if you were dead or alive. Imagine my anxiety!"

"Where am I uncle? What happened? I guess, from what I can see around me, that the news is not pleasant. Am I right?" Guillaume's face darkened and he looked down at the floor awkwardly. He wished he didn't have to give his nephew such bad news…

"Sadly you are nephew. We were on the large south tower of the Krak and I am sorry to tell you that it is the only one that still belongs to us Christians."

"How? That can't be… So the battle was lost?"

"We didn't just lose nephew" said Guillaume, sighing. "It was an absolute rout. We suffered many losses and many casualties. They attacked us with all their strength, you see, and ours was not enough…"

"Yes, that was plain to see."

A heart-rending scream tore the air, making Foulques and his uncle turn their heads back suddenly to see, in horror, a knight lying on the floor, in a pool of blood, screaming, as an arrow was pulled out of a deep wound to his chest, taking with it whole pieces of flesh. Guillaume immediately turned his head back in disgust and looked his nephew straight in the eye, trying not to pay attention to the cries of the poor knight: "I must congratulate you though. You fought very bravely. We did everything we could, but there were too few of us. When we realized that nothing could be done all the survivors retreated, obeying the order of the Lord Master, to this tower. You can't imagine how I felt when I found you lying on the ground. I didn't give it a second's thought, though. Dead or alive I would not leave you in their hands."

"Thank you uncle! If it weren't for you now I would be either captured or dead. So what do we do now? What about the reinforcements we were expecting?" Guillaume shook his head sadly, looking at the injured knight who was dying and the Brothers who were making desperate efforts to stem the river of blood flowing from his chest.

"Don't thank me," he said after a while. "As we were retreating we took all the wounded, as many as we could that is, as there was not much time. As for reinforcements nephew, they are not coming. Do you remember that Stephan I introduced you to in the battle?"

Foulques remembered, despite the concussion he had suffered, so he answered without hesitation:

"Of course. He also killed a large number of infidels from what I remember. Is he alive?"

"Yes. Stephan was the messenger from Bohemund. He arrived at the Krak shortly before the attack began. Hugo, Guillaume and I were reading the letter he brought with him when we heard about the surprise attack from the Muslims so we did not make the sad content of the letter known, to avoid panic. It was too late by then. Now we cannot do anything. Hugo intends to send messengers to the Sultan so that we can hand them the Krak on the condition that we can leave in safety. This pointless bloodshed must stop."

"But, uncle, will Baybars keep his word?" asked Foulques. "Will he let us go?"

"I think so, nephew. At least that's what I wish to hope. He does hate Christians but I don't think anyone can deny that we fought bravely. You know, Guillaume de Boulogne is also dead. We are waiting for permission to bury him, and all our other dead, before we leave."

"That's a pity. He was a brave man, said Foulques, lying down again. I'm sorry I'm lying down uncle, but my headache is getting worse and I feel unbearably dizzy. It's unbearable."

"That's understandable. Lie down and sleep, nephew."

At that moment a loud clatter and voices from below them could be heard. "That is if you manage to!" Guillaume added. "As you can hear the fighting has yet to stop. They would definitely prefer to kill us all rather than parley with us."

"Then I should go and help too. I am not seriously injured," said Foulques, trying to get up.

His uncle stopped him, shaking his head in disagreement and putting his hands on Foulques's shoulders: "Stay where you are. You were unconscious for nearly two days and you want to fight? Anyway we are going to propose peace. I'm going to the Lord Master now to tell him to speed up the process because I fear that soon none of our men will be alive. The procedure involved in surrender and the negotiation of the terms will take some days anyway. Get well soon, nephew. I will come again to bring you the news when I can." Guillaume stopped talking and set off. Out of the corner of his eye he saw someone putting a sheet over the knight they had seen before. Obviously the nurses hadn't managed to stop the bleeding so one more warrior had been added to the sad list of the dead. As soon as Guillaume was out of his sight Foulques lay down again, bringing his hand to his forehead. His head hurt him so much, as if someone was mercilessly hammering his head with sledgehammers. Deeply disappointed by their failure to hold the Krak and disgusted by so many

deaths, he fell into a troubled, dreamless sleep.

***

The eighth day of April had just dawned. The sun was already hot. Foulques was saddling his horse and preparing it for the journey. There was a lot going on around him. Many knights were doing as he was, while servants were helping the injured onto carts and others were moving the corpses of Christians so that they could bury them outside the walls, under the ravenous vultures which were circling above the castle, dissatisfied that their feast had stopped so suddenly. The Muslims were also burying their dead, on the order of the Sultan's, as the stench from the corpses had become unbearable and there was danger of them causing deadly epidemics in the camp.

The surrender had just been signed the night before. The Knights were allowed to leave Tripoli together with their injured and their horses, most of which had thankfully been saved as they were at the centre of the fortress far from the walls where the fighting had been, and arrows and rocks had been fired with deadly results, and, anyway, they had not been used in battle.

When everything was ready, the knights mounted their horses and opened the gates. The horse and carts started moving when the Grand Master gave the order, under the triumphant and mocking regard of the Muslims. Foulques exchanged a sad look with his uncle, who was trotting beside him. When the sad procession was outside the castle and the doors were closed, and cries of joy were heard from the inside: "La hail illa-la, wa Mohamed rasulu-ill a!"[26] The Knights of the Order of St. John went on their way in silence under the blazing sun. The riders did not break into a gallop so that they could accompany the carts. When they had gone far enough, Foulques looked back and looked for one last time at the famous Krak of the Knights which had been lost to the Christians once and for all. Then he looked to the front. It was a long way to Tripoli. Apart from Acre, he had visited no other town in Outremer. He would go to Tripoli with the bitter taste of defeat in his mouth. He silently prayed to God that such a calamity would never occur again...

7

Knights Templar Commandery, Coulommiers, April 15, 1277

hilippe was trotting, nonchalantly, on Calpurnia, through the dense forest, next to the cart with the oil that he had gone to fetch from the Church's estates. His mission was to take it to the commandery safely. He appeared to be enjoying the chirping of the birds as they were returning to their nests and the colours of nature at dusk. The darkness had started to set in, little light now shining through the foliage of the tall trees with difficulty. The driver of the cart, however, was not so nonchalant.

"We had better hurry. I wouldn't like to find myself in this place at night," he said, looking quite distressed. "These woods are a known refuge for all manner of scum and there is just you here if they attack us."

Philippe laughed.

"Don't worry my friend. I've been doing this job for many years. There has never been an occasion on which I have not been able to see off the fellows that frequent this place. They are just thieves; they don't know how to fight." He placed a hand on his sword, tapping it softly and went on: "This here is worth more than their knives, to be sure."

The driver did not seem reassured.

"Yes, but if night comes and we are still here, except for the thieves, the demons of the forest might also attack us. And then there are the wolves and bears."

Philippe continued to appear calm but the fact was that he had started to get angry with the fearful driver.

"Which demons? Those superstitions of yours! Let me tell you again – don't worry about anything, we are not far away anyway. We will be at the commandery in an hour!" Yet he could see the driver out of the corner of his eye and understand that he was still worried, so he added confidently, trying to reassure him: "All these years I've managed very well with thieves. Be sure that, especially today, I will not allow anybody to stop us from getting to the commandery."

"And why are you going to do that today? What is it that makes today special?" The peasant asked Philippe, who kept on looking around suspiciously. Philippe's face lit up.

"Because tomorrow, after so many years of waiting, I'm leaving for the Holy Land at last, with our Lord Master, so I'm telling you I will not let any bandit, demon or anything else prevent me from making my dream come true."

"Well done lad, I am happy for you! You're going to the land where Christ lived! If you go to pray in our Holy City, say a prayer for me too!" The driver said, showing him a little more trust now.

"I don't know if I shall go to our Holy City. As you may have already heard, the infidels have held it for thirty years, so it is now dangerous to go on pilgrimage in times of war, and such times have been very common of late."

"Either way, I hope you go lad!" The driver said, hitting the mule lightly so that it would walk faster and, in a talkative mood now, went on: "Did you say you were going with your Lord Master? Isn't he in the East?"

"He honoured us by paying us a visit concerning financial matters of the Church and now he is going back to Outremer, taking some of us with him. It's an opportunity. So today, is the last time I…"

Philippe's sentence remained unfinished because of a loud cry that startled the knight and made the driver's blood freeze in his veins. They both pulled the reins of their animals, stopping them and turning their heads towards the point from which they had heard the scream. And indeed, in a clearing behind the trees, they saw a carriage.

A tall man in rags was holding the reins of the horse that was drawing it. The animal looked very frightened. Next to the horse lay a man with his throat slit, obviously the driver of the carriage, the robbers' first victim.. The door of the carriage was open and you could see another figure inside while a man in rags was keeping hold of a man who was screaming for help. He appeared to be a nobleman from his fine clothes and the luxurious carriage. The man in rags had brought his knife to the nobleman's neck, apparently to make him stop shouting out.

The eyes of the peasant were now bulging with fear and his whole body was trembling like a leaf in the wind. Without a second thought he got ready to shake the reins hard and said to Philippe:

"Robbers! And there are three of them! Let's get out of here quickly! We're sure to be next!"

"We're not going anywhere. I cannot desert this man. I have a duty to uphold the Law at any cost. Don't move an inch until I come back!" said Philippe, angry at the peasant's cowardice, with a look that showed that he would not take no for an answer, and spurred on Calpurnia towards the robbers, drawing his sword out of its scabbard with his right hand at the same time and raising it in the air.

The robbers turned, startled, in the direction from which the galloping sound came and stood petrified at the sight of an armed knight charging towards them. Philippe headed towards the one who was holding the noble first. The bandit lowered the knife from the nobleman's neck and lifted it so that he could defend himself. His puny knife and Philippe's sword were mismatched.

A heavy blow from the knight's sword cut the hand with which the man was holding the knife off from the wrist. The robber gave a dreadful cry and fell to the ground, writhing in pain, next to his severed hand, still twitching and holding the knife.

When the other two robbers saw what had befallen their accomplice, one left the horse and the other the chest he had been taking from the carriage and they began to run in panic for the trees. The chest fell down with a crash and opened, revealing the loot which the robbers had just failed to obtain: a mass of silver coins, with which the chest was stuffed.

Philippe got off his horse, stood above the wounded thief and said to him in a severe voice:

"I 'm not going to kill you because our Rule does not allow us to take the life of a Christian. For you, however, and for your accomplices, I could make an exception but I give you the opportunity to repent! Now get out of my sight!" The robber leader stood up with difficulty. He tore off a piece of his clothing to bind his wound and stop the bleeding and disappeared behind the trees, moaning and swearing at the misfortune that had led him to come across the knight and showing, of course, no signs of remorse.

Philippe turned to the nobleman, who had not yet recovered from the sudden change in his emotions. There had been unspeakable terror and dread at first, then surprise and finally gratitude and relief thanks to his good fortune. He stood over the dead driver and looked at him sadly. He threw some soil symbolically over his body, closed the dead person's eyes and then turned to Philippe with his arms outstretched and a completely different expression:

"My hero! Let me embrace you! May God keep you well, always! You have saved my life and my fortune! How can I pay you back?"

Philippe received the man's kiss with a smile.

"There is need to thank me sir, I just did my duty. I'm just sorry your driver has lost his life," he said and turned towards the peasant that was driving the cart with the oil, as if he had suddenly remembered him. He had come down from the cart, and was holding his mule by its bridle, looking at Philippe in admiration.

"Now I think you will stop being scared at last!" Philippe said to him sternly. "Go and pick up the coins and don't even consider taking any of them of course."

"Oh, of course he will, as you will my boy. It's the least I can do to thank you for saving my life and my daughter's dowry!" said the nobleman, who had tears in his eyes because he felt real gratitude towards Philippe. He was a good man, which could be seen from his appearance. Short, fat and just after his first youth. His round face exuded warm feelings and love for people.

"You have a daughter of marriageable age? But you look so young!" Philippe said to the man, sheathing his sword and watching the peasant, who had tied the mule to a tree and was walking towards them, out of the corner of his eye.

"I married very young and my daughter will do the same thing tomorrow. And thanks to you she shall receive her wedding gift! But I haven't introduced myself,

I forgot. My name is Gilles Aicelin and I live in Paris, in Louis' palace. My father has been in the service of the King for years, Chamberlain and Grand Keeper of the Royal Seal, a position reserved for me in the future. And by whom have I had the honour to be saved may I ask?"

"Brother Philippe of the Order of the Knights Templar," replied Philippe, glancing sideways at the peasant, who had started to collect the coins.

"Ah that's why you use your sword like that!" said Gilles in admiration. "Of which family, if I may ask?"

"We Brothers are not allowed to use our family name but I will tell you if that makes you happy. My full name is Philippe de Ridefort." Gilles took out a purse from under his robes and gave it to Philippe. It was easy to guess its contents because it felt heavy and made a clinking sound as the nobleman was taking it out of his tunic.

"Thank you very much but I cannot accept it. Whatever I did, I did for the good of justice and, anyway, I have no property of my own. Everything belongs to the order," said Philippe, making a negative gesture with his hand.

The peasant looked greedily at the pouch and then at Philippe, in wonder mixed with admiration and thought to himself:" Will you look at that! And I thought the Knights Templar were greedy!" Gilles continued to hold the purse in front of the knight:

"Never mind, then donate it to your order."

"That I can do and thank you very much. Our Brothers in Outremer are always in need of money." Philippe hung the purse on his armour. Gilles turned to the peasant who had finished collecting the coins and gave him also two silver coins. The peasant, finding it difficult to believe how lucky he was, thanked the nobleman profusely and then put the chest on the carriage. He would be able to live on those coins for months.

Gilles warmly squeezed Philippe's wrist.

"Come and visit me at the palace sometime. I shall order them to open the gates immediately at the sound of your name."

"I would really like to see you again, but I don't know if my superiors would approve of such a visit. You know, we don't leave the fortress of the Order alone very often. Besides that, I'm leaving for the Holy Land tomorrow. I don't know if I will return. My order might need me there permanently."

"Then have a good journey my son. You have my blessing and you never know what life may bring – if you come back, you should definitely come and visit me. I shall ask God to give me the opportunity to pay you back for what you did for me."

"If you want it that much I promise you that I will come to see you if God helps me to see my country again and if I am allowed to, of course," Philippe said, smiling and, pulling his wrist free, turned to the carter and indicated to him that it was time for them to leave. Then he turned and said goodbye to Gilles.

"We must get going, otherwise the night will catch up on us. You should hurry too. Will you manage to drive the carriage yourself? And you're all alone. It was unwise of you not to take a soldier with you in the first place."

"You are right my boy. But don't worry about me. I know how to drive a carriage just fine and a little further on is my manor-house, where I am going to spend the night, and tomorrow, I shall leave for Paris at first light with a man from my manor to protect me. I was foolish, I know, but nothing like this has ever happened to me before. From now on I will be more careful," replied Gilles and climbing on the carriage he held the reins tightly as if to prove that he would do fine on his own. He raised his hand in a gesture of farewell, saying:

"I owe you one lad! Bye!"

Philippe also raised his hand, as did the peasant. Gilles shook the reins and called the horse's name and the carriage sped off down the narrow path. The knight and the peasant remained, watching it until it was out of sight.

***

The ship had just set sail. Philippe was leaning on the rail, looking at the people and the houses of Marseilles growing smaller and smaller as the ship went out to sea. Further along, Luigi was talking to Francois and Jean in a low voice.

Philippe was deep in thought. Three days had passed since the incident with the robbers in the woods. Philippe and the peasant had returned to the commandery without any other unexpected incident occurring. There the peasant had had the best words to say about Philippe and his bravery, praising him to his commander and Grand Master, who, when the cart was late in arriving, had started to worry.

Philippe had given the purse to the Grand Master who, as he was present, was Humbert's superior. The Grand Master had been delighted with the young knight's achievement and had asked him to stay with him permanently in Outremer. Philippe had gladly accepted, believing that this would allow him to later ask for more freedom to search for his "uncle".

The next morning Philippe had collected his few belongings – in other words his armour, as different clothes and eating utensils would be given to him in Outremer and, wearing a shirt, breeches and a summer robe for the trip, they had began their journey to the port of Marseilles on horseback together with Brother Jean, Francois, Luigi and of course, the Grand Master, Guillaume de Beaujeu, who had been commanding the order for about four years now. After a journey with no unexpected incidents, during which a few hours of rest followed many hours of galloping, they had at last, reached Marseilles and had boarded a ship of the order, with the port of Acre, Saint Simeon, as their destination.

The galley had just unloaded precious fabrics and herbs, spices and sugar, oil and fruit – everything from Outremer. Not only knights from other Templar Houses in France that would fight there had boarded it, but also many pilgrims, who usually preferred to travel in ships of the Orders, and not in those of Italian merchants. In the ships of military orders less would be paid for transportation, which was safer anyway as the ships were better maintained, the sailors were selected based on stricter criteria and, above all, there was very little risk of being attacked by pirates as pirates would not dare attack a ship with so many soldiers who were so skilled. So, by travelling in these ships someone was in very little danger of ending his days as a slave in Algiers, where pirates usually sold their "loot".

The galley was overcrowded. The overcrowding was horrible, in the holds the stuffiness was unbearable and the whinnying of the poor horses, crammed together into such a small space, never let up. Francois left the others and approached Philippe, who looked serious and lost deep in thought, despite the pandemonium around him.

"Where is your mind off to again?" he said with feigned severity. "You look as if something is on your mind. Instead of being happy that our dream is coming true, you keep going off into your shell and feeling sorry for yourself! Is that what you are going to be like for the rest of the journey?" Philippe thought for a bit and weighed his words before he answered. Francois and he already knew each other very well. It would not be an exaggeration for him to say that this was the person closest to him in his new military-monastic life. Could he trust him? His instinct told him that he could. So he decided to tell Francois the truth.

"You know, Brother, I have never told you why I wanted to go to the Holy Lands so much," he began hesitantly.

"Well, the reasons are the same for everyone," Francois said cheerfully. "To see the places where our Lord Jesus Christ lived and was martyred, to worship, to fight Infidels and to see that other world – if you like!"

"These are reasons, but I have one more particular reason why I wanted to come to the East."

"Which is?" Francois asked showing more interest and suddenly growing serious.

"You have heard about the two relatives of mine who served the Order before me, right?"

"Of course, Brother. We all know our Order's history, at least a bit of it. Maybe some have not heard about Jocelyn de Ridefort but everyone knows about Gerard de Ridefort, who was also a Lord Master. Weren't they your uncles?"

"Seemingly, yes, they were both my uncles," Philippe answered ambiguously. Francois's curiosity peaked at this answer. He went up even closer to his friend and leaned, in his turn, on the railing around the deck.

"What do you mean seemingly?" he asked Philippe, his emerald eyes open in amazement.

"I'm counting on your absolute secrecy if I am to tell you," Philippe said, lowering his voice considerably. I wouldn't like it if what I told you cost me my place in the Order or led to a harsh punishment. Can I have it then?"

"At all times and in all places, Brother! Don't insult me! Haven't you come to know me all these years?" Francois pretended to be insulted.

"Good. So listen. When I was…"

And so Philippe told Francois everything. He missed out nothing, neither his unloving "father" in comparison to his playful "uncle", nor his mother's inappropriate relationship nor, above all, the revelatory conversation he had accidentally overheard. Francois listened to him with great attention and great surprise.

"…..I therefore plan to ask the Lord Master for permission, at some point, to go to Alexandria and Algiers so that I can look for traces of my "uncle". We received his last letter the year that the battle of Mansurah[27] took place, I think. We don't know what has happened to him since then. Logically, he was either killed in that battle or was captured."

Francois thought for a little after Philippe had finished his story. .Then, he said: "Listen, Brother, I totally understand your desire to see your "uncle" again but, I'm sorry to say this, he is most probably dead. If, however, we assume that he isn't, but was captured in the battle of Mansurah and has not been executed, it is most likely that he died in captivity. Very few people survive for so many years in slavery. But even if he is alive, which is almost impossible, how will you find him in such a huge place? Slaves are not even usually asked their names! Brother, no doubt, only a miracle would help you find him!"

Philippe listened to Francois in silence. He did not want to believe that his friend was right. He knew, deep down, that it was like looking for a needle in a haystack. He believed, however, both in Fate and good Luck. Since those two goddesses, sacred and respected by the Ancients, had allowed him to learn the truth, would they not let him see his father, even for one last time and tell him the things he had kept inside himself all these years? Yes, logic on the one hand, told him that it was impossible for him to find him and he tended to listen to it and give up. On the other hand, he had a feeling that he would see his father again. And Philippe was one of those people who trusted such feelings.

"Off in thought again? Aren't you listening to me?" Francois's voice brought him back to reality, interrupting his thoughts.

"I'm listening, Brother and I know you are right. But something inside me is telling me to try."

"If that's what you feel then do it, but always with the necessary discretion, right? People finding out that you are an illegitimate child would be the worst thing that could happen. You know very well that only knights who are nobles and born within a legitimate marriage are accepted in the Order. You could, however, just ask the older people that we are going to meet if they know anything about your "uncle"."

"Yes. That's a good idea," Philippe said smiling and suddenly changing mood, maybe because his stomach had began to complain loudly. "Why don't we go find the others and have a bite to eat? I imagine you are bored by me and my old stories all this time! We do have a whole trip ahead of us anyway and many prayers! No services, no chores! We must leave something to talk about for the rest of the journey, right?"

"You are right Brother!" Francois said, laughing, and set off. "Let's go!"

8

Hospitaller commandery, Tripoli July 3rd 1277

he church of the Assumption of the Virgin Mary was full of people. The candles of the faithful and the large candles around the coffin placed at the centre of the church lit the stone interior well, adding to the dim light entering through the few windows. Around the coffin the chaplains of the order were chanting and officiating, while the knights, a little further off, were praying silently for the peaceful rest of their dead Grand Master's soul.

Sorrow was evident on Guillaume de Villaret's face. Hugo and he had been through a great deal together and the illness that had caused him such distress in the last weeks, and then his death had brought him intense sadness. However God had 'recalled' his faithful servant for good and Guillaume, despite his sorrow, was now thinking about the dead Grand Master's successor.

In truth, no military order should remain without a leader, not even for one day. Guillaume also knew that, normally, as mareschal, he should temporarily fill the vacuum in authority until the new Grand Master was elected. Because, however, the Grand Master had died not in Acre but in the County of Tripoli, the authority of the deceased Grand Master would temporarily pass into the hands of the commander of the order in Tripoli and not those of the mareschal. This was the man who was now next to Guillaume and none other than Pierre de Moulin. De Moulin had fought next to him at the Krak and had been appointed commander of the order by Hugo two years before in Tripoli, when the previous commander of the Knights of St John in that city had been killed in a battle with the 'infidel'.

Guillaume looked at the dead Grand Master in his coffin. His face looked peaceful and he looked as if he was still alive. It was as if the fever that had constantly caused him distress during the last days of his life had left no sign nor mark of pain on his calm face. In fact, Hugo had suffered both the delirium caused by fever and the pain of the acute dysentery that had eventually cost him his life without complaint. Hugo was wearing his tunic and his robe with the black cross for his last journey. These were the only things he would take with him to the next world. Everything else he possessed, his weapons and the gifts he had received, would go to the order.

The ceremony ended. Whoever had come to say goodbye to the Grand Master – knights or members of the laity – started to make their way out of the church. The coffin was sealed and placed on a cart so that the Grand Master could be buried in a Hospitaller cemetery outside the town. Only some chaplains of the order would attend the burial. The knights would remain here to carry out their important task of electing their new Grand Master.

In fact, as soon as Guillaume came out of the church Pierre approached him:

"Brother, the commander of our Brothers in Acre is here. Let us go to arrange the election day."

There was no disagreement between them or difficulty in choosing a day for the election. In any case, there were only the three of them, the commanders of the order in Acre and Tripoli and the mareschal. There was no commander for the order in Jerusalem, as the city had been in Muslim hands since 1244, nor was there a commander from Antioch, as the city of Antioch had also been lost in 1268. They chose July 20th as the election day. Until then the Brothers would have to say, except for their normal prayers, two hundred more Pater Nosters for the soul of the dead Grand Master and provide one hundred poor people with lunch and dinner.

When the funeral was over, Foulques decided to wait until after the council that was to decide to day of the election before he talked to his uncle. He was feeling uneasy about the news he heard in the church about the Knights Templar and needed his uncle's opinion on this.

He sat on a rock outside the room where the council was taking place and leaned against the stone wall, sighing softly. He had been affected by the funeral and, thinking of the dead Grand Master, without fully realizing he was doing so, had started thinking back over the years he had lived in Outremer.

He had still not been on pilgrimage to the Holy City and did not know if he would ever manage to do so. Relations with the Muslims were constantly getting worse and worse and were making it difficult to cross Muslim territory. He remembered the difficult siege of Krak and the strength Hugo had shown during that time. Would the new Grand Master do as well in such a difficult situation? It was true that Hugo had been deceived by the forged letter, but had not perhaps everybody else been taken in by it?

He brought back to mind Hugo's enraged reaction, when they had arrived in Tripoli after the fall of Krak, around six years before, and had met with Bohemund, then governor of the city, who had known nothing of the letter! He had actually been about to send a group of men to help the Knights of St John at Krak! It was then that they had noticed the absence of Stephan de Perpignan. Indeed, he had not left the Krak with them but, in their sorrow and general agitation during the evacuation of the fort, nobody had realized.

Bohemund had acknowledged that his seal and hand writing had been forged perfectly and remembered some Stephan who had served him some time before and had had a violent argument with the Grand Master of the Hospitallers at the time and had suddenly left, nobody knowing where he had gone. "If I get my hands on him..." Hugo had said to himself, embittered by the betrayal on the part of the Christian and Baybars' sly cunning.

Then followed the unsuccessful armed expedition by Prince Edward[28] of England, who had come to the Holy Lands the summer right after the loss of Krak. Edward was the able heir of Henry III of England, and had come to the Holy Lands hoping to join his forces with those of Louis the Saint, who had come down to Tunis. However, Louis's sudden death had forced the French troops to return to their country, leaving the English, who had arrived in Acre about a month after the fall of Krak, alone.

Edward was bitterly disappointed when he found that the Venetians were supplying Baybars with all the raw materials he needed for his equipment, like metal and wood. Their thirst for profit did not cease although they knew that, in this way, they were harming Outremer's Christians. But he could do nothing about it. He did not succeed in joining forces against Baybars with the Mongols either.

So, not having enough of an army to beat the dynamic Mamluk Sultan for good, he signed a peace treaty with him, through the mediation of Charles d' Anjou, the brother of Louis the Saint, who was already on friendly terms with Baybars. The treaty guaranteed that the Christians, for the next ten years, would keep their few remaining lands, from Acre to Sidon that is, and pilgrims would have the right to use the road to Nazareth.

Despite the truce, however, Edward was not pleased. He was planning to come back at some time with a larger army. When this reached the Sultan's ears he tried to have him assassinated. An assassin dressed as a Christian managed to stab the prince with a knife which had a poisoned blade in June 1272. Edward survived in the end but his life had been at risk for many months. Of course Baybars quickly sent a letter to congratulate the prince on surviving the attack, wishing to show that he had had no involvement whatsoever in this regrettable episode.

Whatever the case, however, Edward decided to risk no more. After his recovery he departed for England, knowing that his father was on the verge of death and, unbeknown to him, he was already king when he arrived there as his father had died in the meantime.

After that unfortunate expedition neither Edward nor any other monarch or noble ever went down to the Holy Lands again. The truth was that the crusade spirit had now died out. Europe had its own problems and its own conflicts between the many small states that were part of it. So Outremer's Christians remained, once again with no outside help. In the years following Edward's expedition, Foulques thought, nothing worth mentioning had happened. Foulques would almost have described his stay there all those years as boring, except perhaps that he had discovered the completely different natural world and amazing landscapes the East offered every curious European.

Day in, day out, week in, week out and month in, month out Foulques had done the same thing. There had been prayers, services, skirmishes with the Muslims and raids on their lands, chores and then everything all over again.

A quick clatter of hooves, as well as happy voices, interrupted his thoughts. Foulques scanned the square in front of him, trying to find the source of the disturbance. He soon saw a man, whose clothes showed that he was Bohemund's man, riding a white horse, shouting and gesturing wildly. Foulques could not hear what he was saying because the hamsin which had started blowing a short while before was carrying his words in the opposite direction from where he was sitting. He was not worried as the man's face was very happy. He did however feel his curiosity rising and so he stood up, dusting off his robe.

"I was so absent-minded! I didn't even realise that the wind had got up!" he said to himself. "What's going on? Why is everybody jumping around like goats? Is maybe an army coming from the West and that's why everybody is happy?" he then thought and decided to go closer to finally find out what on earth had happened. At the same time, the door behind him opened and Foulques's uncle, Pierre and the commander of the Brothers in Acre came out and they too looked around with a puzzled look on their faces. Guillaume motioned to a sergeant, who was rejoicing with a member of the laity a little further off, to approach them. Foulques also went up to his uncle, who was asking the sergeant:

"What's happened, Brother? What are you celebrating for?"

"Haven't you learned the news sir? Sultan Baybars has died! Only two days ago! Our suffering has ended!" the sergeant said, breathlessly.

"He has died? So suddenly? Do you know how?" Guillaume asked, surprised.

"And, more importantly, is it certain that this news is true or is it merely a means of distracting the Sultan's enemies?" added the commander of Acre, a relatively young but large and tall knight by the name of Armand, also surprised.

"That's what the man on the horse says. He found out from the Muslims themselves. There is a successor too - Barakah, his older son who was just crowned Sultan, he says. The funeral of the deceased Sultan took place only yesterday."

"So we were not the only ones to lose our leader then. In any case, if it has in fact taken place, this death is good for us. Barakah is very weak and does not have the reputation his father had to bring together all the infidels against us," said Pierre.

"This is, however, only a temporary respite. Someone more powerful is sure to be found to impose their will," Guillaume disagreed.

"Aren't you being a little pessimistic Brother?" Armand asked him.

"I'm just realistic, Brother. The infidels won't leave us alone until they throw us out of the land they consider to be their own," said Guillaume gravely and turned to the young sergeant once again:

"Do you know why the Sultan died? Was he murdered?"

"Not as far as I know. The truth is that there are many rumours going around about why the Sultan passed away but, no, none of them include murder."

"What rumours?" Pierre asked, clearly interested.

"Some claim Baybars died from the injuries he received in his last campaign. Some others say he drank very large quantities of kumis, you know, that sour mare's milk the Turks and Mongols like so much."

"The idea! For Goodness sake!" Armand interrupted him, laughing.

"The strongest rumour though…" the sergeant went on ignoring the interruption "…says that he had prepared a poison for the prince of Kerak, al-Khair, son of al-Nasir Davoud who served in his army and had offended the Sultan, so they say, and that he then drank from the same cup before it was cleaned!"

"Right. That should have been the real cause of his death. We will never know the real cause of his death for sure but, whatever the case, even temporarily this event is beneficial for us. Thank you for informing us, young man."

After these words from Guillaume the sergeant said goodbye and left. Foulques, who had remained silent all this time, listening carefully to the conversation, set off, nodding his head as if to say goodbye, judging that this was not the most appropriate moment to talk to his uncle, but his uncle grabbed him by the shoulders and, after saying goodbye to the others, left with him.

"I am sorry Uncle," Foulques said apologetically, while they were walking towards the refectory. "I didn't mean to interrupt you. I just also wanted to find out why everyone was so happy."

"Don't worry nephew. We had finished anyway. On the 20th of the month, that is next Friday, we will elect the new Lord Master."

"You are clearly worried about this. Am I wrong, Uncle?" Foulques asked, looking at him knowingly.

Guillaume lowered his eyes to the ground before he replied: "No, nephew, you are not wrong. On the one hand, I am worried about whether he will be capable of controlling the difficult political and military situation we are facing. On the other hand, I would like to continue serving the order as a mareschal. However the new Lord Master might have another person he trusts."

Foulques understood why his uncle did not want to lose his office. Of course he was ambitious, like most people indeed, but, above all he adored his order and wanted to serve Christendom in whichever way he could. So, he said to him: "I think Uncle that, some day, your contribution will be recognised. I don't, however, think that the new Lord Master has any reason to remove you from your office. Everybody admits that, in this position, you have served the order admirably and for quite some number of years. You could even become Lord Master some time, with all the experience you have!"

"God willing I might someday have the honour to serve my Brothers from that position. I do, however, think it is too soon to talk of this."

Neither of the two spoke again. They both remained absorbed in their thoughts until they reached the outside of the refectory, at the buildings of the order. It was time for the midday meal. It was here that Pierre would announce the day of the election of the new Grand Master to the Brothers.

Before they entered, Foulques decided to ask his uncle about what was on his mind: "Uncle, have you heard anything about the disagreement between Bohemund and the Knights Templar? I have not exactly understood the cause of this argument, but it is something that worries me quite considerably."

"You are right to be worried, nephew," Guillaume stopped walking and answered. Of course I have heard about this, I think that everyone has found out by now. Some

Guy of Jebail is probably to blame for the dispute. I think that Bohemund promised the hand in marriage of a young lady to Guy's brother. He then broke his promise and promised her to someone else. Guy then abducted the young lady and married her to his brother. Afterwards,, fearing Bohemund's reaction, he sought the protection of the Knights Templar. This is how the hostilities began - for this silly, in my opinion, reason! It is the worst thing that could happen – for we Christians of the East to be divided now that the Muslims are waiting to strike against us for the last time, after they have recovered from their Sultan's death. Let's hope that this disagreement will be resolved before our enemies consolidate and are unified again."

"We are on Bohemund's side, aren't we Uncle?" Foulques asked.

"Of course we are, nephew! Could we ever be on the same side as the Templars? Aren't we fighting like cocks all the time?" Guillaume said, laughing.

"Since they are so arrogant, who can blame us, Uncle? We cannot trust them."

"I have told you before nephew, don't be so prejudiced against them! The kings here also, like Bohemund, do anything but cultivate harmony! It's just that the present Lord Master of the Templars, this Guillaume de Beaujeu likes getting involved in political intrigues and schemes a little more than ours and Bohemund!"

"And you think this is good do you, Uncle?" Foulques said indignantly.

"Of course not nephew! But that doesn't mean that a Lord Master like that, like my namesake in the Knights Templar, will not cope absolutely well with his military duties! Not only that but I've also heard that he is a very good warrior!"

"You are right, Uncle!" Foulques said, laughing. "How do you manage to find out some much about everybody? Only you know?"

"Secrets of the service, nephew!" Guillaume said, winking conspiratorially. Now that all your questions have been answered, how about we go for dinner?

"Let's go! We've gone on talking enough anyway! And some silence is needed while we are eating!" Foulques replied laughing, and then they immediately disappeared behind the stone gate.

***

July 20th, the day of the election of the new Grand Master, was cloudy at dawn. After Lauds, which all the Brothers attended as always, and while the city had barely woken up and commenced its noisy activities, Pierre chose two elderly Brothers who were highly respected by everyone, Brothers Robert and Bertrand, and went with them to the chapel so that they could pray to God and ask for divine guidance in the important decisions they were about to make. Pierre chose Bertrand to be officer of the election.

After they had prayed, Pierre summoned the Knights' council. In this Foulques and his uncle also took part. Before Pierre began to speak, Foulques cast a sideways glance at his uncle. Guillaume was playing with his fingers. He seemed possessed by great anxiety.

There were forty-five knights in all at that time in Tripoli and they were all present at the council. Five of them, however, were chaplains and so could not be elected to the position of Grand Master. The electors would choose, of course, from the lists which included the names of all the Brothers of the order, in the West and the East. In theory an elector could be elected to the position of Grand Master but this was in fact very rarely the case. "I wonder if my uncle is going to be one of the twelve electors?" Foulques wondered. "Normally speaking, I'm still too young to be in either an elector or candidate."

A knight with a pointed chin, light brown eyes and a crooked nose was next to Foulques. You could tell just by the way he sat at the table that he was proud and very self-confidence. Yet he did not inspire dislike, rather certainty and a feeling of security.

"Who could that be I wonder? I've never seen him before, I think," Foulques thought. "He must be around my uncle's age."

"My Brothers," sounded Pierre's voice, "we have gathered here today to elect, according to the legal procedures laid down by our statutes, our new Master. May everyone make considered decisions, free of bias and antipathy. I therefore order you to decide on, always with the help of God, those who will vote in this procedure. Chose from those who desire peace and harmony in our order."

Then the officer of the election, Bertrand, and Pierre withdrew into a room. They decided that the third person to vote would be Guillaume de Villaret and they called on him to join them in the room. Foulques looked at his uncle as he was walking towards the room. He looked at his face in an attempt to understand whether he was happy to be one of the electors, but that he would also probably not be elected Grand Master. However, his face remained calm and expressionless as he walked. A little later they called on Armand, who rose, disappointment clear on his face. The fifth elector was the elderly Robert. He looked proud to have been chosen for one more time as he knew that he was too old to be a candidate for Grand Master. And certainly, as Foulques watched him stagger forward as if balancing between life and death, he thought that he must surely be over seventy, something very rare at the time.

The twelve electors were chosen in this way, twelve so as to symbolize Christ's Apostles and, finally, those twelve called on the thirteenth member, who had to be a chaplain, and had the honour of representing Jesus himself. The elderly Peter, who had also been an elector in the past, in Outremer and in the West, had this honour. The main function of the thirteenth priest was to calm emotions, in other words maintain harmony between the twelve who would vote.

The electors then presented themselves in front of the others and, reverently following the Rule of the order, prayed together once again for the grace of God and his punishment, meaning the loss of Divine Grace, if they did not do their duty and showed bias towards any Brother for self-serving purposes.

Then the electors withdrew once more, leaving the others to wait anxiously. Foulques knew that after everyone had expressed their opinion, two candidates usually remained and of these two the one with the most votes was elected. Of course, some knight who was in the West could be elected. In this case, however, it would take some time for the knight to find out that he had been chosen and come down to Outremer, and that was why Foulques believed that the Grand Master elected would already be in the East. "The order needs a strong leader urgently, the political situation is too difficult and unpleasant for us to wait for months until someone arrives from the West! The Muslims won't do us the favour of waiting!" Foulques was thinking when suddenly the door opened and there were the electors standing on its sill.

Foulques quickly looked for his uncle among them. Their eyes only met for an instant, but Foulques had enough time to see that his uncle was pleased with the result of the election before Bertrand, as officer of the election began to speak:

"Dear Brothers, give thanks and praise to Our Lady, our Lord Jesus Christ and all the Saints that have deemed us worthy of reaching agreement today for the good of our order. I announce to you, therefore, that, by God's Grace, we have chosen the Lord Master of the Order. Are you happy with our choice?" This question was purely a formality and was posed before the name of the newly elected Grand Master was announced. The Brothers replied in one voice, as was expected:

"Yes, in the name of God!"

Bertrand then went up to Pierre, the temporary commander, and asked him:

"Lord commander, if God and we have elected you Lord Master of our order, do you promise to obey the Rule for the rest of your life, to observe its righteous manners and customs and to work for the good of the Order and the Brothers?

"Yes, God willing," Pierre replied in a steady voice.

This, of course, did not mean that Pierre had been elected Grand Master, this was simply also part of the predefined procedure. Bertrand then posed this same question to many other officials who could have been elected, amongst whom were not only Foulques's uncle and the commander of the Brothers in Acre, but also some wise elders of the order, not as old as Brother Robert, who could also have been elected. Bertrand also asked the knight with brown hair and a crooked nose who had been next to Foulques, but not Foulques and other very young knights.

When Bertrand had stopped asking these questions, bringing, in other words, the procedure of the preliminary oath to its conclusion, he stood at the centre of the room, ready to finally announce the newly elected Grand Master. The suspense amongst everybody present in that room had reached its peak and the tension in the room was so great that Foulques felt dizzy. This was because, according to the Rule, the question had to be posed to the newly elected Grand Master, without him knowing that he had been elected, of course!

This meant that everyone that Bertrand had asked was now wondering if they had been elected! Only the electors remained calm, as they knew the result.

Bertrand strode slowly towards the new Grand Master. When Foulques saw the direction in which Bertrand was heading he was stunned. The elderly man stopped in front of the man with the pointed chin and said to him in an official manner:

"Brother Nicolas, in the name of the Father and the Son and the Holy Spirit, we have elected and we name you Lord Master."

Nicolas stood up, clearly surprised, but also moved by the honour granted him.

Then the elderly man turned to the rest of the Brothers:

"Dear Brothers, thank God, here is our new Grand Master!

The chaplains immediately took up the chant 'Te Deum Laudamus.'[29] Nicolas stood, a slight smile on his face and his back perfectly straight. He inspired energy and trust. Foulques saw calmness and jubilation in his face. He immediately felt, from the impression he gained of this man, as he watched him quietly mouthing the solemn chants, that he was a good choice for the order.

When his eyes met with his uncle's, he saw in them his approval, that he also completely agreed with this choice. He suddenly felt great joy seeing the brothers devoutly going towards the new Grand Master, in order to pick him up and carry him to the chapel. In doing so, the brothers wanted to show their new Master to Christ on the Cross and thank Him for his election. Without thinking, he too ran after them.

When he entered the chapel, he saw the Master kneeling before the altar in reverence. Around him, the chaplains were chanting, praying to God to lead the new Grand Master down the right path. Foulques saw his uncle next to him, kneeling down to pray. He immediately knelt down too, brought his hands together and closed his eyes, praying to God from the depths of his soul that everything would go well from now on.

9

Acre, November 22 1281

 pale sun began to slowly appear behind the mountains, shining its rays on the town's strong walls. As soon as the light went through the fortifications it spread above the stone houses of the town, licking the walls and sweetly awakening its residents – residents of any kind, regardless of nationality and religion – Jews and Muslims, Armenians and Franks, Orthodox, and also Non-orthodox Eastern Christians.

When the sun lit the harbour it was already full of life because of the merchants going back and forth between the ships and the sea, and the Italians shouting loudly at each other could be heard. The harbour had been divided into three parts. One had been given to the Venetians, the other to the Pisans and the other to the Genoese merchants. However, disputes between the Italians and their greed were still proverbial.

Acre had been under Frankish occupation since 1191, when king Richard I of England, the Lionheart, had seized the city during the Third Crusade after three years of siege, taking it from the Fatimids of Egypt. After the second and final loss of Jerusalem it had unquestionably become the capital of the so-called kingdom of Acre and also the seat, and place of coronation, of the Frankish kings. Apart from the kings and the merchants, the three military orders – the Knights Templar, the Hospitallers and the Teutons also had their preceptories in Acre.

In the Knights Templar's commandery, Matins had just ended in the chapel and the brothers were eating silently in the refectory. Philippe was sitting next to Francois and they were eating dates. Both had changed notably. After almost four years in Outremer both their skins had acquired a darker tan, and were rough and hard from hardship and the relentless sun. Ten years had passed since Philippe had joined the order and the first signs of a more mature age had began to show not only in his eyes and on his face, but also on those of Francois, who was also at the end of the third decade of his life.

Now the two knights were greedily sinking their teeth into a sweetmeat made of ginger that the servants had just left in front of them. Philippe's eyes met those of

Francois and Philippe had the sense that the green-eyed knight shared his thoughts completely at that moment: "As much as I eat here I will never tire of this delicious food!"

In truth, for the knights that came from the West the food was only one thing that impressed them greatly. Philippe could still recall his feelings when he first saw the "Promised Land" from the ship. The palm trees, the desert sand, the camels, everything, was magical and new for the excited knights, who were finally seeing for themselves the same things that had been part of their Lord Jesus's everyday life. Even the sky seemed a different shade of light blue from that of their homeland, because of the vastness of the desert.

There were many orange trees and lemon trees, "apple trees of Adam" and "fig trees of the Pharaoh", date trees, abundant sugar cane and nutmeg. When someone scored a line in the acacia tree, the sap, known as "gum arabic", ran plenty. But the most impressive plants all of were the huge cedars of Lebanon and the cedars of the sea. Then there was the stunning wildlife of the area, which amazed the people of the West. Apart from the ordinary animals that they also had in Europe, here the newcomers heard stories of terrible crocodiles, chubby hippos, blood-thirsty tigers and towering giraffes. The only animal the Knights Templar were allowed to hunt was the lion. Many lords who were members of the laity had tamed leopards, which they used as hunting dogs.

All these admittedly wonderful things were in a sharp contrast with what was, for people from the West, the dreadful climate of the Middle East. Hot and humid, it was the worst possible, and most unhealthy, climate for the knights of Northern Europe, who were used to cold weather. When the Hamsin blew you might swallow no small measure of sand, while the stagnant waters, home to mosquitoes and flies, were a source of many illnesses rare in Northern Europe. Cholera, plague, typhus, dysentery and leprosy were common illnesses which spread rapidly and cost many Europeans their lives, their bodies totally unadapted to the heat they were so unused to. Baldwin IV, the king of Jerusalem, ruled from 1174 to 1185 as the famous "Leper King". He had suffered from the illness from the age of nine, was crowned when sixteen and survived until he was twenty-four. He had done the best he could for his kingdom, ridden by disputes, despite his incurable disease. There was always the fear that the successors to the throne would die, as mortality rates among male babies were particularly high. That is why, in the history of Outremer, it was women who often passed on the royal line of succession.

The climate, together with abundant wealth, had made those who had been in the East for many years, and were not knights under strict discipline, creatures of comfort. Their clothes had gold details and were richly embroidered. There was plenty of silk and many ladies adorned their dresses with pearls. The castles were completely unlike those of the West as far as opulence and furnishings were concerned, something that was true for the castles of the orders too. Here there were interior courts with rose gardens, thick Turkish carpets and plenty of porcelain objects, fountains, even scented candles! They were very different from the castles in Europe, which were simple, with huge empty stone halls which had only the basics as far as furnishing was concerned.

Beneath this superficial prosperity, Philippe had seen first-hand during these years how little land remained in the hands of the people from the West. Trade with the 'infidels' was flourishing, thus bringing in all these rich goods, but the Westerners' military situation was hopeless. Philippe had come to the bitter realisation that the Christians were very few in number in comparison with the hordes of 'infidels'.

During the years he had been there he had taken part in many skirmishes with the 'infidels', skirmishes that had taken place despite the peace that supposedly held sway and the relative calm that Baybars death had brought about.

After Baraka's resignation, the ambitious Qalawun[30] had become the new Mamluk leader and was a new threat to the Christians.

Philippe, however, had yet to take part in a great battle or difficult siege. He had become something like the adjutant of the Grand Master. The truth was that Guillaume de Beaujeu had come to like him a great deal and considered him a worthy knight. His feelings certainly had their origin in the episode that had taken place involving Philippe the day before his departure from Coulommiers involving the robbers. The Grand Master had naturally admired Philippe's bravery in the episode with the outlaws, but what he had liked most was the magnanimity and sincerity of the young knight, who had handed in all the money he had received from the noble, without trying to hide and keep a part of it.

So, after the journey, which had allowed them to get to know each other better, Guillaume had developed a close relationship not only with Philippe, but also with Luigi and Francois. Taking advantage of this relationship, Philippe had asked the Grand Master about his "uncle" and had told him about his desire to look for him, but Guillaume's answer had disappointed him greatly. He still remembered the words he had said at the time:

"Brother Philippe, I did not have the honour of meeting either Gerard nor Jocelyn, and that is natural since I am not so old. From what I have heard from those older than myself, however, I have the impression that Jocelyn in particular was a treasure for our order and unbelievably brave. Unfortunately, no one survived the battle of al-Mansurah, where I believe he was lost too, which tells us how bravely he fought, I believe. In accounts of other battles, however, I have been told that he truly brought terror to the infidels. From what I have heard, nevertheless, I believe Jocelyn, unfortunately, to be dead. So it is unlikely that you will ever see him again. I do however understand your desire to look for him. So ask all those who knew him, and if you should learn anything that would enable you to follow his tracks, I, as the Virgin Mary is my witness, will give you as much time as you need to find him. But without wishing to make you sad, I think that only a miracle would allow you to find him again, if, of course, he is still alive."

So following the Grand Master's advice, Philippe had found two very elderly knights in Acre, Brothers Richard and Andre. Brother Andrew had even known one of the five survivors not killed or captured in al-Mansurah. They both had had the best to say about his "uncle" and he had also found out some things about his character and some old battles, but nothing that could help him find him again.

The two Brothers were even sure that Jocelyn was dead or captured. Even if the second case were true, they had told him, he would still be dead after so many years in captivity.

"All these years that I've been fighting, my child," Brother Richard, who did not participate in battles any more but only performed auxiliary tasks because of his old age, had told him, "I have seen only one or two cases in which knights came back from captivity alive. One of them had had his right hand cut off as a punishment when he had tried to escape for the first time and he had only come back when his master had died and released him in his will!"

Richard had also talked to him about his "uncle's" character: "You must be proud to a be relative of Jocelyn's. I have seen very few men in my life that can use a sword so well. He was magnanimous. He spared the life of any infidel that begged him to do so when we had won a battle and he did not take prisoners as slaves. He felt sorry for them I remember. He used to ask what if we were in their place some day. Others were much harsher. They didn't even take prisoners; they killed them straight away. All these things happened in the old days, of course. These days we rarely win great battles, all we do is raid and skirmish. You know yourself. Hatred and intolerance are to blame for everything your uncle always said. All we gave them was blood and pain and they are paying us back now. A tooth for a tooth. Because the Muslims have never forgotten the massacres carried out when we first took Jerusalem[31]. Until then the world had seen no city fall like that. The life of no Jew or Muslim was spared. Only the Mongols in Baghdad did worse than we did, a few years ago."[32] However, Gerard had not spoken so well of Jocelyn's uncle and Philippe's father, Jacques. But Philippe had found out a great deal about the defeat of the Christians at Hattin[33], of which he had had but a vague knowledge until then.

"I was told these things by older men who had taken part in that battle and experienced our internal divisions at first hand. At that time, when the "Leper King", Baldwin IV ruled, we were divided into two factions. On the one hand there was the king with the viceroy Raymond of Tripoli, the Hospitallers and those from the West who had spent many years in Outremer and knew that it was better to stay on the defence and not challenge the infidels. On the other, there were the knights who had just come from the West, who were impatient to throw themselves into battle without thinking of the consequences. We supported them, we Knights Templar, with our Lord Master at the time, Gerard, Reynald of Chatillon, a pretentious, arrogant man, and Guy of Lusignan, who had married princess Isabella and had become king a year before the fateful battle. Some years before, Gerard, Flemish by birth, had gone to Tripoli as a secular knight, before he became a Knight Templar, and had offered his services to Raymond in exchange for his promise that he would marry him to the first suitable heiress in his domain. When, however, Raymond had broken his promise and had given the daughter of the Lord Botrun to a rich Pisan instead of Gerard, the latter had become furious and, having no other alternative, had become a member of the Knights Templar, where he very soon became Lord Master. He never forgave Raymond. I'm telling you all this because the enmity between those two had negative effects when it came to our dealings with the Infidel."

"As for them, they had Salah ad-Din Yusuf ibn Ayyub, known to us Christians as Saladin,[34] as their ruler. He was a very capable man, who also was magnanimous and had principles. Muslims and Christians were at peace under Saladin's leadership. The problem was caused by Raynald, who, six years before the fateful battle, could not bear to see the rich Muslim caravans passing in front of him undisturbed, and attacked one of them. Saladin rightfully complained to Baldwin, who was then king and demanded reparations, something that Raynald refused to make. Saladin then captured one thousand five hundred pilgrims in Egypt and imprisoned them, asking for the return of the goods that had been looted, but Raynald again refused to return anything. Thus the first rift occurred and the great battle between Infidel and Christian took place – with unforeseen results."

"Things had calmed down a little until the moment when Raynald, together with Christian pirates, sank a ship carrying Muslim pilgrims. The Muslims were horrified by such disrespect for their faith and Saladin personally swore not to forgive Raynald for this sacrilege. A year before the fateful battle, when Raynald attacked a caravan of merchants again, killing the Egyptian soldiers that were accompanying it and taking the merchants and the booty to his castle in Kerak, Saladin had had enough. He sent a delegation to Raynald asking for compensation and the release of the merchants. Raynald sent away this delegation without even listening to them. The representatives, in desperation, went to the new king Guy de Lusignan, who listened to them and ordered Raynald to compensate them. Raynald, however, knowing that Guy owed gaining the throne and staying on it to him, paid no attention and the king did not insist."

"So while Raymond of Tripoli made a truce with Saladin, which was considered treasonous by some Christians, but what I would call a perceptive manoeuvrer, Guy, at Gerard's instigation, set off with an army so as to gather his vassals and conquer Galilee before Saladin, unavoidably by then, attacked."

"To cut a long story short, my son, our Brothers then had a small skirmish with the Muslims, months before Hattin, instigated by Gerard. From the ninety knights only three survived, including Gerard. When later Saladin gathered a huge army, Raymond cancelled the peace treaty with him and declared allegiance to Guy, wanting to fight on the Christian side. And that is when the great drama begins."

"On July 2nd, two days before the final battle at Hattin, the Christians set camp at Sephory, a place with plenty of water and good grazing for the horses. Meanwhile Saladin was besieging Tiberias, which Raymond's wife was defending."

"When her messengers reached Sephory and asked for help, a council was held to decide whether the Christian army should leave this good defensive position and rush to the city that was under siege, taking a difficult route with no water and under the blazing July sun. Raymond, thinking wisely, persuaded the king, after several disagreements in the council of course, not to give up their strong position, despite the fact that he wanted to help his wife. Saving the kingdom was more important than his personal possessions, he announced. The king agreed and the subject was closed."

"However, when the council ended, Gerard secretly went back to the king's tent and, telling Guy that Raymond was a traitor and that it was a shame to let a city that was only six leagues away fall, managed to change the king's mind."

"So the soldiers began their difficult march on the morning of July 3rd, under the blazing sun. It was clearly suicide. Soon everyone was suffering from thirst as there was no water anywhere. At night, exhausted, they camped under a hill with two peaks, the so-called horns of Hattin. The well there, however, was dry. Saladin, unable to believe his good luck, surrounded the Christians. That night was a nightmare for them".

"Those who left in search of water were killed by infidels, who, on top of this, set fire to dry bushes, choking the Christians with hot smoke. So, when the attack began a little after dawn, the Christians had no power to fight. Despite their bravery, they suffered a debacle which they, of course, had brought upon themselves. And bringing this heart-breaking tale to its close, it is worth recounting to you the episode that took place in Saladin's tent after the Christians had lost. So it was there Saladin met Guy, Gerard, Raynald and other nobles. Raymond and some lords had, paradoxically, managed to escape. Saladin, always magnanimous, had the king sit next to him and, seeing how thirsty he was, offered him a bowl of frozen rosewater. According to the laws of Arabian hospitality, offering someone in captivity food or drink means that their life is not in danger."

"Guy, after quenching his thirst, gave the bowl to Raynald, who was sitting next to him. When Saladin saw this he said to the interpreter: "Tell the king that he gave that man something to drink, not I," meaning that he could offer no guarantee for Raynald's life. Then he turned to Raynald and reminded him of all the disrespect he had shown and all the crimes that he could not forgive."

"When Raynald answered disrespectfully, Saladin took a sword and beheaded him himself in front of everyone."

"That was the end of a man who had caused so much suffering both to Christians and Muslims. To Guy, who was shaking from fear after what he had seen, Saladin said: "Do not worry. A king does not kill a king, but the perfidy and insolence of this man went beyond all bounds".

"And indeed, he showed admirably leniency towards the rest of the nobles, as he allowed all the barons who were members of the laity to live as prisoners until their ransom was paid. As for the knights, however, he had them all killed except for Gerard, who was also freed, although I believe he deserved to die more than his knights."

Philippe had been left speechless while Richard was talking, so fascinated was he by the old man's account. While he felt proud of his father Jocelyn, he was now ashamed that Gerard was a relative of his. Brother Andre, on the other hand, had told him of the battle of al-Mansurah, which was of great interest to Philippe, as it was after this battle that his father's tracks had finally and irrevocably been lost.

So the elderly Brother had told him about the great hopes that had been placed in Louis the Saint[35] and in the seventh, in time, armed campaign,[36] but which had also ended in a total failure despite the successful capture of Damietta. This time failure was caused by Louis's brother, Robert of Artois's haste in attacking the 'infidels', against the good counsel of the Grand Master of the Temple, Guillaume de Sonnac.

For the first time the Christians had come up against the robust administrative skills of Baybars, later to be Sultan, leading the 'infidels', and they suffered a great defeat – only five out of two hundred and ninety Knights Templar survived! Guillaume de Sonnac was killed in the fierce fighting that took place between February and April 1250, while Louis was captured.

The new Sultan of the 'Infidels', Turanshah, was impressed by Louis's personality and this led to the better treatment of the hundreds of Christian captives on the part of the 'Infidel'. The king bought his own freedom and that of his army by exchanging Damietta and by paying five hundred tournois, that is one million hyperpyra! The deal was made by Queen Margaret, who had given birth to Louis's child after hearing news of the Christians' defeat and naming him Jean Tristan, that is Jean of sorrows.

A little later Turanshah was murdered by Baybars himself, who was thirsty for power. This brought the Mamluk dynasty to the fore and new misfortunes for the Christians. Much of the money for the release of the king was paid by the Knights Templar themselves, although Louis had reprimanded Guillaume de Sonnac in the past concerning the peace treaty with the 'Infidels' and their relationship was not the best possible.

So, Philippe realized that that campaign had cost his order a great deal, a stack of losses in terms of numbers, the life of the Grand Master, which could have been saved had his advice been followed, and a great deal of money.

Brother Andre had told Philippe that maybe more knights had survived and been taken prisoners. No one could have excluded that possibility. However, knights who found themselves in the hands of 'infidels' were usually slaughtered, the latter hating them to death for the courage and selflessness with which they always fought.

"If he survived the deadly battle there is no way he lived afterwards," were Andrew's words, words which echoed in Philippe's ears, causing him to lose hope. It took him some time to accept failure and set new goals in life.

As time went by he managed to put the subject to the back of his mind and forget it, at least so it seemed. This had been the advice Francois had offered when Philippe had told him everything. His friend had truly been there for him, tolerating his crises of melancholy and trying to make him forget through other things. Now Luigi came up to them as they came, their hunger satisfied, out of the refectory. Brother Jean was walking next to him. Luigi addressed them first.

"Brothers, the Lord Master wishes to see us. When Matins were over he told me to find you after you had eaten and for us go together to him."

"Is that so? I wonder what he wants from us?" Francois asked, looking first at Philippe and then at Luigi, in surprise. The two friends had got used to Luigi by now, and as the years had gone by, they had almost become, one might say, friends – but they were always slightly reserved towards him. With Jean, who was now walking silently beside them, weighing them up with his big green eyes, they felt more comfortable.

"I haven't the slightest idea, but he told me to find all three of you and for us to all go to his office together," Luigi replied, shrugging his shoulders.

"So hurry up then so he doesn't have wait for us," said Philippe, starting to walk faster. The Grand Master's office was situated next to the knights' dormitories, not too far from the refectory. In two minutes they were knocking on the heavy door. The knights were surprised when Guillaume himself opened the door. He had sent all his sergeants away and he was alone, something that meant that he had something important to tell them.

"Welcome, my Brothers. Sit down," said Guillaume in his warm bass voice, indicating the wooden stools. When the knights had sat down, he did the same on the wooden chair behind his desk, which was also made of wood.

"Even when he is sitting, this man always retains his grandeur," thought Philippe who, every time he saw the Grand Master, could not cease to be impressed by the grace of his movements and the subtlety of his ways. Guillaume de Beaujeu was not particularly tall, but had prominent cheekbones and a look that captivated anyone who looked at him in the eye. He had been Grand Master since 1273 and, despite the fact that some criticised him for his intrigues, Philippe admired him and considered him a capable leader for the order. He was a proud and ambitious man but also a very active one, something that undoubtedly benefited the order. Guillaume was related to the royal House of France and had supported Charles of Anjou in his effort to create the overseas empire he dreamed of. So he had been strongly opposed the rights of the Regents of Cyprus in Outremer, supporting the representatives of Charles when he had taken part in the Council of Lyons in 1274, which Pope Gregory I had convened, and at which the latter had failed to organize a new crusade and had succeeded in creating a spurious union between the Eastern and Western church. Subsequently, Guillaume had been at the head of the conflict between the Knights Templar and Bohemond VII, Count of Tripoli while, at the same time, he had had contacts with Muslims for political reasons, something for which he was bitterly criticised by his enemies.

Nothing, however, was enough to make him less charming in the eyes of the men he commanded. So, now the four men, enchanted by the calm movements of their Grand Master and his polite behaviour, were, indeed, hanging on his words and patiently waiting for him to tell them for what it was that he now needed their help.

"My Brothers," Guillaume began talking, "you know that our Rule demands that we avoid too much unnecessary talk. That is why I will get to the point and tell you what it is that I need from you. I would like you to accompany me to Alexandria. I know that I could order you to do so. However, I would like you to do this willingly. If you accept, I hope that you will honour me with your discretion and the reason why we are visiting the city remains between the five of us," he concluded, allowing the confidence that he was going to get what he was asking to show. Of course, as a Grand Master he could demand it and he knew that very well, but he also knew, good leader and diplomat that he was, that his chances of getting what he wanted were enhanced by showing his men trust rather than just simply ordering them to do something.

By way of affirmation, Philippe rose immediately and addressed the Grand Master, after looking towards the other brothers and getting their silent approval for what he was about to say.

"It would be our pleasure, my Lord, to serve you and our order. Without reserve, we agree to accompany you. Whatever is said here will, of course, stay between us."

A smile appeared on Guillaume's face. He motioned to Philippe to sit down and began to explain the reasons why they would go on this journey:

"Thank you, Brothers, I knew I could count on you. As you know, things are not going on very well here in Outremer for us Christians and war with the Muslims is on its way, something that means, for our order at least, a heavy toll in blood and money. Am I right?" Guillaume asked, looking at Jean, who said, nodding his head graciously:

"You are right, my Lord."

"Our expenses have increased a great deal lately," Guillaume went on, gravely and with some displeasure in his voice, "and, at this present time, there are some projects for the fortification of those forts that remain in our hands and some ransoms that needs to be paid for various Christians held captive pending. You know very well, I believe, that despite the accusations made against us by some, we contribute as much as we can to the paying of these ransoms. On the other hand, our income has fallen dramatically of late and the order's funds are by no means as large as some wish to believe. The donations to our order have grown considerably less as enthusiasm for armed campaigns here in the East has waned in Europe, as has the admission of new members to the order, which in turn means the property given to us."

At this point Guillaume stopped talking, stood up and unlocked a big metal box which was on the right of his desk. Everyone's eyes widened in astonishment, and a gasp of admiration slipped from Luigi's and Jean's mouth when they saw what Guillaume took out of the box and placed on the desk in front of them. It was a beautiful necklace. The chain was golden and an emerald in the shape of a heart hung from it. No one dared speak and everyone waited for the Grand Master to go on, as he did:

"This is a family heirloom that came to my hands after the death of my sister and which is now property of the order since I am a member of it. I decided, therefore, because of our increased need for money, to exchange it for hyperpyra, which can be used more easily."

"I'm sorry to interfere, my Lord," said Luigi, "but who here has so much money to exchange it for this, if I'm not mistaken, very expensive necklace?"

"That's a reasonable question, Brother," said Guillaume, smiling, "and this is where our trip to Alexandria comes in. Of course no one here has that amount of money, but a rich Jewish merchant, who goes by the name Simeon, lives there. He has the money and is willing to exchange it for the necklace and give it to his daughter. That is why I need four brave knights to accompany me, offering me security and confidentiality."

"Are you sure about this?" Francois dared to ask. "I mean, is it possible that he has so much money to spend? Does he know how much it is worth or does he think it is something less valuable? Because this, I think, is no ordinary piece of jewellery."

"Of course, Brother, we won't risk the trip for nothing. I've been planning all this for months, everything has been arranged and you don't need to worry about anything. I know this man personally. He is honest, trustworthy and, most importantly, discreet, so will not to reveal this transaction to anyone. And, by the way, this is not an ordinary piece of jewellery. You are right Brother. It has been in my family for a very long time. As for the price, I have already stated this in writing to Simeon, who happens to have been, I forgot to tell you, a very good friend of mine for many years," Guillaume said, and with triumphant tone in his voice added:

"The sum is six hundred thousand hyperpyra, a sum that will solve all our current problems and which I reveal to you since you promised me confidentiality on your part and to accompany me."

Stunned by the huge sum, Philippe said:

"Our confidentiality can be taken for granted, my Lord, but how can we, five people, manage to return with such a large amount of money without being noticed, which is what I assume you wish? The necklace can easily be hidden but the money…"

"You are right my dear but I have thought of that too," Guillaume answered reassuringly. "We will not carry the money in a chest so as to become a target, rather each of us will carry some of it in pouches and most of it will be sewn into our clothes. What do you have to say now?"

"I see you have thought of everything. However, it still is a dangerous mission," Philippe commented, bringing the pragmatic aspect of his character to the forefront and putting his emotional nature to one side for a moment.

"That is true," answered the Grand Master, "but as you are a knight here you are constantly in danger anyway, you may get killed in battle or captured. From that point of view I don't think I am asking you to risk more than you already are!"

"That is certain. Let's not talk too much though…" said Jean, already standing. "When are we leaving, my Lord?

"The sooner, the better," said Guillaume also rising to his feet, making the others do the same. "Will you be ready tomorrow?"

"We will make sure we are," said Philippe looking at the rest for their assent. "What do you think? Will we?"

"Of course," Luigi replied on behalf of everyone. "We salute you Excellency," he added bowing slightly. "We will see you at the service."

"Oh and one more question, if I may, my Lord," Philippe broke in. "Shall we prepare the horses or are we going by ship?"

"Oh, yes, I forgot to tell you," Guillaume said, striking his forehead with his hand. "We would have to take a circular route if we took the horses, would lose a lot of time and come across many robbers on our way, while by boat we will travel near the shore, thus avoiding any pirates that might appear. A Venetian galley is leaving for Alexandria tomorrow. It will be perfect. I have informed the captain."

"So you were certain that we would accept from what I understand!" Francois said, laughing.

"To be honest, yes, I know you well by now! You all do your duty! And I thank you for this in advance. May God be with you!" said Guillaume, placing his hand on Francois' shoulder.

"May God be with you too! Let's go," Jean said, opening the door, and their Grand

Master walked to the door and said goodbye to them. They all went out quietly. Nothing was said. Everyone was deep in thought.

"I wish I could inform Abbot Giovanni! He would find this information very interesting! The only thing I haven't found out about is that damn organization, but I will, that is for sure. Something tells me that I need to stay close to the Lord Master. It is not possible for him not to know anything!" Luigi thought and looked at Philippe, deep in his own thoughts, walking a little further off:

"Alexandria. Not bad. If anything, it will be a pleasant change! Let's see..." So they walked, in silence, each of them deep in their own thoughts, until they reached their dormitory.

10

Hospitaller Commandery, Tripoli, November 22, 1281

oulques was waiting patiently outside the Grand Master's office. He could not understand why his uncle had informed him that he should be present at the meeting of the Grand Master with the seneschal, Pierre, and the mareschal, his uncle, who, despite his worries, the new Grand Master, Nicolas Lorgne, had retained in office.

As Foulques had hoped, Nicolas had proved to be a good and worthy leader for the order as his first action was to broker the truce between the Knights Templar and Bohemund IV. Nicolas, well aware the dangerous position of the Christians in Outremer, would often quench the fires of conflict between the Christians and would avoid challenging the Muslims with unnecessary incursions into and pillaging of enemy territory. He believed that peace between Muslims and Christians should, by any means, be kept, precarious though it was, until a new campaign from the West could take place, adding to the number of those Christians remaining in the East. "Undoubtedly a wise tactic," Foulques thought. "What else could anyone do anyway, after our last debacle?"

Foulques brought back to mind everything he had learned about the defeat of the order in the battle of Homs by Qalawun, which had taken place on the thirtieth of the previous month. He had not taken part himself, but some Hospitallers from the commandery of Tripoli, who had fought on the side of the fearsome Mongol Sultan and had been defeated, had returned bitterly disappointed. It was, therefore, a fact that the Mamluks were taking the lead as a military force over the powerful, up until then, Mongols.

"And if the dreaded Mongols did not manage to defeat the Mamluks, can we hope to beat them, a handful of desperate Christians?" was Foulques' last ominous thought before his uncle appeared at the door and invited him in. After saying good afternoon to his superiors, Foulques looked through the window at the sun, which had just disappeared below the horizon, completing another daily cycle, and sat next to the desk where the rest of the men were sitting comfortably.

The Grand Master, without wasting time, got straight to the point. He was sitting at his desk and was holding a piece of paper in his hands. As he spoke, he looked at Foulques, who quickly realized that the rest of the officials were aware of the issue, about which he had no idea, and that the purpose of this meeting was only to inform him.

"Dear Brother," Nicolas began. "You have proved yourself a worthy warrior and that is why, with no need of further explanation, we would like to ask you to accompany us to Alexandria. I mean myself, your uncle and Brother Pierre. To be precise," he added looking at Guillaume, "it was your uncle's idea that you should be the knight that accompanies us. So what do you say? Do you accept?"

Foulques, despite being unprepared and unable to hide the surprise from his face, replied formally: "As you order, my Lord. It is my honour to serve you in any way you think is best."

Guillaume allowed a smile to show on his face, a sign that he was happy with the answer his nephew had given. After that, still smiling, he addressed him: "Nephew, do you not wish to know the reason for this journey?"

"Of course I would, my uncle," Foulques replied, nodding his head,"but I didn't consider it appropriate to ask."

"You acted correctly, Brother," Nicolas broke in "but since you have decided to accompany us you must know the reason for our visit to Alexandria. It is no secret to any Brother of our order, anyway. You have surely heard that in recent years donations to our order and our revenues have somewhat decreased. This is true for all military orders, of course, although I would like to believe that our revenues have not decreased as much as those of the Knights Templar. When, however, an opportunity to gain extra income arises we do not let it slip, do we?"

"That's correct my Lord, as you say," Foulques replied and looked at Pierre, who remained silent and had not moved an inch all this time, but was now beginning to seem impatient and annoyed by Nicolas' explanations. The Grand Master was obviously saying things that Pierre, the mareschal knew well and had often talked about. So it was most probably the case that he was bored to distraction hearing the same thing over and over again. Luckily for him, Nicolas did not seem to be aware of his irritation as he had his eyes fixed on Foulques and was completely engrossed in what he had to tell him:

"A Genoese merchant[37], a permanent resident of Alexandria named Antonio Pescatore, informed me a month ago that his father Alessandro, who recently died, states in his will[38] that he wishes to donate a large amount of money to our order, on condition that we go there to collect it, taking every possible precaution. His son informs me in his letter that the deceased would have in no way wished for his donation to fall prey to robbers, so he advises me to take a few knights with me while the money is being moved so that we do not attract the attention of thieves, but experienced, trustworthy and well-armed knights. Therefore, I chose you three. As for the amount, it is eighty thousand hyperpyra."

Nicolas leant on his chair and stopped talking. Guillaume took advantage of his silence and gave a few last pieces of practical information to his nephew, who listened carefully:

"We shall travel by sea without going out into the open sea, so we will not be in danger from pirates. The most dangerous part will be when we are returning, while we are in the port of Alexandria, before we set sail on the journey back home. Therefore, discretion is necessary so that nobody around us realizes that we are carrying such a huge amount of money."

"That goes without saying, Uncle. Shall I leave to get ready? I assume it will not take us long to set off," Foulques said eagerly as he stood up. The others quickly followed his example so that what else was said was at the door:

"Yes, Brother," Pierre said at last, happy that the conversation had ended. "Tomorrow morning a Genoese ship is leaving for Alexandria so, fortunately, we will not need horses."

At that moment, the bell for Vespers sounded.

"After Vespers and dinner we will all have time to get ready," said the Grand Master. "As soon as the sun comes up I'll be waiting for you here again so that we can go to the harbour. The elderly Bertrand will assume command while we are away." At these words the four knights left the room, closing the door behind them.

11

Alexandria, November 25, 1281

nd what do we do now? How are we going to go? Not one of us knows this city!" said Jean, in a troubled voice. The five Knights Templar had just disembarked at the bustling port of Alexandria. Philippe, Luigi and Francois were looking around them, enthralled, while Guillaume, dusting off his tunic, answered him:

"We are waiting for someone sent by Simeon, Brother. The merchant wrote to me that he was going to send one of his servants to take us to his house as soon as we arrive. I wrote telling him the date and the time, approximately, of our arrival."

"And how will we recognize him? We have never seen him!" Jean said again.

"For God's sake, Brother! We might not know him but he will recognize us. Do you see any other Knights Templar around here?" Guillaume said, a little abruptly, starting to become irritated by Jean's string of questions.

"You are right, my Lord, I hadn't thought of that," Jean replied with deference, looking nonchalantly at some small children who were playing hopscotch and laughing nearby.

Philippe looked around and scrutinized the area. Behind them was the sea, with numerous ships tied to the pier and belonging to Pisan, Genoese, Venetian merchants and, to a lesser extent, from Amalfi. There were also many galleys belonging to Muslim merchants, as well as some which were the property of Jewish and Armenian merchants. At the pier one could see a crowd of people, mainly servants, who were loading and unloading goods onto the ships. It was sad to see old people, but also little children, bent under the weight of the huge sacks they were carrying and stumbling, while the overseers next to them were ready to whip them for even the slightest mistake. The city had been planned over a grid of vertical and horizontal streets, something which made orientation easier for residents and visitors. Philippe turned towards the sea again. In the large harbour there was the small island of Antirhodos and, looking from the beach, the far end of the harbour was marked by small island called Faros, which had given its name to the tower which helped ships to enter the port.

"It is really very beautiful here," Luigi said to himself, looking around too.

Jean and the Grand Master were sitting a little further away from the rest, who kept on chatting about the things they saw around them. Taking advantage of this, Guillaume whispered in Jean's ear:"So what do you think of them, do you think we could introduce them to Fede Santa?"

"I think it is too early for anything like that, my lord," he replied, shaking his head." Let the mission end first. As for Luigi, I am. however, still uncertain."

"Why?" Guillaume asked in surprise. "I would say he is very committed."

"I won't say no, on the contrary. It's just I don't know if Luigi would accept the beliefs that many consider somehow unorthodox. Whenever we have happened to talk about something, he has, I think, proved to be rigid and dogmatic on theological issues."

"All right, Brother, we will see what we will do. Anyway, we have time to…"

"I'm sorry to interrupt you, dear sirs, but are you the friends of my master, Lord Simeon?"

The voice, in halting French, came from right behind the Grand Master and when the two men turned towards it, they saw a small, dark-skinned man, whose age could not be determined at first sight, smiling at them kindly. He was so short that his head barely reached Guillaume's chest.

"Yes, that is us," Guillaume replied, smiling widely and looking at the little man from head to toe in curiosity."

"My name is Farouk. Come with me, I will take you to my master. I presume those young men down there are with you?"

"Yes," replied Jean beckoning to the others.

"My name is Guillaume de Beaujeu and I have the honour of being in command of the Temple Order," the Grand Master said, extending his hand to the servant. "This is Brother Jean, Luigi, Francois and Philippe," he then added, indicating the three knights coming towards them.

"A pleasure to meet you," replied Farouk, shaking Guillaume's hand tightly. "From what I can see you like our city very much, do you not?"

"Very much," replied Francois unable to hide his admiration for the renowned city.

"Is this the first time you have come here?" Farouk asked, addressing everyone.

"Only I have been here before, but that was some years ago now," Guillaume replied.

"Then," said Farouk, extending his right hand in front of him, "would you like me to give you a short tour of our beautiful city on the way to our destination?"

"With pleasure," Guillaume said, and everyone was happy with his decision.

"All right then. It is our duty to show visitors the beauties of our city," Farouk said, clearly happy he had been given the opportunity to display his knowledge of the city, which was quite extensive. He coughed a little to clear his throat and began to talk, looking at his listeners one by one.

"I'll begin straight away, then, with the best known building in Alexandria, which you see in front of you, the famous Lighthouse which was built by Ptolemy I Soter or Philadelphus II.[39] The architect was Sostratus of Cnidus. Its height, before the top fell in the earthquake in the 10th century, was one hundred and twenty meters. This tower, which got its name from the island, shed light at night for ships and was visible at a distance of three hundred stadions. Since then, all the towers constructed for this reason have been named Faros. As you can see, today it is being restored, so that the new damage caused by the recent earthquake can be fixed while the tower is not in use [40]. Right behind you is the Poseidonion, the temple of Poseidon, where sailors made sacrifices. At the end of the promontory you can see jutting out from it, the Roman Mark Antony had the Timonium built, a small palace in which he lived with Queen Cleopatra." He paused a bit and, after he had taken off his white turban, ran his fingers through his slightly sweaty and greyish hair. Then, he put his turban back on again and motioned to them with his hand:

"And now follow me. The Jewish quarter is right behind us, on the eastern part of the shore, but we will take a circular route so that I may show you the things I want to."

They began, therefore, to walk towards the western part of the shore. Everyone seemed to be enjoying Farouk's tour and they continued to look insatiably at everything around them, unable to have enough of the city's beauty, bathed in the morning winter sun. Finally, after they had walked in silence for about five minutes, they stopped in front of a luxurious building with two Egyptian obelisks, and Farouk, his face shining with pride, went on with the tour:

"This, my friends, is the palace Cleopatra built in memory of the Roman Julius Caesar. They used to call it the Caesarium but today everyone calls it the Sebasteion. It now serves, as you can see, as a Christian temple, as there are many of you Christians now and there are not enough churches. The city is, of course, multinational and multicultural."

Farouk pointed at the minarets all around and went on:

"The truth is of course that the Mamluks were more tolerant of both Christians and Jews before you came here with armed troops from the West. Now things are somewhat harder because the Muslims are fanatics. Every time you win a victory in Palestine, your Christian brothers and we as well, often suffer in retaliation."

Philippe and Francois looked at each other, surprised. The truth is that they had never thought about these consequences of the war with the 'infidels'. Farouk, however, left the subject and continued to talk:

"I am now showing you the ancient pagan Alexandria because any beauty our city possesses comes from that time, I think. I don't think you need any information about the mosques, the patriarchate or our synagogue, do you?"

"Yes, exactly as you say. Undoubtedly the pre-Christian city has a unique beauty," said Guillaume.

"May I ask you something Farouk?" Philippe's voice sounded out suddenly while the group paused in front of the yards and warehouses of the port.

"Of course, whatever you want my brave knight."

"You said "our" synagogue before. If I am not mistaken though, your name is Muslim. Aren't you an Arab Muslim?"

Farouk laughed:

"Your observation is right, young man. The truth is that I started my life as a Muslim. I come from a very poor Arab family. My family was forced to sell me as a slave because they could not raise me and my eight brothers. However, I was lucky because Simeon bought me. He is a lovely man that does not consider us to be his slaves, rather his servants, and treats us very well. I have been with him for about twenty years, from when I was still young. I converted to Judaism, without him ever forcing me to do so, because I wanted to. Anyway, as you will see for yourselves, my master respects religions, especially those of the Book[41] and is not at all dogmatic when it comes to matters of faith, unlike, excuse me for saying this, most Christians. So, have I answered your question?"

"Of course, I got more than I asked for," said Philippe, clearly satisfied.

"So we continue. Now we shall walk towards the centre of the city, south that is. The warehouses and the yards are not so interesting, apart from the fact that they have been here since the time of the Ptolemies."

When they arrived in front of a somewhat strange mosque with a column at its side, Farouk stopped walking and began to talk again:

"Here you can see the old Serapeum. It was originally built by Ptolemy III Euergetes[42] in honour of the Egyptian god Serapis, then became a Christian church and has now ended up as a mosque. Next to it stands the column of Pompey II[43], a monolithic column made of granite with a height of twenty six meters. A Corinthian capital stands at its top. It was built in honour of the Roman empire Diocletian III[44] by the prefect of the city at the time, Pompey, in recognition of some beneficial measures he had taken for the city. The Mouseion of Alexandria, with its famous library, was situated somewhere near here. Both were probably built by Ptolemy I Soter[45]. At this moment Farouk paused and Philippe, filled with curiosity, fearing that the servant would say nothing else about the Mouseion, asked him:

"Can you tell us something more about the Mouseion? And the famous library?" Farouk's eyes lit up. It was evident that he was very happy that Philippe was showing interest in these ancient monuments, so he answered straight away:

"Of course, with great pleasure. But let's walk at the same time because we are far from the house and my master will be worried that we have shown no sign of life all this time." And with these words they began to walk towards the east again, but this time through the interior of the city. Jean and Luigi were at the front, walking slowly and turning back all the time to hear Farouk, who was walking with Guillaume on one side and Francois and Philippe on the other. They constantly crossed paths with others in the streets – servants running around doing errands for their masters, elegant Arabs in white robes and carts laden with merchandise dragged by camels or horses.

"Well, the Mouseion," Farouk went on "was part of the palace of Ptolemy and functioned as an institution for the highest intellectual pursuits. Great scientists and men of letters and the arts passed through here, such as the mathematicians Euclid and Archimedes, the astronomers Aristarchus and Hipparchus, the geographer Eratosthenes, the painter Apelles and the poets Theocritus and Callimachus – to name only the best-known. It seems, however, that Ptolemy I founded the Mouseion at the instigation of the Athenian philosopher and politician Demetrius Phalerium and the fact is that it was greatly expanded during the reign of his son, Ptolemy II Philadelphus. It had a number of halls and laboratories, a botanical garden and zoo, an observatory and even sleeping quarters for the visitors. The most important part of the Mouseion was its famous library. It is estimated that when Ptolemy I died, it had around two hundred thousand books and continued to be enriched with new manuscripts during the reigns of Ptolemy II and III, and ended up with about seven hundred thousand books. It is said that when Ptolemy II reigned he gave orders that manuscripts should be confiscated from every ship that entered the port of Alexandria, and that copies be given to their owners."

"And nothing remains of the Mouseion and the library today?" Philippe asked Farouk, anxiously awaiting his answer.

"Unfortunately all that huge wealth of knowledge is now lost, we don't know when or how exactly. Probably the destruction was gradual. Some support the view that the library was burnt when Julius Caesar[46] reigned, while others say it was during the reign of Caracalla[47]. It has been proved that Caracalla confiscated the property of the Mouseion and sent its wise men away. Another catastrophe was caused by the Christians, who ferociously destroyed everything pagan at the instigation of the patriarch Theophilos, when the emperor Theodosius issued a decree concerning the destruction of pagan buildings[48]. Finally, the coup de grace was delivered by the Arabs when they conquered the city[49]. It is most likely that these events are real and that the library was gradually reduced in size. Whatever the case, it is very sad that this has happened. Just imagine how many unknown manuscripts we would have access to today if this library still existed!"

"It is truly very sad," Guillaume said to himself and one could see real sorrow in his eyes as he listened to what Farouk was saying.

They had now reached a large central square in the city. It was overcrowded as the market was there, and the knights looked at all the different products on the wooden stalls in amazement as they heard the dark-skinned merchants shouting and hawking their wares. The sun was now directly overhead when the company paused once more, standing in front of a stall with spices. Farouk displayed his knowledge once more, on the subject of gastronomy this time, enlightening the knights on subjects about which they were completely ignorant, but that were interesting enough to make them use up a little more of their time.

***

A little further down, on the opposite side of the square, Alcmene was choosing oranges and grapefruit from the fruit stall. She was a good-looking girl with Mediterranean characteristics, no more than eighteen years old. Her lush, pitch-black hair streamed like a torrent over her shoulders and reached her waist, while her black eyes, combined with her slim body and the fine features of her face, made it very difficult for any man whose eyes happened to meet hers to remain unaffected.

Her brother, Iacobus, who was at her side while she was choosing citrus fruit, teased her about her special beauty. "The outside is gorgeous but I doubt whether anyone will like the inside! Let's see how we are going to find you a husband now that the time has come!" He would say, referring to her temperamental character, which was certainly not ideal for a girl of her time.

It was true, Alcmene was a sweet girl who could be very bad tempered when she felt she was being treated unfairly or simply when she wanted her own way. She was a wild one! And this was very bad for a girl of marriageable age who was a member of the Greek Monophysite[50] community of Alexandria, in which women had to always obey their husbands and never disagree with them.

Today Alcmene and her brother were very sad, although they were trying hard not to show it. Exactly one year before their father had died when their house was being looted by Muslim fanatics. Other local Christians had also died then, women had been raped, churches had closed and whole fortunes had been lost in one night. Alcmene wished that she could erase that dreadful day from her memory. Hordes of enraged Arabs had poured out in the streets, out to punish Christians in retaliation for the slaughter and the looting of one of their caravans by the Knights Templar.

She herself and her brother had been away from the house on that fateful night and their absence had saved their lives. They had returned home terrified amid the fire and screams that could be heard from the whole Greek Christian district, to find their mother completely naked, covered in bruises, crying over their father's lifeless body lying in a pool of blood in the middle of the house. Their mother had lost her honour and dignity, but at least she had survived. Alcmene could not forget that horrible scene, which still haunted her sleep at night, as she tried hard to adapt to this new life without her father, her mother's mind in tatters and her brother trying to bring new life to the fabric store their father had left behind, and had also been destroyed that night.

When Alcmene had finished choosing the fruit, she turned to her brother standing behind her. Then her eyes fell on the group of Knights Templar who were opposite, at the stall with spices. Her expression immediately hardened and the smile left her face. Her brother saw the change on her face and looked in the same direction. He then turned serious too and, putting his hand on her shoulder, said:

"Conceited Azymites[51]. Let's go." Alcmene would not move an inch. She had remained still, looking at the knights, her eyes full of rage. Sensitive as she was today, due to the sad anniversary of the death of her father, she could not put those terrible images of her dead father and her unhappy mother out of her mind. Her mind and eyes grew cloudy:

"If those damned people hadn't come here nothing would have happened. Father would be alive, we would have enough money and we would worship freely, as we did in the old days. They are responsible for all our ills," she said, her voice breaking, but also tinged with rage. Iacobus, seeing her pain, tried to reassure her by stroking her hair and talking to her gently:

"You are right but what can we do about it? Don't think about the past any more. What is done is done and will not change."

Alcmene was not, however, one to calm down easily. She soon felt her sorrow turn into rage and to a hatred so great for those responsible for her problems that she could no longer control herself. Without no thought whatsoever, she grabbed a heavy stone from the ground, near her feet, and in a lightening fast movement threw it at the knights. Her brother did not have the time to stop her. Only his voice could be heard as his arms remained in the air in a vain attempt to stop the stone's inevitable flight:

"Alcmene, wait! What are you doing?" he screamed.

***

Foulques was walking with difficulty through the square of Alexandria, which was full of people. He had got carried away looking at a stall with tin and copper utensils of every size and every use and was now in danger of losing his comrades and the Italian servant who was leading them towards Antonio Pescatore's house, through the crowd. Luckily for him, the knights had stopped at a spice merchants and so Foulques managed to catch up with them.

"Ah, there you are nephew. I thought you were lost," his uncle said, as soon as Foulques came near.

"Yes, the truth is that I got carried away," Foulques replied, embarrassed and blushing slightly.

"I told you that, with so many people and temptations here, the only easy thing to do is to get lost," Domenico, their Italian guide, a chubby young man with bright white teeth and a kind smile, said, laughing. The Knights of St John had also arrived in Alexandria late in the morning. Domenico, Pescatore's young servant, had waited for them to take them to his master, but none of the four knights had ever been to Alexandria before, so they had also taken their time on the way there, becoming acquainted with a world so different from the one to the East.

"What is this, Domenico?" Pierre asked the servant, placing some small brown seeds that looked like small nuts in his palm.

"That is nutmeg. You don't know what it looks like but you have definitely tasted it as you have been in the East for years!"

"Yes!" Nicolas said, laughing. "The truth is that the food here is much tastier and completely different from ours."

"And this here?" Guillaume asked, showing him some tiny seeds which were hard and brown.

"That's pepper, which is so rare in the West. It tastes nice in almost every type of food," Domenico said. "That next to it is cardamom. There is white and green cardamom and the Arabs use it a lot in their meatballs."

Foulques looked around the square. He preferred to look at the colourful crowd rather than the spices. He was tired from the journey and had no appetite. On the square there were stalls with every sort of merchandize: from vegetables, abundant citrus fruit and dates, to valuable silk and small carved wooden objects.

His eyes fell on some Knights Templar. They were here too, what a coincidence, looking at spices at another stall on the other side of the square. He huffed disapprovingly and said to himself: "Look there! Knights Templar! I wonder what they are doing here. Maybe they came to arrange some sort of alliance with the infidels again?"

Then his eyes turned to the other side of the square, at the top of the imaginary triangle that his company formed with the Knights Templar. The stalls with fruit and vegetables were there. Straight away he noticed a girl who stood out of the rest of the crowd because of her beauty. She looked upset. A young man next to her was stroking her hair. "What a tender scene!" thought Foulques and straight away turned to Pierre, who was next to him and had started whispering the Lord's Prayer. "Of course, it is noon and we are not at the service. Time to pray," he thought and wasted no time in joining in with Pierre:

"Thy will be done..."

Suddenly they heard a scream and a groan of pain. He immediately looked to the other side of the square, from where the shouting could heard. One of the Knights Templar was on the ground, on his knees, with a crowd already starting to gather around him and another young man was striding towards the beautiful girl Foulques had seen before. He seemed furious. When he reached her, he violently forced her arms behind her back, despite the obvious protestations of the young man next to her.

"That's too much," Foulques thought. "They have gone too far now, treating women like that. The poor soul... I must do something..."

With no further thought about it, Foulques headed towards the knight and the girl, without saying a word to his companions who were watching the scene, stunned by what they saw. When Guillaume came to his senses and realised what his nephew was about to do, it was already too late.

"Nephew, wait! Where are you going?" he shouted at him, but in vain. Foulques had already reached the girl.

"Let's go too," Guillaume said to the other, and they all started to run towards him.

***

Philippe, tired of Farouk's tour, was looking around the square and had not seen Alcmene throwing the stone. Before, however, he had time to do anything, its weight had broken Guillaume's left shoulder, its pointed edge opening a wound from which blood flowed. The Grand Master fell to his knees groaning, with Jean and Francois bending down to help him. Luigi remained standing, pointing towards the girl, and said to the other knights, bringing his eyebrows together into a scowl:

"She threw it. I saw her!"

When Philippe realized that if the stone had hit the Grand Master's head it would have killed him, as well as the fact that he was responsible for his safety, he lost control. Without a second thought, he said to Luigi:

"Yes, I saw her too."

Then, blinded by rage, he ran to get the young woman.

She stood proud, looking at him with eyes full of hatred as he drew near. On the

other hand, the young man next to her looked upset.

When Philippe grabbed her arms she threw a contemptuous look at him and, without any resistance, without even saying a word to him, turned her head the other way.

"So you pick on innocent women now? Infidels are not enough?"

Philippe turned to his right, towards where the voice had come from and was surprised to see a young Hospitaller knight glaring at him with intense anger and contempt on his face.

"This woman you call innocent almost killed our Grand Master! She should be put on trial for attempted murder!" he answered, without releasing his grip and looking back at him angrily in turn. Alcmene still did not speak and silently thanked Foulques with her eyes.

"And who are you? A judge? What right have you to arrest her?" Foulques replied.

"With the right of the person who is responsible for his Lord Master's safety!" answered Philippe.

"And what is it to you and why are you getting involved?" Luigi said, joining the conversation. He had come up to them in the meantime and was now drawing his sword from its scabbard. "Why would a monk-knight, dedicated to God, show such interest in a young woman?"

"I am just trying to protect her from you!" Foulques said, also drawing his sword, in response to Luigi's challenge.

"Calm down! Nephew, sheathe your sword at once! The Knights Templar are right, you shouldn't have interfered!" Guillaume said in a strong voice that left no room for objection. He had just reached Foulques, who was arguing with Philippe. Behind him came Nicolas and Pierre with Domenico, while Guillaume de Beaujeu had risen to his feet and, holding his bleeding shoulder with one hand, was also approaching, staggering from the pain, but maintaining his dignity. Francois and Jean were walking behind him, moving curious bystanders away. The crowd needed to disperse and the matter resolved calmly, the two of them told the people there, who were looking at the knights in amazement and some trepidation.

"May I know what in God's name has happened here? Brother Foulques I would like to know why you have become involved in an incident that, from the little I've understood, is not of your concern," Nicolas said severely, looking Foulques straight in the eye.

He nodded in resignation, lowering his sword.

Then Nicolas, turning to the injured Grand Master and recognizing him as someone who shared his title from a ring he was wearing, added:

"Guillaume de Beaujeu, if I am not mistaken, the Lord Master of the Knights Templar."

"Yes. To whom do I have the honour of speaking?" Guillaume replied, while Jean was cleaning his wound with a handkerchief.

"Nicolas Lorgne, I have the same title as you in the order of the Knights of Saint John. Now, can someone please tell me what happened?"

"I can," Iacobus spoke up boldly.

"Who are you young man?" Guillaume asked him.

"Iacobus Philanthropinos, the brother of the young lady here who has caused all the fuss," he said, looking severely at his sister, who immediately lowered her eyes to the ground. Philippe had now freed her hands, while Luigi had also put his sword back into its scabbard. They all felt that they were slowly calming down with the passing of time.

"So we're listening," Nicolas said, indicating that he should start talking.

"I haven't got much to say," he said, looking at the Grand Master in the eye in a way that guaranteed honesty. "Only that, for personal reasons, my sister threw a stone at the Templar Knights, injuring their Grand Master, fortunately not very seriously, from what I can see. It was wrong of her and she will apologize immediately."

Iacobus looked at his sister again in a way that brooked no objections. In reality he was anxious about her fate, because he knew that attempting to murder a knight, especially a Grand Master, was punishable by hanging. Nevertheless he hid his unease, believing that his sister would be spared thanks to the knights' good will and because of the fact that she was a woman.

On the other hand, Alcmene had begun to realize what she had done in a moment of frenzy and against common sense. Deep down she had begun to fear the consequences of her irrational action but, at the same time, she hated all Westerners, and especially the Knights Templar, and that could not be hidden easily. Despite this, she forced herself to ask for forgiveness because her fear was greater than her dislike of the knights at that moment.

"I apologize sir. An unfortunate moment," she said in a cold voice, which could barely be heard, "and in truth very sad."

"I accept your apology," said Guillaume, his answer bringing relief to all those present.

In truth, since no fatality had ensued, nobody wished for things to be taken to their extreme. Even Philippe seemed to have calmed down. He did, however, still feel deep antipathy towards the Hospitaller knight who had got involved, uninvited, in a matter that was none of his business. On the other hand, the Hospitallers' Grand Master seemed very likeable to the Knight Templar in charge of Guillaume's security.

"I would say God protected me and I thank Him for that. It's certain that He guided your hand so that no greater harm would be caused," Guillaume went on to say, while Jean, after having stopped the wound from bleeding, was now putting the Grand Masters arm into a splint by tying it from elbow to shoulder with a scarf tied with a knot.

"I always believed that I would die on the battle field," Guillaume continued, "and from what I gather, my wish will be granted since the Lord saved me today! However, young lady, since you have given me some time in which I will be unable to move my left arm as it must remain still, something that will make things very difficult for me if I have to fight during such time, I would like you to explain the personal reasons that led you to this action."

Iacobus swallowed:

"My Lord, I don't think this is really necessary. We have already delayed you long enough."

"Don't be afraid. I will not change my mind whatever I hear," said Guillaume smiling and looking Alcmene in the eye. I will however take this opportunity to find out what the local Christians think of us. I think you owe me an explanation since you almost killed me, miss, isn't that so? I'm listening, therefore, and don't hide any of your true feelings."

Alcmene, feeling that she could trust the Grand master's words, unleashed her pain without leaving any aspect of her tragic story out, under her brother's terrified regard. He was expecting that his sister's narration would anger the knights, who would finally choose to punish her. In the end this did not happen because everyone present felt compassion for the girl and understood her improper behaviour. When Alcmene had finished, everyone remained silent. The crowd around them had left some time before, as people did not find anything interesting in a conflict that had been resolved peacefully in the end and life in the square went on as normal. After this short pause, the Grand Master started talking again, rubbing his arm in pain:

"I will bear everything you said about the Muslims' retaliation against the Christians here in mind, Miss. I admit that it is an issue I was not at all aware of, until now. I would, however, ask you to be more careful in the future and to give the consequences of your actions more thought," he said in conclusion, making the young woman hide her face in shame behind her brother's back. Then he added, speaking to Nicolas:

"My dear fellow Master, it was a pleasure to meet you. I wish you a pleasant stay and I believe that we shall soon meet again in some battle."

"It was a pleasure for me too. Goodbye and I wish you a speedy recovery," Nicolas said warmly to the Grand Master of the Knights Templar. All the rest of the knights, except for Guillaume de Villaret, did not share their leaders' liking for the knights of the other order and so said goodbye coldly. Philippe and Foulques had barely even exchanged a look, which showed their mutual contempt and dislike for each other.

So Alcmene and Iacobus remained in the square, relieved that this incident had passed off without any unpleasant consequences for them, while both groups of knights went off on their way.

***

The Knights Templar went on their way. It was late afternoon when they drew near to the merchant's house.

"How obnoxious those Hospitallers are," Luigi commented after a long silence.

"And they all interfere where they shouldn't," Francois added.

"And especially that young lad who interfered so suddenly!" Philippe said, without hiding his dislike.

The three knights who brought up the rear kept on talking about the event. In contrast, Farouk, Jean and Guillaume were walking at the front and were talking about trade in Alexandria. It seemed as if they had completely forgotten about the unfortunate incident. When Farouk stopped in front of a two-storey, bright white mansion with ornate metal railings on the balconies and silk curtains that could be made out behind the windows, the knights stopped any conversation and looked at the house, their eyes wide open in surprise.

"So what everybody says about the wealth of the East is true," Philippe thought. In the West the richest lord does not own a palace like that.

Farouk opened the door of the yard and the knights found themselves in a beautiful garden with flowers of every kind, tall cedars and palm trees. There were even small fountains. After they crossed this little Eden, Farouk knocked on the main door of the house. A young servant, in a white robe that made a striking contrast with his dark skin, opened the door and smiled at them.

"Welcome," he said to them. "The master is waiting for you," he added, and led them through the luxurious living room with its carved wooden furniture, to the merchant's office, which was no less luxurious than the rest of the house. The floor was made of expensive white marble and the walls were covered with a fine material that was gold in colour. Huge vases on the floor, some painted with flowers and others with animals of various kinds, adorned each corner of the room. A middle-aged man with grey hair was sitting behind a dark brown luxurious desk and was reading. As soon as he realized that he was no longer alone he stood up to shake hands with every one, smiling broadly:

"Welcome my friends, make yourselves at home," he said addressing everybody, while embracing Guillaume, who looked just as happy to meet his old friend.

"It's been so many years... but what's wrong my friend? An injury in battle? It looks recent!" the merchant said, shocked when his eyes fell on Guillaume's shoulder.

"Never mind, my friend, an unfortunate moment," Guillaume replied.

"The gentleman must have had a saint to protect him," Farouk said and began to briefly narrate the story to Simeon. When the narration was over, the merchant said, nodding his head:

"I see. We must therefore thank the Lord that the worse did not happen." Then, he added, looking at Guillaume:

"And which young man is so loyal to you, my friend, so as to immediately arrest the one responsible for all this fuss, ignoring the beauty of her sex?"

Guillaume placed his hand on Philippe's shoulder, who seemed uncomfortable with all these compliments, and said with pride:

"This is my devoted servant!"

"I see. And his name?" Simeon asked again, now looking at Philippe who, quite uncomfortable by now, said:

"Brother Philippe, Sir. Philippe de Ridefort."

"What? What did you say?" said the merchant, suddenly seeming agitated.

"Philippe de Ridefort," the knight repeated and seeing the surprise on the merchant's face growing, asked:

"Is there something wrong, sir?"

"Young man, this will seem incredible but I have a man who has been working for me here for years, his name is Ridefort and I know that he used to be a Knight Templar. Do you, by any chance, know him?"

Philippe froze. "Might it be… no it can't be… it must be a coincidence," Philippe thought, too shaken to reply.

The rest were equally as surprised. Guillaume was the first to pull himself together and asked Simeon:

"Is your servant named Jocelyn?"

"Precisely!" the merchant said, surprised, and added, filled with amazement:

"But how do you know?"

Philippe could not believe his ears! Was it possible? But, Jocelyn de Ridefort… the same name… Could it be someone else?

"My friend," said the Grand Master clearing his throat "I believe that your servant is Philippe's uncle. He was lost in a battle some thirty years ago."

"Yes, that is exactly what Jocelyn told me!" Simeon said. "It is… incredible!" He turned to Farouk and said: "Quickly, run and bring Jocelyn here. Don't tell him what this is about, though," he added. Farouk ran away to do as his master had ordered.

"But how did he get here?" Philippe asked, his voice shaking, not knowing what to do with his hands – he was so shaken – and kept moving them up and down.

"It's a long story," Simeon said, straightening his white robe. Then he rubbed his eyes and looked at the knights, who were absolutely hanging on his every word, and went on to say:

"Based on what he told me, he narrowly escaped being beheaded because the executioner who was in charge of the executions of the knights after the battle of al-Mansurah either took pity on Jocelyn and another well-built Christian knight, or wanted them to work in his fields for him, and took them as his slaves. After that he sold them to some other Muslim, who offered him a large amount of money for him. He was, you see, very strong when he was young and could do the work of two slaves. He worked hard in the fields until some rich Arab from Alexandria bought him and brought him here. To cut a long story short, this Arab was very harsh master and Jocelyn suffered greatly at his hands, but he managed at some point to escape, risking his life. Then my servants took him in off the streets, where he was hiding, ill and hungry. Don't be surprised by this last part of the story because we have often helped poor people on the streets. I actually have another two Christians who were slaves and escaped, did not know where to go and found refuge here."

"But, how long have you had him here?"

Simeon thought a little before he answered:

"Around twenty years."

"So how old is he now?" Philippe managed to whisper in a voice that could barely be heard, his face having by now turned quite pale.

"He is quite old. He must be more than seventy or around that age. He will tell you himself," the merchant said, indicating that Philippe should look behind him at the door that was now opening wide. Philippe swallowed and slowly turned towards the door.

An old man stood in front of him who, despite the wrinkles on his face and his sparse white hair, still looked slender and robust, as he had in his youth. His left cheek was scarred and his hands were calloused and deformed from old age and the hard work he had been doing all these years.

His eyes, however, watery now, after the initial astonishment of seeing and recognising Philippe, clearly retained all the vitality of his youth. One could see in them his determination to not yet give up on life. His eyes were like those of Philippe's and it was they that left no doubt in the young knight's mind as to whether this old man that stood before him really was Jocelyn, his long-lost father. Seeing him alive, in front of him now, Philippe realised that, all these years, he had never really believed that his father had died, however unlikely that was, whatever others had told him. Somehow he had known that he was alive, without, of course, imagining that he would ever meet him. Jocelyn on the other hand, immediately recognized his son. The little child that he remembered was now a young man. Overcome with emotion, he had difficulty catching his breath.

"Philippe?" he managed to whisper questioningly and, without further delay, found himself in his son's arms.

***

Many candles, placed in gilded candlesticks on the walls, shed their light on the large dining room in the house of merchant Alessandro Pescatore. At the table, laid with a white linen cloth, the group of Hospitallers were enjoying the attention of the house's servants, something that these men, who were used to austerity and hardship, were experiencing for the first time. The young merchant, sitting at the head of the table, was talking to his guests about the political situation in his country, Genoa. Next to him, on the right, sat his graceful wife, near the end of her pregnancy, and next to her was Foulques. Pierre and Guillaume were opposite him, while the place of honour at the head of the table was reserved for the Grand Master. The knights had arrived at the merchant's house in the afternoon where Giuseppina, Alessandro's wife, had welcomed them, as the merchant had left in order to finish some urgent business. After that they had rested in the sleeping quarters that had been given to them and had agreed to join Alessandro for dinner.

"Lord Master, how do you see the situation in Outremer?" Giuseppina was now asking Nicolas, as the conversation had turned to the political situation in the East. At the same time a servant was refilling the glasses of those others dining with wine. Nicolas gently wiped the wine off his lips with a white napkin, placing it next to his plate and spoke in an official tone of voice:

"Undoubtedly things are difficult, my lady. We were recently defeated by the Mamluks. Not even the formidable Mongols can defeat them now. Not to mention that help from the West is rare now. It's been ten years since an organized campaign came here, since Edward of England came."

"So there won't be any more organized campaigns from the West from now on?" Alessandro then asked, leaving the bone from the piece of chicken he had just enjoyed on the edge of his plate.

"We don't know that," the Grand Master said and shrugged. "It is certain, however, that the zeal for campaigns against the Infidels has diminished greatly in the West.

Each duchy and each kingdom has its own priorities and needs an army for its own business. There are not enough soldiers to send here!"

"Excuse me for interrupting," said their hostess "but you must allow me to serve you all with some meat! I see you have only eaten salad!"

"Thank you very much my lady, but none of us are going to eat meat. We are fasting for Christmas, you see," Foulques replied with a smile.

"But I thought that you eat meat during fasts because you are also soldiers!" Giuseppina said, puzzled.

"You are right," Guillaume replied. "That is true, but we make exceptions only on certain days – not whenever we want to!"

"The fact that we are outside the monastery doesn't mean that our discipline should become slack, should it my Lord?" Pierre added, looking at Nicolas and expecting him to reply.

"That's quite right, Brother. Anyway, today we will have a little bit more to drink than usual. This indulgence is enough for today," he said, bringing a glass of wine to his lips.

"So cheers my brave men! May God keep you well so that you can protect our properties in the East!" Alessandro said, raising his glass.

"Amen," said Nicolas and they all drank to the toast the host had proposed after they had brought their glasses together.

"So which cities do the Christians still possess?" Giuseppina asked, returning to the subject.

Nicolas leaned backwards on the chair before he answered:

"Tyre, Acre, Haifa and Tripoli of the big cities. Then there are the forts we still have. We Hospitallers have Marqab and the Knights Templar have Tortosa, Athlit and Sidon. May our Lord give us courage to keep those at least."

"Let's turn to the matter at hand," Alessandro said, indicating to the servants that they should take away the plates and bring the dessert. When it comes down to it, the money from my father will help you in this effort."

"Undoubtedly," Nicolas agreed.

"My father was a great admirer of yours. He always wanted to make a donation to your order but never wrote to you. So he specified this in his will and it is my responsibility to respect his will. I have the money counted in my office, ready to hand over to you. Tell me though, have you thought about how you will carry it in safety to Tripoli?" The servants had now placed a platter of dates and honey in the centre of the table. Nicolas had one, then wiped himself carefully and said in a grave tone of voice:

"There are four of us. We will divide up the money and stitch it into our robes. I believe this is the safest way to avoid attracting the attention of those who might rob us. Of course, we shall place some money in each of our pouches so that, even if something happens, only that money is lost. We shall do that tonight so that in the morning we can depart straight away."

"So you shall not stay with us any longer?" Giuseppina asked, clearly saddened by this.

"This is not possible, my lady. As I told you, the situation calls for our quick return to Tripoli," Nicolas replied.

"Very well. I too believe that the money will be transferred safely," the merchant said and then went on, addressing the Grand Master:

"Let's go to my office so I can hand it over to you right now."

The two men rose and left the room while Guillaume proposed another toast to the hostess:

"I hope the heir is born soon! I drink to his health and yours!"

"Amen, with the Virgin Mother's help. And may you return safely!" Giuseppina said, and everyone brought their glasses together once more.

***

It had now grown well and truly dark. When the knights and Jocelyn had recovered from the surprise and the excitement caused by their unexpected meeting, they went to the dining room where they had eaten with the merchant's family. Simeon had treated them as if they were lords, and not monk-warriors, with typical oriental dishes and desserts. They were all very happy, though Philippe and Jocelyn were still very shaken and were not very talkative at the table. They felt as if they had a great deal to say and that this should happen when they were alone. So, when dinner was over Guillaume permitted the two men to leave so that they could talk, while he and the rest and Simeon went to the merchant's office to finish the job for which they had come to Alexandria.

Philippe was walking with his father in the gardens of Simeon's mansion, which were dimly lit by some torches. That they were both deeply moved was clear from their eyes. They remained silent because they both had so many things to say about the years that they had lived apart from each other that they did not know where to start and where to end. First of all, Philippe wanted his father to know that he too knew the secret Jocelyn had shared with his mother, but he did not know how to broach the subject, because when the elderly Jocelyn learnt of this, he was sure to suffer another great shock.

"How is your mother? My brother?" Jocelyn asked, as if he had read Philippe's mind, unwittingly starting, in this way, a conversation Philippe had wanted to start and could not find the way. Nevertheless, it took the young man a long time to reply because he knew that the news of his parents' death would make the elderly man sad. He could not, however, hide the truth from him.

"My mother is no longer alive. Neither is my father," he replied bluntly and unemotionally. Philippe, looking at his father's face, who, when hearing the unfortunate news, stopped walking and looked Philippe in the eye with a surprised look that was also profoundly sad. He added, therefore, trying to ease the man's grief:

"Why does this sound strange to you? So many years have passed."

"That's true but that I should live after so many battles and hardships, and that they should have died in the peace and quiet of their own home? Isn't it somewhat unnatural?" Jocelyn said, with a faint smile on his face.

"The way you put it, you are right, but the Lord decides when he will call us to him and no one knows what His will may be. Maybe He did not let you die precisely so that we would meet here today and have this conversation."

"How did they die?" Jocelyn asked again, as he sat on a large rock under a palm tree. Philippe sat down too.

"My father died from a problem with his heart. My mother died a little later. Her own heart may well have not been able not bear so many griefs."

"Griefs? Why? Did something else happen to the family? Your sisters?"

"No," Philippe answered hastily, not knowing how to spit out what had been burning on his lips all this time. He hadn't meant to say "griefs"..

"My sisters are fine, at least that's what they said in their last letter. It has been some months since I received it. They have their own families now."

"And your property?" Jocelyn said. "I mean, why did you become a Knight Templar? I thought your father had other dreams for you."

"Definitely. But he died before I became a member of the order. Whatever part of the fortune that my sisters did not use as dowry for their marriages I gave to the order. As for my decision to become a Knight Templar, you played your part in that too. When you came and told us about your life as a knight and about your military achievements, I imagined myself living the life of a knight and wanted to become one of you."

"Yes. I remember those visits of mine," Jocelyn said wistfully, fixing his eyes on the trunk of a tree opposite them. "Those years were so pleasant. I can still remember us vividly, fighting and playing with those wooden swords I had given you as a present. Do you remember?"

"Of course. I only ever played like that with you. My mother also helped me take my final decision to become a member of the order."

Jocelyn looked at the young man, puzzled.

"Margaret? How did that come to pass?"

"She knew of my secret desire to become a knight." Philippe now began to talk with difficulty. While he spoke his eyes looked not at Jocelyn but at the soil under their feet.

"As she was dying she made me swear to become a knight and come to the East to look for you…"

"Me? But why?"

Philippe cleared his throat. He lifted his eyes from the ground and looked his father in the eye:

"Because she loved you. Since you left for the East and never returned she withered away. I am sure she died of grief at losing you and not because of my father's death."

Jocelyn felt as if he had been struck by lightning. As he had his eyes fixed on Philippe's, he thought: "But how can he know this?" He tried desperately to think of something to say but could not think of anything appropriate. But Philippe, to his surprise, put his finger to his lips, indicating that he should say nothing and, holding both his hands in his own, squeezed them tightly and went on to say:

"Don't trouble yourself with how I came to know this. I happened to hear your conversation on the night that you were saying goodbye to my mother, when you were leaving to become a Knight Templar. I did not mean to. I just couldn't sleep that night. So I got out of bed and happened to go past my mother's bedroom, where you were too."

The colour had now completely drained from Jocelyn's face. The memories of that night, which he had kept so vivid within him for so many years, welled up from within him as from the bottom of an ancient chest that had been left aside, forgotten for years, and flooded his entire being. He too continued to squeeze his son's hands and whispered:

"But then you must know that…"

"You are my father…" Philippe added and the two men fell into each other's arms, sobbing together once more.

Crying was something that freed both of them. Philippe felt calm at last. He had let out what he had hidden inside him for so many years, he had fulfilled his mother's last desire and most importantly – he had found his father again, his real father. Jocelyn, on the other hand, felt great relief and indescribable joy. After so many hardships he could once again hug his son, without having to hide his real feelings and with nothing bad having been caused by this revelation since Philippe's legal father had died, without, thankfully, having ever found out the truth.

"I am certain that God has kept me alive just to experience this moment!" Jocelyn said, his voice breaking. "Your mother would be so happy to see us now! Of course I always felt guilt and shame with regard to my brother, and believed that God would punish me for my dishonour. Instead of this, he has judged me worthy of seeing you again!"

"What's done is done now, Father," Philippe said, wiping his eyes and pronouncing this last word with unimaginable joy.

"Deep down I always knew you were alive even though everyone told me I would never find you again!"

Jocelyn wiped his eyes too with his palms and said to Philippe:

"Son, have you told anyone that I am your father? It wouldn't be good if the order knew you are an illegitimate child. I don't think anything too bad would happen, but this had better stay between us."

"Of course, Father," Philippe said, making a negative gesture with his hand. "You needn't worry about that. I have only told François, and he and I are bound by true friendship, so he would never tell others of this. As for the rest, they will never know, as I will continue to call you uncle in front of them. But tell me, what do you intend to do now?"

Jocelyn stood up. He was about to speak but he did not have enough time as they heard others approaching. Guillaume and Jean were coming towards them. Guillaume said to them, smiling:

"Well? Is everything all right? Did you have time to talk as uncle and nephew?"

"I think a lifetime won't be enough to say everything but, yes, basically we talked," Jocelyn answered, giving Philippe, who also stood up, a knowing look.

"How is your arm my lord?" he then added so as to change the subject. Guillaume touched his shoulder, which was still tied with bandages and replied:

"It hurts a little but the swelling has gone down somewhat."

Then the Grand Master turned to Philippe:

"We have stitched the money into our robes. Only yours remain, Brother."

Then, as if he had suddenly remembered something, he turned to Jocelyn again.

"What do you intend to do Brother? Are you coming with us?"

"That is exactly what I was asking him before you came," Philippe said.

Jocelyn sighed. He started walking slowly around the small group of people. He had made his decision. From the moment he had seen his son, memories had been flooding back. He eventually stopped walking, stood next to his son and said in a low voice:

"I owe Simeon a lot. If it weren't for him I wouldn't be alive now. Yet now that I have found you again it seems unthinkable for me not to go with you. I believe that God has somehow sent you here. Of course I am too old to fight but I will help you in any way I can in war and peace. I still have strength, although, to be honest, I don't think I have many years of life ahead of me. I would, therefore, like to die as a Knight Templar and offer my services to the order, and also to God."

When Jocelyn had said these words he extended the index and the middle finger of his left hand and, after putting them together while bending all the rest of his fingers, he lifted his hand and brought it for a moment to his forehead, without Philippe noticing, as he was to his right. Guillaume, however, and Jean who were both opposite Jocelyn, noticed the gesture. A faint smile appeared on their faces and Guillaume was the first to speak:

"Very well, Brother, so welcome back to our order! We are sure to find something for you to do. First of all, you could become your nephew's groom so that you don't feel useless."

Then he turned to Philippe.

"What do you think of that, Brother?"

Philippe felt uncomfortable about the idea. Him giving orders to his father? It should be the other way round! Jocelyn understood his son's hesitation and quickly reassured him:

"Don't worry, I will not be your servant if this displeases you. But, at my age, nephew, these are the only things I can do to be of any use! Not to mention that it been years since I held a sword!"

"If that's the case, so be it," Philippe said calmly, while thinking that at least in this way the two of them would have plenty of time to spend together.

"Well," Guillaume said to Philippe, "we shall set off early in the morning. So go and stitch in the money and get yourself ready. Luigi and Francois will help you. As for your uncle, don't worry. You will see him all the time from now on!"

"To make up for all those years lost to us, nephew! Goodnight then!" said Jocelyn, squeezing the young man's hands. Philippe could not help hugging his father again. Then he said goodnight and walked towards the house.

As soon as Philippe had left, Jean turned to Jocelyn and said, triumphantly:

"From the first minute I saw you, Brother, I imagined that you would be one of us.

Who would have expected that we would find a lost member of Fede Santa after so many years! So we welcome you again!"

"I am happy to be with you, my Brothers. So our brotherhood still exists! I am happy about that!" Jocelyn said happily and put his hands firmly onto the Grand Master and Jean's shoulders. He could not believe that, apart from his son and his order, he had also found people with whom he shared a deep faith and a well-kept secret.

"We intend to include your nephew too," said Guillaume. "Do you think he is ready? We are also thinking of Luigi and Francois. They have all proved they can be trusted."

Jocelyn hesitated for a moment and then replied:

"I am certain that my nephew will see his induction into Fede Santa in a positive light because he is a seeker and man attracted to mysticism, at least as far as I remember. I can't say about the others because I do not know them well. However, I believe that, except for being trustworthy, they must be open-minded and have somewhat supernatural, let's say, concerns."

"Of course, you are right, Brother. When we reach Acre you shall talk to Philippe first and we shall see about the others," Guillaume said, making a vague movement with his hand.

"I shall do that, my Lord. I want my nephew to partake of this knowledge. In all the years here, you should know that I have not missed out on philosophical and inter-faith discussions. Simeon is a man who could certainly be a member of our organization if he were a Knight Templar. He has an intimate knowledge of the Kabbalah and is open-minded as far as Christianity or Islam are concerned. In all this time we have shared wonderful conversations, and times of reflection and meditation. I shall miss his company."

"Yes, he is very well-educated and good to talk to. I have also found out for myself from our conversations," Guillaume agreed.

"You were certainly very lucky to have met him," Jean said. The three men fell silent. They remained looking at the full moon, which had just risen and, under its silver light, each of them became lost in thought. After some time of complete silence, Guillaume's voice sounded, light and relaxed:

"What do you think? Shall we go inside? I think you too, Brother Jocelyn, should go to get ready and talk to Simeon."

"You are right my Lord," Jocelyn said, sighing and looking at the full moon. "Shall we go?"

***

In the sweet dew of dawn that always exists before the sun comes up, the house of the merchant Simeon was buzzing like a beehive. The servants were running up and down as part of their everyday chores and, only today, to prepare the food to give to the visitors who were soon departing. In the salon of the great mansion the knights were packing their things, while Simeon's wife Esther and, his daughter, Sara, two petite women with pitch black hair, were saying goodbye to Jocelyn, with tears in their eyes. Next to them stood Simeon, who was also clearly moved.

"We will miss you a lot!" said Esther to Jocelyn.

"I will miss you too! We've spent so many years together," he replied and then turned to Simeon with eyes full of gratitude

"I don't know how to thank you for all that you have done for me all these years. If it weren't for you I wouldn't be alive now!"

Next to them Philippe was straightening his robe, looking at them tenderly.

"You are exaggerating!" Simeon said, making a face. "If it hadn't been me, someone else would have helped you."

"No one! People like you can be counted on the fingers of one hand. May God always keep all of you well."

At that moment Guillaume came up to them and said, addressing the merchant:

"Thank you for the wonderful hospitality and help. We are in your debt!"

Simeon had bought the necklace at the price they had arranged. So the trip had achieved its purpose and more. The kindness and hospitality the merchant had shown them were very rarely offered so freely.

"It was my pleasure, my Lord Master!" Simeon said exchanging a warm handshake of goodbye with Guillaume.

A thin maid with rosy cheeks came up to Luigi and gave him a packet with food for the journey. He said goodbye to her kindly and she shyly looked down at the floor.

"So are we ready? Can we leave?" Guillaume asked everyone there.

"Yes, my Lord. Let's go," Francois and Jean replied with one voice.

"Farouk will accompany you to the harbour. In the mornings Venetian ships always depart for Outremer so you will definitely find one to get on and leave," Simeon said to Guillaume. Jocelyn hugged the ladies of the house goodbye. His heart bore the pain of parting with the people who had been his family for so many years with difficulty. He had shared with them not only the sorrows and difficulties of his turbulent life, but also his feelings and his thoughts. He knew the people he was now parting from so suddenly as well as the back of his hand. All these years he had also shared his philosophical concerns and thoughts with them. Until the day before he would have sworn that he would die in this house; he had been certain. But now his life had once again taken one of its surprising turns.

"So farewell, my friend. On the one hand I am very sorry you are leaving, on the other I can't help but be happy for you at finding your nephew and your people after all these years and making your return to where you belong."

Jocelyn nodded his head in agreement, acknowledging the truth in Simeon's words. Then, giving the merchant a warm embrace, he turned to Guillaume:

"Let's go!" he said decisively. He knew he was now turning a new page in his life, and leaving behind him the bitter memories he had from his captivity. The knights followed Farouk across the garden and found themselves back in the bustling streets of the city that was waking from its nightly slumber. Jocelyn looked back at the house in which he had lived for almost twenty years for the last time and then, briefly squeezing the shoulder of his son, who was walking beside him, looked in front of him, at the blue-green sea. From now on, for whatever remained of his life, he would look only ahead, never backwards.

***

The sun was now straight overhead as the Venetian galley taking the knights back to Acre left the port of Alexandria behind. All of them were leaning against gunwale, listening to Jocelyn, as he told them of his turbulent life in his years as a slave, as if he wanted, by journeying back into the past, to exorcise the bad memories and put them out of his mind.

"So, Uncle, will you tell us exactly how you ended up at Simeon's?" Philippe had asked Jocelyn, burning with curiosity, as soon as the ship had raised anchor.

"It's a long story" Jocelyn had replied.

"We have plenty of time on our hands!" Francois had said to him, moving around some ropes coiled in the corner where the group of knights had been sitting with his foot.

"Very well then. But you should know that it is not pleasant for me to talk about these things," Jocelyn had replied, making a gesture of resignation with his hand and taking up his story.

"There weren't many of us prisoners after our defeat at al-Mansurah. Most people had died in the battle. I was not that lucky. I was to suffer much more in my life. Surprisingly, I did not have serious injuries from the battle, only a superficial cut on my right shoulder. They had us, then, with our hands tied behind our backs in a tent. All of us that had survived were exhausted. Sweaty, covered in dust and thirsty, we were waiting for our turn to die with dignity and meet our Lord. Muslims do not spare the life of any knight who finds himself in their hands, neither do they ask for ransom for release as they do for members of laity, but you already know this. What you probably don't know is how much they hate us knights. They consider us fanatics because we are ready to die without question for our faith."

"We had, then, been left in the tent, and only myself and a well-built Brother, whose name I do not remember any more, remained. We were praying when the executioner entered the tent, holding a blade from which the blood of our Brothers was dripping. Neither of us could help but shudder. The Arab, however, asked us something in his language. Not understanding what he was saying to us, having not yet learnt Arabic, we remained silent. Then he violently pulled us up. We then believed that our final moment had come. Yet the Arab took us out of the tent while looking around anxiously. We then saw the headless bodies of our comrades and, to our horror, realized that we were stepping in their blood. The executioner pushed us into another tent, which must have been his own. We stayed there the whole night, expecting to die at any moment. We could hear voices outside and people enjoying themselves. The Infidels were celebrating their victory over us. Nobody came to get us, though."

"Finally, when God brought the new day to the world, the executioner came again. Now silence reigned over the whole Muslim camp. The Infidels were obviously sleeping after they had been celebrating until the early hours of the night before. The executioner brought his finger to his lips, indicating that we should make no sound. He put white turbans on our heads and dressed us in white linen robes. We could not understand anything any more. After that, he put both of us on a horse, tying our hands to its saddle, mounted his own horse, which was tied in front of ours, and we left the camp. It was only when we were far away that the Arab made the animals gallop."

"I never learned why he had done this and saved our lives. Over the next years, with all the hardships I suffered, I cursed him for it. It would have been better, I used to say, if he had killed me then. I wouldn't have had to experience the miserable life of a slave. Now I know that God shone his light on him, so that he would spare our lives and I can be with you this moment talking to you!"

They remained silent, reflecting on Jocelyn's words. Alexandria was now lost from sight behind them and the galley was now maintaining its course, sailing along the coast.

"Where did that Arab take you in the end?" Francois asked. after some moments of silence.

"To Damietta. He made us work in his fields. He had thirteen slaves in total, including us, for this job. I have nothing exciting to tell you about our life there. Every day we did the same. The overseer would wake us up at dawn and we would work until noon when they would let us rest for half an hour and give us water and bread and some kind of gruel. After that we would work until night when they would give us plain gruel again. Especially in the summer, work in the fields is truly an ordeal. Of course, back then I did not know it but, elsewhere, working conditions were worse. And other overseers, elsewhere, were much stricter. They whipped you for the slightest thing."

"So where was it worse to be a slave?" Philippe asked and Guillaume next to him motioned to him not to interrupt.

"In mines and shipyards conditions are much worse, not only working conditions but also hygiene. In galleys, however, it is the worst of all. Thousands of slaves die of disease, exhaustion or drown when the ship to which they are tied sinks[52]."

"It is truly horrific. Of course Muslims would go through the same things if they found themselves in our hands. Isn't that the case?" Jean asked.

"Of course. A slave is neither a man nor an animal. He is probably considered as something in between. Neither Christian nor Muslim masters hold his life to be important. To cut a long story short, however, the other knight and I remained there for around five years, which went by excruciatingly slowly. I only saw the Arab who had saved our lives when he was inspecting the fields."

"In the summer when I was thirty-six years old, a rich Arab – he must have been some relative or other of the man in whose fields we worked – came and walked around with him in the fields while we were working. I was tilling the soil with a hoe, suffering in the unbearable heat. The rich Arab stopped in front of me and looked me down from head to toe. Then he talked to our owner and then they left."

"That night, the overseer ordered me to collect my few belongings, my rags that is, and the things I used for eating and, with no explanation, put me on a cart and took me to the man I had seen in the morning. I didn't even have time to say goodbye to the knight with whom I had been saved. I never found out what happened to him but he probably stayed there until he died."

"My new home was a hut like my previous one, and was dripping with water in even the slightest rain. Working conditions were more or less the same. The food, though, was a little better because the owner was richer. They usually gave us vegetable soup, sometimes meat soup, at noon and night, and bread at both meals of the day. I remained at there for around ten years."

"In the end that Arab probably faced financial difficulties at some point, because, one day, he put me and another three well-built slaves into a cart and took us to the slave market in Damietta. where he sold us to a slave trader. And that's when the worst period of my life began."

Jocelyn paused. It was now noon and time for midday prayer. So, all the knights crossed their arms and quietly said the Pater Noster as they were supposed to do, under the curious gaze of their fellow travellers, some of them actually prayed with them.

When they had finished, Luigi took some bread and cheese out of his saddlebag and they all had lunch in silence. Nothing betrayed the enormous sum of money that the knights had hidden on them Fortunately for them, they seemed to be an ordinary group of Knights Templar returning to Acre after a visit to Egypt, as many other travellers were doing. As soon as they had finished their meal, Jocelyn went on with his story:

"The slave market is one of the worst things mankind has created. It demeans human dignity. The slave trader took all our clothes off, leaving us not one single cloth with which to hide our private parts and had us up on the platform. Next to us were not only other unfortunate men and women, but also little children who must have been captured in some Barbary[53] pirate raid or other."

"At one point two buyers for rich Arabs came and started feeling up a beautiful woman. The poor woman must have been a lady and was not used to such treatment. She was weeping and when the men reached her private parts she could not bear the shame and passed out. Then the buyers started looking at a little girl who could have not been more than ten years old. She was screaming as if possessed and resisted when the slave trader held her so that they could open her mouth and count her teeth. Finally, the buyers came to me. After they had counted my teeth and looked me over well, they spoke to the slave trader for some time. I understood that they were bargaining over the price."

"When they finally came to a decision, the slave trader, after taking the money and giving us our clothes to wear, tied me, another man unknown to me, the woman who had passed-out, and had meanwhile recovered, and the little girl, one behind the other and we set off for our new home."

At this point Jocelyn stopped talking, sighed deeply and wiped his eyes, which had filled with tears as he had brought such unpleasant memories back to mind. The ship had turned and was continuing its course towards the North, with the shore on the one side and the endless sea on the other. The rest of the knights appeared numb and upset by what they were hearing. In the end Luigi broke the silence:

"It has been so many years since then. How do you remember all these things so well, Brother?"

"I think, Brother, that the worst memories of our life, just like the best, are indelibly recorded on our memory. And for me the slave market was definitely one of the most horrible memories of my life and that is why I remember it as if it was only yesterday."

Then, Jocelyn, stroking his white hair for a moment, gave Philippe a loving look and, fixing his eyes on the open sea, went on:

"The Arabs that had bought us were overseers for a rich Muslim merchant from Alexandria. So they put us, once more, on a cart, and we began our long journey to Alexandria. I later found out that the overseers had come to Damietta. to do some work for their master and had not initially intended to buy slaves from that city as Alexandria has a slave market of its own, and a large one at that. They had bought us with money from their salaries so that they could offer their master a gift for his birthday! So, after a torturous journey, during which they gave us water very infrequently and some dry bits of stale bread for food, we reached Alexandria, where they presented us to our new master, a very thin man with big eyebrows who seemed a heartless and cruel man from the very beginning. He didn't even address us. For him we were nothing more than mules that he would work as hard as possible. I never saw the womenfolk again. Clearly they must have been kept for housework."

"The other Christian slave and I were taken to a straw hut together with other slaves where another slave, who acted as an interpreter since he knew Arabic and Frankish, explained to us that we would work in the building of the master's new house. That kind of work is worse than working in the fields because it is highly likely that an accident will take place and someone will be seriously or even fatally injured. The carved stones and marbles used for the building of a palace which serve for its exterior decoration are very heavy and there is very great danger that a stone tied with a rope might slip and crush those lifting it."

"So every day we risked our lives because the master wanted to build this majestic and extremely tall building. He aspired to building the tallest building in Alexandria. I, for one, was lucky. During the two years I endured that horrible place, I saw the man with whom I had been bought together and another five men lose their lives after being crushed by a huge stone. I also saw men having their legs crushed by stones and staying crippled for their whole lives, if, of course, they too didn't die from the bleeding. Don't think that they took great care of those unfortunate enough to get injured or sick. The doctor only came once to do what he had to do. If the patient survived, fine. If not... it didn't matter, one mule less."

"This one time, a slab of marble hit a slave on the shoulder, causing him serious injuries. The man was bleeding and crawling, and it was clear that he could not go on working. The overseers, however, thought that he could and when the man fell down, unable to carry on, they began to whip him so that he would get up again."

"I could take no more. I intervened and told them to stop hitting him, since the man clearly could not work any more. This made them angry and they punished me for my insolence: baring my back, they tied me between two columns and gave me thirty lashes as a punishment. I still have the scars on my back. The doctor eventually came to see the unfortunate man that night and put some cream on my wounds too. I learned my lesson though, and never interfered again, no matter how pained I was by the injustices around me."

"The next night I tried to escape. I left the hut unnoticed but was discovered because of the guard dog tied next to our hut for the express purpose of preventing escape. As soon as I came out it started barking like crazy. I needn't say much. Just that the penalty for attempting to escape the first time is a hundred strokes of the rod on the soles of your feet, the second time the cutting off of a member of your body and the third time death. When they took me to an executioner, experienced in the meeting out of my punishment, they had the other slaves watch, as an example was being made of me."

"They tied me, face down, on a wooden bench and the executioner started to hit me on the bare soles of my feet, slowly and painfully with a stick, counting the strokes aloud. At some point I lost consciousness from the unbearable pain. When I woke up, a doctor was taking care of my wounded feet in the hut. I lay on my back for a week, unable to walk at all. My feet had become deformed forever. The overseers were patient and waited for me to recover because I was strong and did a lot of work. When I returned to work I asked God to make some rock crush me because I could not bare the thought that this would be my life from now on. I almost went crazy, my mind was in tatters."

The narrator stopped to have some water and take a breath. A woman was standing next to them. She seemed to be listening too, moved by the elderly knight's story. She couldn't have been very old, but looked older than her years. She must have been a beautiful woman when young. Her eyes were full of tears when they met those of the elderly knight. Then the woman came up and said to Jocelyn:

"Forgive me, I wasn't eavesdropping, but happened to be next to you and couldn't help but hear your story. I feel very sorry for you and I wonder if my husband and son who were taken by pirates ten years ago have gone through or are still going through the same thing. Since then I've barely survived, waiting for them to come back, maybe, one day. That's why I was listening to your story. I thought that maybe they too escaped slavery, as you managed to."

Philippe exchanged a sad look with Francois. Jocelyn sighed. He knew he was extremely lucky to have escaped as that very rarely happened. Most slaves remained slaves for their whole lives if they did not die young, which was very likely, given the hardships. How could he, however, take all hope from this poor woman, who looked as if she had no other reason to exist than to hope. So he replied:

"Have faith in God and you never know. He is omnipotent and might perform a miracle for you too." The woman's face was lit by a faint, timid smile. Jocelyn looked at Guillaume who was talking to Jean in a low voice, then he took up his story again.

"So it was then that I met Paulo, a Calabrian who had been captured by pirates five years before. He gave me back a taste for life by planting the idea in me of trying to escape once again. And that's what we did. We carefully planned our escape over many nights and hid some bread at each meal to take with us. But we didn't know what to do about the guard dog. In the end we decided to throw enough food at it so that we could run away in the other direction before it got wind of us. I didn't tell you that the dog was also constantly hungry because they gave it very little food, just as they did with us."

"So, when we had saved enough food, we chose a moonless night on which the Hamsin was blowing in the opposite direction from where the dog was so that the wind would not carry our smell to it, and we escaped after having given it plenty of food. Everything went as planned and no one noticed us as the dog didn't bark. We crawled through the grass until we reached the wooden fence that surrounded the Arab's property. We jumped over it and were, at last, free."

"But our difficulties were far from over. Anyone could tell that we were runaway slaves by our clothes, and what bread we had with us was only enough for a few days. After that what would we do? We had no money to buy our way onto a ship and leave Alexandria. So we had to either find a job, something very difficult for two runaways in tattered clothes, or to sneak in secret onto a ship and go to some other place where, wherever it was, we would be safer and would be able to make a fresh start in life. So we chose the second solution."

"So we headed for the harbour, since it was still night, intending to sneak onto a boat and wait there, hidden, until it set sail. We also thought that, if we were lucky, we would find a boat from Italy or Marseilles and could ask for help from the Christians. Come to think of it now, I think that had we actually boarded a Christian boat, they would felt sorry for us and taken us to the West with them for free. But we were not to be so lucky. We could only hear Arabic when we reached the mole. The ships that were anchored there belonged to Muslims. So we decided to move slowly past them and go on to the Italian ships."

"We walked silently past the boats and could hear the sailors laughing and drinking wine, despite their Prophet's injunction against alcohol. At some point we found ourselves too close to one of these groups of sailors. We hid behind a crate and decided to wait, as we couldn't go past them without being noticed. The sailors were probably very drunk, we could hear them dancing and having fun. During the years we had spent in slavery we had both learned Arabic so we could hear them talking about women."

"Suddenly, one of them said he was going for a piss. We could hear him coming our way. We drew ourselves up against the crate and could hardly breathe for fear of being discovered. I remember briefly closing my eyes and praying to God, but when I opened them again, I found myself face to face with the sailor who was looking at me, surprised, holding his member in his hand, about to piss!"

"I had lost it, but Paulo next to me was faster: he immediately grabbed a plank that was leaning against the crate and landed it hard on the dumbfounded sailor's head. He started screaming in pain, holding his head in his hands, while we ran off, with our hearts in our mouths, unable to believe we had had so much bad luck! Our hiding place had been discovered only because a drunken sailor had decided to piss there! The rest of the sailors set off after us when they realized what was happening."

"We were almost out of the harbour when Paulo tripped over some rolled up canvas and fell to the ground. I turned round to pick him up but saw his face tighten in his effort to get up. He couldn't. He must have sprained his ankle badly. The men chasing us were about to catch up with us."

"Paulo looked me in the eye and said to me, out of breath:

'Go Jocelyn, go! I won't make it! At least save yourself!'

'But I can't leave you here!' I replied in panic, pulling his hand so that he would get up.

'I can't run, I am done for whatever happens! So you go! Farewell my friend!' These were his last words, I remember them clearly, his expression pleading with me to leave. I looked at him for a moment, which felt like an eternity. Then I looked up, saw the men getting near and my instinct for self-preservation came into play. I let go of Paulo's hand and set off running again. Without a doubt, it was Paulo's capture that saved me because the sailors, content with catching at least one of us, stopped chasing me. So I hid in the narrow streets of the old town, shaking with fear and stayed there until dawn."

"And what became of Paulo?" Philippe asked anxiously.

"I have no illusions about his fate. He was a runaway slave that had hit a Muslim. If the sailors did not kill him on the spot, they probably handed him over to his owner to face the set punishment. The guilt of getting up and leaving him there will stay with me forever."

"Yes, but what else could you have done?" Luigi said.

"Nothing, but I was racked by guilt for months afterwards. Anyway, we had escaped together and without his help and support I would never have made it!" Jocelyn said, looking down, a few tears in his eyes, and stopped talking. Bringing back to mind the last part of the story had obviously made him very sad. The woman, a little further off, frozen stiff, looked at him compassionately.

"And how did you end up at Simeon's?" Guillaume asked after a while. Jocelyn finished his story, keeping his eyes fixed on the ship's deck:

"In the morning, having somewhat recovered from the fright, I remembered that I was carrying the skin with water and that Paulo had had the bread, and consequently I now had nothing to eat! I thought, now mistakenly I believe, that the sailors were also looking for me and was afraid to go to central places, let alone to the harbour. I was still too upset by what had happened to calmly think about what to do. So I walked the streets, alone and devastated by Paulo's loss. The truth is that I did not care about my life any more. I wanted my life and my suffering to end. I had neither the courage nor the desire to try to save myself. That same night I got the chills. I was ill and was starting to get a fever. I must have been near Simeon's house and was dragging myself along with difficulty when I lost consciousness. I woke up and realized that I was lying on a real bed in a luxurious house. At first I thought I was dreaming. Simeon's people had taken me in from the street, saving me, of course, from certain death. I lay in bed for some days until I had recovered from the hardships and suffering of so many years. I think you know the rest of the story."

Jocelyn looked up and saw the woman in front of him. She smiled at him, wished him good health and huddled up a little further off to sleep. The sun was now setting. The rest of the knights stood up, silent, and stretched limbs now numb from so many hours of sitting still. After they had said the Pater Noster for the evening, together with Jocelyn, they began to talk: Guillaume and Jean about administrative matters and Francois and Luigi about military matters. Only Philippe went up to stand at his father's side. Gazing out to sea, they stayed there for some time, communicating in silence.

12

Fort Marqab of the Hospitaller knights, May 23, 1285

hick smoke had turned the sky black and hid the sun above the fort. The fire had already caused what was known as the Tower of Hope at the north end of the fortress to collapse and knights and sergeants were running up and down, throwing soil and whatever water they had left onto it, trying to stop it from spreading. When the fire was finally out, Foulques, black from the smoke, as he had actively participated in putting it out, sat on a stone from the pile of rubble and held his head in his hands in despair. He sat still, trying to calm down, unable to believe the new calamity that had befallen them.

After the pleasant break of the trip to Alexandria, Foulques had returned to his monastic duties, on which he had been spending less and less time compared to that he spent on his military duties given the alarming increased frequency of battles and skirmishes with the "Infidels" in recent years. Qalawun, Baybars' most capable emir, who had defeated the Armenians in Cilicia in August 1266, was proclaimed Sultan in 1279 after Baybars' death following a brief dispute with his successors, and was carrying on the work of his predecessor with great success. Everything indicated that his last triumph would be the conquest of this fort. He wanted to conquer it by any means because of its size and because of the fact that the Hospitallers frequently formed alliances with the neighbouring Mongols, and thus constituted the greatest obstacle to the Mamluks' efforts to drive the invaders away from their land.

It was for this reason that the new Grand Master of the Hospitallers, Jean de Villiers, elected a year before to fill the position on the death of Lorgne, had appointed Guillaume de Villaret commander of Marqab in the beginning of the spring of 1285. Guillaume, always taking his nephew with him, had gone to assume his new duties with a great of optimism and enthusiasm. Yet he was now forced to admit that the hopes of the order keeping Marqab, and stopping Qalawun's momentum, were rather forlorn.

The siege had began on the seventeenth of the previous month and up until a few days before it had seemed that the care taken and excellent preparations made by Guillaume in anticipation of the siege would pay off. The Sultan had appeared with a huge army and many siege engines.. The knights, however, were unperturbed when they saw the catapults since, they too, had such devices and had, in fact, by placing them on the walls, a better and wider range of fire than that of the Muslims.

So, after a month-long siege, the Sultan had made no progress, while many of his siege engines had been destroyed by direct hits from the knights' catapults. During that month, Foulques had learned to use the catapults to perfection in his effort to be useful since direct attacks by the enemy army on the fortress had yet to take place. However. it seemed that the Sultan did not want to sacrifice his men's lives needlessly on such very strong walls before his siege engines broke them down, at least in one place.

Guillaume, in charge of defences, brimmed with optimism until he became aware of the new danger that was facing them.. This danger was no other than the tunnels of the enemy's engineers, many of which had yet to be located by those under siege. It was then that he began to worry in earnest. It was a tunnel such as this that the enemy dug under the Tower of Hope and filled it with flammable timber without the Christians noticing. A great fire was lit and the Tower had been brought to the ground. Still sitting among the ruins of the tower, Foulques heard the troubled voice of the guard:

"Raise the alarm! The enemy is attacking us through a breach in the walls!"

When indeed Foulques lifted his eyes he saw many "infidels" walking towards him, brandishing their swords menacingly and trying to climb the ruins. Foulques pulled his sword from its scabbard in an instant, ready to defend the order's fortress. Around came other knights and sergeants doing the same. The knights still had no shortage of men as, up until that time, only two sergeants had been killed and some men injured, as no hand to hand combat had yet taken place.

Despite the fact that the tower had collapsed, the pile of ruins was particularly high and the Muslims were having difficulty climbing it under the hail of stones the sergeants were raining down on them from above. When Foulques realized that there was no point in using his sword this time either, he shouted loudly:

"Bring boiling oil!"

Then he put his sword back in its scabbard and started throwing rubble and stones from the pile of ruins at the attackers. The others quickly followed suit. Skulls cracked, limbs broke and wounds opened up on the bodies of the Muslims, whose charge lost something of its impetus when they saw that they were not achieving anything. When Guillaume appeared at the breach with servants holding the pot of boiling oil, panic spread among the attackers. With one swift movement, the servants tipped the pot and the boiling oil fell on those Muslims who had not run away. They began to scream, scalded, completely discouraging those thinking of trying to climb up again.

The knights celebrated their victory and retreated to the interior of the fort. Foulques took off his helmet and, holding it in his hands, approached his uncle, who was examining the ground a little further off, concerned. Still further Pierre off was doing the same, his face tight with worry. Foulques started examining the ground too and soon realised why his uncle and Pierre were worried. He stamped his foot on the ground and the soil there collapsed, pulling Foulques into the hole. Pierre ran to him and stretched out his hand to help him out. Foulques grabbed it and clambered up at once.

"Damn it," he said. "It's full of tunnels underground."

"Yes," Guillaume agreed while also climbing up. "We are doomed whatever we do. I knew there were tunnels but I had no idea there were so many," he added, dusting off his clothes.

"It is a matter of time until they penetrate our defensive positions and we will not be able to do anything to stop them. They will spring up everywhere!" Pierre said with obvious frustration on his face.

"Our impregnable walls are useless now! That is why they gave way so easily before! They knew that if they didn't take the fortress from the walls, they would sneak up from behind and surprise us. They might even have made this attack as a diversion and filled the tunnels with men so that they can suddenly attack at a moment when we are not expecting them," Foulques agreed.

Guillaume kicked the wall hard.

"Damn it! You are right, nephew," he said to himself, angrily. "They have been digging under our noses all this time! I admit I was a little worried but I did not believe that these damned people had created a whole underground city under our fort! Qalawun is smarter than I thought!"

"Even if we had discovered this earlier, we wouldn't have been able to do much. The soil around the fort is soft and easy to dig out. We've always known that that is its weak point. As many tunnels as we destroy, the Sultan has so many engineers that they will always create new ones. You are wrong to be sad, uncle, this was God's will," Foulques said, trying to somehow ease his uncle's disappointment.

"So what do we do now?" Pierre asked.

Guillaume sighed:

"Unfortunately we are forced to surrender. We are lost. I find it utterly pointless to waste men's lives in a defence with a foregone conclusion here, when we have a huge shortage of manpower in all our strongholds and a war with the infidels on all fronts."

"You are absolutely right, Brother," said Pierre. "I am sure that our Lord Master would do the same thing if he were here. Resistance and war until the end are for situations in which there is hope. Unnecessary sacrifices will not save Outremer."

"We should then inform the council of the situation and send messengers for terms of surrender to Qalawun, shouldn't we uncle?" Foulques said, disappointment clear in his eyes.

Guillaume motioned that they should follow him with the same sad look:

"Yes, nephew. We shall request to be allowed to leave with all our equipment, at least we knights that are here. The sergeants can leave unarmed."

The three of them started walking towards the commandery. Foulques looked around the grounds. Knights and sergeants were going up and down the walls. Others were talking quietly, sitting on the ground and others were taking their armour and helmets off with the help of their servants. When they reached the door of the commandery Guillaume said to the sergeant who was at the door:

"Call all the senior knights for an urgent council." The sergeant ran to do what Guillaume ordered. Turning the door handle, Guillaume said to himself: "This time Qalawun has beaten us.. However, I have a feeling that we will face each other again, very soon."

All three men disappeared inside the building, grimly silent, closing the door behind them.

13

Acre, October 29, 1287

he slightly cool breeze that had just risen up reminded Philippe that another winter was about to come upon Acre. His hair stood on end and he wrapped his cloak tightly around him while he continued walking quickly towards the dormitory. Dinner and Vespers had just finished and the knights were getting ready for bedtime. Philippe reached his straw mattress, carefully took off his robe from his shoulders and left it next to him, carefully folded.

While he was sitting on the bench, he saw Francois gesticulating vigorously at the other side of the dormitory. He could not however hear what he was saying because next to him two young knights were constantly talking. "I'm sure that something bad has happened again," Philippe thought as he lay down on the mattress. Luigi was already lying down next to him, trying to get to sleep without success. Philippe sighed and closed his eyes. Soon, however, he felt a hand squeezing his shoulder. He opened his eyes and saw Francois above him. Luigi was now sitting on his mattress. He obviously could not sleep either because of the two knights who were talking.

"What has happened this time?" Luigi asked in a bored tone of voice, resting his head on his hand.

"Bohemund of Tripoli has died," Francois said straight away, ignoring Luigi's sour look.

"Died?" Luigi repeated as he were an echo, with evident interest.

"Bad news," Philippe remarked. "Who will command Tripoli now? He was single and had no children."

"Power would normally pass to his sister Lucia, but she lives in Puglia[54] and it will take her long to come down to Outremer if, of course, she decides to do so."

"What do the lords there say?" asked Luigi.

"They don't want her of course. Meanwhile, some Bartolemeo Embriaco has assumed power," Francois replied, taking his robe off too and walking towards his straw mattress, which was next to Philippe's.

"So nothing is final yet," commented Philippe, lying on his back and putting his hands behind his head.

"Nothing," said Francois lying down. "However, I'm afraid that that discord among the followers of this Embriaco and Lucia may well, once more, benefit Qalawun, who never misses opportunities like these."

"You are right. Let's pray that Acre keeps out of disputes in Tripoli," Philippe concluded and the three knights did not talk any more but remained immersed each in their own thoughts. And while most knights – including Francois – quickly fell into the arms of Morpheus, Luigi and Philippe stayed awake.

Philippe fixed his eyes on the empty mattress opposite him, now in moonlight. "Where could he be?" he wondered, considering his father's absence from the dormitory at such a late hour. He must be with the Grand Master again..

Since they had returned from Alexandria, Philippe's father had been taking care of his son's horse and going to the services normally but spending most of the rest of his time with Guillaume. They would often disappear for hours on end. In the beginning, Philippe would worry about him, until he realized there was no point any more in looking for him. When Jocelyn's meetings with the Grand Master came to an end, he would always return unusually calm, serenity and a permanent smile on his face. Philippe had often asked him what he had been doing with Guillaume for such a long time but Jocelyn would always answer: "You will find out when the time comes. I must be sure that you are absolutely ready before I tell you anything."

So Philippe could do nothing but wait patiently and, as time passed, he stopped asking anything whatsoever. He turned on his side on his mattress again and changed position, but he couldn't sleep. "Might it be the full moon? What's wrong with me?" he thought.

Next to him Luigi was not sleeping either. He was, however, keeping still with his eyes closed, trying to calm down. He was feeling far from tired and that is probably why he could not fall asleep. Suddenly he heard whispers, but forced himself not to open his eyes. Jocelyn had returned.

"Aren't you sleeping nephew?" he quietly asked Philippe.

"I can't uncle, I don't know why. Do you think it might be the full moon?" Philippe replied jokingly.

Jocelyn was about to take his robe off but, as if a thought had suddenly come to him, did not do this in the end. He decisively addressed Philippe in a conspiratorial way:

"Now is the opportunity. Everyone is asleep and we have all night in front of us. What do you say?"

Philippe put his elbows on the mattress and sat up.

"An opportunity for what?" he asked, puzzled.

"To tell you the things I want to, at last. I think you are ready now."

Philippe was more than willing. Instead of giving him an answer, he instantly got up from the bed and threw his robe over his shoulders, walking towards the door, behind his father, who had already gone out.

"Ready for what I wonder," thought Luigi and opened his eyes the moment Philippe disappeared through the door.

He sat on the mattress and looked around him. Everybody else was sleeping and there was complete silence in the dormitory. "I mustn't miss this conversation," thought Luigi and sprang up, also putting on his robe so as not to get cold. Then, with silent steps like a great cat, he made for the doorway, where he stood motionless and looked out. He soon spotted the two knights. They had sat down on two rocks under a large cedar tree right opposite him and, fortunately for Luigi, had their backs turned to him. A faint smile appeared on the knight's lips: "Nice. The only thing I have to do is hide behind that thick trunk and be completely silent".

So, like a bloodthirsty panther stalking its prey, he quickly covered, with great, silent steps, the few meters between the dormitory and the cedar and took up position behind the trunk of the old tree, just as the screech of an owl broke the silence of the night. The two knights had not exchanged a single word, since Jocelyn was thinking of where it would be wise to begin. Philippe understood that his father had many things to tell him and let him put his thoughts in order, helping him remain silent. They had the whole night in front of them anyway.

He looked at the moon. It was like a huge snowball in the starless pitch-black sky. It seemed as if it were also looking at them, as if it were taking part in their conversation, patiently waiting for Jocelyn to begin. Philippe smiled at the thought that they had "company" and looked at his father, who appeared to be very deep in thought. He was unaware, however, that someone else, apart from the huge snowball, was impatiently waiting for Jocelyn to start talking.

Jocelyn took a deep breath and looked his son in the eye:

"First of all, I want you to tell me, my son: what is God to you?"

Behind the trunk Luigi suppressed a gasp of surprise when Jocelyn addressed Philippe as "my son". "The two of them are probably hiding more than I thought!"

Philippe was surprised by Jocelyn's question. The only thing he had not expected was to start a theological debate with his father under the moonlight. He understood, however, that his father was taking the conversation somewhere else and, for that reason, thought very carefully before he answered.

"God is everything. He is everywhere, everything is done according to His will. He directs us and leads us." He paused and added:

"I think that God is within every one of us but I don't think I can answer your question. What is God? I think that, in reality, we know very little about this. God is an intangible spirit, three persons in one nature."

Philippe shrugged his shoulders in resignation:

"Has my answer satisfied you? I believe I can't think of anything else to tell you. I have never given it any thought and no-one has ever asked me what God is before."

Jocelyn smiled contentedly. Philippe's answer had given him the opportunity to steer the conversation in the direction that he had intended.

"For a start, son, you said: "No one has ever asked me what God is before," and "I have never given it any thought." Do you think that is right for a monk like you? I mean, wouldn't it be more spiritual on your part to have already asked yourself, before I ask you?"

Philippe was baffled:

"Certainly. But why would I do that? We attend services every day, we pray to God and try to do his will. Isn't that enough?"

"From a formalistic point of view that is definitely correct," said Jocelyn, looking deep into his son's eyes. "From a spiritual point of view though? You said before that God is three persons in one nature. Do you know this from personal experience?"

"Of course not! I have known this since I was a little child. That's what we have been told!" Philippe said indignantly.

"Who told you?"

"Everyone. My mother, my father, the priests."

"And you think that they have seen that God is three persons in one nature?"

"Of course not! They have known it and believed it all along! What are you asking me?" Philippe almost shouted, somewhat irritated, finding no meaning in these questions.

"Don't be angry," the elderly knight replied, laughing. "I am just asking you these things so that you can see that everything you know about God is what others have told you, those who simply believe these things because they too have heard them from others and have no personal experience of them. Right so far?"

"Correct, but I still don't understand what you are getting at."

"So if I told you that I know, from personal experience, that God is simply a spirit and that the three persons, the Holy Trinity and all the rest are human inventions, would you believe me?"

"What is this ungodly man saying? So many years of living amongst Jews and Infidels have made him a heretic!" thought Luigi angrily, and Philippe had the exact same thought but said it aloud:

"But this is heretical thinking father! You, a monk who has so often fought for God, can't be saying such things!"

A faint smile appeared on Jocelyn's face again, and he said to Philippe, nodding his head:

"The word heresy comes from Ancient Greek and means choice. Since when should a man's attempt to think freely and to seek his spirituality alone, outside the established system of worship which we call the Church, be condemned?"

Philippe remained silent, deep in thought. He saw that his father was right. A little further off, out of sight, Luigi thought, with satisfaction,:

"Now I have something really good to tell Abbot Giovanni!"

After some time of silence, Jocelyn spoke first:

"I know that deep down you agree with me son, don't you? What I want from you is to simply set yourself free, away from the blinkers and reins with which the Church narrows our horizons. You know, contrary to what people usually believe, the Church has deliberately hidden a great deal about Jesus and has led us into darkness, hiding the true light from us, preventing us from having personal contact with God and leading us to sterile, standardised worship with no spiritual depth."

Philippe, his interest aroused and his curiosity at its peak, motioned to his father to continue, as he did:

"Well, son, in order for you to understand the things I want to tell you well, we must take things from the beginning. Fortunately we have time. First of all, I assume you know that the ancient world, which was entirely pagan, had reached a very high level of intellect in philosophy, art and, to cut a long story short, all aspects of public life."

"Yes, there were wise men like Plato and Aristotle. Some of their texts have been preserved and we study them even today, don't we?"

"Exactly, son. And there are many other wise men from those times. Have you ever heard the names Porphyry, Plotinus, Origen, Iamblichus?"

Philippe shook his head.

"You might not know then that the ancients reached a very high level of spirituality, notwithstanding their remarkable achievements in the arts and philosophy. Have you ever heard of the Eleusinian Mysteries?"

"To be honest, no," said Philippe after a little thought.

"Well, since ancient times," continued Jocelyn, "there have been people who had the desire to experience the divine themselves and, through a process of initiation, reach a condition called ecstasy or, more simply, theosis, to come to know God themselves and sense Him in all their being, to become one with Him."

"A noble desire but one also difficult to achieve, I imagine," commented Philippe.

"Exactly. Through that initiation process, however, the believer would be reborn and eventually transform into a better man. He experienced, in other words, a spiritual rebirth, his own personal resurrection one might say. In order to achieve this, one should first of all have self-awareness and know himself."

"That's all well and good, but I don't understand what it has to do with us," Philippe broke in again.

"Not so fast, you'll see. Well, some of the ancient sacred texts that tell of the gatherings of these Mysteries have come down to us. These included ritual dances, loud music, huge pyres, bodily immersion and alternating light and dark to help the initiate reach deification, after, of course, a great deal of personal effort. But these things were for the few, for the elite who were willing to try to experience the divine.

For the ordinary people there were the so-called myths, entertaining stories, but which for the initiate held deep spiritual teachings. They were, that is, spiritual allegories, which the uninitiated might understand to be literally true. These myths constitute the first stage, the Outer Mysteries. Whoever understood the myth better would move on to the second stage – the Inner Mysteries – which I described to you before. These mysteries came from ancient Egypt. The Egyptians were the first to represent them in the passion and resurrection of the god Osiris."

Philippe let out an exclamation of surprise and Luigi had difficulty in restraining himself from doing the same.

"But," Philippe exclaimed intensely, "we also have the passion and resurrection of Jesus!"

"Exactly! Disregard the fact that almost no one knows about this today. The truth is that Christianity has more in common with Paganism that it has differences!"

"This cannot be!" Philippe almost shouted in disbelief.

"It is," Jocelyn nodded reassuringly. "Let me go on and you'll see. Well, the pyramids in Egypt, except for being the tombs of the kings, were also used for this mystic cult of Osiris. From Egypt this cult spread throughout the Mediterranean basin. So we have a god who died and rose again in all areas of the Mediterranean: Greeks worshipped Dionysus Zagrea in place of Osiris, in Italy it was Bacchus, in Asia Minor Attis, Mithras in Persia and the god Adonis in Syria. The story of these gods is more or less similar, with only minor variations. To be specific, Dionysus was born of a virgin on December 25th, turned water to wine, was hung on a tree or crucified, and rose from the dead. Those faithful to him would, indeed, partake of wine as his body and blood, as Holy Communion. Does that remind you of anything?"'

"But that's exactly the same story as Jesus'! Can this be true?"

"Of course it is son. I know it is difficult for you to believe but Jesus is nothing more than one more god amongst the many other gods that were worshipped in this way in ancient times."

"And how do you know that it was really like this?" shouted Philippe in disbelief. "I mean to say, father, how do you know it wasn't the other way round and that ancient myths did not copy the story of Jesus in retrospect?"

Jocelyn stood up and motioned to Philippe to follow him. Philippe stood up too, puzzled, and followed his father, who was walking towards the Grand Master's office while talking at the same time:

"This is something that the Christian Fathers said later, not knowing how to cover up the all too obvious similarities between their newly established religion and Paganism." When they reached the Grand Master's office a little further down, Philippe was surprised to see his father taking out some keys from his robe and unlocking the door without any concern.

"You have keys? I thought only the Lord Master and the seneschal had keys!"

"So you thought wrong!" Jocelyn replied, laughing while he opened the door wide, and motioned to Philippe to come in.

"But are we allowed to enter without the Lord Master knowing? Shouldn't we ask for his permission first?"

"Don't worry. All members of Fede Santa have unrestricted access to the manuscripts you are about to see now as their study and knowledge of them are two of our primary concerns. Come in and..." said Jocelyn. He left his sentence unfinished because he thought he had heard something, like a branch breaking. He turned his head, concerned, and scanned the yard. Except for the shadows created by the moonlight falling on the trees, he could see nothing. Philippe listened, in turn, as he too had heard the sound. Now, however, complete silence reigned. Even the owl was quiet.

"It must have been a lizard," said Jocelyn. "Let's go."

They entered the office, closing the door carefully behind them. They had, however, forgotten to look at the side wall of the building, under the window, where Luigi was on the floor. He was cursing himself inside for being so careless as to have stepped on the twig that had gone unnoticed in his effort to quickly follow the two knights.

"Whew, I made it again!" he thought, trying to stop his heart from racing. "I might not be able to get in, but I will definitely hear something from here." He then looked anxiously at the building some way off right opposite him. "As long as no one comes out of the dormitory to go to the toilet and sees me." He perched there and listened carefully so as to understand what the two knights were saying.

***

Inside the building, the two knights headed towards a small door that Philippe had never noticed before as it was almost hidden in a recess in the wall with a stone arch on top, behind the Grand Master's wooden desk. After lighting a torch that he gave to Philippe, Jocelyn put another of the keys he had on him in the door. Before, however, he opened it, he turned and gave Philippe a stern look:

"It goes without saying that whatever I tell you will stay between us. You know very well that not all Knights Templar would accept such views. That is why we are very careful about bringing new members into our organization."

Philippe nodded in agreement and then the two men entered the room, closing the door behind them.

Luigi angrily brought his hand down on the stone wall:

"Damn it! What do I do now?"

As soon as he heard the door closing he slowly raised his head and looked through the window. It was dark where the door of the room that the two knights had just entered was, and to the right of the door were stairs that led to the basement, where the treasury and the financial documents were.

Luigi did not hesitate for a moment:

"I'll stand outside the door. I'm sure to hear something of what they say, and when I hear them coming out I'll hide on the stairs. What's more, I won't be seen by anyone coming out of the dormitory. So it's best there."

At once, making no noise, he climbed through the window and, having entered, slithered to the little door and gently placed his ear against it. For now he could hear no sound coming from the room.

Inside Philippe had already hung the torch on the wall and it shed light on a room full of books. There were many wooden bookcases placed tightly next to each other, containing what must have been hundreds of manuscripts. At the other side of the room was a glass display case, but Philippe could not see what was in it from such a distance. He was trying to get over his surprise and was moving his hands awkwardly, unable to find something to say. His father had talked to him about manuscripts, but so many? Jocelyn, who was clearly taking pleasure in his son's surprise, remembered the time he had been initiated into Fede Santa and was smiling, moved. It had been so many years since then! And now he was initiating his own son himself!

"This is the order's real treasure, larger in value than any monetary treasure. Not even the Temple of Paris has as many books as the library in Acre," Jocelyn said to Philippe, unable to hide the enthusiasm in his voice.

"So at this moment you are now standing in Outremer's largest library and, possibly, the largest in the all Christendom. But before we look at the manuscripts and continue our conversation, I want to show you something related to what you asked me before."

Jocelyn walked towards the glass showcase and Philippe followed him, brimming with curiosity. When they came to stand over the glass, Philippe looked down to see a tiny piece of plaster showing someone on a cross[55]. Philippe looked at his father questioningly.

"It's just a depiction of Jesus' martyrdom on the cross. I don't understand what is so strange about that?"

"Did you notice the letters on the amulet?"

Philippe looked more closely and made out an inscription under the crucifix. It was, however, not in Latin, and he could not read it.

"I see them," he replied. "What language is it?"

"Greek. And you know what it says?"

"Jesus Christ I suppose."

"No. Look. The first letter is "o", which is the same as in Latin. See it?"

Surprised, Philippe, leaning over the cast, found that his father was right. He tried to read the rest of the inscription:

"Op…I don't know the next letter."

"It's the Greek "phi". However, the second letter is not read "p" as you did, but "r".

Jocelyn opened the showcase, gently lifted the amulet and placed it in his palm. Then he placed the index finger of his other hand on the tiny letters and slowly read the inscription, showing Philippe the letters one by one:

"O-r-f-e-a-s V-a-k-k-i-k-o-s. It's the other name of the Greek God Dionysus." Philippe could not believe his ears:

"It can't be!" he said, clearly shaken.

"It is." This is the answer to the question you asked me before concerning who copied who. This amulet appears to depict the Passion of Jesus. However, in reality, it depicts the passion of Osiris-Dionysus and one of the hundreds that existed in the pre-Christian years and has come down to us intact. It belonged to one of the first Lord Masters of the order, Bertrand de Blanchefort[56], who donated it to the order. His family had it in their possession for years after it was discovered by chance during a trip somewhere in the East, according to Blanchefort. When this man was initiated into Fede Santa, before he was elected Lord Master of course, he realized exactly what that amulet was and saw its true value."

"I understand. But since when has this organization existed father?" Philippe asked the question he had been thinking of for some time now.

"It was established by Everard des Barres[57], the third Lord Master of our order. He was a wise man and had been initiated into the Mysteries before he joined the order. He had an original library of apocryphal manuscripts, which he donated to the order. It was his idea to preserve the lost knowledge of antiquity through an organization of wise and progressive people who were at the same time, members of the order. And, as you can see, he succeeded and I am sure that future generations, if there is ever freedom of thought and expression, something I wish for with all my heart, will thank him for that."

Philippe remained silent for a while, trying to take in everything he had heard. Meanwhile Jocelyn carefully put the amulet back into the glass case and headed towards the manuscripts.

Philippe followed him. Then he stopped in front of a bookcase, leaned forward and read out the names of authors where he could make them out and the titles were in Latin.

"Ammonius, Pythagoras, Origen, Valentine, Monoimos..."

He was interrupted by Jocelyn: "Take that manuscript by Monoimos and give it to me. I want to read you something."

Philippe took the manuscript, which was bound between two leather covers to protect it from the damp, and gave it to his father.

"What a pity that I don't know Greek...I could read it on my own..." he murmured disappointedly.

"And who says that you can't learn? Many of these have been translated into Latin, many others haven't. I myself shall teach you so that you can study these wise teachings yourself," replied Jocelyn, opening the manuscript and looking for the part he wanted to read to Philippe.

"Latin is certainly not enough. Ah, here it is at last! Well, this Gnostic teacher says: 'Abandon the search for God and creation and things like these. Look for him by taking yourself as the starting point. Learn who it is within you who takes everything as his own and says; "My God, my mind, my thought, my soul, my body." Learn from where sorrow, happiness, love, hatred come. If you look into these matters carefully, you will find him within yourself."'[58]

"I see. So through knowledge of self we can attain knowledge of God if I understand correctly. It sounds interesting," Philippe remarked, his curiosity aroused by this unusual teaching, and his eyes still fixed on the manuscripts.

"Exactly. You're a fast learner I see," said Jocelyn, smiling, closing the manuscript and putting it carefully back in its place.

Philippe continued to browse through the books, tapping them with his finger, and going on to another bookcase, again reading the Latin titles out loud:

"The Apocryphon of James, the Apocalypse of Peter, the Gospel of Thomas[59]." He stopped in his tracks, trying to take in what he had just read:

"The Gospel of Thomas?" He read it again and made sure that his eyes were not deceiving him. Then he looked at the title and continued to read:

"The Gospel of Philip. But what are these Gospels, father? I know of only four!" he raised his head, puzzled, and looked at his father questioningly. Jocelyn folded his arms over his chest and replied:

"You know, as almost everyone else does, of only four of the many Gospels that exist, namely those of Matthew, Mark, Luke and John, those, that is, that Irenaeus put forward as genuine at the end of the 2nd century AD. Nevertheless, the New Testament, as we know it today, only took on its final form in the 4th century AD."

"I always thought that the New Testament was written shortly after Jesus' death."

"And yet there was a great deal of dispute as to which texts would finally be included in it. But we will get there. For now, we were talking about the amazing similarities between Paganism and Christianity."

"There is definitely, however, a great difference," said Philippe, interrupting his father – pagans were polytheists while Christianity established monotheism for the first time."

"I wouldn't say that. Although they do have a lot in common, there are definitely some differences, nothing, however, to do with polytheism. I told you before that the God worshipped in the Mysteries was one, but he had one name in Egypt, for example, and another in Asia Minor. Not only that, the multitude of minor gods were something like the angels of our religion. So, generally speaking, we are talking about about many aspects of the nature of one god. Our Holy Trinity is also a similar compromise promoted by Christianity in its effort to prevail against a very strongly incumbent paganism. Finally, as for the idea of one single god itself, I shall refer again to the ancient Egyptians: they first established monotheism as we mean it today. It is this idea that the Ancient Greeks, especially Pythagoras, borrowed in their turn."

At this point he broke off again and started looking again for some manuscript. Philippe waited patiently, while outside Luigi was just as surprised as the young de Ridefort, as he listened to the conversation between the two knights.

"So five hundred years before Christ," continued Jocelyn, who had found what he was looking for, " the ancient wise man Xenophanes says to us: "There is one god, always dormant and at rest, moving everything with his thoughts." And then there are the words of Pythagoras himself, as Justin the Martyr gives them to us: "There is one god and he does not exist, as some assume, outside the world but in it." For philosophers before Socrates it was a well-established tenet that there is one god," he went on, closing the book and putting it back in its place. Then, seeing that Philippe remained silent he added:

"In their writings the philosophers Celsus and Origen the Pagan often made fun of the Christians' desperate attempt to present these teachings as new in their writings. But, as you see, they did it in the end." Philippe was listening to his father carefully. He thought that Jocelyn was right on the one hand, based on everything he had told him, but on the other he had to raise his objections.

"That's all very well. But then why did Christianity prevail over paganism? And then there are teachings that are clearly Christian like loving your neighbour, moral purity, humility and poverty. And even if the idea of Resurrection and Eucharist are not Christian, there is still Baptism, the idea of Heaven and Hell, and symbols like the cross and the fish which are clearly Christian. Are you maybe forgetting all these Father?"

Jocelyn indicated that his son should sit on one of the two stools in the library. Philippe sat down on one and the elderly knight sat on the other before he began to talk:

"I shall leave your first question for the end. As for all the others, let's take them in turn, shall we? You spoke first of love for one's neighbour. First of all, you should know that in the ancient Mysteries, the people involved called each other brothers, just like Christians."

Once more Jocelyn got up and disappeared from Philippe's sight, looking for another book that would prove what he was saying to his son. When he found it, he continued to talk, standing, with the book open in his hands:

"Sextus, Epictetus and Socrates, those who first taught love for one's neighbour. You might not know the first two, but that's not the case with last one, is it?"

"Right. Everyone has heard of Socrates, I think."

"Let's start with Sextus' saying in his book entitled "The Sentences of Sextus": "May you be able to benefit your enemies". Epictetus in his work "Theses" continues: "This is the way of the philosopher: to be lashed like a donkey and to love the one who lashed him, to be the father and brother of all humanity." And that brings us to Socrates' words, as his student Plato cites them in his work "Crito": "It is never just to hurt someone, it is never just to take revenge on someone nor is it just to do something bad, even in the case that someone has been offended and they try to do the same back." Moreover, the Orphics and Pythagorean philosophers[60] went further than Christianity did: they extended their love to the animal kingdom, condemning the animal sacrifices that some religions performed, and by being vegetarians. To conclude, Christ was not the first to teach this, but the last. Any objection to this?" Jocelyn asked his son in a triumphant tone of voice, closing the manuscripts he was gently holding. Philippe nodded in resignation.

"No objection. It is clear that whatever objections I had were only due to my ignorance on the subject."

"So I shall go on. Let's talk about moral purity. You must know that while Christians accused the Mysteries of being wanton licentious meetings of degenerate people who were prey to their passions, the exact opposite was in fact the case. The Mysteries were a source of moral purification and preparation for death. Iamblichus[61] tells us about this in his work 'On the Mysteries': 'The aim of such displays in the Mysteries is to free us from our violent passions, giving pleasure to the eye and, at the same time, driving away every evil thought through the awesome sanctity that accompanies these rituals.'"Jocelyn took another book from the bookcase and went on to say:

"The Stoic philosophers[62] passed down the concept of "conscience" to the Christians. Seneca[63] tells us: 'Every day I bring complaints against myself, before myself as judge. When the light is gone and my wife, who is aware of this habit of mine, is silent, I reflect on the day that has passed. I go through all my actions and words and weigh them up. I hide nothing, I spare nothing. Why should I hesitate to confront my shortcomings when I can say: 'Take care not to repeat them and I forgive you for today."

Jocelyn closed the book which he had been looking for before in the bookcase, while Philippe stood up and started to walk up and down the room, weighing up everything his father was telling him. His father went on with what he was saying.

"As for the confession of our sins which supposedly Jesus taught first, you should know, my son, that whoever wanted to take part in the Mysteries first had to purify themselves by publicly confessing their weaknesses and their wrongdoings. Even the famous Roman Emperor Nero was forced not to take part when he realized he had to confess to killing his mother!" Philippe, slightly surprised on hearing these words, looked his father straight in the eye and said:

"So I imagine the Mysteries must have been a sacred institution for the ancients – as even a powerful man like Nero chose not to tell lies in front of the priests of the Mysteries, rather than take part and then make a fool of himself if he was later proved to be a liar."

"Exactly, son. It is incidents such as this that show the prestige that the Mysteries enjoyed back then. The confession to the priest of the Mysteries was, as it is in Christianity, an action of piety and not simply a formality. Of course, just as not all Christians today are good people, back then hypocrites also sometimes joined the Mysteries. This, however, does not change the character of the Mysteries."

"Of course. There have always been hypocrites and liars and there always will be."

Philippe folded his arms, leaned on a bookshelf and asked his father:

"What about humility and poverty? What do you have to say about them? Because I have to confess that up until now you have backed up what you have said with strong arguments and won me over."

"Not I, but the philosophers themselves I think!" Jocelyn replied, laughing, and then, becoming serious again, went on:

"Have you ever heard of the school of philosophy called Cynicism?"

"I know the name, but I am afraid I do not know anything particular about them."

"Well, their name comes from from the Cynosarges in Athens, where Antisthenes[64] taught. It was he who established this new teaching, which had many things in common with Jesus' teaching. The cynics lived lives of complete abstinence and were indifferent to established values, which means they held laws, glory and wealth in contempt, and lived as the poor did. In the first century AD, that is when Christ was alive, it was a common sight to see cynics, wearing cloaks and carrying begging sacks and sticks, wandering from city to city, preaching to the people and condemning whatever evil they saw. This picture reminds you of the Christian apostles who later taught in the same way, doesn't it?"

"It certainly does, Father. That's who I thought of. The similarities are incredible."

"So I won't dwell on them. I'll close the subject by giving you a quote from Plato that I remember off by heart and which Jesus himself believed: 'It is impossible for an extremely good man to become extremely rich.' Philippe sat down again and Jocelyn did the same. The young knight, thoughtful, looked out of the window at the moon, which was now very high in the sky, allowing only its silver light to show through the window. Although it was late he was not at all tired. On the contrary, his mind was working overtime, as it took in all the extraordinary and, at the same time, incredible things he had heard that night. Eager to hear more, he looked his father in the eye, urging him to continue.

Luigi, who had heard everything in the meantime from behind the closed door, was feeling somewhat confused. On the one hand he judged the elderly knight to be a heretic for professing such beliefs, while on the other he could not do anything but accept that what Jocelyn was saying made sense and could be true, especially since there were texts that backed it up. So he was also waiting anxiously to hear more, his ear pressed to the door – but also ready to go if he heard steps coming towards him. All he could hear coming from the room was, however, Jocelyn's voice starting to talk again:

"So what does that leave us with? Rituals and symbols if I'm not mistaken. I think you mentioned baptism and the idea of heaven and hell, the fish and cross, if I remember correctly?"

"Exactly, Father".

"Let's start with baptism. According to Saint Paul, entering water means death, immersion in water symbolizes burial and coming out of it resurrection. Isn't that so?"

"Yes, so I believe."

"So baptism is in complete agreement with the spirit of the ancient Mysteries, which spoke about mystical death and symbolic resurrection. This ritual is a purging. In the first years after Jesus' death, Christians went naked to be baptised, and when the ritual was over put on white clothes and walked in a procession holding a candle, with a wreath on their head – just like people did in the procession of the Eleusinian Mysteries."

"So baptism is not a Christian ritual?"

"Of course not. But it's not of ancient Greek origin either. It is an ancient symbolic ritual performed by the Sumerians, a people who lived in Mesopotamia, a place where one of the first advanced civilizations of the world existed. You see, therefore, that, Christianity, unable to uproot all these ancient practices, embraced them and incorporated them so successfully that you can see that everyone today considers baptism to be Christian! The same goes for the famous miracles that Christ performed."

"Now that is impossible! Only Jesus performed miracles!" said Philippe indignantly, gesticulating wildly. Jocelyn indicated that his son should calm down and went on in a calm voice:

"The right thing to say my son would be that we have only been told about Jesus performing miracles. That doesn't mean that there weren't others performing them, we just don't know about them!"

"And who are these people?" Philippe asked in disbelief.

"Many. You have heard of the famous doctor Asclepius, haven't you?"

"Yes."

"It was said that Asclepius, like Jesus, cured the sick and brought people back from the dead. Pythagoras, the famous mystic, is better known as a mathematician, but he also performed miracles, curing people. What's more, Iamblichus in his work 'The Life of Pythagoras' claims that Pythagoras calmed the waves of the sea and the rivers so that his disciples could pass over them. I also suppose you know about the fish with which Jesus filled his disciples. when they were fishing. There were one hundred and fifty three of them, weren't there?"

"I think so, from what I can remember," Philippe replied trying to remember the relevant passage.

"Do you know why there were one hundred and fifty three fish?"

"To be honest, no."

"Because Pythagoras also mentions so many fish in the equivalent miracle!"

"Is that possible?" Philippe exclaimed. "So all of Christ's miracles have their counterparts in antiquity?"

"Almost all of them - if not all. But let me continue. Empedocles from Agrigentum[65] was also declared a god because he performed miracles. Finally, I must mention Apollonius, who also raised the dead and, of course, the god Dionysus, who people believed turned water into wine at his wedding with Ariadne, as Christ did at the wedding in Cana!'"

Jocelyn cleared his throat and, after a short pause, went on:

"The famous Christian symbol of the fish is also linked to Pythagoras. It is a symbol that has its roots in sacred pagan geometry. Two circles join so that the circumference of one touches the centre of the other, forming a fish, the vesica piscis in Latin. The mathematical relation between the height and width of this shape is one hundred and fifty three divided by two hundred and sixty five, a formula also known to the famous mathematician Archimedes."

"Now I see!" Philippe broke in suddenly. "That's why there are one hundred and fifty three fish in the two miracles of Pythagoras and Jesus!"

"Exactly son. I shall end this account of the similarities between Paganism and Christianity with the most famous of all Christian symbols: the cross. It was sacred to the ancients too because its four arms were thought to represent the four elements of the natural world – earth, water, fire and air. The fifth element, the spirit, would materialize from these four elements. Most Christian symbols therefore, are of Pagan origin, my son, and most events in Jesus's life can also be seen in the life of Osiris-Dionysus."

"Such as?" Philippe asked again.

"I already told you of the most important ones – the virgin birth, the death on a cross and resurrection. There are also many other similarities."

"For example?"

"For example Mithras was also born in a cave and was visited by shepherds. Mithras was also led, on a donkey, to his suffering, like Christ when he entered Jerusalem. Dionysus is also the righteous one who stands up to the oppressor, like Jesus, and had, as he did, twelve disciples."

"But why twelve students, and not seven or three, which were, from what I know, sacred numbers?" Philippe asked once more.

"Because the circle of twelve around a sacred person comes from sacred geometry."

"Meaning?"

"Meaning that the ancients had discovered that if a sphere is surrounded by others which have the exact same dimensions and they all touch one another, then the central sphere will be surrounded by exactly twelve other spheres."

"I see. So there is an explanation for everything," Philippe observed. "But why have you pointed out all these similarities to me? Where are you going with all this?"

"First of all, I wanted to prove to you that nothing is what it seems. Secondly, my aim was to give you a different perspective and realise that any issue can be viewed from many different sides. It is important for me that you learn to search for the truth on your own, and are not content to accept what other people tell you, that you do not believe it without further examination, simply because "that's how it is," as we are often told. So now you know all this, I can talk to you about the dispute between the Scholastics and the Gnostics."

"I have never heard these terms before," Philippe remarked and rose from his stool, grimacing at the discomfort he had begun to feel after sitting on wood for all this time.

"I am not surprised. People usually say that Gnosticism is a heresy that came into being after orthodox Christianity. This, however, is totally untrue. Rather, Gnosticism existed before orthodox Scholastic Christianity, but encountered fierce opposition from the latter until it almost disappeared. These people believed in what their name tells us. Their goal was what I told you at the beginning – knowledge beyond faith and self-awareness aiming at deification. Because the scholastics prevailed in the end, today we place emphasis on faith and less on knowledge. The gnostics did the exact opposite. Philippe, who had been walking around the room in small circles all the time that Jocelyn had been talking, stopped walking and raised his hands, indicating to his father that he wanted him to stop.

"If I have understood everything you have said correctly, Father, and put it all together, I have to come to the conclusion that Fede Santa is made up of Gnostics and that you are one of them. Is that correct?"

Jocelyn smiled.

"You could say that. But let me finish. So, Gnostics were influenced by the pagan mysteries and studied ancient Greek philosophy a great deal. They included some of the greatest intellectuals of the first early Christian centuries, like Valentinus, Vasilidis, Clement and Origen, who I mentioned before. Over time they came to be branded heretics. However they called themselves true Christians, and believed that the so-called scholastics had lost the true faith."

"But I don't understand," Philippe interrupted. "Why was there such a dispute? Simply because the Gnostics devoted more time to the study of the ancient philosophers?"

"Of course that wasn't the only problem. Remember when we were sitting outside and I talked to you about the Inner and the Outer Mysteries?

"Yes. So?" Philippe asked impatiently.

"I think I told you that there were some myths for the masses. Most people perceived them to be true events, while the initiated perceived them as allegories with a deeper meaning." Jocelyn stopped talking. He had reached the most critical point in his revelations and now felt the need to hesitate. He concentrated for a moment, looking at the floor with some discomfort. Then he lifted his head and his eyes met those of his son, who had now folded his arms and, leaning gently against the bookcase, appeared impatient to hear the rest. Jocelyn took a deep breath and went on:

"What would you think if I told you that the story of Jesus never actually took place, but is only an allegorical myth with a very deep meaning?"

Philippe's eyes narrowed, his pupils becoming two thin lines. It couldn't be that his father professed such views while being a monk at the same time! He remained silent for a while and, after suppressing the wave of rage that he felt overwhelming him, replied dryly:

"I would say that's going too far," said Philippe giving his father a sharp look

After a moment of weakness, Jocelyn immediately regained his composure and prepared his counterargument, remembering his own reaction when he had been initiated into Fede Santa many years before.

"Calm down son. Your reaction is no different from those of all the others who have heard the same thing in the past, when they have yet to hear the explanation it requires. My reaction was the same when I first heard this."

"But how can you deny the existence of our Saviour?" Philippe asked indignantly. "If you do not believe in the death and the Resurrection of our Lord then you are not a Christian!"

Outside, Luigi would also have expressed his displeasure about Jocelyn's beliefs aloud, if he had been able to. At the same time, however, he was very curious to hear how the elderly knight would back up this claim, if for no other reason than that he had to admit that he had never before come across a more educated man.. The strict figure of Abbot Giovanni came to his mind. He certainly, he thought, would not even listen to Jocelyn's explanations. His thoughts were interrupted by the voice of the elderly knight.

"All these things, my son, are of no importance. The Resurrection must be taken symbolically and not as a true event. Resurrection, as one experiences it through the myth of Jesus, is nothing more than the entry of the faithful into a new life, where one becomes a better person and the death of Jesus is the death of our old "bad" self. This, however, is something difficult to grasp and requires great effort on the part of the believer. It is definitely easier to say that Christ died for us and rose from the dead and just believe it, without having to do anything else but fast a little in order to receive communion, rather than constantly strive to become a better person and exercise constant self-criticism."

"I must admit that you are right about that. I am ready to hear your proof about the fact that Jesus never lived," said Philippe, his voice calmer now. He sat back down on the stool and waited for Jocelyn to continue.

"First of all, son, you must know that no one can give you proof of either the existence or the non-existence of Jesus. Don't ever believe any representative of the Church who tells you that they have proof of this. They simply believe with all their heart that Jesus really existed because they are in the first stage of the initiation and will probably never wish to move on to the second one.

You need to know, son, that there are three levels of knowledge in the Mysteries. In the first one, the factual one, the spiritual Christian has been baptised with water and initiated only into the Outer Mysteries. For this reason they take the story of Jesus to be the true story of a God-man who died and rose again. Our Church remains at this stage today, forbidding, indeed, those who wish to continue to the second stage from doing so, and condemning them as heretics.

In the second stage, the now more spiritual Christian has been baptised with air, the Holy Spirit in other words. He has been initiated into the Inner Mysteries of Christianity and takes the story of Jesus to be an allegorical myth, and not a true story, which encompasses deeper meanings.

The third and last stage, known as Mysticism, involves baptism by fire and the Gnostic, by now, Christian is aware of his identity as Christ or the Word, and is no more need of any teaching. You realise, of course, that in order for someone to reach the third stage, a great deal of effort is needed on his part – and true self-knowledge. So the easily-believed story of Jesus' life was simply a way for the first Christians to attract candidates for initiation – it was a myth for spiritual beginners."

Philippe remained silent for a little. He looked at their silent partner outside the window, the moon, which was about to set. After pondering upon what he had heard briefly, he weighed his words carefully and said to his father:

"Everything you have told me up to now sounds correct and makes sense. But I would like you to give me some clues, at least, -as you say that no evidence exists, that lead to the interpretation that Jesus was a mythical Jesus, and explain to me why the Gnostics, although spiritually superior to the Scholastics, did not finally manage to prevail."

Jocelyn gave himself a few moments of reflection to put his thoughts in order. After a while he stood up and after looking carefully for a book for some time, took it in his hands, took a separate piece of papyrus out of it and gave it to Philippe, saying to him:

"Read it aloud."

The young knight took the papyrus and made out about thirty names written in Latin on it. He raised his head and looked at his father, a puzzled expression on his face. His father, however, indicated that he should start reading and this the young knight did, straight away, shrugging his shoulders in resignation:

"Arrian, Petronius, Seneca, Dion Prusseus, Valerius Flaccus, Lucius Florus, Quintilian, Favorinus, Lucan, Pliny the Elder, Appian... I don't understand. Aren't you going to tell me who they all are, Father?"

Jocelyn indicated that he should carry on reading and Philippe went on in his clear, warm voice, tinged with a large measure of curiosity:

"Juvenal, Theon of Smyrna, Damis, Silius Italicus, Aulus Gellius, Statius, Columella, Martial, Plutarch, Apollonius, Pausanius, Ptolemy, Dio Chrysostom..."

Philippe sighed and, taking a deep breath, read the last three names while putting the paper down on a wooden table opposite the bookcases, against a wall and obviously used for office tasks.

"Hermogenes, Lysias, Valerius Maximus."

"They are all, my son, Roman historians, all of them prolific writers that lived and wrote in the century in which Jesus is supposed to have lived."

"What then do they say about Jesus?" asked Philippe, in suspense.

"That's exactly the point. They say nothing," said Jocelyn, shrugging his shoulders. Once more, Philippe was very surprised..

"Nothing?" he repeated like an echo, unable to believe it himself.

"Nothing whatsoever. That sounds a bit strange for a man who lived such an unusual and hectic life as Jesus, don't you think?"

"Yes, it does.."

"And I think this sounds even stranger when you consider that the Romans, who crucified Christ, were known for the records they kept of every activity they did, let alone cases in law. Nevertheless, not one Roman makes any mention of some Jesus who was put to trial and executed by Pontius Pilate."

"Wasn't Pilate a prefect of Judea?" Philippe asked again.

"He was. From 6 AD to 36 AD. That's, for a whole thirty years. However, nowhere does it say that he tried some Jesus. Very strange in my opinion," Jocelyn concluded and then went on: "Only Tacitus, Plinius the younger and Suetonius, towards the end of the first century AD have anything to say.. But not about Christ himself- about the disturbances created in the empire by the followers of Christ, the so-called Christians."

"So they tell us nothing about Jesus' life?"

"Nothing. They just refer to those called Christians."

"And if there were texts that mentioned Jesus and were lost?" Philippe objected. "That is a possibility we cannot exclude, isn't it?"

"Definitely. Think, however, that if there were such texts, the Church would have done everything it could to save them. And wouldn't the early Scholastics, like Justin the Martyr, have referred to such texts, albeit lost today, to better substantiate their positions? Not one of them, however, refers to such documentation – simply because there isn't any! Strange as it may seem to you, only the Gospels are referred to by scholastics as proof of what they are saying, nothing else. As for Jewish historians, they do not refer to Jesus either[66]."

"So that leaves us only the Gospels?" Philippe asked again.

"Yes. These, of course, are not works of historians, and this can be easily proved by the host of contradictions they contain and incorrect information about the geography of Galilee. This fact, of course, makes them unreliable. Each of the four Evangelists gives us a completely different version of the same – supposedly – story. There are similarities only at the very basic points, apart from later alterations. By the way, have you ever noticed the contradictions they contain? You must have often heard the Gospels and if you are a little sceptical you easily notice the inaccuracies. But were you at all sceptical?"

"I suppose I wasn't," Philippe admitted, somewhat sheepishly. Jocelyn smiled.

"Like everyone. No one dares to question something that has been passed down to us as something infallible, inspired by God. In fact, Mark's Gospel, which is the oldest, was written around 80 AD, Matthew's and Luke's a little later, and John's dates to the beginning of the second century. And, of course, the author of the Gospel according to Mark was not called Mark, nor was he a disciple of Jesus. He is some author, unknown to us, who used the name Mark to give validity to his work, as Mark was supposed to be one of Jesus's disciples. The same goes for the rest of the gospels of course."

"And the differences you said were not immediately obvious?"

"There are so many it would take us many nights to find them all. So I will give you a few that are typical. If, for example, you look at the genealogy that Luke and Matthew give us, you will see that the names, apart from that of Joseph, Jesus's father, are all different, with the exception of David's - to which they all go back! The only thing in common between the two Gospels is that both authors say, after all these names, that Joseph is not Jesus's father, but God himself! So why do they give us all this genealogy? Of course Mark tells us nothing about Bethlehem, nor about Jesus's virgin birth. What's more, the Evangelists fail to agree about when exactly Christ was born! Luke says it was during the census of Quirinius, Matthew says it was during the reign of Herod."

"And which version is the right one?"

"Whichever one someone believes – there is no right and wrong version! If you study the Gospels in this light, you will realise that we have taken a mixture of events from all four Gospels to be the true story of Jesus's life. We believe that an event from a specific Gospel is true and we say that that is the way it happened, without caring that the rest of the Evangelists don't agree! For example, we all say that Christ was born in Bethlehem during the reign of Herod, don't we?"

"Yes."

"So we take Matthew to be correct here, although the others do not agree. More-over, often, where we can, and the two versions don't contradict each other, we accept both to be true, as, for example, with the earthquake that supposedly happened during Resurrection according to Matthew, and the disciples who visited the tomb in Mark. At this point the narratives are also combined. However, when it comes to Jesus's trial and death, the accounts contradict each other."

"How?"

"According to Matthew and Luke, Jesus was tried by Hebrew priests of the Sanhedrin, something that John does not refer to at all. And what were Jesus's last words on the cross? According to John they were "I'm thirsty,", and "It is done." Luke says "Father, into your hands I commit my spirit," while, according to Mark and Matthew they are: "My God, my God, why have you forsaken me?" Which of all these is right? And isn't it strange that Jesus' close disciples, who supposedly wrote the Gospels, do not even remember their master's last words well?"

Philippe did not reply and Jocelyn took the opportunity to continue his chain of thought:

"Other events in Jesus's life on which there is disagreement are where he preached and to whom he first appeared after the Resurrection. Then, episodes like the wedding at Cana and the raising of Lazarus appear only in the Gospel of John, in which, also, Jesus's closest disciples, James, John and Peter play a very small part, unlike in all the other Gospels! In this Gospel we also come across two apostles who are not mentioned by the other Evangelists at all: Nathaniel and Nicodemus. All these things, for me, clearly show that an attempt was made to construct the story of Christ."

"Then there are the Acts of the Apostles. Of course they are concerned not with the historical Jesus, just the Apostles. However, they are not a record of events and are full of exaggerations if they are read carefully. They are, like many other of the letters of the Apostles and the Gospels, fabrications, with information added and left out, depending on what each author wanted to put across. The Gospels accepted as canonical are full of such later accretions."

The most glaring example of this is the Gospel by Mark. In our library we have two Gospels by Mark: an old one, before it underwent censorship, which, however strange this may seem, did not include the Resurrection and a new one in which it magically appears![67] So there are other Acts too, and more Gospels, as I said before, which the official Church does not accept because they challenge the established image of Jesus as we know it.[68] Fortunately, however, some were saved and came down to us so at least we have access to this, historically inaccurate, but amazingly mystic, Jesus!"

"So, if I get it right, the Gospels which are not accepted as canonical..." Philippe began to say and Jocelyn added:

"...are the texts of those who had reached the second and the third level of initiation and accepted Jesus, not as a historic figure, but as a Grand Master of initiation into the Mysteries! These texts were studied by Gnostics in the first early years of Christianity and..." at this point Jocelyn hesitated a bit... "the Cathars of our time.[69]"

Philippe suddenly jumped up. Terror could be clearly seen in his eyes:

"The Heretics? That's why all that bloodbath? That's why they wiped them out?"

Jocelyn nodded sadly.

"The truth is that the Church displayed unprecedented zeal in exterminating them. Now you know the reason. We, as an order, did not take part in this disgraceful genocide."[70]

Philippe did not reply. Everything that Jocelyn had revealed to him made sense and was backed up by evidence. He couldn't deny it. Basically the only thing keeping him from embracing these new ideas was the fear of going against the tide, which was undoubtedly easier and safer to follow. But now he knew the truth. Could he go on in life pretending he knew nothing of this? He thought of the Grand Master and his father...All these members of this organisation were good people, people who inspired calm in others and possessed self-awareness – that was true. Would he like to be one of them?"

He went to the window and looked again at the moon, which was about to set. The darkness was no longer thick and impenetrable. The new day had timidly begun its course. Jocelyn also walked towards the window, put his hands affectionately on the shoulders of Philippe, who was deep in thought, and said:

"Now you know everything."

Philippe smiled hesitantly:

"Almost everything. You did not tell me why the scholastics prevailed in the end."

"That's right. Think. Why do you think they prevailed?"

Philippe turned his back to the window and leant his back against it gently. He thought a little and said:

"Maybe because Scholastic Christianity is an "easier"" religion? I mean to say, as you yourself also said I think, it is easier to believe that the story of Christ is real, simply go to the rituals and do the Outer Mysteries than to constantly think of how to become a better person, to interpret metaphors, something that needs a lot of thought, and try to reach theosis."

Jocelyn, who had stood opposite the young knight, nodded in agreement:

"Yes, that is the reason. However, it is not the only one. The second reason is to do with how Gnostic and Scholastic Christianity were organised. Religions need to be well-organised in order to prevail over other religions and survive, don't they?"

Philippe nodded in agreement and Jocelyn continued:

"Gnostic Christianity had no organisation – basically because it was not interested in anything like that. It did not consider it important. In every ritual, the role of high priest was played by a different believer – man or woman – who was chosen by lot. They did not have bishops or a standardised doctrine that they followed strictly, as the Scholastics did. There was freedom of thought, and the habits and beliefs of each group of Gnostics varied from town to town. There were many ways for someone to reach theosis and every one chose their own way. But a religion so flexible in its structure, which is not fanatically interested in attracting new believers, survives with difficulty. Added to that it offered almost equal status to women in a male dominated society and time. You can easily see why Gnosticism was doomed at the outset."

"That's right. Neither the Greeks nor the Jews gave great freedom to their women and neither do we today. Our priests consider them to be instruments of Satan that lure us into the sins of the flesh," commented Philippe.

"Exactly. And, finally…" continued the elderly knight "…the Roman Empire, under whose protection Christianity became the official religion, promoted Scholastic and not Gnostic Christians."

"But why?"

"As I told you before, monotheism was quite widespread before the introduction of Christianity. The Roman Emperors wanted one faith-one emperor, to impose one common religion. As one of the cults – Dionysus, Adonis, Osiris and the rest – had not managed to prevail over the others, they adopted Scholastic Christianity, a monotheistic religion with external rites like Baptism and Marriage, attractive to and easily understood by the masses. The basic thing was that this religion, in contrast with the Gnostics, had already removed the philosopher intellectuals from positions of power and demanded blind obedience to the Church's leaders from the faithful, thus ensuring the established order in the empire. Because, you should know, that these philosopher-intellectuals often questioned the authority of the state and undermined its power, fomenting unrest. That is why scholastic Christianity was chosen, thus helping to maintain peace and order in the empire."

And so we come, son, to the darkness of today, since, in destroying everything pagan, we have lost all ancient knowledge. The ancient pagan civilisation was superior to ours. The Gnostics did not condemn pagans – instead they co-existed harmoniously with them and their different beliefs were woven together and interacted towards a productive philosophy. Yet with the predominance of the scholastics, the pagans were savagely persecuted, their temples destroyed and their knowledge lost. There has been no greater setback in the world than that brought about by scholastic Christianity. This, sadly, is the truth my son."

Jocelyn raised his arm, indicating the books.

"Fortunately, these were saved. But there were infinitely more that were destroyed forever, deliberately. At least you can come and read the ones that have survived. From tomorrow I can teach you Greek. If you agree, of course."

Philippe had, by now, made his decision:

"I would really like that, father," he replied, stroking his beard and stifling a yawn. Remarkably, this yawn was the first, despite the fact that he had stayed up all night.

"I must admit that everything I have heard is strange, but very interesting."

Jocelyn smiled and, looking happily at his son, put out the torch, covering it for an instant with a metal cone. It was, however, no longer dark in the room, since the sun had almost risen.

"I am glad you found all this fascinating, son. The truth is that your reaction was exactly the one I had hoped for. As I assumed, you are a man who likes to question and who does not hesitate to challenge mainstream tradition. That is enough to make you a member of our organization."

And, he added, making a move to leave:

"Let's go now. Let's get to our beds. The bell for Prime will be sounding shortly.."

As soon as Luigi heard these words, he ran towards the window, quickly climbed up and, after jumping out, began to run, treading lightly, towards the dormitory. Luck was on his side as everyone was still asleep. He quickly took off his robe and lay under the linen blanket, only a second before Philippe and his father came in, walking on tiptoe.

Philippe felt his body numb from that sweet fatigue that someone feels when they haven't given their body a night's rest. All his father had revealed to him was going round and round in his head. He was thinking about how lucky he was to have him in his life. And, with that thought, he fell asleep for a few minutes before he was woken by the bells that loudly summoned him to Prime.

14

Tripoli, February 28 1289

he emir Badr al-Din Baktash al-Fakhri was moving quickly along the long corridor in the Knights Templar commandery that led to the Grand Master's office. When he reached the oak door, the two young sergeants who were guarding it stood aside and politely indicated to him that he could go through as the Grand Master was expecting him.

The emir gently pushed the door and entered the room which was, at that moment, filled by the dying rays of the setting sun and quickly descending into darkness. Two sergeants were walking around the room, lighting torches and hanging them on the walls. Al-Fakri moved towards the end of the room, where he could see three knights sitting at a desk. One of them, the one sitting in the centre, was the Grand Master. When he looked at him, he could not help but think how much he was impressed by his appearance. It was his well-built body and his striking facial features, together with his gaze that captivated whoever saw him. The emir had seen him before recently, as well as the two other young knights next to him, who had been serving as mareschal and seneschal for some time now, Philippe and Jean. Philippe, to be precise, was a deputy under-mareschal and working in the place of the real mareschal during his two month absence in the West. Another knight who was standing a little further off would act as interpreter in the conversation that would follow. The meeting with the emir was the reason why some Knights Templar had moved from Acre to Tripoli only the previous day.

The emir's jet-black eyes lit up with greed when he saw a pouch on the Grand Master's desk. He knew it was full of silver coins and that it was destined for him. It was his reward for the information he would give the knights about the Sultan Qalawun's latest movements.

The emir's thoughts were interrupted by Guillaume, who stood up to welcome him by stretching out his hand and indicating that he should sit down. The emir got straight to the point, making sure, at the same time, that he talked slowly, so that the interpreter would have enough time. When he had finished, the knights' faces were white with fright and the emir was barely able to hide a smile of satisfaction, bringing his hands to his cheeks, which were covered in hair, for a moment. He might be giving information to the Knights Templar in order to get rich, but that didn't mean that he liked them. On the contrary, he was glad that these arrogant 'infidels', who had invaded his homeland, were losing against his fellow countrymen. It just happened that his greed was greater than his patriotism.

The Grand Master, clearly shaken, gave the emir the pouch. He thanked him and told him that he could go. The emir also said goodbye and headed towards the door, weighing the pouch in his hand.

"That was an important piece of information. Fortunately, it received a commensurate reward," he thought with a smile while leaving the room and shoving the pouch into an opening in his robe.

He could hear the knights talking behind him, troubled.

"Do we believe him for sure? Will Qalawun attack Tripoli?"asked Jean, a little doubtful about what the emir had said. Guillaume 's answer, however, was so absolute in tone that it left no room for doubt:

"We have no reason not to believe him. He has given us information so often and it has always been accurate."

"Whatever the case..." Philippe added "... we know that Qalawun has been mobilizing his army for about a week now and is moving towards Syria, but without giving us the slightest hint as to his goal. And we were naturally concerned. We were worried – as was normal. Isn't that why so many of us came here in haste from Acre?"

"Yes, and it was the right thing to do from what it seems. His intention is to attack here and we must inform the commune straight away and prepare our defences," said Guillaume and he stood up straight away, motioning to the others to follow him.

***

In the Hospitaller church, in another part of the town, Vespers had just ended and the knights and sergeants were going out into the courtyard and getting ready to go to the refectory for the evening meal. Most of the Hospitallers, after the loss of Marqab, had gathered in Tripoli and Acre. Guillaume, Foulques and Pierre, like other knights, had also come to Tripoli after the fall of the fortress and had stayed there for years while the Grand Master Jean de Villiers moved back and forth between Acre and Tripoli.

Guillaume and Foulques, having also gone out into the courtyard, were standing, watching the hustle and bustle of the city, slowly fading from sight as night fell. Opposite them under a large cedar tree, sat three knights with white robes on which a black cross was embroidered, similar to that which both the Knights Hospitaller and the Knights Templar had on theirs. Guillaume discretely pointed out one one of them, the largest, to Foulques.

"That man there is the Lord Master of the Teutonic knights, Burchard von Schwanden."

The Teutonic knights were mainly German and had been founded in 1190 by the burghers and merchants of Lübeck and Bremen, who had initially established a hospital for the care of German crusaders on the outskirts of Acre while the city was under siege during the third crusade. Someone by the name of Sibrant had been in charge. The order had grown considerably under the command of Hermann von Salza at the beginning of the 13th century. In the first decades of that century they had also taken action against pagans in Eastern Europe, especially in Livonia,[71] which continued unabated until the 15th century. A host of victorious campaigns came to something of a halt with their defeat in 1242 at Lake Peipus at the hands of Alexander Nevsky, the Russian national hero.

"He came from Acre today," Guillaume continued talking about the Grand Master of the Teutonic Knights. "This, together with the arrival of our Lord Master and Lord Master of the Knights Templar, portends nothing good. Qalawun is planning something."

Foulques was about to say something but, at that moment, they saw a commune official going towards the Teutons. He said something to them and Burchard and two other knights moved off. Then the two Hospitallers noticed that the officer was coming their way. When he got near them, he told them, in a voice that was rather too delicate and high-pitched for a man:

"We have an emergency council. The Lord Master of the Knights Templar would like to make an important announcement. Please tell your Lord Master to come at once to the great hall in the town hall with his officers."

The officer did not wait for Guillaume's reply. He turned around and left quickly. He seemed to be doing his job with great formality and haste. But Guillaume lost no time either. He went to notify the Grand Master, Jean de Villiers and Pierre straight away. Soon Foulques saw them striding away and his curiosity. reached its peak. He could, however, do nothing but wait, as not everyone took part in the council, so that unnecessary noise would be avoided.

***

The tall stone town hall stood out in the great square of Tripoli, together with the bishop's palace, which was right opposite. Two columns with marble ivy leaves framed the otherwise plain entrance. In its interior the decoration was also sparse. The great hall, however, where the council was taking place, inspired awe in anyone who saw it, its size and the absence of many windows making it dark and imposing. Now torches on the walls lit it, creating eerie shadows of every size of the people who had gathered there, while their voices reverberated in loud echoes, since the huge room had no furniture except for a table placed in its middle, against which the Countess Lucia was leaning.

She was a petite woman, with black hair and harmonic facial features except for her hooked nose. Her eyes, however, were the colour of the sea and her elegant movements revealed her graceful femininity.

The countess had married Narjot of Toucy, the former great admiral of Charles d' Anjou, and lived in Puglia before going down to accept her inheritance a year later. Her husband had remained in Acre and she had gone to Tripoli, where it was proving hard for her to assert her legal rights as the sister of Bohemund VII. The commune that had taken power in Tripoli after Bohemund's death under Bartolemeo Embriaco had the support of the Venetians and consequently the Knights Templar, who always maintained good relations with them.

Lucia had, however, managed to win the Genoese over to her side, guaranteeing them commercial privileges and, in this way, gaining the support of the Hospitallers which were, as a rule, allies of Genoa. It was then that the Venetians and Embriaco expressed their displeasure at this development in what later proved to be a disastrous way: they called on the Sultan to intervene on their behalf.[72] Qalawun was naturally very happy to be called on to intervene and did not let this opportunity to go to waste. So he mobilised his troops with the intention, not of helping Embriaco, but of seizing Tripoli.

Next to Lucia stood a Genoese admiral by the name of Zaccaria, a tall and thin man of lofty bearing. Opposite them was Embriaco with the Venetian bailo[73] of Tripoli, looking cold-eyed at Lucia and the Genoese. Around the table, in a circle which had formed with it at its centre, stood the Catholic Bishop, the head of the Orthodox clergy and two senior officers in the city administration, Catholic by religion, who represented not only the Catholics but also the large number of Orthodox in Tripoli. The Grand Masters of the three knights' order, with the two knights who were next in the chain of command, made up the circle. Everyone was talking at the same time and there was a terrible commotion because of the echo in the room.

When those who had to be present at the council had gathered there, Lucia raised her right hand. Surprisingly, those in the huge room immediately fell silent, and Lucia started talking in her thin, colourless voice.

"My dear fellow-citizens, first I would like to wish you all a good evening and officially welcome the Lord Masters who have just arrived in our city. We have met here today urgently, despite the late hour, because the Lord Master of the Templar Knights, Guillaume de Beaujeu says that he has an important piece of news to tell us. So let's hear him."

A low murmur of disapproval spread through the room as Guillaume left the circle and took his position in the centre, next to the table. The Grand Master, despite the bravery he had shown at crucial moments, was not liked by the laity nor knights of other orders, noted as he was for deviousness and greed.

Ignoring the murmur, Guillaume started to talk in a booming voice, which echoed around the empty walls of the room and was tinged with a measure of concern:

"My fellow-citizens, once I too, in my turn, have wished you a good evening, I would like to share with you a very unfortunate piece of news – that I have at least heard in time – from a reliable source: Sultan Qalawun is about to attack Tripoli."

An icy silence greeted Guillaume's announcement. Embriaco was the first to break the silence. Moving towards the Grand Master, he looked at him derisively.

"And how would you know this?" he asked sceptically.

Guillaume was intimidated neither by the attitude of the person that he was talking to, nor by the obvious contempt that Embriaco showed towards his office.

"I have good informants," he replied, brief but polite. One of the two Sultan's emirs himself warned me. That is why we must waste no time. We should prepare for the siege immediately."

"And why should we believe you? Do you have proof of what you are saying?" Embriaco continued in the same ironic tone of voice.

"My God, what a fool!" Philippe thought while following what was going on from his place in the circle, and, at the same time, wondering if he should interject and confirm what the Grand Master said. After all, he himself had witnessed what the emir had said.

Guillaume was ready to answer Embriaco but he had no time to do this as his opponent continued undaunted to attack him verbally, looking at the crowd and making dramatic gestures.

"It is known to everybody here that the Lord Master loves to make up stories in order to reap the benefits of being a mediator."[74]

"Am I wrong?" Bartolemeo concluded, looking towards the crowd for support. Indeed, disbelief was evident on the faces of most of the people in the room. No one had believed the Grand Master.

"You're not wrong, Bartolemeo," the Catholic bishop of the city agreed, speaking out suddenly and fixing his old eyes on Guillaume, who he had always disliked, as, of course, he did all Templar Knights. Who knows what new plots he is hatching again!" he continued, raising his wrinkled hand, covered with precious rings, into the air.

"In God's name, you must believe me for the good of this city! I am telling the truth!" Guillaume shouted in despair, but in vain. Shouts of disapproval and jeers filled the room.

Philippe had had enough. He would not tolerate such an unjust attack on the Grand Master. In an instant he was himself in the centre of the circle and, raising both his hands, shouted at the top of his lungs, to make himself heard over the other voices.:

"Stop! The Lord Master is telling the truth! You must listen to him for your own good!"

More whistling and cries of disapproval followed Philippe's intervention, Guillaume's eyes silently thanking him. Guillaume de Villaret looked at the two knights in sympathy. He had seen the concern on the Grand Master's face, and understood that Guillaume was telling the truth. Now, however, the initial mild disagreement of the crowd had turned to unrestrained rage after Philippe had spoken and it would be futile to try to convince them. Next to him, Jean de Villiers and Pierre were also looking at the Templar Knights disbelievingly. Pierre had recognised the faces of the three Templar Knights in the room as those of the knights with whom they had met in the unfortunate incident in Alexandria.

Lucia was now also raising her hands, trying to bring order to the chaos around her. However, no one would pay attention to her any longer, while fresh voices could now be heard, those of the many officials who supported Embriaco, dealing Guillaume the final blow.

"Get out of here!"

"You greedy braggart!"

"Get out!"

"Traitor!"

Guillaume could take no more insults. His face twisted, and eyes flaming with rage, he limply lifted his hand as a sign of resignation and put it down straight away, at the same time indicating to Philippe and Jean to follow him, which they did. The three knights sullenly made their way through the crowd, while around them people were still swearing. Seeing the Templars depart, Jean de Villiers turned to Guillaume de Villaret, bending close his ear in order to be heard above all the pandemonium.

"What do you think about all this, Brother?"

Guillaume watched the Templar Knights disappear behind the heavy oak door, sighed and turned to the Grand Master:

"I am afraid, my lord, that such arrogance and ingratitude on the part of the crowd will not go unpunished by the Almighty."

"I'm afraid I too am going to agree with you," said Hugo, moving towards the door himself, troubled by dark thoughts.

***

That dawn, at the end of March, was sweeter than at other times. This was because there had been a significant improvement in the weather and the wind was full of intoxicating scents as Nature was in bloom. Even after sunset, the night primroses did not cease to make the locals dizzy with their delicate fragrance. That is why the guard at the city's walls had leant against the stone and had fallen asleep despite the hard mattress it offered him. The song of a bird welcoming the new day woke him from his torpor. The soldier rubbed his eyes and looked at the pink sky. Then he got up and looked around him, worried that someone might be nearby. He knew very well that he shouldn't have fallen asleep. After making sure that no one was around, he let his eyes stray beyond the moat outside the walls to where the red horizon met the earth. And then the guard blinked, certain that his eyes were deceiving him. But no. The whole horizon in the distance was covered by infantry and cavalry, a sea of men.

"Qalawun's army!" the guard whispered in a voice that shook. "The Templar Knight was right!" Aware of the panic rising inside him he ran down the stairs that lead to the walls, stumbling twice, and began to frantically ring the bell. The head of the guard ran there straight away and heard the unhappy news, realising, as did everyone else, even if it was too late, that Guillaume had spoken the truth. The next days went by with both sides preparing for the difficult battle ahead. The 'Infidels' set up their siege engines outside the walls and organised their camp. The Christians, on the other hand, gathered supplies and received a little help from King Henry of Cyprus, who sent his brother Amalric to the besieged city with an escort of knights and four galleys. Some non-combatants, to Lucia's and Embriaco's relief, fled to Cyprus in time, before the stranglehold tightened, giving the city less useless mouths to feed. A French regiment from Acre also arrived, after a request had been made, with Jean of Grailly at its head, who immediately took command of the army. In the harbour there were four more Genoese galleys under Zaccaria's command, and two Venetian ones. The Grand Masters of the orders had departed for Acre but all three orders had left knights in the city, the Knights Templar under the command of Geoffroy de Vantac, the Hospitallers under the command of Matthew of Clermont. Philippe together with Jean and Foulques with Pierre were also included in these forces. Both Philippe's father, to his son's great relief, and Luigi remained in Acre.

April had arrived when the first stone from Qalawun's deadly siege engines shook the walls to their foundations, spreading panic amongst the inhabitants of the city. It fell on what was known as the Tower of the Bishop, in the south-east corner of the walls facing inland, which the Knights Templar had undertaken to defend. The Hospitallers were responsible for another sensitive spot in the defences next to the Tower of the Bishop to the sea, which actually bore their name since it was called the Tower of the Hospitallers. The Venetians, Genoese and city guard were responsible for the defence of the rest of the walls, but soon it became clear that once again the Christian forces were inadequate for the defence of this huge fortress, having at the same time to face forces that far outnumbered their own. Nevertheless, the Christians put up a brave defence for about two weeks, tirelessly repairing the walls, carrying stones, soil, wood and whatever else could be used for this purpose. Even the women who had remained in the city were helping as best they could, also filling in the holes in the walls and taking water to the exhausted men defending the city..

As time went by, victims from the arrows and the rocks launched by siege artillery that fell, by chance, or even intentionally, in the city and not on the walls, rose dramatically – thus reducing the small number of those defending Tripoli even further. The Muslims had also made some surprise attacks. These may not have proved, as expected, successful in gaining them entrance to the city that they wanted so badly, and had cost them men, but they had inflicted a large number of casualties on the Christians, who were finding it more and more difficult to make up their losses. In contrast, those undertaking the siege appeared not only not to be getting less, but actually growing in number as if a cornucopia were in their possession. It was in a raid such as this that Geoffroy de Vantac, the commander of the Knights Templar lost his life.

It was in mist at dusk that some of those besieging the city had managed, despite all the barriers that those defending it had placed in their way – bringing down their ladders and showering them with boiling water, to enter the walls, taking the Christians by surprise and causing momentary panic among them until they had managed to react. There were not many intruders and all were soon killed but, before this happened, they took the lives of some of those defending the walls, among them that of Geoffroy.

Philippe was there at this difficult time and was fighting hand to hand with some of the invaders, his sword literally drenched in blood. He had not been able to do anything to help the unfortunate man. Geoffroy was fighting hard with a large, well-built opponent when another Muslim nearby decided to help his comrade by instantly plunging his sword into the knight's back before he had time to even realize it. Philippe had seen the Knight Templar fall to the ground covered in blood, which he vomited before he was left staring up at the sky with eyes wide open in terror, in a belated plea for divine assistance.

At that very moment all those who had entered at that spot had been annihilated and, as night was now falling, the battle raging along the walls now gradually subsided. The sound of the battle was followed by an apparent calm, broken only by the groans of the wounded. The stench of human waste and the dead filled the air. Philippe himself had undertaken the task of dragging Geoffroy's body to the hospital to ensure that his body was buried there. As he was dragging the body down from the stone stairs he had come across another knight, a Hospitaller, who was performing the same grim task. When Philippe's sad eyes fell on the Hospitaller's face, he had immediately recognised the knight with whom he had argued in Alexandria.

Foulques seemed to remember Philippe, only now his look of haughty disdain had been replaced by one of compassion and mutual understanding. The moment allowed no room for foolish, petty egos with so many dead comrades around them. They remained still, looking at each other for a while, and it was Philippe who spoke first when his eyes saw what seemed to be a superficial cut on Foulques's thigh.

"I see you are hurt, Brother. Do you need help with this grim task of yours?" Philippe said, offering to help Foulques to carry the dead man down the steep stone staircase.

"Thank you, Brother," Foulques replied with a tired smile. "It's just a minor cut. But two are better than one. Come, let's take yours down first and then mine."

Rather than reply, Philippe had let Geoffroy's body fall softly to the ground and taken the legs of the dead man that Foulques was carrying. They carried him down the stairs carefully and then did the same with Geoffroy.

"May God keep you well, Brother. What is your name?" Foulques asked before each of them headed towards their respective hospital.

"Philippe. And yours?"

"Foulques. I hope to see you again."

"Me too. Good luck."

They exchanged these few words and looks of sympathy and each went his own way.

***

"You can't be such cowards! You can't! Embriaco's hoarse voice could be heard all over the central square of Tripoli, now full of rubble caused by the many rocks that had been launched into the walls. The Venetian bailo looked at Embriaco coldly and replied:

"I will not sacrifice my men. Why should they give their lives for a city that has been already lost?"

"It would not be doomed if you were not leaving. In God's name, I beseech you!" Embriaco screamed again, beside himself, and looked at Pere de Moncada, the new commander of the Knights Templar, silently imploring him to intervene, since the Venetians were always on good terms with the Knights Templar. He was a very short man who was not known for his good looks, but he was a very good warrior. So the Knight Templar started talking:

"Bartolemeo is right. If we stay united, with God's help, we can beat the Infidels. You know that if you leave, this will have a negative impact on the rest of the men's morale." The Venetian bailo, in a gesture of flagrant indifference towards those with whom he was in conversation, took a white handkerchief from his lapel and wiped the sweat off his forehead, making a show of ignoring them. Then he put it back slowly in its place, and only then did he deign to answer Embriaco and Pere:

"Unfortunately no one is going to rebuild the broken walls so that we will be safe, not even very God himself, on whom you call. I will waste no more time on meaningless talk. The best thing you can do is get out of here while you can."

And with these words, he turned his back and began to walk behind his soldiers who, carrying their belongings, were heading towards their ships in the port.

"Coward! Traitor!" Bartolemeo continued to yell in vain behind him, while Moncada watched him leave in silence, despair etched on his face. The Countess Lucia also watched the scene in silence, as did Foulques and Pierre, who had left the walls for a while since the attacks had become somewhat less frequent. This was, however, anything but a good sign. It probably meant that the enemy were mustering strength for their final assault, which they were to make at the point which was once called the Tower of the Bishop, of which there was almost nothing left now, after stones had landed there unabated for almost three weeks now, as long as the siege had lasted. It was the collapse of the walls that had prompted the Venetians' departure.

"Deep down we know that the Venetians are right – but we don't want to admit it, do we?" Pierre whispered in Foulques's ear, and received a nod in agreement..

Foulques was looking worriedly towards where the Genoese were standing. The Genoese had also witnessed the scene and were now murmuring and gesticulating. Suddenly, their admiral Zaccaria jumped forward and bluntly announced:

"We are leaving too! I cannot leave my ships to the Venetians! These traitors might steal them given the chance!"

They all remained speechless on hearing these words. It was Countess Lucia's turn to break the silence and now plead with Zaccaria, since the Genoese were her allies.

"Please Zaccaria, reconsider! You can't allow your rivalry with the Venetians to influence your judgement at such a difficult time for Christians! Think of the civilian population! What will happen to all of them if the Mamluks enter the city?"

There were now tears in the countess's light blue eyes, and she had taken on the appearance of a Madonna in a painting. However, Zaccaria appeared unmoved by this exquisite creature's request, since he had already made his decision. However, one could detect a trace of compassion in his voice as he answered her:

"My countess, the civilians are the best reason for you to also leave not an hour later and save yourselves."

"But if the Venetians were not leaving, neither would you. I ask you, therefore, to reconsider in the name of our alliance." Zaccaria looked at Lucia and then at his compatriots. On their faces one could see only the desire to leave. One of them, seeing that the admiral was in two minds, stepped forward and said to Zaccaria:

"My Admiral, except for our lives, there are also our ships. You wouldn't want them to fall into the hands of the Mamluks! Or I imagine, as you said before, into the hands of the Venetians. Isn't that so?"

Those words did not leave Zaccaria any margin for further thought. He looked sadly at Lucia and said to her:

"I am sorry, it can't be otherwise. If you stay, I wish you good luck. May God be with you," and he headed off with the rest, so that they could collect their belongings. An icy silence fell over the square.

"You can consider the city taken," Foulques said to Pierre as he saw the Genoese leaving.

***

The next morning, as everyone had expected, the Sultan ordered a general attack with his whole army. There was brief resistance from the Christians, but it soon became evident that the Italians had been right. Morale had fallen when the Venetians and the Genoese had left, but, whatever the case, the walls could not hold the unstoppable hordes of the Mamluks for long. The Christians were bravely fighting among the ruins. However, when some of their enemy began to enter, this tipped the balance of power, and those defenders who chose not to abandon their posts immediately found themselves in a very difficult position. The enemy were large in number, with three of them for each man defending the city. Soon the scene on the walls of the city resembled that of a slaughterhouse.

At the Tower of the Bishop most Hospitallers had left for some time now, since their commander had sounded the retreat, aware that any further resistance was futile. Pierre had been killed at the beginning of the general assault by a stray arrow, which had gone straight to his heart.

Nevertheless, Foulques would not give up the fight and had not left with the others, in defiance of his usually impeccable judgement. He slew his enemies with fury, hacking down with his sword any man unfortunate enough to find himself in his path. However, one sturdy opponent, before Foulques managed to take his life by cutting off his head, plunged his sword into the knight's thigh, literally the minute before he died and his head was severed from his body. The pain from the wound was unbearable for the already weary knight and the blood was flowing out of him like a river, exhausting him even more, since he had been fighting for some hours in the sun without food and water.

"Damn it!" he thought, enraged. "My God, help me!" he managed to whisper. Seconds later, his sword fell from his hands and he fell on his knees, a moment before he lost consciousness.

A little further off, Philippe, also covered in blood, decided that any resistance was futile when he saw Jean and Pere de Moncada slaughtered before his eyes, as was Embriaco. The instinct of self-preservation then kicked in a flash, instantly driving away the clenching feeling that had welled up in his chest at the loss of his friend. In any case, Pere's replacement, another high-ranking knight who had immediately assumed command, had already ordered a retreat.

"If I die here now, my sacrifice will make no sense; and I won't be able to offer my order anything more. So I must find some way of getting out of here alive. My father is also in Acre," he thought.

He left the walls straight away and, going a little further back, looked towards the harbour. In the distance he could make out the countess Lucia, the mareschal of the Hospitallers and Amalric of Cyprus in a boat, getting ready to sail off to Cyprus.

"They are heading towards the ships. At least they have managed to get away and Henry has sent ships, because otherwise, with the Italians having betrayed us, we would have no means of escape," he thought.

On the shore he could make out other boats, loaded with both soldiers and civilians, heading towards Henry of Cyprus's ships. They were loaded to the hilt and rocking so much that one would have thought they would sink before they reached the ships.

The sailors on the ships were helping civilians to get on them as much as they could, while the cries of the less fortunate on the shore reached their ears. Not everyone was managing to get away. Philippe looked at the waterfront again and saw a mamluk grabbing a young woman, who was about to jump into the water and holding a baby in her arms, by the hair. The soldier threw her down and the next moment pierced her baby's body with his sword. Then he took the unfortunate woman by the hair again, as she screamed hysterically and tried to pick up her baby, now dead, and dragged her away from the waterfront. Philippe was quite far away but he could see that the woman was beautiful. It was a heart-breaking sight.

"At least she will not lose her life, only her honour," he thought, without, however, knowing whether it would have indeed been better. The most beautiful of the women who had not had time to escape would end up in Qalawun's and the pashas' harems.

Philippe did not know what was best for him to do. The boats on the shore were growing dangerously fewer and fewer and he did not know whether he would have time to get down to the harbour before the last one left. He looked at the walls again. Enemy soldiers were now entering without hindrance – since the defence had now collapsed completely – and the 'Infidels', now drunk with victory, had spoils on their minds. Suddenly, a life-saving idea came to him.

"Calpurnia!" he exclaimed.

He looked towards the centre of the city. The enemy had most probably not gone to the stables yet, since the Muslims were interested firstly in capturing slaves and then plundering the houses, taking their time. Without a second thought, he threw down his shield and as many pieces of armour as he could take off himself so as not to be a target and started running towards the stables, wisely avoiding any mamluks he encountered. However, when two enemies approached him threateningly, he was forced to fight them and, with the power that the will to stay alive endows, to send them quickly to their deaths, then go on his way.

It was relatively quiet in the stables. Philippe looked at the surrounding houses, which had many different valuables placed outside them, from carpets and jewellery to loose coins, but he could see no-one, anywhere.

"The people who live there are most probably hiding and the objects placed outside are probably to prevent intruders from entering the houses – unless they had time to get down to the harbour. I wish I could help them," Philippe thought, opening the stable door wide. He was relieved to see that the horses were still there.

"My girl?" he whispered and received a long whinny in reply. He quickly walked towards Calpurnia while the other horses looked at him in curiosity. He stroked her muzzle and began to saddle her quickly, while voices could be heard outside.

"They are here!" the knight whispered in fear and, a moment before he mounted his horse, said:

"Our salvation is in your legs, my beauty. Gee up!" and as, the knight brought his heels against the horse's sides, it replied with a nicker and then lunged forward.

Coming out in the sunlight, the first thing he saw was three 'Infidels' who had obviously found the residents of the house next door where they were hiding. They had just killed an old man, whose dead body was in front of the house, and were now about to have their way with a dark-haired teenager who was screaming hysterically as they tore off her clothes.

The sight of Philippe on the horse took the three men by surprise, and he, knowing that on horseback he had the advantage over the others on foot, did not hesitate: he took out his sword and drove it into the back of one of his enemies, in an attempt to save the girl. She got up and, mad from fear as she was, began, half-naked, to run away. The other two, now expecting Philippe's attack, took up defensive positions and began to swear in Arabic at the knight who had allowed their prize to get away. Philippe managed, at the last moment, to avoid a sword-thrust destined for Calpurnia's chest by getting the horse to rise up onto its hind legs. He managed to inflict an injury on the second man's shoulder but, after that, as the girl was nowhere to be seen, decided he was needlessly placing his own flight to safety at risk. In one sudden movement, he pulled Calpurnia's reins and she began to gallop towards the walls, leaving the third man behind, trying to help his injured comrade.

Philippe thought that the girl might have been saved thanks to his intervention but he doubted that she would avoid dishonour and captivity next time. "She shouldn't have run off. I could have taken her with me," he thought. Shortly afterwards, however, he started getting angry with himself for having delayed, and began to try to avoid those he encountered on his way so as not to get involved in other fights, which would further delay him.

He soon reached the ruins of the Tower of the Bishop. They were desolate and full of dead bodies. "Clearly whoever was to enter by this way has already done so. They will definitely have opened the central gate from the inside by now, so everyone should be coming in by that way now," thought Philippe. "The Sultan is probably getting ready to enter the city."

Philippe stopped Calpurnia galloping and made her carefully climb over the rubble, looking at the ground. He saw a dead body with no hands and he shuddered. Further down he saw another dead body, with a sword stuck in its eye. The smell was truly unbearable and the knight had to be careful so that the horse would not slip in the blood and all manner of other human body fluids that covered the ground.

He had now reached the top of what used to be a tower and he got off his horse, holding Calpurnia's reins so as not to make it more difficult for the horse during this difficult descent. He looked beyond the walls and, to his relief, saw that the bulk of the enemy had left that area. There were only tents left from the camp, with the servants walking around and the deadly siege engines glinting in the light of the sun. He turned back and looked at the once magnificent city for one last time. Now the only thing he could see was rubble and buildings in ruins, the picture of chaos. The wind carried the cries of panic of the crowd and the sound of looting. Philippe felt his heart heavy for once.

He was about to start his descent, when he heard a moan behind him. He turned his head and, looking to find which dead body was showing signs of life, saw Foulques on the ground, with his thigh covered in blood. Philippe was surprised. He let go of the reins and leaned over the injured knight.

"Brother?" he whispered to make sure that the voice was the Hospitaller's. "Are you alive?" He received another moan for an answer. Philippe tore off part of his robe and tied it round the Hospitaller's thigh tightly in order to stop the bleeding, which had drained him of energy. The knight opened his eyes and looked around as if in a daze.

"Where am I?" he said in a hoarse voice.

"You are lucky your injury is no worse. You have probably been unconsciousness for some time now. But we must leave straight away. The looting has begun and we are no longer safe here," Philippe explained to him, helping him up.

"Water," the injured knight murmured, not having fully recovered yet, while trying to move with difficulty.

"We'll find some on the way if we're lucky. Now you must get up and get on the horse, if you want us to get out of here alive," the Knight Templar replied, pulling his hand to help him stand up, while looking uneasily around him. The Hospitaller got up, unsteady on his feet. Philippe took his armour off and helped him mount Calpurnia, who was snorting anxiously because of the smell of blood that had reached her nostrils.

"The only thing you have to do is to hold on tightly and be patient," Philippe said and took Calpurnia's reins again, leading her carefully down the dangerous descent through the rubble. When they found themselves outside the walls, Philippe also mounted the horse and brought her to a gallop.

"I don't know how to thank you," Foulques said, having now fully regained consciousness. "If it weren't for you.."

Philippe did not let him continue:

"You shouldn't thank me but Calpurnia. Anyway, you would do the same thing for me, wouldn't you?"

Foulques agreed with a tired, affirmative nod of the head. They had arrived in front of the "Infidels'" tents. Philippe tensed up.

"If we make out of here alive, I believe we can get to Acre."

Indeed, it had immediately come to others' attention that they were getting away, as the Knight Templar had feared, and some servants were running up and down, pointing at them and gesticulating frantically. But none of them were on horseback, which was very fortunate for the knights, so Calpurnia continued to gallop undisturbed until the city finally disappeared from the knights' sight. They had escaped the present danger but, on their three-day trip to Acre, many unforeseen events could still take place since they were at war with the Muslims.

"Thank you again," said Foulques. "You know, when we first came across each other in Alexandria, I disliked you! Now I owe you my life!"

"If it makes you feel any better, I also disliked you. It's natural, isn't it? Knights from different orders do not normally get on well." Philippe replied, turning his head back so that his voice could be heard over the loud noise of the horse galloping.

"That is not good, however. My uncle, who is also a member of the order, always used to say that we would do wonders if we were united."

"Was he here, in Tripoli?" asked Philippe.

"No, fortunately. He stayed in Acre and will be glad to see me get back alive."

"I also have an uncle who is a Knight Templar in Acre. Have you been with the Hospitallers for years, Brother?"

"Yes. I also fought in the Krak against Baybars. You? Have you been in your order for years?"

"Yes," Philippe replied and then, changing the subject, went on:

"I hope we find some water somewhere and a safe place to spend the night. I am very thirsty."

"Me too. However I think that as long as we gallop along the shore we are bound to come across a camp."

They said nothing more. It was now late in the afternoon. When darkness had fallen for good, they could see an oasis from far off. The Bedouins' white tents stood between the date palms that grew at random around a small lake, lit by a great fire, which the Arabs had lit in the centre of their camp.

Before they approached, the knights took the rest of the pieces of their armour off, helping one another, and hid Philippe's sword inside the sack they had hung on Calpurnia's saddle. They both knew very well that the Bedouins were generally very hospitable towards all travellers, even those of different religion. They doubted, however, whether they would welcome them if they realized that they were knights. All Muslims had a profound dislike for both Knights Templar and Hospitaller knights, and considered them to be groups of fanatics who would not hesitate to slaughter even innocent civilians.

So Foulques and Philippe pretended to be simple travellers and gained the Arabs' hospitality for that night. Foulques, who knew Arabic, managed to communicate with them perfectly well. Philippe had also learned some words after having stayed in Outremer for so many years. While they were quenching their thirst and eating around the fire, the looting in Tripoli ended and Qalawun entered the city in triumph.

Philippe was incredibly sad about the new tragedy facing Christendom, but he was happy to have escaped and be able to carry on the fight and, above all, that luck had brought Foulques, who would now be dead without his intervention, his way. As he watched him eat dates around the fire, he had the feeling that his life, from now on, would be bound together tightly with that of the young Hospitaller. He did not know how this would happen, but he just had that feeling.

Foulques, on the other hand, felt infinite gratitude towards the Knight Templar, and a great liking for him. As he brought a cup of cool water to his lips, he put all unpleasant thoughts to one side and smiled politely at the man who had saved him.

15

Acre, April 30, 1289

o do you think that the departure of the Italians is what brought about the disaster?"

"I don't think so. It just meant that the city fell sooner. The walls were so badly damaged in some places that it was only a matter of time until the Infidels entered, I believe."

"Except for the Countess and Amalric, were there many other survivors?"

"I can't say, my Lord. Undoubtedly most were killed. Some civilians fled to Cyprus. Maybe some knights were among them. I am not, however, able to say how many."

"Very well, you can go."

The voices were those of Jean de Villiers, the Grand Master of the Hospitallers and a Hospitaller who had survived and managed to reach Acre at dawn the next day. When it was almost noon, the Grand Master gave permission to the knight to leave. With the exception of two civilians, survivors who had reached Acre the previous evening, this Hospitaller was the first of his order who had managed to get out of the ruins of Tripoli alive.

Except for Jean, present at this conversation, taking place in the central square of the city, in front of the palace of the Patriarch, were Guillaume de Villaret and some Knights Templar, including Guillaume de Beaujeu and Jocelyn. Also present were Patriarch Nicolas and the man who was in command of the city, since King Henry's brother and the king himself were in Cyprus – Jean de Grailly, and another high ranking member of the hierarchy, Otto de Grandson. There was no doubt that news of the fall of Tripoli had alarmed everyone.

As soon as the Hospitaller left, Jean gave Guillaume a desperate look that betrayed his agitation, and said in a trembling voice:

"It was a huge disaster. Do you think any of our men are alive?"

Guillaume stood, his eyes fixed, staring into space. He was thinking of Foulques.

"I hope so, but it is very unlikely that anyone survived Qalawun's fury."

"My Lords,"Jean de Grailly broke in, addressing both the Grand Masters, "do you think that Qalawun might turn against us now?" Guillaume de Villaret looked at

Jean, playing nervously with his fingertips, and then turned to Jean, giving him the answer he had not wished to hear:

"I am afraid I do. If he does not attack us soon, I believe he will do so in the next three years."

"But," Otto de Grandson said, gesturing intensely, "King Henry has signed peace with Qalawun! He cannot attack us!"

"Of course he can, and I assure you he will not rest until he has driven all Christians from Outremer. Mark my words," Jean replied calmly.

"A horse with two riders is approaching the southern gate!"

The pessimistic discussion was sharply interrupted by the breathless guard now next to them.

"Civilians?" Jean asked the guard.

"That's what they appear to be. They might be civilians that got away from Acre."

"Definitely. Bring them here as soon as they arrive. They must have something new to tell us."

"Yes, my Lord."

A quarter of an hour had not passed and Calpurnia had reached the square, with the two knights on her back. Jocelyn was the first to recognise the horse from afar, and then its riders. At first he blinked, sure that it could not be Calpurnia. After rubbing his eyes, he took a closer look and managed to see his son in civilian clothes. At once the face of the desperate father, who had lost all hope, lit up with happiness, and his old heart almost broke.

"Well, it's Philippe!" he shouted, and began to run towards the horse.

"And Foulques behind him! Wearing civilian clothes too!" the Grand Master of the Hospitallers noticed too, causing Guillaume to also run towards Calpurnia

Philippe had barely time to set foot on the ground when he felt the warm embrace of his father, who burst into tears. He was so moved that his elderly body could not bear it in silence. He was rent by sobs.

"It's all right, father, calm yourself," Philippe whispered gently into the old man's ear as he hugged him.

Guillaume, on the other hand, after hugging his nephew, could not hide his joy. A huge smile was written across his face, all those gloomy discussions that had gone before now forgotten

"But… why are you wearing civilians' clothes?" Otto asked, when the thrill and excitement had died down.

"We stopped at a Bedouin caravan," said Philippe, pulling away from Jocelyn's embrace and bringing his hands to his father's shoulders. They were very hospitable towards us, but I don't think that would have been the case if they had known that we are knights, would it?"

"No, it wouldn't. Now, tell us, how did you manage to get away?" Guillaume de Villaret said, still smiling.

"Philippe saved my life, uncle!" said Foulques.

"You are exaggerating!" Philippe interjected, while, at the same time, stroking his tired horse, which was out of breath. "We both owe our salvation to Calpurnia – to her legs, to be precise."

"That's for sure," said Jocelyn, softly rubbing Calpurnia's muzzle and, straight away, indicating to a sergeant nearby, that he should attend to the exhausted animal.

The sergeant took Calpurnia and the two knights told not only their story, but also of many things that had happened during the unfortunate siege. Those present listened with great interest.

Philippe and Foulques were finishing their story, and the Hospitaller was about to go to the hospital so that they could take better care of the injury to his thigh, when the news of a second arrival came to stir the residents of Acre. The same guard came running down the walls once more, to announce the arrival of King Henry himself!

***

"Tell him then that he can tell me what he has to say. I'm all ears."

Henry's booming voice, addressed to the interpreter, echoed out on the heavy stones of the audience hall. The king's heavy, metallic voice matched his appearance perfectly as he was unusually tall, with a determined chin and prominent cheekbones framed by a dense and coarse black beard.

Sitting on the throne in the centre of the room, he fixed his eyes on Qalawun's envoy, placed his elbow on the arm of the throne covered with luxurious fabric, and his head now supported, inclined it slightly to the left, indicating that the Arab should start talking. At the same time, he made sure he hid the anxiety that had been eating him up inside since he had heard about the Fall of Tripoli. Only the day before had he come to Acre to see, with his own eyes, how threatening the situation was for his kingdom, and today, with no warning at all, an envoy from the Sultan had arrived.

The diminutive Bedouin began to talk slowly so that the interpreter would have time to interpret, looking at him and then the king with complete confidence.

"Your Majesty, I am here to convey to you my Lord's protest at the help you and the military orders of knights offered Tripoli. Need we remind you that you have agreed a truce with him?"

On hearing these words, Henry placed both his hands on the arms of the throne and gripped them tightly, trying to control the rage that was overwhelming him. When, finally, he replied to the envoy, his voice sounded calm and steady:

"Please, in turn, remind your Lord that the truce we have agreed concerns only the Kingdom of Jerusalem, that is Acre and the areas around it. The County of Tripoli was not included in the Kingdom and if the truce had included Tripoli then you, quite simply, would not have attacked it! So, ambassador, do not give me such humbug!"

The interpreter translated Henry's last words with some trepidation and anxiously waited for the Arab, who seemed to have swallowed the king's last insult without becoming the least upset, to reply. Bringing his index finger and thumb to his chin, he began to slowly rub it, giving Henry a sly, sideways look that seemed to be hiding a great deal. After some time, he folded his hands over his stomach, and said in a confident voice that bore no trace of apology:

141

"I must admit you are right, your Grace. What you have said may have slipped the Sultan's attention. I suggest, therefore, always following my master's wishes, that we renew our truce for ten years, ten months and ten days. Are we in agreement? I believe that a truce suits us all."

Henry remained silent. He was not so foolish as to not understand that the Sultan was playing cat and mouse with him. If, however, he failed to agree to this peace – in name only, he would give the Sultan the pretext he needed to attack Acre, even the next day. Such a thing was not at all in his interest. He needed time on his side. The longer Qalawun remained inactive, the more time Henry would have to gather men and strengthen the walls, giving Acre a chance of being saved. This was because he was in no longer in any doubt: the attack on Acre had been decided and would take place. The question was when and for what reason. He should not, therefore, provoke the Sultan by giving him the excuse he so needed. So, adopting a formal tone, he looked at the cunning ambassador and said:

"Tell your master that I accept the truce and let him not forget that it was he himself that asked for it to be extended. Give also your master my kindest regards."

"Very well, let it be so. Until we meet again, Majesty," the ambassador replied, bowing and looking at the king menacingly before he turned and left the room.

Henry closed his eyes and brought his hands to his face, troubled. He motioned to the interpreter to leave. He wanted to be alone, to ponder the situation. What had God decided to do with Acre? He wondered if his efforts to save the city were worth it. Or had the Christians of Outremer committed so many sins that God was about to punish them all? His mind raced to examine all the alternatives he had at his disposal. The Mongols could definitely help him. But if he called them the Sultan would definitely consider it a violation of their truce and that would offer him a perfect excuse to attack. So he would have to do something else that would not provoke Qalawun.

Sighing deeply, he got up slowly and began to pace up and down in the great hall. He was walking almost silently, as if the sound of his steps might have interrupted his thoughts. As for himself, he could stay in Acre for a few more months to organise its defence. Cyprus had no need him for now.

Suddenly he stopped, he clenched his right fist and brought it down hard onto his left hand.

"That's it!" he said.

He could send Jean de Grailly to the rulers of the West and explain the difficult situation to them. Yes, he had time, he definitely had time. It would take Qalawun many months to strengthen his army again. Jean could, therefore, tour extensively, asking for help.

"I'll send him to Pope Nicolas too," he thought. "He always shows Outremer's problems greater understanding."

He sat on his throne again. Happy with himself, he put the negative thoughts he had had at the ambassador's visit behind him, and called one of his servants. He would call the Grand Masters and civil officials to inform them about the ambassador's visit and Jean's forthcoming tour. After that he would be able to give his full attention to gathering supplies and making repairs to Acre's fortifications. Yes, there was still hope for Acre and Henry had decided to play his last card to save it.

***

"I shall be saved."
"And I shall save."
"Amen."
"I shall be freed."
"And I shall free."
"Amen."
"I shall be pierced."
"And I shall pierce."
"Amen."
"I shall be born. "
"And I shall give birth."
"Amen."
"I shall eat."
"And I shall be eaten."
"Amen."
"I shall hear."
"And I shall be heard."
"Amen."[75]

The underground chamber was brightly lit by many candles, creating the impression that it was day. The air was filled with the sweet smell of incense mixed with clove and cinnamon as it burnt in an open bowl at the end of the room. Three relatively young knights sat crossed-legged on the floor, each rhythmically beating their own large drum. The knights held hands, forming a small circle. It looked as if they were hovering above the ground, swaying slightly as they were to the rhythm of the music and moving their clasped hands at the same time.

In the centre of the circle stood the candidate for initiation into Fede Santa, his eyes covered with a handkerchief. It was the knight Geoffroy de Charney, a small man with ebony eyes and red cheeks, now even redder from the heat caused by the breath of so many people in the room and the handkerchief hiding his eyes and partially covering them. Sweat was running down his face from the effort he was making for his voice to be heard over the drums, as he was the first to speak in every triplet, saying what he had been told by the others beforehand. In his turn, Guillaume de Beaujeu, who was here playing the role of Christ, would, from inside the circle, follow with the fixed response and the chorus then intoned "Amen" at the end of each triplet.

There were five knights in the chorus, three of whom were Philippe, Francois and Luigi. Francois and Luigi had become members of the organisation about a year after Philippe and, while they had taken part in Fede Santa discussion meetings a number of times, this was the first time they were taking part in the initiation ceremony of

143

a new member, except, naturally, the time they themselves had been initiated into the organisation. Philippe had, of course, experienced the initiation ceremony as an initiate a few days after Jocelyn's revelations to him, before he had left for Tripoli.

The three young knights had been surprised to see for themselves not only how many knights actually held such unorthodox beliefs that deviated so much from the conventional ones, but also how deeply certain knights were steeped in Ancient Greek philosophy and mysticism. Many of them had attained the highest level of initiation, as had Jocelyn and Guillaume.

However, on that particular day, only Luigi's body was present throughout the whole ceremony. After the Fall of Tripoli, his mind had been constantly prey to fear for the fate of Acre and, as a consequence, his own. His mission had been accomplished, and with success beyond expectations.

He had, in the end, managed to feign interest, and in philosophical and theological discussions perfectly, without anyone noticing. So, by constantly asking the Grand Master and the other senior knights about such subjects, he had managed to come to be considered an open-minded and inquiring mind and succeeded in being made a member of the organisation. And, having achieved that, he had managed to collect large amounts of secret information. He had managed to send Abbot Giovanni some of the information he had collected about Fede Santa and the financial affairs of the Knight's Templar.

However, he now felt he had achieved his goal and was desperately looking for a way to get out of Outremer. He had to admit that he had grown to quite like the Knights Templar but there was no way he would give his life to the order. He had decided, therefore, to lie to the Grand Master and say that his father was on the verge of dying so that he would let him go. It had just so happened that, only the day before, letters had arrived from the West and Luigi saw that this was a unique opportunity to lie to the Grand Master and say that the letter he had received from Soumpiako was from his father, and not from the monastery.

The room was suddenly plunged into darkness, rousing Luigi from his thoughts. The knights playing the drums had got up and covered all the candles in the room with big metal bowls at the same time. After waiting for ten seconds, they uncovered the candles and took up a slower rhythm on their drums, which marked the final phase of the process. Guillaume left the circle, went up to Geoffroy and stood facing him, placing both his hands on his shoulders. The rest of the knights started to move in time again and Christ-Guillaume said:

"I am the lamp for those that see Me."

Geoffroy remained silent while the knight-helpers said once more:

"Amen."

Christ-Guillaume continued, speaking the words slowly, graciously and majestically in a voice that sounded as if it was coming from the afterlife:

"I am a mirror for those that perceive Me."

"Amen."

"I am the door for those that will knock at Me."

"Amen."

"I am the way for the wayfarer."

"Amen."[76]

Guillaume-as-Christ slowly and calmly took the handkerchief off the neophyte's eyes. Then he took the knight's hand and, holding it tightly, sat next to him and said, looking into his eyes:

"Now respond to my dance. See yourself in Me talking and when you have seen the things I do, be silent about My Mysteries."[77]

At this point the drums took up a very fast rhythm. The knights in the circle began to dance fast and Geoffroy and Guillaume did the same in the centre of the circle, always holding hands. The firm grasp of their hands symbolised the unbreakable bond that united all the initiated. The dance continued for a few more minutes. The knights' legs were moving so fast when making the steps that they looked as if they were flying, with their feet touching the ground for only a few moments.

When the dance reached its end and the room was once more plunged into darkness in the same way once again, the knights stopped holding hands and, taking their lead from the Grand Master, all embraced the new member and kissed him on both cheeks. The three knights who were playing the drums did the same. The ceremony had reached its end and the knights began to talk in small groups. Guillaume was talking to Geoffroy when Luigi came up him. The Grand Master, who was wiping the sweat off his forehead with a handkerchief, turned and smiled at Luigi.

"My Lord, I would like to talk to you in private."

"Of course, Brother. Let's go upstairs."

The Grand Master smiled at Geoffroy, nodded goodbye to him and began to climb the stairs, with Luigi following him.

Philippe, who was talking to Francois a little further off, commented on the scene, abruptly changing the subject of the conversation:

"See? Luigi is leaving with the Lord Master. Hasn't he been looking a bit anxious lately? I hope he can trust the Lord Master with what is on his mind." Francois turned as well and watched them climb the stairs. He agreed with Philippe with a slight nod of the head:

"Yes. He's always acted a little strangely, but of late he has been extremely agitated. Who knows what is on his mind? Maybe it's simply our military defeats. If that's the case, I wouldn't say he is worried for no reason!"

"Yes, you're right! We are all worried about those! That's it."

Philippe gave a slight wave as a sign of resignation and the two knights changed the subject of their conversation again, while, directly above them, in the Grand Master's office, Guillaume and Luigi were sitting opposite each other, the first on the chair behind his desk and the other on the stool opposite.

"Well I'm listening, Brother," Guillaume said, glancing through the window at the hues of purple, orange and yellow on the horizon that marked the end of another day in Acre.

Luigi's confidence rose for a moment so he sat up and looked the Grand Master in the eye, trying to make his voice sound as convincing as possible and to hide his growing unease.

"My Lord, you know of course that yesterday we received correspondence from the West." Guillaume stroked his shaved head and nodded in agreement.

"I received a letter from my mother, from Soumpiako." The young knight paused so that he could draw Guillaume's attention to what he was about to say and stirred nervously in his seat:

"My father is dying and would like to see me. My mother wrote that it would be very good for him if he saw me for one last time."The Grand Master folded his hands together on the desk, his expression giving not the slightest indication of what he was thinking, and he went on, helping Luigi out of a difficult position:

"So you would like me to allow you to go and see him, wouldn't you?"

Luigi nodded in agreement, his anxiety growing. Guillaume's face remained completely expressionless, not leaving any room for the young knight to guess what the answer he was waiting for so impatiently would be. Finally, the Grand Master's voice broke the short silence:

"Brother, I share your pain and understand how difficult this situation might be for you. What you ask, however, leave to go on a trip that will keep you away from Acre for at least a month and a half, while the city is about to be besieged, is not something I am able to give."

"Yes, but..." Luigi was about to try once more, but the Grand Master interrupted him and his tone of voice had now become more severe and would not, indeed, brook any objections.

"Yet Brother, you know very well that I need every last man. And I would ask you not to insist because you are breaking our vows. Must I remind you that our order and our obligations towards it and towards the Lord are above any kind of family obligation, however serious that may be."

Luigi was looking at the floor, trying to hide his great disappointment.

"No, my Lord, I am well aware of this."

Guillaume got up, disappointment and contempt clearly visible in his eyes.

"Then let's go to Vespers. And I don't want to hear anything about leaving, from any of you, ever again. Especially at such a difficult time for the city. From no one! I consider it outright cowardice. Am I clear?"

"Of course, my Lord."

By the time the knight had got up from the stool Guillaume had disappeared. Dragging his feet, the young man went out and headed towards the church.

"Damn it! I'm too late! So must I die so young for the Knights Templar? This can't be. There must be some way I can leave this damn city," he thought and decided to be patient for the time being. The thought that Qalawun would not, logically, attack the city before spring gave him some encouragement and, entering the church, he sat next to Francois. Maybe the liturgy would help him relax.

From the front pews Guillaume was looking at Luigi. "Can he really be such a coward?" he thought disappointedly. "And he is a member of Fede Santa too!" He folded his hands in prayer on his thighs and tried to focus on the chants, but without success. He knew very well that if he allowed Luigi to leave, there was no way he would return to a doomed city in spring. So he didn't trust him? Probably not.

Clearly not everyone would react in the same way in a situation like this one. Some would balk out of fear, others would not. Whatever the case, to allow someone to leave at such a difficult time for the city would be a dangerous temptation for the rest. So, not only to Luigi, but to no one would he give permission to leave the city. That was the right thing to do and that was what he would do to fulfil the vow he had made to God: to protect His possessions. He leaned his head downwards and prayed to God to give courage not only to the Knights Templar, but to all who were in Acre.

***

September had now set in and, although the weather was still hot, the first rains had fallen when Henry decided to return to Cyprus, leaving his brother as bailli in Acre. Having strengthened the fortifications of the city as much as he could, laid in as many supplies as he could and having sent Jean de Grailly at the same time to get help from the West, he thought he had truly done the best that he could for the city.

Meanwhile, the knights from all orders were helping with the fortifications and the collection of supplies, but were also relatively inactive. So Philippe had all the time to study Greek with his father, as he had promised him. He could, therefore, be better attuned not only to the mystical teachings but also to the philosophy of the ancients, broadening, in this way, his mental horizons and filling his free time in a pleasant way. Because, except for their daily monastic duties and some physical exercise to keep them battle-ready, the knights had little to do other than wait for Qalawun to make the first move.

This also gave Foulques and Philippe the opportunity to meet often, something that, from some point onwards, they both sought, since they felt as if they had known each other for years and felt a great affinity for one another although they were completely different characters. Foulques was more absolute in matters of order and ethics and, though sensitive at heart, was tougher in everyday life than the sensitive Philippe, who always put emotion above reason.

However, since in life it is always true that opposites attract, the two knights had found, it seemed, that their personalities complemented each other and they spent their time well, sharing their innermost thoughts. They had actually designated the great cedar near the walls as the spot that would play host to their conversations. This old tree, with its lush foliage, was at the inside corner of the walls on land, at the so-called Accursed Tower, the most vulnerable spot in Acre's defences.

So, as they had so often before, today they had arranged to meet to talk about the news that had reached Acre from the West, breaking, once more, the rule that monks had to remain silent. Wearing their summer shirts, the two knights sat next to the each other, leaning their backs on the tree trunk, with their elbows on their knees.

"Well, Brother," Foulques spoke first, "you've heard the news in the letter from Grailly that came this morning, haven't you?"

Philippe made a face and shook his head unhappily:

"Yes. Grailly says that Pope Nicolas welcomed him with understanding, and that everyone was upset when they heard about what had happened at Tripoli."

"But as long as the Sicilian problem exists, he is sorry but he cannot help!" added Foulques, fixing his eyes on the walls opposite him.

"He also writes that that they are all expecting Edward of England to launch an expedition first, because he has already participated in a military venture and is thought to have experience in the East."

"From what it seems, however, Edward, despite his promises to come to Outremer again, does not seem to have the resources necessary to undertake such a venture as this again. The conquest of Scotland and Wales is also more important to him."

The Knight Templar stopped staring at the sun, which was about to sink into the sea, and turned to the Hospitaller, clearly puzzled:

"So have you understood exactly what is going on with the Sicilians, what it is that means that everybody in the West is talking about them?"

Foulques folded his arms behind his head, leant against the trunk of the cedar and replied to Philippe, with his eyes still fixed on the walls:

"Basically Charles d' Anjou is to blame for everything. Although he is now dead, the Pope gave Sicily to the Angevins in the end and the Sicilians have now turned against them. The French, on the other hand, want the island so that they can fight the power of the maritime republics, including Aragon, which consequently prefers to take the side of the Sicilians. Anyway, no maritime republic was ever on good terms with the Pope."

"I understand. So the French and the Pope against Genoa, Aragon and the rest of the maritime republics. So the Sicilians' rebellion a few years ago was for nothing, the problem was not solved it seems."[78]

"On the other hand," Foulques continued, "I don't know if you've heard about the alliances between Qalawun and those in the West."

"Alliances? No, I don't know about that," Philippe replied, surprised and nervously rubbing his beard.

"The Genoese were harmed a great deal by the fall of Tripoli. So to compensate for what had been lost, they seized an Egyptian merchant ship in the port of Tineh on the Nile Delta. Qalawun responded by forbidding them to use the port of Alexandria. So the Genoese were forced to sign a peace treaty with him! And you haven't heard the best part yet: when the Genoese envoys reached Cairo, they came across embassies of the Greek and German emperors there - waiting to see the Sultan!"[79]

"That doesn't surprise me. The Greeks have always been traitors, and, as for the Italian merchants, I believe that in order to make money, they would make peace with the devil himself!"[80] Philippe remarked.

"I agree!"

The two knights remained silent for a little, looking at the red sun sinking into the light blue water, each of them deep in thought about the fate of Acre. Foulques eyes, however, despite the glorious wonder of Nature taking place before him, kept turning towards the walls. Philippe noticed this:

"Is there something going on with the walls that I don't know? Because from the moment we came here you haven't taken your eyes off them!"

Foulques did not reply straight away. When he spoke, after a while, his voice was a whisper:

"You know, they say that the fortifications of the city are extremely good, except for this corner. Now that I can see it from up close, I realize, unfortunately, how right they are."

Philippe also looked at the walls carefully. From North to the corner in the South he could see the following towers in order: the Tower of the Countess of Blois, the Tower of the English and right on the corner,the Tower of King Hugh and the Tower of King Henry II on the outer side of the walls, with the Accursed Tower on the inside. After the corner, moving from South to West, the towers were considerably further away from each other and there were three until the sea: the Tower of Saint Nicolas, the Tower of the Legate and, where the walls ended at the sea, the Tower of the Patriarch. Then he told Foulques what he thought:

"If there are so many towers at the same corner you are probably right. But, since there are so many why should we be worried?"

"I think that the spot is very convenient for those attacking because those defending are exposed to the enemy on two sides. When Qalawun besieges us, we will have problems here, I am sure of it."

The sun had now disappeared into the sea and darkness had gradually begun to fall. After some minutes of reflection, Philippe whispered:

"Are you afraid of death?"

The silence of dusk was disturbed only by some birds nesting in the cedar and coming back to roost. Occasionally the cry of some animal would sound out. An owl had began her hunting for the night and was hooting rhythmically. And if someone listened carefully they would hear the light sound of waves, which could be heard from there. However, no sound of human activity could be heard. Foulques, who felt as if he had been completely immersed in these sounds, replied after a long silence:

"No. If I die for a noble cause I don't care."

He laughed slightly and stood up:

"Of course I am still young and would wish to delay it as long as possible. But I wouldn't say it is something I am constantly afraid will happen. Whatever happens, happens. He took Philippe, who had also stood up in the meantime, by the shoulders, and added:

"And of course that doesn't mean I am not grateful to you for saving my life! Thanks to you I will be able to help, as much I can, here in Acre. How about you?"

Philippe laughed in turn:

"I am not as brave as you are. Which means I would never leave Acre to avoid doing my duty, but if someone told me that I would die tomorrow, I would tremble like a fish! The idea that I will find myself near God and that supposed afterlife, doesn't make me feel much better, you know. At least I hope that, if I am to die in this siege, it will happen all of a sudden and in an instant!"

At that moment the bells for Vespers sounded. The two knights began to walk back and changed the topics of the conversation to lighter ones. The orange half-moon, which rose timidly behind them, watched them walking from above, as if it was laughing when it did this. By the time it had reached its height and turned white, the two young men would be in their respective churches, leaving their worries about the fate of the city and their own destiny behind.

16

Acre, August 10, 1290

ere comes the army from the West! Here comes help!"
The guard was ringing the bell wildly with excitement and his loud voice was echoing over the high walls, which were soon full, although it was very early in the morning, of every kind of knight, political official, civilian – even woman and child, who ran to see the arrival of the crusader fleet on which they had been placing all their hopes of repelling the forthcoming attack by Qalawun[81]

Indeed, on the horizon, on the calm sea, one could see the crusaders' galleys wrapped in a faint morning mist, approaching fast. Their large white sails were filled by the strong west wind pushing them from behind towards the port like some huge invisible hand. The oarsmen, taking advantage of the wind, were enjoying some rest, a rare occurrence for them.

In the end, the Pope's churches had received some positive response among the peasants and unemployed townsfolk of Lombardy and Tuscany. The Pope himself had not, of course, seemed very excited by this, since no earl or baron had shared the same desire as the villagers nor participated in the crusade. This army, a mob thirsty for an adventure that would lend it honour, the salvation of heaven and, preferably, the more tangible reward of loot, was not exactly what he had expected. He placed it under the command of the Bishop of Tripoli, who had escaped the destruction and had come, as a refugee, to Rome, with the hope that he would be able to discipline this uncontrollable rabble.

The Venetians, on the other hand, had the commercial hegemony in Acre, and, while not very sorry to see their rival Genoa lose its base in Tripoli, had decided to send twenty galleys under the command of the Doge's son, Nicolas Tiepolo, assisted by Jean de Grailly and Roux de Sully. On the way, they were joined by five galleys sent by the king of Aragon, James, who wanted to help despite the fact that he was at war with the Pope and the Venetians.

Meanwhile, in the year that had passed, Acre had been in its last heyday. The truce that King Henry and Qalawun had signed, although based on the pretence of friendship between the two parties, had greatly benefited trade in Acre, which had resumed.

The harvest of 1290 was good one in Galilee and the Muslim villagers brought large quantities of their produce to the markets in the city. Even the merchants of Damascus had began to send their caravans to the city again.

This brought Acre unprecedented energy and activity. Outremer's Christian cities always had love-hate relationships with the Muslims: trade, paralysed when the two sides were at war, was exactly what gave them life and supported them..

This fundamental contradiction had sealed Outremer's fate from the beginning. Trade was essential to the survival of these cities, and this trade was with the very 'Infidel' with whom their Western inhabitants had come to the East to fight!

Philippe and Foulques were among the crowd that had run to the walls next to the sea to see the arrival of the fleet. Next to them were Francois, Jocelyn and Luigi, who were constantly commenting on what they could see. The galleys docked slowly in the harbour and it was nearly noon when the army began to disembark.

"There's Jean de Grailly! He was brave enough to return, and his mission met with some success," shouted Francois, when he saw the small man on the beach. He was one of the first to disembark.

At that moment everyone's eyes turned to a slender man in shining armour, with eyes that shone with confidence, who had just set foot on the shore. In one hand he held his helmet while with the other he shook the hand of the bailli of Acre, who had come to greet the fleet. The Grand Masters of the three Orders were also on the waterfront to welcome the newcomers.

"That must be the Doge's son, Nicolas Tiepolo," Foulques remarked.

Jocelyn looked at him, deep in thought. Finally he said:

"I just hope that he is not arrogant and listens to what he is told."

"Why do you say that uncle?" Philippe asked him, puzzled.

"I think that after all these years in the East nephew, you will have seen the negative effects a stubborn commander who has no experience in war with the Infidels in Outremer can have on the defence of a city."

"Yes, they are usually in a hurry to attack the Infidels, too sure of their strength and, of course, make a mess of everything as a result, with dire consequences for the rest of us!" Foulques said.

"Exactly!" Jocelyn agreed.

The peasants had now begun to disembark and the knights were looking at the undisciplined rabble with justifiable distrust. Many men were getting off the ships with their swords held high in the air shouting:

"Death to the Infidel!"

Others were getting off with their arms around each other, laughing, obviously having consumed very generous amounts of wine during the trip. Others were looking around at the city in a daze.

The first to express his doubts about this rabble of an army was Philippe:

"They will cause more problems here rather than help us."

They all agreed, nodding their heads and looking at the crowd with disappointment. They realised that they could only rely on themselves and the Venetian soldiers. When the disembarkation had ended, everyone went back to their duties, as if nothing had changed. However, everything was about to change, unfortunately for the worse.

***

That dusk, on one of the last days of August, the sound of steel on steel echoed beneath the great cedar near the Accursed Tower, as did the panting of the knights. Philippe and Foulques often practised their swordplay both to stay in shape, and for their own enjoyment.

Philippe felt his strength leaving him. The mock combat between the two knights had lasted a long time since they handled their swords almost equally well. Foulques had also begun to feel exhausted. Sweat had soaked their clothes, making their breeches and shirts stick to their bodies.

In the end Philippe caught Foulques off guard, and in one lightning-fast movement, had the tip of his sword pressed against the exhausted Hospitaller's throat.

"Aha!" Philippe said laughing. "I think that Knights Templar fight better than Hospitallers!"

Then he put the sword into its scabbard and fell to the ground, out of breath.

Foulques, next to him, did the same, feeling a brief twinge in his, now fully recovered, thigh.

"Don't be so sure! In the next fight, you'll see who's better!" he replied in a playful mood, while taking deep breaths. They remained lying down with their eyes closed for a while. Only their rapid breathing could be heard, together with the tweeting of the birds.

At some point Philippe muttered something to Foulques, who was relaxing:
"Brother?"

"What is it?" replied the knight without opening his eyes.

"I would like you to clarify something for me about your order."

"Of course. Let me hear your question."

Foulques still had his eyes closed and his hands folded on his chest, while his face looked calm and completely relaxed, something that it certainly hadn't been in a long time.

"Is your order dedicated to Saint John the Baptist?"

Foulques opened his eyes, looked the Knight Templar in the eye and laughed kindly.

"What kind of question is that Brother? How can you not know that? Everyone knows, just as they do that your order is dedicated to the Virgin Mary!"

Philippe stopped for a while and then continued hesitantly:

"It's just that, I heard once that initially you were dedicated to the Greek Saint John the Merciful. That's why I am asking – to see if anything like that is true. The Hospitaller looked at Philippe in obvious surprise:

"Where did you hear that?"

"Well... I once heard a conversation back home between some Brothers who were saying this and, because I know that there is some hostility between our orders and that many of the things said are not true, I thought I'd ask you."

"I will tell you, but it will stay between us, won't it Brother?" Foulques asked in a serious tone of voice, got up and sat cross- legged on the grass.

Philippe nodded in agreement and sat in the same way, all ears.

"As you know our order is the oldest, but initially its members were infirmarians, not knights."

"Yes, we were the first to combine the roles of soldier and monk," agreed the Knight Templar.

"So the truth is that our order existed long before it was founded officially by Gerard in 1113. Before Jerusalem was captured, some merchants from Amalfi had established a hostelry for Latin pilgrims in the Holy City. After our forces took Jerusalem back from the Arabs, it was turned into a hospital-cum-monastery, where pilgrims and the sick were taken care of.

"This is all very well," Philippe interrupted "and, I admit, new to me, but what does it have to do with what I asked you?"

"Always in a hurry! You'll see!" Foulques laughed, and went on:

"The original building where the merchants had their hospital while the city was in the hands of the infidels was given to them by the Greeks, who were already using it as a hospital, and who, as you must know, thanks to their emperor's protection, had a much larger presence in the Holy Land than us.

"That's right. Anyway, in the old days, Jerusalem belonged to the Greek Empire.[82]"

"So the Greeks, who always owned a substantial number of properties in the city that they had acquired, having reached an understanding with the infidels, gave the building to the Amalfian merchants, and they in return, dedicated their brotherhood to Saint John the Merciful, a Greek Patriarch of Alexandria who had been made a saint.[83] This, of course, with the capture of Jerusalem by our forces, changed over the years. I believe you can imagine why."

"Indeed. Neither the Pope nor you yourselves would be able to bear it if it became widely-known that your order had Greek origins, would you?"

"Exactly. That's why our patron saint changed," Foulques added, smiling. "So what you heard about our order was not slander, but the truth. It's been covered up, but not very well it would seem!" Foulques stood up suddenly, taking hold of his sword. "And now that I've answered your question, I owe you a return bout."

Philippe also stood up, also smiling, and took hold of his sword in turn. He didn't really want to fight again, but he would for the sake of his friend. "You feel like it! I'm exhausted!"

"So am I, but that doesn't matter. Practice! You know that we often need to fight even when we are very weak!"

Philippe said nothing more, he just tried to concentrate and attacked Foulques, who skillfully dodged the blow by leaning to one side. It was now his turn to attack the Knight Templar. Holding his sword with only one hand, he swung it through the air. Its edge would have reached Philippe's throat if he hadn't fallen to his knees in an instant. The sword-play went on in this way, with no clear winner, for some time, until the Hospitaller managed to do what he wanted to do so badly and win the return bout. Catching the exhausted Knight Templar off guard, he had the tip of his sword right at his heart. Philippe had no time to defend himself and threw his sword to the ground, his voice rasping with the effort:

"Alright, you've won! A draw!"

Yet at that very moment, and before Foulques even had time to lower his sword, the bell sounded, ringing frantically. The two knights looked at each other, still out of breath.

"It's the alarm! They may well be attacking us!" shouted Philippe and, after he had picked his sword up, quickly climbed onto the walls to see, his heart heavy with suspense. He scanned the countryside outside the walls, as far as the horizon, but could see not a single soul. The bell, however, continued to ring. Philippe shouted to Foulques, who was looking at him anxiously, waiting for his reply:

"There is nobody out there! Something else must have happened!"

"Why are we standing here then? Let's go and see!" replied the Hospitaller and the two knights began to run towards the central square of the Patriarchate. As they got closer, screams reached their ears, which the two knights heard with growing concern.

When they reached the square, they stumbled on Foulques' uncle who, together with Grand Master Jean were screaming a series of orders to some other Hospitallers. As soon as Guillaume de Villaret, saw his nephew, he gave him no time to ask anything. He turned his face, red with rage and consternation, towards the two friends and said to Foulques:

"Thank God you've come! The soldiers from the West have gone wild and are attacking the Muslim merchants in the city! Quick! Save as many as you can!"

"We shall lock them in the towers on the walls with us!" added Jean.

Then he looked at Philippe sideways and said to him:

"You too! All the orders are doing the same so that we may manage to avoid incurring Qalawun's wrath!"

Philippe did not wait to hear anything more. He at once rushed towards the soldiers that he could see opposite him, cutting five unfortunate Muslims who had fallen to their knees, begging for mercy, to pieces. Foulques followed him, obviously angry and muttering through his teeth:

"These stupid peasants! I was sure they would cause us problems!"

Philippe saw a young boy in a turban hiding under some stairs. Knowing that it was a matter of time until the furious mob found him, he pulled him out saying to him:

"Don't be afraid, stay next to me and everything will be alright!"

It took the boy, who was paralysed with fear, a few seconds to realize that the knight meant him no harm and decide to follow him.

Around them the slaughter went on and the blood of the merchants had painted many streets in Acre red. The soldiers from the West, literally out of their minds after so many months of inactivity in the city, were putting every citizen with a beard they came across to the slaughter. This also resulted in the loss of many local Christians since they also had beards. The knights and the barons of the city tried, in vain, to save the unfortunate merchants. They only succeeded in saving some of them by taking some of them to the towers.

"We came to slaughter Infidels," screamed the undisciplined mob.

They could not wait any more. As for their commanders, who had not managed to stop their men from constantly getting drunk in taverns, they had failed to control them once more. Their only success being that they had managed to seize some those who had started the slaughter.

Everything had happened so suddenly that no one understood how the riot had started. Some claimed that it had all started during one more drinking session, others that an "Infidel" had seduced a Christian woman, and her husband had asked his neighbours to take revenge. Whichever way, however, the slaughter had started, the result was the same: the harm was done now and the wrath of Qalawun was now ready to come down like thunder upon the city.

***

Qalawun's two envoys kept nervously walking up and down in the room. The food they had been offered remained untouched on the small table in the corner of the room. They were eagerly waiting for the "fair devils"'answer, which they would then report to their master, and were in no mood either to eat or talk.

Qalawun had been justifiably enraged by the slaughter of the innocent Muslim merchants about half a month before. So he sent envoys, who asked the barons of Acre to hand over the instigators of this slaughter so that they could be punished. Meanwhile, Constable Amalric, Jean de Grailly, the representatives of the church and the Grand Masters of the three orders were having a meeting in the great hall of the Patriarchate in order to decide what answer they would give Qalawun's envoys.

"What can we do? The Sultan is bound to attack us," argued Amalric, a man of average height with a thin voice and a wide forehead.

"There is one way we can avert an attack by Qalawun," declaimed Guillaume de Beaujeu.

"And what is that, Brother?" asked Burchard von Schwanden, the Grand Master of the Teutonic knights, stroking his beard. Guillaume looked all those present in the eye. He knew that no one there would like what he was about to say but, for the good of the city, it was worth a try. So he cleared his throat and began:

"If we hand Qalawun the criminals we have locked up in Acre's prisons, in place of the instigators of this evil, then I am sure he will calm down, at least for a while. Anyway, the only thing he is asking for is justice and no one can blame him for that." A cold silence greeted his words. Guillaume knew they would reject his proposal. It was only in Jean de Villier's eyes that he saw a glint of approval. In the end the Catholic bishop of Acre spoke:

"My child, what you are saying is a sin. To hand Christians over to Infidels when we know that they are certain to meet death at their hands? What will we say when the moment of judgement comes, before God?"

Jean de Grailly was quick to offer his support: "That's right. The bishop is right.".

"May I just remind you that these are common criminals, many of whom we also intend to put to death," said Guillaume, with a touch of irony in his voice.

"Apart from that, should we remind you, My Lord, what will happen, not only to the criminals, but to innocent civilians if Qalawun enters the city?" Jean de Villiers agreed with Guillaume, the same touch of subtle irony in his voice. He looked the elderly bishop in the eye, and eyes set in wrinkles glared back at him.

Guillaume gave Jean de Villiers a look full of gratitude for his support. Burchard gave his support to neither opinion. In any case, he was a man of limited abilities and reluctant to take risks.

"Let's ask the townsfolk what they think of our proposal, Grand Master," the Constable Almaric suggested.

Guillaume objected. "That's absolutely stupid. The crowd has no understanding of politics and will never agree to it. Whatever is done must be done in secret."

"That's right," Jean agreed. "No one has to know."

"I will not let you hand those who share our faith over to these barbaric dogs!" the bishop shouted as loud as his age would allow him to.

"Alright, calm yourself My Lord. We shall ask the crowd," Amalric broke in reassuringly.

Jean and Guillaume exchanged looks of disappointment. They knew the crowd would never approve of such a proposal. At least they had tried to save the city. When, later, they put this dilemma before the crowd, they started shouting, categorically rejecting the Grand Master of the Templars' proposal, and even hurling abuse at him for putting it forward. The people would have happily watched the executions of these people by the city's authorities in the administration of justice, but they did not want to see them put to death and humiliated by 'the Infidel'.

So the envoys went back to their master and gave him the Christians' answer to his request: not only would they not hand over the perpetrators of the slaughter to him but, on top of this, the Christians maintained, with shameless hypocrisy, that those responsible were the Muslim merchants themselves, so they were to blame!

Now the Sultan had every right to break the truce, according to his lawyers. So, thanks to the fiasco of the Tenth Crusade, he began to prepare his army in secret so that he could finally drive away all the Frankish Infidels who had invaded the land of his ancestors.

From then on history repeated itself, just as in Tripoli. The emir Al-Fakhri, once more , staying faithful to his agreement with the Grand Master of the Knights Templar, notified Guillaume that Qalawun was planning to attack the city very soon. Guillaume called a council to notify the authorities in Acre straight away but, once again, no one believed him.

Then the Grand Master of the Knights Templar decided to send someone to Qalawun to sound out the Sultan's intentions and try to achieve some kind of agreement so that the Muslims would not attack the city. Philippe was the envoy who, believing that Guillaume had truly done whatever he could to save the city, readily agreed to make the tiring trip on horseback to Cairo. And he actually came back to Acre with a proposal from Qalawun, of which Guillaume informed the High Court in Acre straight away. Qalawun was willing not to touch the city if he received as many Venetian zecchini as there were inhabitants in return. However, the members of the court and the political officials rejected this proposal with contempt, believing that they could resist Qalawun. For a third time, the Grand Master of the Knights Templar was sworn at by the mob, who called him a coward and a traitor as he left the chamber.

Guillaume went to his office, bitterly disappointed and utterly humiliated. His pessimism was shared, and not without reason, by not only all the Knights Templar but also members of other orders, who were always more perceptive than the laity. Now nothing could be done. Acre would be laid siege by Qalawun. Everyone in the city waited in the numb expectation of seeing him appear outside the walls. Yet God, for some unknown reason, had decided to give the doomed city one last breath of life.

17

Cairo, November 4, 1290

lthough it was November, it was a sunny day and very hot for that time of the year, even for the Middle East, where relatively mild winters are common. The helmets on Qalawun's soldiers shone in the blazing sun, as did the large number of catapults that the Sultan would take with him to besiege Acre. All the army had assembled outside the palace and was waiting for its leader to come out and inspect the troops so that they could finally march against the 'Infidels'.

Indeed, dressed in Arab battle dress, armour lighter than that of the Franks and a cone shaped helmet, the Sultan appeared. He came down the stairs at the entrance to the palace quickly, followed by his young son, Al-Ashraf Khalil. The commanders of this great army bowed as soon as they saw the Sultan and his son approaching them.

Qalawun greeted them with a movement of his head and then he looked around at the arrayed troops. Satisfaction quickly registered in his eyes, and so the man with hawk-like facial features mounted in one skillful move the bright white Arabian stallion waiting for him. Then he took his scimitar out of its scabbard and raised it into the air.

"Death to the Infidel! Glory to Allah!"

At the same time the soldiers did the same with their own swords and repeated these words in one voice. Then the Sultan, followed by his son and the commanders of his army riding behind him, drove forward and the army set off on its long march towards Acre. The oxen dragging the heavy catapults raised great clouds of dust into the air. After some hours on the road, the Sultan appeared to be in some discomfort, although his horse was not going very fast so that soldiers on foot could keep up. His face had turned deathly pale and sweat was running down his forehead. His hands appeared to be shaking on the reins. These changes did not go unnoticed by Qalawun's son, who was riding close by. He went up to his his father and in a worried voice asked him:

"Father, are you all right?"

Qalawun looked at his son, his wet eyes glistening from fever. His voice was far from a whisper, but it did not boom out as it had before. It was, however, also easy to detect a slight tremble in it:

"I'm all right son," he lied, although he was feeling extremely unwell. He did not want to jeopardise morale among his men in any way. He knew, however, that he looked too unwell to hide the truth completely. So he went on with feigned confidence.

"It's just a little autumn fever. Don't worry. We will crush the Infidels."

Al-Ashraf nodded in agreement, but the sceptical expression on his face revealed that he was not absolutely convinced that it was a "little fever" that was giving Qalawun so much trouble. A sense of foreboding preyed on his mind. Nevertheless, he forced himself to smile and to give courage to his father:

"We shall reach Marjat at-Tin tonight. I am sure that you will get some rest there and get your strength back."

"Thank you, son, I believe so too," the Sultan replied untruthfully. As time went by, his condition seemed to be getting worse rather than better.

Al-Ashraf pulled on the reins of his brown horse to turn back to his position, but changed his mind and asked a question that had just entered his head:

"Father, is it true that in your letter to the king of Armenia you say that you will leave no Christian alive in Acre?"

Qalawun smiled:

"Yes, my son. The Infidels will pay for all their treachery."

A loud dry cough followed the end of his sentence. Khalil did not reply, but returned to his position. and continued to watch his father out of the corner of his eye, together with the rest of the generals. His father was ready to drop, but he continued to ride his horse without complaint, despite his obvious discomfort.

***

Long drawn out chants and soft wailing broke the stillness of the night. The Sultan's tent, dimly lit by candles, was full of people who wanted to pay their last respects to their ruler, who was now dying. Holy men were chanting so that Allah would welcome the soul of his servant, about to make its last journey. They prayed as they censed the air, filling it with smoke and intense odours. The senior generals grasped their leader's hand for one last time. On their faces you could see his imminent death brought them genuine sorrow and a feeling of shattering loss.

Qalawun might have been relentless and merciless towards his enemies, but for his people there was no doubt that he was a great Sultan, who had achieved a great deal during his reign and had ruled wisely. At his side was his son, following the last moments of his father's life with heartfelt sorrow.

The Sultan lay on a bed in the centre of the tent. His eyes were closed and there was a wet cloth on his forehead to cool the fever which had now been racking his body for days. The doctors had done the best they could but now they had withdrawn, having realized there was nothing they could do in the face of death's dreadful power. As soon as the army had arrived five days earlier, at Marjat at-Tin, the Sultan had taken to his bed, exhausted, never to rise from it again.

Now, gathering his last strength and after all the generals had said goodbye to him, Qalawun opened his eyes and, in a whisper that could barely be heard, called his son. Khalil, with tears in his eyes, took his hand and put his face up close to his father's to hear his last words.

"I am now leaving for the long journey, my son," said the Sultan and smiled at Al-Ashraf with difficulty.

"Yes, father, I know," he replied, his voice choked with sorrow, squeezing his hand.

"I want you to promise me that, whatever happens, you will continue the campaign and drive the Infidels away from our land."

"I promise you, father," Khalil answered solemnly. "In the name of Allah, I swear I will not leave your work unfinished. When I close my eyes, our land will be free."

"That is what I wanted to hear. Thank you, my son!"

The Sultan, happy that his last wish had been granted by his son and, feeling weaker and weaker as time went by, leant his head wearily to one side and closed his eyes, but never let go of his son's hand. Khalil bent his head. For a while they stayed that way, holding hands while around them only the chanting of the holy men could be heard. After a while Al-Ashraf felt his father's grip release completely. Qalawun had died.

Then the young heir stood up and, with tears running gently from his eyes, kissed his father on the cheek for the last time. He closed his eyes for a minute and tried to control the tears he could feel welling up in his chest. Now was not the time for tears, but for action, just as he had promised his father.

"We are going back to Cairo. We will bury him with all the honours befitting a great leader," he declaimed.

The holy men nodded in agreement and Khalil left to let them prepare his father's body for transport. Al-Ashraf's mind worked feverishly. He had to be very careful from now on if he wanted to stay in power. As always happened after the death of a great leader, there were many that would hope to usurp his power and the danger of civil war was ever present. Khalil would have to have his wits about him if he wanted to fulfil his oath. He did not know exactly how, but he was determined to honour his promise at any price.

18

Acre, March 26, 1291

 here was no moon that spring night. About three hours after midnight, and before there was the slightest hint of the next day's dawn, a tomb-like silence and stillness reigned in the city.

The shadow, taking every precaution, had become one with the fortifications. He moved slowly, feeling his way along the wall near the Accursed Tower, his back turned towards it and facing out. The black clothes he was wearing made it even harder to see him in the dark. The shriek of a night bird startled the shadow for an instant and caused him to slow his pace. Quickly, however, he realized what it was that he had heard and that his presence had not been detected as he had feared. So the shadow continued to grope his way along the wall, searching for the ledge he had discovered some days earlier, from where he could climb up, and which led to freedom, avoiding the guards.

At last, he discovered the small gap he was looking for in the stone. The shadow raised his hand high, and began to feel the wall further up so that he could find exactly where the second step was. When he had found it, with slow and very careful movements, he held onto the second step and brought his right leg up to the first.

Luigi knew that what he was doing was very hard and dangerous. Climbing was also difficult and the chances of him being discovered were by no means remote. He had, however, to take the risk, if he ever wanted to get out of this damned city alive and see his homeland ever again.

He had delayed his departure greatly, and inside he was cursing himself for not having dared to do this earlier. But it was the fear of doing it and the hope that the city would escape the siege in the end that had kept him from putting his bold plan into action.

The truth was that Luigi, just like everybody else in the city, of course, except for the more perceptive members of the Orders, had been taken in by Qalawun's death and thought that their troubles were over. In Cairo the usual palace conspiracy had taken place, which almost led to civil war among the Muslims. When, however, Al-Ashraf, showing an unusually iron hand, arrested the leader of the conspiracy, emir

Turuntai , the Christians realised that they should not have taken the new Sultan so lightly.

The people of Acre had, therefore, sent one more embassy to Al-Ashraf, to sound out his intentions. The four people who made it up had been chosen with great care, with the intention of making the best possible impression on the Sultan. Its members were a notable of the city who spoke Arabic, Philippe Mainboeuf , a secretary called George, a Hospitaller and a Knight Templar, Bartholomew Pizan. The way Al-Ashraf welcomed this embassy left the Christians dumbfounded: he refused to listen to them and ordered them to be thrown into prison, from where they never left.

This made it clear to the people of Acre that the new Sultan would show them no mercy and that he would attack the city, something that his father had had no time to do. In fact, some of the city's leaders even regretted having rejected the proposal made by the Grand Master of the Knights Templar the previous year, and not making an agreement with Qalawun so that the city could be saved.

Now rumours circulating that the 'Infidel' army had already set off on its march against the city had plunged all of its inhabitants into despair and Luigi had decided, finally, to escape.

Luigi emptied his mind of these thoughts and tried to focus on his goal. He had almost reached the top of the walls and was now close to freedom. This was now the hardest part since there was a certain part of the walls, right under the top, where there was nothing against which to support oneself.

If there had been no guards on the towers, he could have avoided all this dangerous climbing and, having climbed the battlements, could have come down on the outer side of the walls. But there were guards on all the battlements so this difficult climb was the only way for someone to leave the city in secret.

So Luigi took a deep breath and stretched himself out as far as he could, holding onto the edge of the stone which stood out at the top of the walls with the tips of his fingers. He released his feet from their last footholds and swung into space. He wanted to use them to climb the last meters but his grip was not firm enough and he was unable to lift the full weight of his body, not even for the few moments necessary for his attempt to meet with any success. The knight felt his fingers slip and his body fall backwards. He tried in vain to choke a muffled cry and crashed to the ground, falling on his left leg.

At once he felt acute pain piercing that part of his body and, when he tried to put his weight on the leg and get up, he realised that this was impossible.

"Damn it!" he muttered through his teeth. "I must get out of here before the guard on the Accursed Tower comes!"

A few meters away, at the corner of the walls, the guard had heard the cry and the dull thud Luigi's body had made when he had fallen to the ground from so many meters high and had run towards it straight away. A young, diminutive man, he thought he would come across some brawl or other, the usual result of a long bout of overindulgence in wine. When, however, breathless, he reached the spot from where the sound had come, he was amazed to see a man in black trying to crawl away from the walls.

"What on earth is going on here?" he shouted.

Luigi, unable to stand, looked at the guard pleadingly:

"Please...let me explain!"

"Explain what? You were going to run away because you are spying for the Infidels,"[84] said the guard, making a gesture of disgust with his hand. "Guards! Come quickly! Alarm!" he then shouted at the top of his voice.

Then he grabbed Luigi by the arm and forced him to his feet. His broken leg, however, prevented him from keeping his balance, so the guard had him sit on a large stone.

Luigi was already bathed in a cold sweat but also felt a sense of resignation. He knew that now that he had been discovered, there was no chance he would ever see his homeland again...unless...his mind ran through the possibilities. What punishment awaited him now? Maybe imprisonment, but expulsion from the order was not out of the question either. When a knight concealed another commitment, such as marriage or membership of another order, the most common punishment was expulsion from the Order. So maybe if he confessed the truth – that he was a member of the Benedictine order – they would expel him from the order, and so he would succeed in his purpose by indirect means?

At that moment a voice roused him from his thoughts. It was one of the guards nearby that had heard his comrade shouting and had run to see what was happening. As soon as he saw Luigi he cried out:

"But he is a Knight Templar! We must call their Grand Master straight away. Emmanuel, you go!" he ordered. A third guard who had run to the spot set off immediately. After a period of uncomfortable silence, he turned to the small man who had first discovered Luigi.

"Do you believe he is a spy for the Infidels?"

"If you say that he is a Knight Templar, it is not impossible. Their order has always had sordid dealings with them." Luigi, visibly annoyed by this aspersion and rather more relaxed after he had given his situation some thought, turned to the guards with a disdainful look:

"Yes, so that they can hold onto your territory, you fools!"

The diminutive guard could see Guillaume de Beaujeu and Jean de Grailly coming towards him with Emmanuel and did not have time to answer. He just glared at Luigi in dislike, and then turned to Guillaume to give him the explanation needed:

"My Lord, I found this man on the ground a while ago. He was obviously trying to get away in secret, but he fell from the wall while climbing it. If you look at his right leg, you'll see that it is broken and this is the best proof of that what I am saying is the case. He was going to the Infidels to inform them about the state of our forces! You must arrest him immediately!"

Guillaume gave Jean a look that showed that he felt the guard had had too much to say for himself. Jean then said:

"Thank you very much Nicolas for your services. And your fellow guards too. You can now return to your posts. We shall clarify the situation."

The guards, clearly disappointed that they would miss what would happen next, reluctantly returned to their positions, leaving the three men alone. It was only then that Guillaume was able to see the Knight Templar's face:

"Brother Luigi?" he whispered, shaken and his mind turning straight to Fede Santa. If the Knight Templar who had tried to ran away in the night was a member of Fede Santa, then things were by no means, by no means at all simple. Luigi looked at Guillaume sadly and started to apologise:

"My Lord, I am very sorry. I…"

Guillaume interrupted him sharply: "Whatever you have to say, Brother Luigi, you shall say it in front of me, the seneschal, the mareschal and the other brothers tomorrow. For the time being, although it saddens me to do so, I have to lock you up." Luigi thought it better to take it all stoically and raise no objection. So he said nothing more.

The three of them set off for the prison but Jean, who set off last, saw a piece of paper on the ground. He picked it up and said to Guillaume:

"Grand Master, take a look at this piece of paper. I found it on the ground. Then Luigi in one swift movement, after turning pale when he remembered the letter for the abbot that he had had on him and letting a short expletive leave his mouth, grabbed the piece of paper from Jean's hand saying:

"That is mine. It is something personal about my father. Give it back!"

Jean gave him a scornful look and, in a movement that was just as quick and unexpected, took the piece of paper back and hissed:

"Whoever runs away in the night like a common criminal no longer has the right to personal items? Isn't that so, Lord Master?"

"It is," said Guillaume, looking at the knight severely as he took the piece of paper from Jean's hand and put it into his own shirt pocket. He no longer trusted Luigi at all and certainly doubted whether this piece of paper had anything to do with his father. He went on, addressing Jean:

"I shall look into this later. Let's search him to see if he is hiding anything else." Luigi had realised that all was now lost, since the Grand Master would read the letter, in which he revealed details of Fede Santa's last ritual, which had taken place only the previous day, to Abbot Giovanni. Deathly pale , he raised his hands up, completely resigned to his fate, allowing Jean to find a small flask and some bread and cheese which he had saved for his journey, and which had not fallen out of his robe when he fell.

"I see you were well-organised, young man!" Jean said, handing what he had found to Guillaume, who looked them over and then said:

"Let's go. Tomorrow with the help of the Almighty we shall clarify the situation."

After they had locked Luigi in an empty cell, leaving him to curse the idea of carrying such a letter on him, and now certain that his plan had met with complete failure. Guillaume and Jean bade each other goodnight, Guillaume having promised that he would tell Jean what Luigi intentions were the next day, if he were able to find this out. Guillaume entered his office and, after closing the door, carefully took his cloak off his shoulders, placed it over a stool and collapsed into his chair with a gasp of frustration. He was profoundly sad that a member of Fede Santa had betrayed his trust, but also angry at what was proving to be his bad judgment as to the knight's character. He had not for a moment, however, believed that Luigi was spying for the 'Infidels'. "As if Al-Ashraf and the siege weren't enough, I have my own men's disloyalty to put right. How could I have been so wrong about Luigi?" he said to himself.

Slowly and carefully, he unfolded the paper and began to read.

***

The next day, all the Knights Templar of Acre, including Philippe, Francois, Jocelyn and other members of Fede Santa, such as the mareschal Pierre and the new seneschal Andre, who had been appointed to Jean's position after his death, attended their Brother Luigi's trial. It took place in the large ceremonial hall the Knights Templar had, in a building next to the one that housed the Grand Master's office. It was the only hall that could accommodate all the Knights Templar in Acre.

When Phillippe entered, he saw Luigi sitting on a stool in the centre of the room, his head bowed. His left leg was bandaged since he had been taken to the hospital before being brought to trial. He did not know whether he should feel pity for his -now former - Brother, or contempt. He sat next to Francois, together with the rest of the knights, who were waiting expectantly to hear what their Brother had to say in his defence. Hatred aroused by the Templar's treason was written on some faces; others, fewer in number, betrayed only compassion and sympathy.

The Grand Master, together with the seneschal and the mareschal, were sitting opposite Luigi at a large table. All the Knights Templar, even Luigi, were wearing their white robes with the red cross, lending the room an impression of absolute uniformity. Guillaume raised his hand for silence and in a serious voice, coloured with a touch of sadness, said:

"My Brothers, a very sad event brings us here at these difficult times for the city." He paused briefly and then got to the matter at hand:

"Last night the guards of the city caught Brother Luigi trying to escape by climbing over the walls. Proof of his intention, apart of course from the act of running away itself, was a flask of water and some bread and cheese that he was carrying on him for the journey."

His words were met by fierce jeers from the rest of the Brothers. He fixed his eyes on Luigi, whose head was still bowed, and addressed him:

"Brother Luigi, do you accept these accusations?"

The Italian raised his head up wearily and replied:

"There would be no use in trying to deny them."

"Very well. However, I must ask about the motive behind your escape before I move on."

"Cowardice. Fear of the impending battle," Luigi said with no trace of hesitation, exciting more murmurs of disapproval amongst his Brothers. He no longer cared what would happen. He knew that since Guillaume had seen the letter to Abbot Giovanni, his fate was sealed.

The Grand Master remained thoughtful for a brief while. The day before, when he had read the letter that Luigi had had on him, he had been astounded by the fact that the monk was making revelations about Fede Santa. He had realised that Luigi was nothing other than a spy secretly placed amongst the Brothers, not by the 'Infidel', but by the Church itself, which had always been hostile towards their order. He ought, therefore, to show the letter and finish making the charges brought against Luigi, but without referring to Fede Santa in front of everyone.

In the end, he held up the piece of the paper and spoke again, in the belief that the mareschal and seneschal, who would look at it, were also members of the organisation and they too would understand what they should not reveal in front of their Brothers.

"The problem with Brother Luigi is not only his cowardice, to which he himself confesses anyway, but also the fact that he has hidden his membership of another order from us, as this letter we found on him proves. As you all know, false testimony and perjury to our order are severely punished. So, Brother Luigi here, before becoming a member of our order, was already a monk belonging to the Order of St. Benedict, in the monastery of Soumpiako in Lombardy to be precise."

Brother Pierre and Andre's reaction was immediate and they asked to look at the letter straight away. These words also prompted yet more loud outcry in the room among the rest of the knights since other religious orders were not held in high regard by the Knights Templar. Brother Pierre stood up right after he had finishing reading and, once a glance from the Grand Master had indicated that he had permission to speak, said in a loud voice:

"My Brothers, things are just as our Lord says. I must, therefore, ask Brother Luigi again if it is true that he is also a member of the Benedictine Order."

Meanwhile the constant jeers of disapproval reaching Luigi's ears had wounded his pride. He suddenly felt a deep hatred for that order which would, it seemed, deprive him of freedom for the rest of his free life. After all, he wasn't the only one hiding something. What about Philippe and Jocelyn? Weren't they hiding information? The knight got to his feet, and adopting a tone completely different from that he had before, said in a voice full of contempt and hatred:

"It is true that I am a Benedictine but it is also true that other Brothers have been hiding things from you."

"What do you mean Brother Luigi?" Guillaume asked, looking at the knight in disbelief and feeling his heart race at the same time, without knowing why.

Without a second's thought, Luigi decided to tell the secret he had discovered by chance, as a last means of defence:

"I mean that Brother Philippe is illegitimate. His father is a Knight Templar, and is none other than Brother Jocelyn."

Straight away, everyone looked at Philippe and his father. Philippe's face turned ashen, as did Jocelyn's, and he felt the world slipping away from under his feet. He managed, however, to get hold of himself quickly and, knowing that there was no point in denying something that was true, said with a voice that betrayed his agitation:

"It is true. Of course, I don't know how Brother Luigi found out, but it is true. I ask for forgiveness, my Lord. Even so, I wished to serve God."

Guillaume was also surprised by the news, but he knew that it was nothing very serious, at least for a knight that had repeatedly proven his worth, like Philippe.

The truth was that during its early years the Knights Templar Order, like all the knights orders, had accepted only noble offspring, excluding any candidate about whom there was even suspicion that they were illegitimate. As years went by, however, that rule became somewhat more relaxed and was not always applied.

Guillaume also remembered the case a predecessor of his, Armand de Perigord, had come across, about fifty years before. Many Knights Templar who were highly thought of amongst the Brothers, had been received into the order through simony and confessed this to Armand. Armand found himself in a very difficult position and put the case before the Pope, who placed it under the Archbishop of Caesaria, who , in the end, offered the solution. The Brothers were put on trial, expelled from the Order and then readmitted since they had been pious and beyond reproach   One of them, Guillaume de Sonnac, who died at the Battle of Mansurah, was later voted Grand Master.

Guillaume therefore knew that Philippe's misdeed was not so serious, especially at a time when the order was facing such difficulties in terms of manpower and particularly when it concerned a knight whose behaviour had been faultless. So he stood up and delivered these words, looking Philippe in the eye:

"Brother Philippe, your behaviour until now has been impeccable so I shall ignore your concealment from the Order that you are not the fruit of a legitimate marriage. I wish, however, wish to impose a light form of punishment on you. What do you think, Brother Pierre?"

"I agree with you, my Lord. I suggest that Brother Philippe eats on the floor for a month."

"Punishment agreed. Brother Philippe, you may sit down now. Let us return to the matter of Brother Luigi."

Philippe sat in his seat, his heart still beating fast. His eyes had met Luigi's and his expression had revealed his disappointment at the light punishment that had been imposed on him in the end. He could still not believe that Luigi knew his secret, which was, of course, no secret any more! His father, opposite him, was looking at him with the same surprised expression. He looked at the Grand Master, who was whispering something with Brothers Peter and Andre, probably about the sentence they would impose on Luigi and considered himself lucky. He believed a very severe punishment would be imposed on Luigi.

The Grand Master, who had sat down again, stood up once more and announced Brother Luigi's sentence.

"Brother Luigi, for the fact that you belonged to the Benedictine Order before you became a Knight Templar, something you hid on your reception into our order, but also for the cowardice you have displayed during the current critical situation in the city, you are sentenced to life in prison."

Luigi did not react in any way on hearing this terrible news. It was something he had been expecting so he did not even look the Grand Master in the eye. He kept

staring into space and maintained the same attitude of resignation even when two sergeants approached him to take him to prison.

Philippe watched Luigi as he moved towards the exit with his head bowed. He felt infinite sorrow at the fate that awaited the Benedictine. A life without the light of the sun, in a dark, damp cell. He shuddered involuntarily. Next to him, Francois, whispered in his ear:

"So there was something not right about him from the very start! We were right!" Philippe just nodded his head. It was now time for lunch and those present at the trial had already begun to leave the room and head towards the refectory. Most of them were silent, as the Rule of the Knights Templar stated that they should be.

Philippe saw some of his Brothers look askance at him after Luigi's revelation, but he did not care. He walked slowly to the exit with Francois at his side, looking around for his father.. The old man Jocelyn had, however, already left, also having received strange looks from his Brothers.

When Philippe got out and breathed fresh air he felt somewhat better after being indoors for so many hours amongst so many people. Nevertheless, a burden lay on his heart that refused to be lifted and a feeling of pessimism had crept over him. He thought that, deep down, Luigi was right to want to leave. Philippe had no liking for the options open to him, nor did he want to die so young. But what could he do? That evening he would try to meet up with Foulques, who was always more of a fighter. Maybe he would give him courage, he thought. Carrying these thoughts with him, he was the last knight to enter the refectory, where his punishment would take place, while the sun was right at its highest point in sky.

19

Acre, April 5, 1291

 hat are we going to do, my Lord?"

"Do you need to ask, Brother? What can we do, we will defend ourselves to the death!"

"But… my Lord, there are almost three times as many of
them as there are us!"

"So be it. Run and get the rest. From today, everyone, apart
from those to whom I give leave, will be at their posts on the
walls. What are you waiting for?"

"Right away, my Lord."

Guillaume de Beaujeu looked sideways at the guard running to carry out the order, then hid his face in his palms and let out a deep sigh. Sometimes, when nobody
else was around, he allowed himself to show all the despair that overwhelmed him.
In front of others, however, especially in front of his Brothers, he tried to always look
strong and, as much as circumstances allowed, optimistic. Once more he raised
his head and looked at the sea of men that was outside the walls. It was Al-Ashraf's
army who had, since dawn, made its appearance by stealth outside the walls of Acre.
The ramparts were full of people from the orders, political officials and women and
children, who watched in complete despair as thousands of Al-Ashraf's men gathered. Finally, at some point around dusk, all his troops had arrived. No one had ever
believed that the Sultan could raise such a large army.

"Foolish citizens…" the Grand Master said to himself after lowering his hands from
his face, looking at the women weeping nearby, their arms around their children.

"If you hadn't been too stingy to pay Qalawun when I had told you, now your lives
would not be hanging by a thread. And not just yours, but also my men's," he kept
on saying to himself in disappointment. Guillaume tried to make a rough estimate
of enemy numbers.

"Around fifty thousand horsemen and at least one hundred and twenty thousand
soldiers on foot,"he whispered, "and I have less than one thousand knights and sergeants from all the orders and approximately fourteen thousand foot soldiers …and
there are no more than than forty thousand civilians, including women and children.

I am afraid these numbers do not favour us at all." He did not, however, remain there to think about it more. He cast one last glance at the Sultan's army and sped down the stairs that led to the open space under the ramparts. He knew that the doors of the castle had now closed and that the Sultan's catapults would begin to pound the walls mercilessly. "Thankfully at least the precious manuscripts are now safe in Paris," he thought.

Indeed, it had been about a month now since the very rich collection of books in the library at Acre had been transferred to the capital of France at that time. The decision of the members of Fede Santa, concerned for the safety of the valuable manuscripts that had been preserved, had been unanimous. In this way, at least, the members of the organization had one less thing to worry about, amongst all the others, ahead of the impending siege. Today, therefore, was a day of preparation for the forces from both sides. In the morning, as soon as the first enemy soldier had appeared, a meeting had been arranged at dusk with Jean de Grailly, together with the rest of the political officials and the members of orders at the Patriarchate to divide up the areas to be defended in the best possible way.

As Guillaume strode towards the Patriarchate, he saw scenes of frenzy and panic in the city. Men were running up and down carrying food or jugs of water, sergeants and knights from all the orders were going back and forth carrying out various orders from their superiors, women with babies in their arms were crying and screaming in panic. The whole of Acre, in other words, was a hive of activity.

Upon reaching the Patriarchate he saw the same activity in the harbour. Supplies were being unloaded from the ships and Venetian and Parisian merchants were talking intensely. There were no Genoese in Acre. They had been driven out of the city by the Venetians some time before, during one more of the usual commercial disputes between the Italians, and had signed a separate peace treaty with the Sultan. "At least we have control of the sea. So we shall not have no shortage of food," the Grand Master thought on a positive note, the first in an otherwise black day, as he looked at the large number of ships anchored in the harbour.

Entering the building and seeing the other three participants - Jean, Otto and the Grand Master of the Hospitallers - he saw that everyone else was already there and realised that he had been so absorbed in his thoughts that they had delayed him so much that he had been the last to arrive. After he had greeted those few people around him, they all sat around a big table. Then Guillaume noticed that the Teutonic Grand Master, Burchard von Scwanden was not there. He asked why he was absent.

"So you haven't heard?" Jean said.

"Hear what? I was on the walls all day," the Grand Master asked again, surprised.

"The whole Teutonic community is talking about it: Burchard resigned as Lord Master and the knights are electing his successor as we speak."

"What? Why? He didn't have any health problems from what I know."

"He cited the seriousness of the situation as an excuse and claims he thinks that we the Hospitaller and you the Knights Templar are more organised to face the danger than the Teutonic Knights."

"All right, but are those reasons to resign?" Guillaume asked again, unable to believe his ears.

"Sheer cowardice, Lord Guillaume, don't give it too much thought," Jean said. "So, now to the subject at hand."

After a long discussion, those present were finally confident that they had shared out the defence of the city as best they could and man the walls adequately, despite their severe lack of numbers. Thus the corner of the Accursed Tower, which was considered by everyone to be the weakest point of the defence, was entrusted to the troops King Henry had sent from Cyprus, with his brother, Amalric, in charge. On their right, towards the sea, at the Legate Tower, outside which Al-Ashraf had placed his tent, the French and English knights were placed under the command of Jean de Grailly. Further down, at the Tower of the Patriarch, which was on the coast, the Venetians and the Parisians under Otto de Grandson's command were to be positioned. The Teutonic knights were given an supplementary role, in the royal regiments of the Accursed Tower, due to their limited numbers, but also due to a lack of trust after the unfortunate event of their Grand Master's resignation. On the other side of the walls on land, the Hospitaller knights were placed, facing the army of Damascus opposite them. Finally, the large number of Knights Templar were responsible for the so-called walls of Montmusart, which reached until the other shore on the other side of the city. Outside the walls, the armies of Hama and Egypt had made camp.

After that, the four men dined together, talking about what each of them thought about the enemy's forces, and then they walked around the walls, inspecting the watchtowers and telling their commanders who was to defend each section. A little before they parted, late at night, they heard from a Hospitaller sergeant that someone by the name of Konrad von Feuchtwangen, a man who had gained great military experience in his time in Prussia, had been elected as the new Teutonic Grand Master. Then they went to rest for a few hours because the days that dawned from now on would be difficult for everyone.

***

At first light next day, the bombardment of the walls began, making the white flags of Outremer with their yellow crosses and the blue flags of the French Royal House with their yellow lilies that were on the walls, flutter wildly all the time. The Sultan's catapults were working all day, throwing heavy stones or clay pots full of explosives onto the walls. From their posts, Philippe and Foulques also saw clouds of arrows coming towards them from Al-Ashraf's highly skilled archers. At the same time, the wily Sultan had thousands of engineers at each tower, who would dig day and night from now on, undermining the vital defensive positions of the Christians, of whom there were not enough in any case to adequately man the walls. Philippe and Foulques spent all day on the walls, each at his respective order's defensive sector. That night, after diner and Vespers, and of course getting the permission of their superiors, they met under their cedar in an attempt to escape the atmosphere of death that prevailed on the walls briefly. The two knights had taken their armour

172

off and were gazing up at the stars, lying on the ground. They were both exhausted.

"For how long do you think what was happening today will go on?" asked Philippe, his eyes fixed on the endless black of the sky.

"The question is not for how long it will go on, but how it will end," Foulques replied laughing.

"And do you have optimistic thoughts about how it will end?" asked Philippe wondering how Foulques could joke and laugh at a time like this, when the future looked so bleak.

"It is too early for me to tell you for sure but my thoughts on the subject are anything but rosy," the Hospitaller knight replied pragmatically, showing the Knight Templar that he had misinterpreted his friend's laughter:

"And why should they be rosy? Only today I saw five of our sergeants die, and in horrible ways too. And think that today a general assault was not launched- only attacks at certain places on the walls. Of course, on the other hand, I saw at least three times as many Infidels lose their lives as well. I wonder when my turn will come," he added with a sigh.

"Don't think that way. Have courage," said Foulques, looking deep into Philippe's eyes to give him courage. "Say something else now. I would like to escape this grim atmosphere of war for a bit."

"You are right. Would you like to spar to pass the time?" Philippe asked, laughing, knowing that what he was suggesting was mad after a long day of intense activity and physical exhaustion. Foulques, knowing that the Knight Templar was joking, gave a faint smile and the two knights remained silent for a while. The Hospitaller knight broke the silence first, changing the subject:

"Would you ever like to become Lord Master?"

The Knight Templar looked at Foulques, puzzled:

"What kind of question is that?"

"Change of subject we were saying before," said Foulques, shrugging his shoulders indifferently. "Tell me please."

Philippe, after thinking about it for a little, said without hesitating:

"No. I am not made to carry so many responsibilities on my shoulders. You?"

"I would like to become one sometime and serve my order from that extremely important position. Deep down it is my secret dream," said the Hospitaller, his eyes fixed on the stars.

"I am sure your dream will come true," Philippe replied with certainty.

"How do you know?"

Foulques threw Philippe a glance of surprise, turning his head.

"Let me know what is going to happen for once! I might not have political experience, but I do have intuition, which, until now, has never proved wrong!" Philippe replied laughing.

"I hope so!" Foulques sighed and, after standing up, started walking around the cedar. Suddenly he remembered something and turned to Philippe again:

"I heard that one of you Templars was sentenced to life because he was a Benedictine at the same time. Is that true?"

"Yes. Brother Luigi. In fact I got punished because of him. I will eat on the floor for a month!"

"You? Got punished because of the Benedictine? But why?" The Hospitaller asked, obviously puzzled. Philippe bit his lip. That last sentence had truly slipped his tongue. However, he felt that he could reveal the truth about his father to Foulques. He had true feelings of friendship for the brave knight. In any case, what had once been his secret was now known to the whole of his order.

On hearing this disclosure, which lasted some time, the Hospitaller knight reacted calmly, shrugging his shoulders:

"You are neither the first nor the last of illegitimate origin to serve an order. There are many such cases I know of in our order. Think of how many there are that I don't know. But how did Luigi find out?"

"I don't know! I really want to find out! When I find the time, I think I am going to pay Luigi a visit in prison, maybe he will tell me."

"Why not? Shall we go now? We have a day just as hard, if not harder, ahead of us tomorrow."

"Let's go," Philippe agreed and stood up himself. They bade each other goodnight without another word, and made their way to their respective dormitories, each in the hope that they would stay well and meet again.

***

The moon shone in the sky on the night of April 15th. At the foot of the Tower of the Templars, on the walls of Montmusart, near a small wooden door, shut tight at the moment, around twenty Knights Templar and ten of Otto's soldiers were huddled together. Amongst them were Francois , Philippe and the Grand Master Guillaume who, together with Otto, was in charge of the mission that was about to begin. The Christians were going to make a short sortie to inflict some damage on the army of Hama… Philippe's felt as if his blood had frozen in his veins. He could stand to wait no longer. He gave Francois, who was next to him, an anxious look. The knights had been ordered to remain silent and Francois looked back at him, shaking his head imperceptibly at the same time.

Guillaume opened the door, carefully and silently. One by one the knights began to go out into the Muslim camp, where complete silence reigned. It seemed that, except for the guards, they were all sleeping, so the Christians would indeed take them by surprise.

Philippe's turn to go out came and, as soon as he did, he saw the Muslims' tents a few meters off and a guard from behind. Philippe pinned himself against the wall, just as the others did, so as not to be noticed by the guard. Philippe felt that his heart was about to burst. He knew that everyone's life now depended on luck. If the guard saw them, he would immediately raise the alarm and then 'the Infidels' would slaughter them before they even had time to react.

Fortunately, however, nothing like that happened and the Christians made their exit successfully without being noticed by anyone. The guard was now sitting down unconcerned on a rock with his head down. He looked as if he was sleeping. This was quite possible, and made it much easier for Guillaume, who was the last to appear at the little door.

Wasting no time, Guillaume began to move silently towards the guard, keeping as close to the walls as he could. When he came up close to him, the blade of a small knife glinted for a split second in the moonlight before it was plunged without mercy into neck of the unsuspecting guard, granting him instant and silent death.

After wiping the blade of his knife on the ground, Guillaume placed it to the side of his armour and motioned to the rest to follow him to the tents, and so they did. The enemy soldiers were sleeping and nothing seemed to be moving in that particular part of the camp. On Guillaume's command the slaughter began.

The Christians knew they had limited time on their hands before the alarm was raised so they made sure to be as quick as they could. Philippe tried not to think while his knife mercilessly cut the throats of the Sultan's sleeping soldiers. He performed the movements automatically, closing his ears to sounds of distress that might have been heard. This was, for Philippe, something completely different from the battle one on one on the walls. There you would fight for your existence and every enemy you killed meant gaining your own life. Now it was all a case of the brutal murder of people who posed no threat to your physical well-being, at least not at that specific moment. However, things quickly changed here too.

When almost all the soldiers in two tents had been killed, almost one hundred men, the soldiers from the nearby tents were alerted by some who had woken up in time and had not been slaughtered, so the Christians realised that it was time to go. Otto shouted the command exactly at the time when armed 'Infidels' were entering the tent.

"Back quickly!" Guillaume screamed and rushed on, urging his men to follow him. Philippe, now feeling like a deer surrounded by wolves, left the tent grasping his bloody dagger. Before, however, he even realised where he was, he felt the ground disappear under his feet and fell to the ground with a crash. He looked to see what it was that made him lose his balance and saw a thick rope which held the tents to the ground next to him.

"Be careful!" he then shouted, but it was too late. Philippe had time to see many of his comrades get tangled up in ropes and fall, amongst them Francois. Unfortunately not all of them had time to get up and leave, unlike the two friends.

Philippe and Francois were the last to return to the safety of the castle, getting away literally at the last minute from a big man who was chasing them. Otto sealed the door behind them straight away, only to realise, very much to their regret, that a large number of their comrades had been left behind, to be captured or killed on the spot.

"Damn it! Damn ropes!" Guillaume shouted, while Philippe and Francois were, in horror, thinking of the fate that awaited those that had been taken hostage.[85]

Now it was time to take care of the injured. Philippe, Francois and several more had got away unhurt. Truly lucky, they had not been involved in a melee with an enemy. Some other knights, however, and some members of the laity, having fought with some Muslim, had managed to get away but had paid a price. Next to Philippe lay a knight that had lost consciousness because of the constant bleeding from a deep cut in his chest. Further off another had lost his hand and was moaning horribly. This made Philippe want to get away from there so that he would no longer have to hear those horrible cries. However he managed to suppress the feelings of nausea and, with Francois, helped the nurses that had started to arrive with their difficult work as much as they could.

Dawn was breaking when the weary Philippe reached his dormitory. His last thoughts before he fell asleep were: "Was it all worth it? Had it had any effect on enemy morale – or had the lives of so many of our men been lost for no reason?" With these thoughts he fell into a short, troubled sleep, at the same time thanking God that he was still alive so that he could return again to the walls in a few hours.

***

May had now come after April but the new month had not, until now at least, seemed to have any hope to offer to the heavily besieged city. Although the ships in the harbour continued to supply the city as normal, thanks to the Christians' undoubted superiority at sea, great cracks had began to appear in the walls from the Sultan's catapults, and those under siege did not always have time to repair them satisfactorily. The Sultan's engineers had already reached under many towers and had began undermining them. It was a matter of time before some collapsed. And if all that was not enough, it was inevitable that the number of people defending the city was constantly being reduced by losses in battles. The Christians were not renewing their man power as Al-Ashraf was doing. His soldiers seemed to be growing more and more despite heavy losses, as new soldiers were constantly taking the place of dead ones.

In the light of these facts, and after a second, completely unsuccessful raid carried out by the Hospitallers, those under siege decided to make no further sorties as they realised that they were paying a disproportionate cost in human lives in comparison to what they had to offer the helpless city. And so the Christians turned solely to defence, their morale falling more and more each day, now having abandoned every offensive venture.

Philippe had leave all afternoon on that particular day. He had fought without break on the previous day, fending off an attack on a great scale that his sector had suffered - one that had cost the Christians many lives. The attack had been made on many fronts at the same time and had also cost the Muslims many lives, so today was a day of rest from aggression for both sides. The only thing that continued was the relentless bombardment of the walls. Nevertheless, the residents were no longer troubled by the bombardment, since they had become used to living with it.

So after Philippe had got as much rest as he could, he decided, before his meeting with Foulques, who was also on leave and exhausted, to pay Luigi a visit in jail.

Before Philippe went there, he made sure he got permission from Guillaume, who gave it to him unconditionally. So the guard with the curly hair had no objection to letting him through. He unlocked the heavy iron door slowly and told the knight to knock three times when he had finished his visit. When Philippe entered the dark chamber, a strong smell of human excrement filled his nostrils. His eyes needed some time to get used to the gloom since there were very few torches shedding their light on the space.

The prison in Acre was a long corridor where the condemned were chained to the wall by means of a short chain around one of their legs. They slept, ate and went to the toilet on the same spot, just like those condemned to the galleys. Very little fresh air entered and a little light came through some cracks high on the walls. In these conditions very few prisoners survived for more than a year.

Philippe's nostrils gradually grew accustomed to the horrible smell, but he was finding it hard to get used to the horrible scenes he saw. He walked down the narrow corridor looking for Luigi as eyes from sunken sockets and gaunt faces looked at him in curiosity. An old man who looked as if he was from another world, with his long white hair and skinny body, tried to grab the knight's leg as he went past and Philippe stepped back in fear at the last moment. At the end of the corridor he saw a young man.

"That must be him," he thought.

The prisoner had his head down and looked as if he was sleeping. However, as soon as Philippe stood in front of him he raised his head so that Philippe was able to recognise what was left of the once mighty knight. Luigi had grown horribly thin, the light blue eyes that had once resembled the sea had lost their shine because of malnutrition. Philippe realised, to his horror, that huge sores covered his face and hands. Before the knight had time to say a word the convict in the ragged clothes gave Philippe a forced smile, showing his now black teeth, and said in a choked voice:

"Yes, it's leprosy. Happy now? Are you pleased? I think God has punished me enough."

Philippe sighed. He might not have ever liked Luigi a great deal but he felt great sorrow to see him in such a condition. After all, he was someone with whom they had been through a great deal and had often fought together. Without meaning to he thought of the trip they had gone on together to Alexandria so many years before. He bit his lower lip hard at the memory of that pleasant event that now belonged to the distant past. How agreeable everything was then!

"Luigi, I am truly very sorry," was the only thing he could say extemporaneously.

"You came to ask me how I came to know your secret, didn't you?" Luigi asked him, with slight irony in his voice.

"You are right there, but I assume you will not tell me," said Philippe somewhat coldly, having detected the irony. He remained silent for a while, his arms folded. Then he added:

"You hate us all, don't you?"

Luigi shrugged his shoulders with indifference.

"No more than I hate myself or Abbot Giovanni, at my monastery, who sent me on a suicide mission like this." He tried to to stagger to his feet, but without success. He held the edge of Philippe's tunic and pulled it hard on it, looking at him imploringly.

Philippe shivered involuntarily.

"Will you do me a favour? A very great favour?"

"Tell me what it is," Philippe replied, his voice shaking almost imperceptibly.

"I shall tell you what you want to know, and then you will kill me."

Philippe's eyes widened.

"Luigi, what are you saying?"

"Does it sound absurd to you? Look around you!" the former Knight Templar began, his tone of voice betraying his deep despair.

"I am a leper; I can't bear to melt away in this living grave. Philippe I know you well, have mercy on me! You wouldn't stand this place for one day!"

Philippe looked around. He felt a stabbing pain in his heart. Luigi, and everyone there, was paying the price for an action of theirs. They deserved the punishment. However, if someone had stayed in a place like that for a whole month, hadn't he been punished enough? Death was definitely relief for someone who lived there. He looked Luigi straight in the eye and said to him:

"I understand you but you are asking me to commit murder. To kill a Christian, even a convict, is an action that is forbidden."

Then, Luigi, without saying a word, pulled up his tattered robe. Philippe saw, in horror, that the convict's legs and chest were all an open scarlet wound. The illness had literally cut swathes from him and it was clear that he had but a few days left to live. The wounds looked very deep.

"No one will know. I am so ill that everyone knows, guards and convicts, that I do not have much time left."

Pausing, Luigi changed the subject abruptly, believing that he had convinced Philippe by now, or that by using this revelation as a last card he would achieve his miserable goal.

"I heard you talk with your father on the night that he told you about Fede Santa. Then I learned everything about you and the organization."

Philippe brought that particular night to mind. While he remembered it in so much detail, there was no room for Luigi in his memories of those moments.

"But how?" he wondered. "We were alone!"

"You think so!" Luigi smiled cunningly at him. "I was behind you when you were talking outside and I went behind the library door when you went inside. At the end I ran and lay down first, so that you wouldn't notice me."

Then, in a completely different tone of voice, he went on:

"I owe you an apology for revealing your secret, it was my mistake. At that moment I was so blinded by rage that I could not do otherwise."

"You don't need to apologise, I understand," said Philippe, clearly in an understanding mood. "Anyway you didn't cause me any great harm! You heard the punishment: I simply ate on the floor for a month!"

"Yes, you are right. That does not compare with the torment I am going through. Of course, you didn't do anything bad. It is not your fault that you are an illegitimate child!" the convict agreed, smiling.

Philippe did not comment, but he continued to regard Luigi with a neutral expression. The atmosphere between them had lightened enough by now, despite the grim backdrop, and Luigi decided to change the subject again:

"How is the siege going?"

Philippe's face darkened at once. "Not very well I'm afraid."

"As I expected," Luigi replied. "That's why I wanted to leave, but it seems that God had other plans for me."

Then, suddenly turning serious himself , he looked around. The other convicts, despite having looked inquisitively at Philippe in the beginning and having appeared to be eavesdropping on their conversation, had now grown bored. The knight's visit had been a long one and most of them now seemed to be half asleep.

"Now is the right time" whispered Luigi to Philippe, looking around him. "No one is paying attention to us. I shall loudly tell you to leave now so that I can sleep and you will draw close to me for short time and stab me in the wound I have on my chest, exactly over the heart. I'll show you where. After that, when you get out of here, make sure you tell the guard and the Lord Master that I am very ill and, of course, wash yourself very well straight away and, of course, clean your knife too. I wouldn't want the man who saved me to die from the same illness!"

Philippe seemed hesitant. He knew that Luigi was right and that no one would find out, but he was in two minds. The prisoner looked deep into his eyes and drew close to him. Then he said, in a loud voice:

"And now get out, knight, I want to sleep!"

Philippe, having by now made his decision, took hold of the stiletto under his robe with no hesitation whatsoever, and held it at about waist height with its point towards the convict. He almost failed to notice when, in an instant and with no diffi-culty, Luigi buried his rotting flesh onto the point of the knife, exactly at the height of the heart, letting out a faint moan and biting his lips so as not to shout. Then, taking a step back, he lay on the floor and, looking at Philippe with complete gratitude, whispered to him:

"Thank you for putting me out of my misery. May God reward you! Goodbye!"

Then he closed his eyes and stayed still as if he was sleeping.

"He is sure to be dead in the next five minutes," Philippe thought and, putting the dagger under his robe, turned round and headed towards the exit. The strange thing was that he felt no remorse for his actions, only relief. He truly believed that in the end he had done what was right.

After that, he knocked on the door at the beginning of the corridor three times and the guard opened it straight away. While the latter was locking the door, Philippe told him:

"The convict I visited, Brother Luigi, is in the advanced stages of leprosy. I don't think he has many days to live."

The guard shrugged his shoulders while replacing the padlock.

"It doesn't matter. One mouth less to feed. He wouldn't live much longer in there anyway."

After washing himself thoroughly in a well, Philippe also went to Guillaume, who was on the walls, and told him about Luigi's condition. The Grand Master appeared sad for a moment, but did not show his feelings. He looked happy for some reason though, now unknown to Philippe. Foulques revealed it to him later, when he welcomed him at their meeting place with a warm smile..

"You are late! I have been waiting for you for some time now! Everything alright?" he asked him as soon as he saw him.

"I'll tell you," Philippe replied and sat on the ground, leaning back against the trunk of the cedar.

"I shall tell you first! This time I have very good news!"

The whole of Foulques's face shone. He was standing up and gesturing intently. His joy was clear.

"I'm all ears. Although I would have preferred it if you had waited a bit."

Philippe stood up, remembering that he had wanted to empty his bladder from the moment he had entered the jail, so he went a little further off and then sat back down at the same spot, more relaxed, and said to the Hospitaller:

"I'm ready to hear the good news."

"Help is coming from Acre!" Foulques said straight away, without delay.

"Seriously?"

Now it was Philippe's turn to be happy.

"King Henry of Cyprus himself left Cyprus by ship with a hundred horsemen, two thousand infantry and forty ships! He is arriving tomorrow!"

"That's why our Lord was so happy when I saw him before, now I understand!"

"The envoy came today. Also, Jean of Ancona, the Archbishop of Nicosia is joining him. His presence, together with that of the king, will definitely encourage the defenders of the city."

"Perhaps God has had mercy on us," Philippe commented happily.

"Now it's your turn. You have news too. I can understand it from the expression on your face. I'm listening."

Philippe told him about his visit to the prison, not telling him, however, about the fact that he had saved Luigi from more horror. Foulques heard what Philippe told him about how Luigi had discovered his secret with real interest. He didn't appear to be very sorry about his condition and the rest of the convicts since he was, by nature, stricter concerning matters of order and punishment and less emotional than the Knight Templar.

Also, Philippe did not reveal to him the existence of Fede Santa, which was actually the real reason why he and his father had stayed up all night then. He just told his friend that he had had an important conversation with Jocelyn that night about their common past. He didn't know if he would ever be able to share the serenity and peace of mind that his involvement in the organization had brought him, for which he was grateful, with the Hospitaller.

After a while, after the two knights had talked about all kinds of different subjects, they went their separate ways, with greater optimism for the future this once.

***

Dawn had brought in the seventh day of May a few hours ago now. A little cloudy and cold, it was a day that did not remind one of the spring but autumn, the sky constantly giving the impression a heavy downpour was going to follow. In the Patriarchate's great hall Jean de Grailly, Otto de Grandson, the three orders' Grand Masters and, of course, the king and his brother Amalric, met once more.

The meeting was deemed necessary since, much to the great distress of those defending the city, Henry's arrival, three days ago, had not appeared to tip the scale decisively in favour of the Christians, as everyone had hoped. On the contrary, it had become clear to everyone that there were too few reinforcements to prevent an outcome of the siege detrimental to the citizens of Acre, which, as the days went by, seemed more and more likely for the doomed city.

With no ideas left and no solutions in sight, and many towers on the walls brought to the verge of collapse by the Sultan's pioneers, those present finally agreed to Henry's proposal. They would try to persuade the Sultan to raise the siege and, in return, satisfy his every demand.

As Henry sat gracefully on his throne, wearing his golden crown and his luxurious cloak, he gave the impression of a mighty monarch with a plethora of territories and great power. The truth was, however, quite different, since Henry no longer had anything but the island of Cyprus and the last, pitiful remnants of the once huge Outremer, now Christian enclaves in a vast, Islamic territory now hostile towards them - the present city of Acre, Tyre, Sidon, Haifa and Beirut. Around him stood the rest of the men, forming a large semi-circle in front of the throne.

Guillaume de Beaujeu was talking now, putting forward the names of two of his own people to meet with the Sultan:

"I think that Guillaume de Cafran and Guillaume de Villiers are the most suitable for the mission. Besides having a perfect command of Arabic, they have both been members of the order for many years and have proved their worth on similar missions. They are also at an age that makes them accommodating and slow to anger. I don't think they will insult the Sultan, intentionally or unintentionally.

Henry listened to the Grand Master attentively, resting his right elbow on the arm of the throne and slowly stroking his beard. When Guillaume had finished putting forward those he was suggesting for the mission, the king put his other elbow on the left arm of the throne, leant towards the same side and, continuing to stroke his beard, said in a deep voice:

"They seem fine. Unless someone else has better candidates to suggest."

The king looked around at the faces of the rest of the people there, but no one looked as they had anything else to suggest.

"Alright then. The knights should be told of their mission straight away."

"When do you think they should visit the Sultan, my Lord?" Jean de Grailly asked respectfully.

"As soon as they have been informed of the mission. There is no time to waste."

***

181

A little later a white flag was raised near the Tower of the Legate, right on top of one of the central gates of the city. The Gate of St Anthony, was next to that of the French royal residence, and its great heavy doors were being opened carefully. When they had opened two Knights Templar appeared on horseback, one of whom also had a white flag. The two middle-aged knights waited for the drawbridge to come down over the moat and then brought their heels into their horses' sides so that they would set off. Voices were heard from the enemy camp opposite, and some movement could be discerned at once in the Sultan's tent, right opposite this gate.

On reaching the enemy camp, the two knights were welcomed and greeted in Arabic by one of the Sultan's trusted emirs, Emir al-Shuja'i. The two knights got off their horses and the emir announced to them that the Sultan would see them in a very short time.

Before a minute had passed, the flap of the tent was lifted and Al-Ashraf immediately appeared. He walked briskly, his face showing that he knew that he was in a position of superiority. The two knights noticed this immediately and exchanged a worried look as if to say to one another that things would not be very easy for them and the mission that had been assigned to them to carry out a difficult one.

The Sultan greeted them in his language and the knights responded to his greeting with a very respectful bow. Before, however, they could say a word, the Sultan abruptly asked them if they had brought the keys of the city. The two men looked at each other in panic and Guillaume de Villiers replied that they had not. Then Al-Ashraf began to talk again:

"In any case..."he said to them, spitting out the words one by one in Arabic, "I shall take back this city and I do not care about the fate of its inhabitants. If you surrender now, in recognition of your courageous king who came to fight, I shall spare the lives of the people of Acre.. Well?" The Sultan finished talking and folded his arms over his chest, waiting for the two knights' reply. He looked as if he was enjoying their discomfort, regarding them with a cold and, at the same time, sadistic expression. As the Sultan had foreseen, cold sweat started to bathe the two Knights Templar, as they asked for two minutes to confer before they gave an answer.

"If we promise to surrender the city, we shall be considered traitors by our people. We do not have such orders from our Lord Master," whispered Guillaume de Villiers to Guillaume de Cafran.

"You are right," he whispered back.

"So let's tell him the truth – that we do not have such orders."

"Alright then, let's get out of here as soon as possible."

Guillaume de Cafran, a barely perceptible tremor in his voice, told Al-Ashraf that if they promised to surrender at that moment, their people would be consider them traitors. Before he even had time to finish his sentence, a whistling sound came through the sky. Before everyone there had even realised what was actually happening, a huge rock landed right next to them. It brought up a huge cloud of dust into the air, without hitting anyone in the end.

The two knights froze, while the Sultan, enraged drew his sword from its scabbard and headed threateningly towards them saying:

"Here shall be your grave! You unfaithful dogs, do you mock me by supposedly coming here to surrender and then those on your side launch missiles to dispose of me? Now you shall see!"

The two Knights Templar had frozen on the spot, unable to defend themselves as they had come to the camp unarmed. Al-Ashraf had already raised his sword, ready to strike Guillaume de Cafran when the voice of Emir al-Shuja'i restrained him, literally at the last minute:

"Wait my Lord. It is not worth infecting your sword with these pigs' blood! Let them go! You will be able to take your revenge when the city is yours." The Sultan stood still, his sword in the air, pondering upon what the emir had said for some seconds, seconds that passed excruciatingly slowly for the knights. In the end, he cast them a glance full of contempt, put his sword back in its scabbard and said to them in a threatening voice:

"You can go back to your king and tell him that it would be better for him if I didn't find him alive in the city when I take it. Have I made myself clear?"

"Of course, my Lord," Guillaume de Villaret said straight away, his face regaining its normal colour and nodding to the other knight that it was time for them to go. The other Guillaume lowered his head for a second, bowing to the Sultan and the two knights headed towards their horses at once. As soon as they had mounted them they headed quickly towards the gate, under the eyes of their enemy, full of contempt.[86]

***

"Be careful, Brother!" Francois screamed so that he could be heard over the roar of the battle, making Philippe turn his head the last minute before an Arab soldier could kill him with a fatal blow. The Arab struck the air. Philippe took advantage of this and plunged his sword deep into the 'Infidel's' chest. Drops of warm blood sprayed the Knight Templar's face, before the eyes of the dying soldier opened wide and he fell to the ground dead. Straight away Philippe ran to help the Grand Master. He had been surrounded by the enemy, who he was putting to the sword with incredible energy, an open wound on his arm.

A little further off, at the Gate of St Anthony, which was under fierce attack, the mareschal of the Hospitallers, Matthew de Clermont, was fighting just as bravely. He was helping his Grand Master, the tireless Foulques and his uncle at his side. It was only when night started to fall that the Muslims, who had been repelled thanks to the Hospitaller and Knights Templars' bravery, abandoned their efforts to take the city for the day. Those defending the city had retreated to the inner line of walls that morning as the collapse of the walls was rapidly being brought about by the Sultan's catapults from above and undermining from below.

Almost ten days had passed since the Christians' unsuccessful attempt to negotiate a truce. No one had yet found out who had launched the rock into the Muslim camp at the most critical moment, putting the life of the Templar envoys at risk. Thus, the 'Infidels' had continued to besiege the city, and the walls were caving in

more and more, making things harder and harder for the Christians.

A week before the attack at the Gate of St Anthony, the Christians had decided that they could no longer hold the Tower of King Hugh, so they set it on fire and allowed it to collapse. Then it was the turn of the Tower of the English and the Tower of the Countess of Blois to be undermined. Not only the walls near the Gate of St Anthony, where today's attack had taken place, but also the walls near the Tower of St Nicholas had already begun to collapse. Despite their retreat to the inner wall, those defending the city had won the battle that day, but what would happen the next?

When all their enemies had been successfully repelled, Philippe fell with his face to the ground and remained there, exhausted, feeling unable to make any kind of movement. His muscles refused to obey after so many hours of tireless effort. The knight had his eyes closed but he felt a shadow over him. He lifted his head with difficulty, still on the ground, and saw his father offering him a waterskin. He took it from Jocelyn's hands at once and drank from it thirstily.

Because of his age, Jocelyn had taken up auxiliary work, such as carrying water or rocks on the field of battle, or taking the injured to the hospital.

"Congratulations my son. Today you fought truly bravely!" he said to his son, looking at him with pride."

"Thank you, but I don't think I'll be up to doing it again," replied Philippe with a tired smile, handing the water to another knight who had come up to them.

"Unfortunately, I doubt it if any us will be up to doing it again. The hospital is full, as, of course, is the one belonging to the Hospitallers, and the doctors don't know who to save first. I go to help as much as I can too. You rest. I am sure tomorrow will see a new attack so it is very important to relax a little now and get some sleep."

Philippe nodded in agreement and put his head back to the ground. He stank of urine, sweat and blood, mixed with the smell of soil, from miles away, and it disgusted him. He wished he could close his nostrils to those horrible smells, his eyes to those terrible scenes of men with limbs cut off, and his ears to the cries of the wounded.

He was glad, however, that in all this, he had his father with him. Without him by his side he was certain that he would not feel as strong. Eventually, he was able to fall asleep there. It was a disturbed sleep, full of nightmares. Philippe did not know, but this was to be the last time he would sleep in Acre and the last night that Acre was to be in Christian hands.

20

Acre, May 18, 1291

he darkness was still thick when those few defending the city relieved the watch and took their places on the walls after troubled sleep, fully prepared for the bloodbath that everyone knew would ensue as soon as dawn broke. The Christians had been told by their spies in the 'Infidel' camps that the Sultan would order a general assault that day, and they had ensured that they were as well- prepared as possible to ward off the attack.

Philippe, who had just woken up and was already feeling tired, despite the fact that he had managed to sleep for five hours on his mattress, tried to stifle one yawn after the other and stay calm, taking up his usual post on the walls of Montmusart.

The night before he had been woken from his troubled sleep at the Gate of St Anthony by a visit from Guillaume. He had talked to the Grand Master for some time, and was informed that Luigi had been found dead in prison, his death brought on by the advanced stages of leprosy. Philippe had listened to this piece of news calmly and his reaction had, in no way, betrayed any involvement of his in Luigi's death.

In fact, the Grand Master had told him that Luigi's death had gone completely unnoticed, until a young man discovered to have been the traitor only the day before had been led to the prison. It was he who had quite deliberately launched the projectile when the two Knights Templar were discussing peace with the Sultan.

When the envoys had returned to Acre, they had demanded that the fool who, through this reckless act, had almost got them killed be found. Soldiers, after laborious investigation and ten days of thorough research, had arrested a young member of laity. He had claimed that he was trying , through this act, to save the city, intending to kill the Sultan with the huge rock.

However, his explanation convinced neither of the two Guillaumes, nor their superiors. So the young man was taken to Acre's hell-hole of a prison, where the guards, in the course of their attempts to find somewhere to put their new inmate, had come across Luigi's body, which had by now begun to rot.

The Grand Master, in the end, had also congratulated Philippe on the bravery he had shown in battle and had wished him good luck.

When Philippe said goodbye to Guillaume a strange sense of melancholy came over him. Something inside him told him that this was to be his last conversation with the Grand Master. As for Foulques, he hadn't seen him face to face in days, since an increase in their duties had forced the two friends to devote whatever time they were not fighting to rest.

The chilling sound of an arrow speeding through the air, suddenly piercing the dirt next to Philippe, instantly roused the knight from his thoughts. In that instant all his senses were at the ready. He grasped his sword, lying a little further off, tightly and made sure he was covered well behind the arrow slit in the wall. Dozens of other men over the whole of Acre did this at the same time.

The faint morning light had begun, timidly, to appear and Philippe was able to see hundreds of men attacking the walls along their whole length, letting out horrifying cries and holding their scimitars above their heads, as far as he could see.

"Men! Make ready! With God's help victory can be ours!" Guillaume's penetrating voice rang out and the exact same moment, the ground began to shake from the drums and cymbals of the enemy which the Sultan had ordered to be played throughout the attack to embolden the 'Infidel'. This was soon followed by the horrifying sound of the projectiles raining down on the already crumbling walls.

It soon became evident that, despite the Christians huge losses and the resulting lack of men, the attackers were being repulsed successfully, although with great difficulty, along the whole length of the walls, except in one spot where the 'Infidels' were carrying out their main attack and had put the largest number of soldiers: the Accursed Tower. It was only a matter of time before the Mamluks broke through there.

Soon the first attacker was climbing the walls, followed by another three, who the Christians did not manage to repulse. Syrians and Cypriot Franks made up the garrison in Tower. There were too few of them to be able to withstand the enemy's strong attack. So the garrison was driven back to the Gate of St Anthony, which once more became the scene of fierce fighting. When King Henry's brother, Amalric, saw how desperate the situation they had found themselves in was, he called on the members of orders to help.

Indeed, the knights from the two great orders ran there straight away, and found themselves fighting as if they were only one order, as if there hadn't been so many years of fierce antagonism between them. It was thanks to this that Foulques found himself fighting side by side with Philippe.

"Men! Everyone follow me! We shall take the Tower back!" screamed the mareschal of the Hospitallers, Matthew de Clermont. and the knights from both orders, together with the two Grand Masters, followed him, united in one last effort. The area around the Accursed Tower became a blue and white sea of men, wearing red and white cloaks and shiny armour, desperately trying to stop their enemy, huge in number.

However, the counterattack failed. There were already too many of the enemy to repulse, even by such good fighters as the knights of the orders.

Thus Acre had now been taken and her struggle was coming to its end. However, the great bloodbath that was about to follow had yet to take place. At the eastern wall,

Otto de Grandson and Jean de Grailly held their positions for a few more hours after the Accursed Tower fell. They were soon surrounded by the enemy, who had now taken the whole length of the walls, and were entering the city itself.

In the general chaos, the two friends continued to fight, tireless, next to their Grand Masters. The end to this, meaningless by now, bloodshed, came when Guillaume himself was wounded. Philippe saw the mamluk who was aiming at the Grand Master's back but had no time to do anything. Guillaume was fighting with a ferocious mamluk, who thrust a scimitar deep into his back and then drew it out suddenly. He let out a horrifying cry of pain and then fell to the ground in a pool of blood. Philippe and the other Knights Templar ran quickly to their dying Grand Master and some of them took him to one of buildings belonging to the Order, where he died almost instantly.

The Templar and Hospitaller knights were left numb after Guillaume's fatal wound. Foulques' uncle, together with some other Hospitallers, decided not to let their Grand Master meet the same end. When Jean received a slight wound to his arm, his knights, despite his loud protestations, took him to the harbour, where they put him on one of the ships that had begun to depart from the city, now given up to the enemy.

Philippe continued undaunted to spread death amongst his enemies, as did Foulques. Many other knights from both orders were also determined not to give up the fight, despite the fact that it was clearly hopeless. Philippe had successfully fended off an attack by two slender mamluks when he heard Francois, who had been keeping up the fight nearby, despite having been hit by an arrow, still stuck into his shoulder, call his name:

"Philippe! Come quickly!"

Without a second's thought, Philippe ran behind the rock from which he had heard his friend's voice. He was certain that Francois needed his help to face some enemy. This was why he was completely unprepared for what he saw when he rounded the rock. It was not Francois surrounded by enemy soldiers that he saw, but his father on the ground in a pool of blood, with Francois over him, comforting him. Philippe bent down over Jocelyn at once. His eyes quickly fell on his father's chest, where, at lung height, there was a deep wound from which heavy bleeding was sapping the life out of the old man. Besides this, however, it was clear that the wounded old man was having difficulty breathing, since the scimitar that had pierced him had gone deep into his lungs.

The young man's face was masked with pain. He bit his lower lip hard, making it bleed, in an attempt to choke back the sobs he felt rising up in him since it was patently clear that Jocelyn had but a few more minutes to live.

"Why?" was the only word he could say.

Jocelyn looked with glazed eyes at his son, kneeling over him. He brought his bloody hand to Philippe's chest and, gathering his last few ounces of strength, said to him in a hoarse voice:

"Never mind... I...have lived my life... But you, do me the favour of saving yourself... Leave! Please..."

The elderly man could say nothing more. Jocelyn's hand simply fell to the ground from Philippe's chest, and his eyes remained fixed on what he had loved most in his life on earth – his only son.

Philippe, no longer able to hold back his tears, now running down his cheeks, closed his father's eyes gently with the tips of his fingers, forgetting the chaos around him for a moment and whispering:

"Goodbye, Father. Farewell."

It was Francois' hand, who had been standing a little further off while Philippe was saying goodbye to Jocelyn, keeping an eye open for any attack against them, that the knight felt on his shoulder, bringing him back to reality. People were running up and down in panic, knights were still fighting and some of the 'Infidels' had already begun looting.

"I am sorry to break in at a moment like this," Francois said softly, "but things are getting worse. If you want to satisfy your father's last wish, you must leave his body here and we should go to the harbour at once. The last available ship is sure to vanish soon."

As much as he did not want to, Philippe knew that, if he wanted to live, he had to leave his father's body there, much to his grief, unburied, and leave Acre straight away. It was one of the few times in his life that Philippe decided to give precedence to logic over emotion. It seemed, however, that the instinct to survive proved to be, in the end, stronger than anything else in life. So, with a heavy heart, the young Knight Templar closed his father's eyelids with his fingertips and, choking back one last sob, stood up, saying goodbye one last time to his father.

"Goodbye again. We shall meet again one day."

Francois stood waiting behind Philippe, looking around him nervously, appearing more and more impatient to leave. And it proved to be for good reason.

At the exact moment, when the two young men were about to set off running towards the harbour, three middle-aged Arabs came up to them holding their scimitars menacingly. The two knights, however, relatively rested by the brief respite that saying goodbye to Jocelyn had given them, made short work of them, killing two and seeing off the third, who ran away to look for easier prey.

Philippe then immediately took the arrow out of Francois' shoulder - relatively painlessly as, fortunately, it had not gone in too deep. He bound the wound as tightly as he could, and the two knights set off for the harbour, their swords always at the ready to face any possible danger. On their way to safety they often had to show disregard for the Christians being slaughtered around them, knowing that if they helped everyone who needed help they would never leave the city themselves.

When, however, the two knights came upon three children curled up in a hole in the walls and literally shaking from fear, they couldn't prevent themselves stopping and exchanging looks heavy with meaning and compassion. There were two boys around ten years old, and a girl with fair hair who was a lot younger and looked like an angel, although her eyes were red from crying.

Without saying a single word to each other and having reached agreement only by exchanging looks, the two knights went up to the children and Francois, taking the little girl in his arms, said to the two boys:

"Follow us quickly if you want to live."

The two little boys, obviously trusting those two older armed men wearing armour, obediently followed them straight away, holding back their sobs. As the group got nearer to the harbour, things became more and more dangerous, and fights to the death between members of the laity and 'Infidels' more and more frequent. The two knights were attacked more often. They had the children with them, and the 'Infidels' eyed them up as spoils of war for the slave trade. Fortunately, however, they warded off all such attacks with success.

They had now reached the top of the sea walls and were now ready to start their descent towards the ships when Philippe suddenly caught sight of Foulques through a crenel in the fortifications. The Hospitaller was now fighting completely alone, since everyone else around him had either left or been killed, against three hefty mamluks. He was fending them off with great agility. His red robe with its white cross was torn, while blood covered the whole of his left arm, from which the shaft of an arrow was sticking out. This time the scales in Philippe's psyche tipped in favour of his heart. So, without any further thought, he said at once, leaving the astonished Francois no room for disagreement:

"You go on. I will follow shortly," and he ran towards the injured Hospitaller at once. He arrived at the very moment when one of the three mamluks, unnoticed by Foulques, was about to plunge his scimitar deep into knight's back from behind.

At literally the last moment, before the deadly weapon had touched Foulques skin, the Templar leapt with a shout in front of the surprised mamluk and ran him through the heart with his sword. It caused him to fall back with horror etched into eyes wide with surprise at Philippe's intervention and take, almost instantly, his last breath.

Foulques was surprised but, realizing what would had happened to him if Philippe hadn't interfered, smiled at him in gratitude. Then, wasting no time, he quickly took advantage of the other two terrified mamluks' shock at the sight of their comrade's demise. He struck one of the two on the shoulder with his sword, the second one on the leg. Wounded and aware that they now had to fight two knights, they thought it better to leave straight away rather than risk their lives. Foulques then looked Philippe in the eye and said:

"You have saved my life once again."

"And if you wish me to do it again in the future you must follow me straight away to the ships," Philippe replied gravely, looking at his friend's injured arm. He then asked Foulques to keep still, and quickly pulled the arrow out of his arm, making the injured knight scream in pain. Tearing off a piece of his already ruined shirt, he bound the wound quickly so as to stop the bleeding. When he saw that the Hospitaller was reluctant to leave, Philippe went on, without taking a breath, in an even more serious tone of voice , trying at the same time to sound convincing:

"Brother, I will not leave you here to throw your life away for no good reason. If God has kept you alive until now, it means you have much more to offer your order. Our Lord Master is already dead. But I think yours is alive and I am sure that in the future he will be delighted to accept the services of such a very brave knight as you."

Seeing that the Hospitaller had now been convinced, he added:

"And your uncle, who is now, if I'm not mistaken, safe with your Lord Master, will be certainly very pleased to see you alive. Shall we then?"

"Let's go!" said Foulques looking at the carnage around him with inexpressible sadness before he ran after Philippe towards the ships. "It is true," he thought. "The city has fallen. Any resistance is now futile."

On reaching the dock, the knights were witness to frenzied scenes. Elderly people, women with bawling children in their arms were trying to fit into small rowing boats, and men of every sort, civilians and soldiers, were trying to reach the ships, and, consequently, salvation, in any way possible.

The two friends, in horror, watched in horror as the boat of the elderly patriarch Nicolas, packed with refugees which he had been putting on it himself for some time now out of compassion, was unable to bear the weight of so many souls and sank, taking almost everyone on board into the arms of Death. A little further off, a Catalan adventurer Roger de Flor, who had fought bravely as a Knight Templar throughout the duration of the siege, had taken over a galley and was getting rich by offering salvation to the noble women of Acre for considerable amounts of money.

Philippe quickly scanned the ships and boats, looking for Francois. He had begun to feel desperate when he finally spotted the fair-haired knight in a boat, together with the children, heading towards a Venetian ship. The boat was half empty and was not yet very far from the shore. Francois, standing up in the boat, had also spotted Philippe and was gesturing to him to swim to the boat.

Without a second thought, Philippe said to Foulques:

"Will you manage, wounded as you are, to swim to the boat? I will also help you as much as I can."

Foulques looked at some armed Muslims who appeared to be slowly coming towards them and said:

"I must. From what it seems, I have no choice."

With swift movements the two knights quickly helped one another take their armour off and dived into the water straight away, leaving their heavy swords and all their equipment on the shore. With a little help from Philippe, Foulques also managed to reach the boat, which Francois and his men helped them board. The fair haired angel that Philippe had saved before with Francois was sitting next to him in the boat and she gave Philippe a beautiful smile, showing him, in this way, how happy she was to see him again.

When they boarded the ship, the three knights noticed that king Henry himself and his brother Amalric were on board and that they were very lucky to have been saved, since there had really been far too few ships to save all those fleeing the city.

Indeed, the slaughter was great, but so was the number of Christians sold into slavery in the East. No one was able to calculate the number of the dead nor the prisoners, but in the next days the price of girls in the slave markets of Damascus was to fall again by one dirham, because of the abundant supply.

And so the three knights remained, despondent, on the ship's deck as it sailed away, to watch, in dejection, the sad fall of the last major city of the once great Outremer, as it slowly disappeared below the horizon.

"Farewell Calpurnia! Goodbye the East!" Philippe whispered leaning on the gunwale, saying goodbye to the land in which he had spent the best years of his life.

He hoped his beloved horse, which he had been forced to leave behind, as had of course many other knights, would find a good owner. He bade farewell to his Brothers, the Grand Master and his beloved father, who had died in Acre, one more time... Now that the stress of the battle had passed and Philippe had now reached safety, there was no reason to hold back his feelings. He started crying silently, his eyes fixed on the shore, receding further into the distance..

Next to him Foulques and Francois were experiencing similar feelings. In defeat, the knights had absolutely no idea what the future held, nor what they would do in life from now on. For they had lost the purpose for which they had been nurtured to serve with courage for so many years now: the defence of the Holy Lands, where the one they knew as Christ was said to have lived and grown up.

The day Acre fell, it seemed as if the Muslims, after bloody conflict, would at last drive the invaders who had, for many years, caused havoc and destruction, off their land. For the time being, Allah had won, but the Christians thought this was a temporary victory. It would take another twelve years for them to understand that their hopes were forlorn, at least as far as the recovery of the Holy Lands was concerned.

21

Knights Templar fortress, Isle of Ruad, January 15, 1303

he sun had almost sunk into the calm sea, allowing the black veil of the night to slowly cover the tiny island that was two miles from the shore of what used to be Outremer, right opposite Tortosa.

Philippe, who was on guard duty that night, had just taken his place on the southern edge of the walls. He was rubbing his hands, trying to warm himself up, as around him a strong ice-cold howled, causing waves to batter against the castle walls.

In the twelve years that had passed since Acre had been lost, the once mighty knight seemed to have suddenly aged. In two years' time he would reach the age of fifty. The first streaks of grey had appeared in his hair and around his eyes the first wrinkles had begun to form.

Even so, Philippe would not have looked his age had it not been for the dull and vacant expression fixed on his face. It showed so clearly that he had given up on life, an attitude that had completely engulfed him these last few years. The now middle-aged knight had knelt down on the ground and begun to pick the sparse grass that grew there and throw it around. For the thousandth time he wondered what on earth he was doing on that dry island and begged God to take him unto Himself quickly so that he would escape the tedium of his life as soon as possible.

A deep sigh issued from his lips and his mind filled once more with pictures from the past, from that terrible May of 1291, the scenes of the siege, the occupation of the city and everything that had followed. Philippe had heard this later from survivors and travellers who had witnessed it, and had passed through on their way to Cyprus.

On that night of 18th May, when he himself, Francois and Foulques had managed to leave Acre by sea, Al-Ashraf had made his triumphant entry into the ruined city. The whole of it was now in his hands, except for the headquarters of the Knights

Templar, protruding out into the sea and on the southwestern side of the city.

Many of the Knights Templar, together with civilians, men and women, had taken refuge there and held out bravely against the Mamluks for one more week after the the rest of the city had been taken. In charge of its defence was Pierre de Sevrey, the mareschal of the Temple. After a week , Al-Ashraf, wanting to avoid further losses to his forces, made his proposal to Pierre. Those defending the fortress would be given free passage to Cyprus in exchange for the fortress that he needed to complete his conquest of the city. Those defending it, knowing that any further sacrifice was absolutely pointless, agreed.

When, however, one hundred mamluks entered the fortress with an emir in charge to make sure that the terms agreed were followed, they gave into their desires and began to lay hands on the Christians, despite what had been agreed. Outraged, the knights fell upon them and, after they had put them all to the sword without mercy, prepared to defend themselves to the death.

In the meantime Pierre had managed to send the treasure of the Order to Sidon, together with a few non-combatants and Thibaud Gaudin, later Grand Master of the Order. The Sultan, not knowing what else to do, put forward the same terms again and Pierre came out the fortress together with a few men, with the assurance that they would not be touched, to talk about the terms of the surrender. As soon as they reached the Sultan's tent, the poor knights were seized and beheaded.

After that the rest of the knights locked themselves in the fortress again and continued their desperate battle until the Sultan's pioneers managed to undermine the fortress from underground. In the end, while the battle for it was in progress, the fortress collapsed on those attacking and those defending it alike, thus playing out the final act in the drama of Acre.

The end of the tragic story was the Sultan's decision to destroy Acre completely so that the city would never become a spearhead in the future for any new Christian attacks on Syria.

And so its once bustling markets and houses were laid waste, the proud buildings belonging to the Orders torched and the sturdy towers that surrounded the city left to crumble. Decades later, only the church of Saint Andrew would remain standing in the city, as did the tomb of the Dominican Jordan of Saxony, who was saved from the Muslims' wrath because his body had been found perfectly preserved. Only some ragged peasants roamed about amongst the ruins.

Tyre had been given up to Al-Ashraf without a fight by Adam de Cafran, the bailli of the city who had lost his nerve when he saw the Sultan's mighty army outside the walls of the city. In Sidon the surviving Knights Templar elected Thibaud Gaudin as their new Grand Master and fought bravely, before they realised that further resistance was futile, abandoned the city to Emir Shujai, and sailed to Tortosa. Beirut and Haifa suffered the same fate and were handed over almost without a fight, as were the Templar fortresses of Tortosa and Atlit, evacuated so that meaningless losses would be avoided.

Philippe himself had left his friends amidst a sorrowful atmosphere in Famagusta, Cyprus. Only a few months after the fall of Acre, Thibaud had chosen him, together with other knights and sergeants, to be one of the members of the guard on the island of Ruad, which the Christians aimed to use as a base for later attempts to reconquer Outremer. Philippe had not seen his friends again since then, but he had learnt that Foulques, like all the other Hospitallers, had remained in Cyprus, while Francois had gone to Paris.

So years without purpose had passed by on this dry island for Philippe, who, having lost his father, and with his two closest friends far away, sank deeper and deeper into depression.

In 1293 Thibaud passed away and a new Grand Master had been elected, Jacques de Molay, a brave man but one with average capabilities, Philippe had heard, and without the insight and imagination these difficult times for the order demanded.

Philippe was so absorbed in his thoughts that he completely failed to hear the steps coming towards him from behind. They were those of Brother Armand, one the closest advisors to the commander of the castle, Hughes d'Empuries, who had fought in Sidon before it finally fell to the Muslims.

"Brother?" the muscular, skinny man said in his soft, silky voice to Philippe, who turned around, surprised.

"Oh it's you Brother Armand! I must say you gave me a fright!"

"I realised that! You looked very absorbed in your thoughts. What were you thinking, if I may ask?"

"Nothing in particular. I was just thinking back over the unfortunate events of the past years. I'm trying to get over my boredom and sadness."

"As are we all."

Armand shrugged his shoulders and continued to talk, allowing a faint smile to show on his face:

"Then you will probably be happy with the news I am bringing you. Our superiors have decided that knights that fought in Acre, are over forty years old and have been in the Holy Lands for more than fifteen years, are to go to Limassol to serve our order from there from now on."

Philippe remained thoughtful for a while, pondering Armand's words. Then, with a voice that showed neither happiness nor sorrow, but only surprise, he asked:

"I see. And why is that? I thought that our order wishes to keep as many soldiers on this island as possible."

"Yes, that's true since there is always the hope that the island can be used as a bridgehead for the opposite shore. But the young knights who came to Ruad the year before last will suffice when it comes to such a campaign, and, most importantly, are full of energy and desire to fight the Infidel. We, however, are old and have become tired by now, and have no appetite for anything. I'm afraid we won't be very good fighters in battles to come! Am I wrong?"

A sad smile crossed Philippe's face.

"No. It's just sometimes I forget how much I have aged! Aren't you leaving?"

Armand smiled in his turn and said:

"I, Brother, am thirty eight years old and, besides, I would not leave without Hughes. He is in need of my help and, as you know, he considers me his right hand here. The young knight gently patted Philippe's shoulder and went on:

"So go get your things ready then, I'll stay on watch. The ship that will transfer you to Limassol will leave at dawn. Goodbye Brother!"

"Have courage Brother Armand! Farewell!" Philippe responded, saying goodbye to him, and headed towards his dormitory to pack his things, not knowing whether he should be pleased or not about this sudden piece of news.

As he walked in the half light of the moon, which had just risen, he turned and looked at Armand, who was standing with his eyes fixed on the stormy sea, in defiance of the cold wind. Without knowing why, he had a strange intuition, like the one he had had when Acre had fallen, that he would not see him again and, involuntarily, shuddered. Trying to put these thoughts out of his head, he turned his mind to the next day's journey. "At least I will be able to see Foulques," he thought to himself and felt, for the first time in some years, somewhat happy at this prospect.

He reached the entrance to the dormitory but stopped outside when he saw light in Hughes' office, and thought he would go to say goodbye to him. As he lifted his hand to knock on the wooden door, a genuine smile finally lit up his face as he was thought of his new life. His mood now having completely changed, he silently thanked God for this gift to him.

22

Limassol, Cyprus, Templar Headquarters, January 16, 1303

he Venetian ship taking Philippe and the other veteran Knights Templar to Limassol was about to dock in the harbour of the ancient city. It was late in the afternoon, but Philippe did not feel at all tired, despite the fact that he had been travelling since the morning. He had never felt so happy and optimistic since the fall of Acre. He was standing and gently leaning against the gunwale of the ship and, like other passengers around him, admiring the island of Venus, which in comparison to the dry barren desert and parched earth to which he had got used all these years, seemed very green to him.

This city seemed to him quite different from Famagusta, where most ships had gone after the Fall of Acre since it was the closest city to former Outremer. He let his eyes wander around the abundant vineyards on the outskirts of the city, the rich, well-built aristocratic houses in its centre, but also the strong fortifications that surrounded it. There were also many, mainly Orthodox since the vast majority of the island's inhabitants were Greek Orthodox, churches and monasteries scattered about, as far as the eye could see.

Philippe's eyes also wandered to the great castle in which he would spend his days from now on. The castle was of Byzantine style and had been built in 1193. Philippe looked at the other castle that towered over Limassol, on the outskirts of the city, the Kolossi, in which the rivals of his order, the Knights Hospitaller ,were temporarily based, It had been built by Frankish conquerors some years earlier. "That's where Foulques must be," thought Philippe and, absorbed in these beautiful images as he was, it took him some time to realise that he was the only one left on deck, since the ship had now docked and disembarkation had almost come to an end.

He stepped off the ship quickly, jumping cat-like onto the mole and headed towards his comrades who had gathered a little further off. They were listening to the Knight Templar who was to take them to the castle. He was a relatively young, curly-haired knight with sparkling grey-green eyes.

"Welcome to Limassol my Brothers. I am Brother Ponsard, from Gizy. Follow me to our castle where I will present our commander to you, Ayme de Osiliers." The knights started walking around Ponsard in silence. One of them, Geoffroy de Gonneville suddenly asked Ponsard:

"Brother Ponsard, is our Lord Master, Jacques de Molay, here in Limassol?"

"No, Brother, he is in Paris at this time, but he will be coming back to Cyprus soon. Three years after the fall of Acre, he began a grand tour to recruit people to our order and to try to convince monarchs to support a new crusade. He travelled to the Papal States, and the whole of France and England, where he spoke with King Edward."

Geoffroy nodded.

"We heard this while we were in Ruad but we heard nothing about whether his efforts met with any success."

Ponsard's expression turned sad before he spoke:

"Bad news of this kind does not travel quickly. That is why you heard nothing. Besides some vague promises of an armed campaign in former Outremer, things are not going very well for our order. Here on the island the locals really dislike us, as you shall soon realise for yourselves. In the West most people believe there is no reason for our existence if we do not manage to recover the Holy Lands, and that, sadly, is impossible at this moment."

The knight spoke no more and everyone remained silent, considering what he had said. Philippe thought that Ponsard must be right, judging by the poisonous looks all the locals they had met on their way had thrown at them. Soon they reached the castle gates, which were wide open to welcome the veterans from the East. There the rest of the Templars Brothers welcomed the travellers with genuine delight.

***

The next day, in the morning, after breakfast and attending Mass, all the new arrivals having properly settled in, Philippe, with permission from commander Ayme, saddled his new horse and went out for a trot in the city. It was sunny and, although it was winter, not very cold. His new horse, named Pilgrim, was bright white with a grey mane and had belonged to a knight that had been sent to Ruad. Philippe stroked it lovingly before they set off so that they would get used to one another. Deep down, however, he missed Calpurnia, who he had been forced to leave behind in Acre.

"I hope she is in good hands at least," he thought.

All the knights had the right to go out now and again, but Philippe did not simply intend to simply wander around the city. He wanted to go to Kolossi and see Foulques, from whom he had had no news since he had left Famagusta. He wanted to let him know that he too was now in Limassol, hoping that it would be possible for them to see one another now and again, although with the expulsion of the Christians from the Holy Lands, the hatred and competition between the two orders had grown. Their common goal now lost, both were trying to survive as best they could in times that were so difficult for the military orders.

Philippe urged his horse to trot on slowly towards the Hospitaller's castle, which could be seen in the distance. Pilgrim, obedient and quite fast, immediately responded to his new owner's commands. As he was riding, the Knight Templar brought to mind images of the previous day, filled with new ones.

Ayme de Osiliers, the commander of the castle, had welcomed them cordially, but the truth was that he had conveyed no optimism to him as far as the future of the order was concerned. He had told them a little about the political situation on the island and the Mediterranean and, after that, a Brother sergeant had given them horses and showed them their dormitories in the spacious Byzantine castle. After Vespers and dinner, Philippe had fallen into a sleep that was peaceful and deep, something he had never experienced while he was in Ruad.

Philippe had almost reached the entrance to the castle, which was guarded by two young sergeants. Philippe dismounted, tied Pilgrim to a tree and went up to the guards. Before he had time to say good morning to them, the younger of the two, after throwing a look full of contempt at the red cross embroidered on his robe, said to him:

"What do you want here Templar? Your people are not in this castle! On your way!"

Philippe, who had been prepared for a cold but not quite such an inhospitable welcome, remained frozen to the spot, not knowing what he could say to the guards to let him enter the castle or call Foulques themselves.

While he was thinking what to do, the heavy, dark brown door opened from the inside loudly and a man on a big black horse appeared. He was wearing the usual black robe[87] with the white cross that the Hospitallers wore in times of peace[88] but, from the two guards' reaction, who at once humbly bowed their heads, one could easily understand that this was the Grand Master of the Hospitallers.

Philippe fixed his eyes on the Grand Master's face and smiled faintly when he realised who was before him. The man, after saluting the two guards, looked in his turn at the knight standing opposite him and at once shouted, smiling and getting off his horse to go up to the person he was addressing.

"Brother Philippe! I'm so happy to see you again!"

Guillaume de Villaret went up Philippe and gave him a paternal hug around the shoulders.

"I'm very happy too my Lord! Am I mistaken to call you this or have I guessed correctly?"

"You have! I have the joy of having served my order as Lord Master for about eight years now. Where are you?"

"I have just come from the Isle of Ruad. From now on I shall be in our castle here in Cyprus."

Guillaume laughed again and put his hand on Philippe's right shoulder said:

"The man who saved Foulques! I don't know how to thank you for getting him out of that hell in Acre! If it weren't for you I would not be enjoying the wonderful service he is giving our order as a mareschal!"

He paused a little to take a breath and continued:

"My nephew will be very pleased to see you! Shall I assume that that is the reason why you have come here?"

"Yes, but if you hadn't happened to come out my Lord, I don't think I would have achieved my purpose! I received a rather cold welcome," Philippe replied, looking sideways at the two guards who, having watched the scene in surprise all this time, now at once bowed their heads, looking at the ground.

Guillaume turned to them straight away and said to them sternly:

"This eternal hatred! How much wrong would have been avoided if it did not exist! However much rivalry and competition there might be between us, it doesn't mean that we must avoid all contact!"

He then turned to Philippe:

"I've been saying these things for years but no one listens to me! A voice of one shouting in the wilderness! What can one say?"

Then he went to his horse and, mounting it, added, still giving the guards a stern look:

"Tell the mareschal at once to come to the entrance!"

Then he turned to the Knight Templar:

"The best thing for both of you would be to talk to each other outside at your leisure."

He took hold of the reins and after the horse had already set off, said goodbye to Philippe, raising his hand:

"You must excuse me. Unfinished business! It was very good to see you, Brother, come whenever you want!"

"I was very happy to see you too and thank you!" Philippe replied, also raising his hand up as a gesture of farewell.

It wasn't long until a guard appeared, followed by Foulques.

The years Foulques had spent in the East seemed to have made him more mature and stronger. His bearing had acquired newfound determination and maturity – unlike Philippe who gave the impression of a man that was mentally and physically tired. Of course, time had also left its marks on the Hospitaller knight's face, but the Hospitaller appeared ten years younger, even though he was the same age as the Knight Templar. The fact that his hair remained black, although it had thinned a little, played an important role in this.

As soon as a surprised Foulques saw Philippe, he smiled broadly and ran to embrace him, saying in a voice that revealed the strength of his feelings:

"Brother! You're here? I did not expect to see you again, to tell you the truth!"

Philippe hugged the Hospitaller tenderly and answered him in a voice that shook with joy at seeing his friend, like a brother to him, again.

"It looks like you won't get rid of me that easily!"

"I hope not! I would never want that!" Foulques said, laughing, taking him by the shoulders and indicating the road ahead:

"Shall we walk while we talk? It's such a lovely day!"

Philippe nodded and Foulques turned to the two guards:

"Give hay and water to Brother Philippe's horse and keep an eye on it until we return!"

"Yes, sir," the older of the two replied dutifully and ran off to do what he had been ordered.

The two friends began to walk along a dirt path. Foulques was the one who spoke first, after a short pause:

"So, tell me your news. Will you be in Cyprus from now on?"

"Yes," replied Philippe and added, growing serious:

"The years on Ruad were truly awful. A monotonous life on a barren dry island. I am very glad I came here. But tell me your news. I saw that your uncle has become Lord Master, and he told me about you. How is life here with your new duties?"

Foulques nodded, a little discontentedly.

"Don't think that it hasn't been difficult for all of us. We are still working things out. For the time being we are fulfilling our role as infirmarians and, in this way, to a certain extent, keeping those who would have us crucified for the loss of Outremer quiet. I imagine that for you, since you do not have that role, it must be more difficult to adjust."

"Unfortunately, that is so. Anyway, I heard recently that the Teutonic knights have, for the time being, settled in Venice."

"Yes, and if you want my opinion, I think that their Grand Master, Siegfried von Feuchtwangen, is handling the situation better than all of us. Reliable sources tell me that he is gradually turning focus north to the Baltic, to Livonia to be precise, which is teeming with Pagans."

A cart full of wood went past them, driven by a villager, who looked at them askance. Philippe noticed this out of the corner of his eye and replied:

"A smart move on his part. They have found an immediate objective, something that we lack at the moment. Of course they have been active there for almost a century, which is why they never had so many people as we had in Outremer."

"And that is why, after all, they have been left out of the different proposals that have recently been made as far as merging our orders is concerned. Have you heard about this?"

Philippe looked at Foulques in surprise and stopped walking:

"No, never. A merger of the orders?"

He indicated the shade under a big olive tree and then walked in front of Foulques to sit in it. The Hospitaller followed him and sat next to him, continuing, however, to talk:

"The mystic writer Ramon Llull[89] first put forward the idea , before the fall of Acre, at the Council of Lyons[90], although King Louis the Saint gave birth to it. I also know that Llull presented his ideas to the current king of France, Philippe. You know this is something that would probably have taken place if today's Pope Boniface had shown the same interest in this merger as his predecessor Gregory, who was in Lyons."

"So do you think anything of this sort could happen?" Philippe asked, interrupting the Hospitaller.

Foulques shook his head:

"To be honest, I don't believe it could, and I think that neither our order nor yours would want it to. That, of course, does not mean that, deep down, the idea is not a good one."

Philippe made a grimace and a vague bored movement with his hand, changing the subject:

"Let's talk about something lighter I am sick and tired of talking about the bleak future. This uncertainty has worn me out." Foulques jumped up and pulled his sword from its scabbard, cutting the air.

"Come on, for old times' sake!"

Philippe stood up too, smiling broadly and, after taking his sword out too, stuck it with its point into the ground and leaned his right hand on it.

"Come on then! I'm waiting for you!"

And, at once, he raised his blade, waiting for the Hospitaller to attack first.

After almost an hour of intense sparring, the result of the fight was still uncertain and the sun was now high in the sky. Philippe looked towards Foulques and pleaded with him breathlessly:

"Enough! I have to go back for the service at noon." Foulques threw his sword on the ground straight away and sat down on it suddenly, taking deep breaths.

"You are right! Me too! I got carried away!"

He took out a small handkerchief and wiped the sweat off his brow, adding, out of breath:

"But it was nice! A draw!"

Philippe, already standing, nodded to Foulques, smiling:

"Come on mareschal, let's go! But we shall do this again. I'll be back in shape by then, and will beat you quickly!"

"We shall see about that!" said the Hospitaller cheerfully, getting up. He put his sword back in its scabbard, and the two knights quickly went on their way back.

23

Hospitaller Castle Kolossi, Limassol, March 8, 1306

arch, known to be a cold month, confirmed its reputation and started off very cold. The huge stone audience hall in the Hospitaller castle was still freezing cold, despite the fire burning in its large fireplace.

Right in front of the fire place, in a wide velvet armchair, rubbing his hands to warm them as best he could, sat the new Grand Master of the order, Foulques de Villaret, elected only a year before. His predecessor, and uncle, Guillaume had fallen ill with pneumonia, which had, sadly, proved fatal. The Hospitaller knights of Cyprus had solemnly elected Foulques in his place. As a mareschal, he had been very successful at Guillaume's side and was considered to be one of the most mature, wisest and bravest men amongst the Hospitaller knights of Cyprus.

Next to him, in two chairs, sat the two officers next in seniority in the order, Thomas and Nicolas, who were also listening with great interest to what the Genoese corsair opposite them, Vignolo di Vignioli, was suggesting.

The curly-haired, well-built man with a cut on his cheek and one eye lost in battle, had decided to visit Kolossi for the very purpose of putting forward his proposal to the Grand Master, which he was now doing in a hoarse voice:

"…You see, therefore, that my action aims to benefit all of us in some way. I would not have suggested it unless, as you already know, the Greek emperor Andronikos[91] had not already given me the islands of Kos and Leros as fiefs. They will serve as bases for us to take the rest of the Dodecanese."

Foulques remained silent for a while, considering what he had heard. His uncle came mind. How much he missed his insights at times like these! What would he have to say about all this if he were here now? He rested his elbows on the arms of the chair and tapped his fingers nervously, bringing the tips together before he finally decided to speak:

"So what you are suggesting, if I have understood correctly what you have said until now, is that we help you with our fleet to take the rest of the Dodecanese and you will keep one third of the islands we manage to take. Is that so?"

Vignolo nodded and leaned back in his chair with a look of absolute confidence. He believed that the Grand Master would accept his proposal. He then leaned forward again and addressed Foulques in a conspiratorial tone:

"I know that your order is in need of a base, an island from which it will be able to continue its battle against the infidels with their large fleet[92]. I think that Rhodes, in the centre of the Aegean, will serve your purpose very well."

Instead of replying, Foulques turned and looked at Nicolas and Thomas and they, in turn, nodded to the Grand Master, indicating that they agreed with the pirate's suggestion.

Foulques, however, wanted to think about it more. So he stood up and said to Vignolo:

"Don't misunderstand me, but this is a very important matter for our order. Allow me, therefore, to give you an answer tomorrow. Come at the same time and you will have my answer then."

Vignolo stood in turn, unable to hide his disappointment that his proposal had not been accepted right away. He could not, however, do anything other than come the next day. So he respectfully said goodbye to the Hospitallers and left the room. As soon as the door closed, Thomas addressed the Grand Master who had, in the meantime, sat down again:

"With all due respect, my Lord, why did you not accept Vignolo's proposal? It is a wonderful opportunity!"

Nicolas agreed with Thomas, adding:

"And what if Vignolo goes to the Knights Templar now and they accept right away?"

"Out of the question," Thomas said emphatically."The Knights Templar do not have a fleet large enough for such an undertaking."

"I did not say I will say no," Foulques suddenly said, ending the dialogue between his subordinates. I just wanted to weigh up all the advantages and disadvantages of this action, given that Vignolo is not a man to be trusted. Don't forget that he is an adventurer."

"I agree, my lord," said Nicolas, "but I don't believe he would dare not keep his promise to us and find himself in chains on one of our galleys pulling an oar!"

"That's true, my Lord, agreed Thomas. His fleet is not even near as large as ours!"

"So you believe that if we agree to his proposal, our order will have the base that it hopes for so much?" Foulques asked.

"Yes, my Lord," said both officials in unison.

Foulques stood up and, hands together behind his back, began to walk up and down the room. Nicolas and Thomas remained silent, seemingly a little impatient to hear Foulques' final decision.

The Grand Master, deep in thought, approached the fireplace. He noticed that the fire had almost gone out since the logs had almost burnt up completely. He bent down at once to the right of the fireplace, to put on two more logs.

Thomas then stood up and rushed to perform this task for the Grand Master, but Foulques, still silent, stopped him, raising his hand and looking him straight in the eye. He did not like it that the others were always doing the manual work instead of him just because he was the Grand Master and their superior. Nicolas and Thomas knew this so they did not insist.

Foulques lifted two heavy pieces of wood himself and fed the insatiable flames with them. The flames showed their gratitude at once by burning harder. While Foulques was looking at the wild flames licking the crackling logs, he warmed his hands in front of them and said to himself in a voice that could barely be heard:

"Knights of Rhodes then. That can't be bad."

***

In the middle of March, a week after Foulques' meeting with Vignolo, the weather on the island was still quite cold for that time of year. Philippe, wrapped tightly in his habit, was saying goodbye to Cyprus again, from the deck of one of the Knights Templar's ships this time.

"So, here I am, going back to my homeland," thought Philippe. "After so many years! I did not believe I would ever go back, to be honest!"

After about three years in Limassol, Philippe and many other Knights Templar had been ordered to return to Paris which had, in the meantime, become the Templars' main base, at least for the time being. These three years had been relaxed and without military duties for Philippe, who, despite the morass in which the order found itself, had been feeling better than he had on the isle of Ruad. The reason for this had undoubtedly been his meetings with Foulques, which had provided an outlet for him, added to the fact that he had been in a relatively large city, full of life, which did not allow any room for boredom.

Many of the brothers, like commander Ayme, were also members of Fede Santa. So Philippe had not missed meetings where the knights performed their rituals and talked about philosophy and mysticism, even without having at their disposal the rich collection of manuscripts, now in Paris so that they could be studied there.

He had even managed to reach the highest level of initiation by now and believed that, up to a point at least, he had managed to tame some of his impulses and become a better person.

Philippe was staring at the sea, and images of the Brothers in Ruad that he would never see again came into his mind. A short time before Philippe's departure from Cyprus, tragic news had reached Limassol: sixteen Mamluk galleys had besieged the island. The Knights Templar had fought back bravely, until they had faced starvation. Hugues d'Empuries, the commander, had then agreed to give up the island on condition that the knights were allowed to leave in safety. Once again, however, the Mamluks had gone back on their word, and all the Knights Templar had either been killed or imprisoned.

Everyone in Cyprus was very upset and discouraged on hearing this news. The little hope that the Christians had of taking back the Holy Lands, was now fading into nothingness. The uncertainty the orders were facing had now become even greater.

As Philippe watched the harbour of Limassol disappearing into the dense fog that covered the city that cloudy day, he brought back to mind the last time he had met his beloved friend, Foulques. The Hospitaller had been very sad that Philippe was about to leave, but the two friends had promised each other that they would keep in touch by writing to each other.

Foulques had then confided in the Knight Templar, telling him about his order's forthcoming campaign against the Dodecanese, and the trip he would make to Europe to get the Pope's approval for it. Philippe had marvelled at the venture and had said that he wished his order had such a clear goal. Foulques had promised his friend, as he was saying goodbye to him, that, whatever happened and however long it might take him, he would write to him from Rhodes – if everything went well, of course.

Philippe looked at the Brothers who were travelling with him and were talking right opposite him. He saw Ponsard de Gizy, Geoffroy de Gonneville and Ayme de Osiliers, who were travelling with him, all members of Fede Santa. Most of them were his age, and that of Francois, who he would see again in Paris. He smiled faintly when he thought of his old friend, who he hadn't seen in such a long time.

"I hope he is well," he said quietly to himself. "Francois, I am on my way!"

Then he began to walk towards the rest of the Brothers. He believed that this time he would stay in Paris permanently.

"I really want to stay somewhere for good at last," was his last thought before he went up to his Brothers. He did not know that, at the same time, kilometres away, someone was taking care to shatter his dreams once more.

24

Paris, March 18, 1306

he audience hall with its tall gothic arches in the royal palace was heated by two large fireplaces and decorated with deep red velvet curtains and beautiful, wooden carved furniture. In the middle of the room was a throne for the king of France , with carved dark brown wood and golden trimmings on its edges, on purple velvet. The "Grande Salle" (Great Hall), as it was called, was known throughout Europe for its gothic beauty and grandeur, inspiring awe in anyone who entered it. It was a part of the royal palace on the Île de la Cité - that had been rebuilt the previous century by Louis IX on the ruins of what had once been the seat of the Roman commander of the city. The present king of France, Philippe, had also significantly expanded the palace[93].

Esquieu de Floyran could not restrain an exclamation of wonder as the great oak doors opened and he entered the Great Hall, accompanied by two guards. Two middle-aged men entered right after them, politely greeting Esquieu, and sat on the two armchairs to the right and left of the throne where the king was about to sit. One was Guillaume de Plaisians, a small man with a pleasant appearance, an eminent jurist and lawyer of the king of France.

The other one was named Guillaume de Nogaret. Harsh in appearance, with a pointed chin, he was liked by few people in the palace, except the king himself. He was short and fat, with thick eyebrows that arched above his cold, light blue eyes. Guillaume was also a lawyer and had taught Law at the University of Montpelier.

This man was ruthless and specialised in defaming his victims with accusations of witchcraft, heresy and sexual perversion. Some of his victims were members of the clergy, and Pope Benedict XI had been forced to excommunicate him. Not that this was of great importance to Guillaume, who bore a profound hatred for the Papacy. Many different rumours attributed his cruelty and hatred towards the Holy Father to a tragic incident in his childhood.

Some said that Nogaret's parents were Cathars and that they had been burnt alive during the Albigensian Crusade in the previous century. This childhood trauma had scarred Guillaume for life, turning him into a particularly twisted individual.

Esquieu knew all this and, meeting this man face to face for the first time, saw for himself that the rumours circulating about his ruthlessness were certainly absolutely true.

Suddenly, the two men stood up and bent forward into a bow. Esquieu turned to the door and faced the king of France, who was entering the room at that moment, greeting them. Esquieu also bowed his head in respect and raised it only when the king had sat down on his throne. Esquieu kept looking at the monarch for some time, impressed by his appearance, as he leant forward and whispered with his lawyers.

Philippe IV was truly a very handsome man and he had already, from the first years of his reign, acquired the epithet "The Fair". He was tall and slim with blue-green eyes, while fair curls gently crowned his rose red cheeks. His almost feminine beauty contrasted strongly with his contradictory character.

The distrust and suspicion that characterised him had their roots in a childhood that had not been easy. Son of Philippe III, "The Bold", he had lost his mother, Isabella of Aragon, when only three years old. He had not seen a great deal of his father, who had married again to Marie of Brabant. When Philippe's older brother, Louis, died, unexpectedly making him the heir to the French throne, rumours were that the unfortunate young man had been poisoned by his step-mother and that she was planning to do the same to his brother.

He had, therefore, learned to be suspicious and wary of the people around him. Grandson of Louis IX, later called "The Saint", he had inherited his grandfather's piety as far as theological issues were concerned – something he shared with his beloved wife Joan of Navarre - but no respect for the Papacy. His disputes with Pope Boniface VIII, but also with his successors, were well-known. Philippe held the firm belief that a monarch was appointed by God to rule over the faithful and that the Pope should be subject to the will of the crown.

"So I'm listening Master…what did we say your name was?[94]" the King said in his thin voice, tinged with a little curiosity, addressing the stranger, when he had finished muttering with his lawyers.

"Esquieu, your majesty. Esquieu de Floyran. At your service," he replied, bowing his head again obsequiously, but pausing to think how best to begin his speech.

In the end he coughed, clearing his throat, and began to make strong gestures to lend emphasis to his words:

"I would like to draw your attention, your majesty, to a very serious matter. It concerns vipers feeding at your breast, unbeknown to you, who are so pious as to be unaware of the danger they pose to you, and to the realm over which you have divine authority."

Philippe, somewhat annoyed by the speaker's wordiness, tapped his fingers on the arm of the throne impatiently:

"To the point please, Master Esquieu, to the point."

Esquieu gulped and immediately said in one breath:

"I mean the Knights Templar."

The king and his lawyers' eyes grew wide with astonishment and looked at each other, perplexed. De Floyran gave them no time to think further and went on:

"They are a nest of heretics who spit and trample on the most sacred symbol of Christianity, the cross. Instead of our Lord Jesus Christ they worship a satanic idol. During the ceremony of their initiation into the order, all the knights tie a cord around the idol, which they then wear around their waist to honour him. I think it is a shame that you, such a devout lord, should be surrounded by such heretics."

The King and his lawyers were looking at Esquieu with expressions full of distrust. Then Nogaret's eyes suddenly lit up and a faint smile appeared on his face before he leant towards Philippe's ear:

"Your Majesty, if I may, I am sure that all the things this man is telling us are nothing but slander." The king nodded his head in agreement and Nogaret went on, while Esquieu looked at them in anticipation, mingled with some measure of fear.

"But we can take advantage of this slander to fill our empty coffers. So let's pretend we believe him, see what else he has to tell us and I will share all my thoughts with you as soon as he leaves."

King Philippe gave a crafty smile and nodded once more, rubbing his chin. He knew very well what Nogaret meant. So, to continue the conversation, he asked Esquieu:

"And how do you know all this Master Esquieu?"

"I know it first hand, your majesty, since I have been a member of this heretical order and was often forced to perform such obscenities. Sodomy is one more hateful act that often takes place in it. Also, imagine that, as part of his initiation into the order, the candidate must kiss the knight who presides over the ceremony, on the navel, buttocks or the penis, depending on the occasion."

"So you performed all those outrages and trampled on the cross?" Guillaume asked, no emotion in his voice, but the expression on his face severe.

"I could not do otherwise. Had I not, I would not have been admitted to the order. I do, however, sincerely repent of it. Remorse and duty to God have brought me here today to tell you all this"

"Very well then," said Philippe lifting his hand for a minute to show that the audience had ended. "I shall order an investigation into this sinful order, after I contact the Pope, and we shall settle the matter. You can rest assured."

Esquieu bowed very low:

"Thank you, your majesty, for the time you have spent listening to me. May God grant you long life."

Then he got up and left the room, smiling malevolently and muttering:

"This time I believe I have achieved my purpose!"

Back in the audience hall, the king, after some time deep in thought, staring into the flames in the fireplace, finally turned to Nogaret:

"So, my dear, I am ready to hear your thoughts on this matter although, to be honest, I think we are of the same mind."

Nogaret smiled conspiratorially and stood up. De Plaisians sat up in his armchair and also fixed his eyes on Nogaret, full of curiosity. The lawyer walked up and down with his hands behind his back and began to share his thoughts with Philippe:

"Let's take things from the beginning, your majesty, when two months ago you decided that France should return to the old currency from the time of your grandfather Louis the Saint[95],and riots took place in Paris[96], where did you take refuge?"

"In the Temple, my dear, as you know very well," replied the king, somewhat bored.

"There, as you told us yourself, you saw, with your own eyes, the immense wealth of the Knights Templar, didn't you?"

"Of course. Those riches would solve the financial problem my kingdom is facing."

Nogaret smiled slyly, looking the King in the eye and went on:

"So as this Order, whether heretical or not, no longer serves any purpose for Christendom, it would suit us very well if it were dissolved and we were able to seize its fortune, wouldn't it?"

"Absolutely right, my dear. I completely agree. The problem is – how are we to prove these accusations which are, as far as we know, untrue, except maybe for some isolated cases."

"All three of us know that Esquieu is a former Knight Templar who was expelled from the order for misbehaviour," de Plaisians broke in, "so he has every reason to accuse the order. We also know that before he came to us he visited James II of Aragon, and made the same accusations to him as well. James, of course, sent him on his way, not believing a word of what he said."

Guillaume raised his hands, shaking his head:

"But it is not necessary for these accusations to be true for us to act. Only the fact that they have been made is enough for us. Your majesty, you referred to isolated cases of corruption in the order before. Of course cases like these are not confined to the Knights Templar. We know very well that people who are supposed to be people of God and who sin are everywhere, in every order and in every monastery. However, we must try to find cases like these to achieve our purpose or, even better, more expelled Templars like Esquieu, who will willingly testify against their former order."

The king stroked his chin for a moment and said:

"That is not a bad idea. But where will we find such Brothers?"

"That is my job, your majesty. First of all, Esquieu himself will not find it hard at all to bring some of his former Brothers here to us. Give me time to prepare the indictment and when everything is ready, we shall notify the Pope. In any case Clement[97] will not raise any great objection to our plans." De Plaisians nodded in approval, giving the king the all-clear. He brought his hands down on the arms of his throne, saying:

"Very good, Guillaume, I therefore assign you the task of preparing a convincing indictment against the Knights Templar. You have the experience necessary for such a task. De Plaisians will, of course, also help you. And, of course, you shall receive commensurate reward if you succeed in your purpose."

Nogaret rubbed his hands, pleased.

"Rest assured, your Majesty. Jacques de Molay will be last to hear of all this, when it is too late.

***

It was almost summer, after a particularly rainy spring in Paris, and whole weeks of sun had followed dull cloudy days, giving Francois and Philippe the opportunity to go on their walks in the bustling city centre around Les Halles[98], the famous Parisian market, more often. On sunny days the two friends loved to go down past the strong fortress that king Philippe II had built the previous century[99], then walk by the Seine, ending up at the Sorbonne College[100], the centre of religious studies in France.

Philippe had already adapted to his new life which was, undoubtedly, easier and more enjoyable than the one he had had in Outremer. When the Grand Master Jacques de Molay was out of town, which was very often, discipline in the Temple, already now not as strict, would become even more lax, and the knights, except for services and the now mere formality of training to keep in shape, had plenty of time to go on outings into the magnificent city.

So many of the once hardened Knights Templar were led to long drinking sessions and debauchery, to say nothing of the temptations of the flesh placed by the exquisite creatures with loose morals that were ever-present in the busy shopping streets to lure the weakest characters into sin. The harsher punishments imposed from time to time on knights who had gone astray, were not enough to put them back on the" straight and narrow" as they lost all reason for their existence, and were now extremely bored due to lack of activity and excessive amounts of free time.

The two friends, for the time being, steered clear of such debauchery and were satisfied with long walks and quiet conversations on a wide variety of subjects, together with some wine in the little taverns of the city, which were always full. They had also become reacquainted with the famous manuscripts of Acre. The two friends would often go to the library and kept up their rituals, many times a week, thus answering their spiritual concerns.

They had, in fact, happened to go out a couple of times with two other members of the organisation that Francois had met in Paris before Philippe's arrival, Brother Hughes de Pairaud and Brother Pierre de Bologna, and had talked for hours on end about Ancient Greek philosophy.

So today, one of the last days of May, the two knights were on their own and, after their usual walk, decided to go to a new tavern on the banks of the Seine. They did not always have money for wine and good food since knights were not supposed to own anything. In fact, however, with the decline of recent years, they had managed to obtain some money here and there, either from selling some old object of theirs, whose existence they had kept a secret from the order, or from their parents' fortunes which, since many knights were now near home, they could plunder with impunity.

Philippe himself had had, as did Francois, a large reserve of cash since he had returned to Paris. He had met one of his sisters, Isabel, a few days after his arrival. She had given him a substantial amount of money for his "pocket money" as she had called it. He had taken the opportunity to hear news of Claudia, his older sister, who he had not seen in years.

Both of Philippe's sisters were now married to members of old noble families in France, and Philippe now had many nephews and nieces he had never met, neither had he met his sisters' husbands. But he had learnt to live all these years without a family – so the truth was that he did not miss his sisters a great deal. His Brothers, with whom he shared many more common memories than with the members of his family, had become his relatives now.

The two knights stood outside a picturesque little tavern for a while, looking at the wooden windows which were full of geraniums, and the tasteful, as it seemed through the drawn, curtains, interior. The tavern was called "Belle Nuit", "beautiful night", undoubtedly a well-chosen name. There was a tavern on the ground floor, and the two upper floors served as a small inn.

"It's on me today," Philippe announced, an expression on his face that showed that he would not take no for an answer, as he opened the door to the tavern, which, although new, was quite crowded with people eating and drinking there. The two knights chose one of the only two free little tables next to the kitchen and, right away, sat down on the wooden benches.

"If that's the case we must eat until we drop tonight!" Francois said, making a joke as a somewhat delayed reply to his friend's suggestion.

Philippe smiled and prepared to joke back, in turn, when his eyes fell on the young lady taking orders from the next table and, for a moment, had nothing to say.

The petite young lady standing opposite him, who couldn't have been more than twenty five years old, had her long brown hair tied into two braids on the right and left side of her head, which gently crowned her lily white neck. She wore a green dress covered by a white apron at the front. Philippe's eyes fell on her breasts – not so large but well-shaped, her slender waist and her well-shaped hips which, undoubtedly, failed to meet the standards of beauty of the time, which required women to be fat, with curves, so that they would be, so people believed, fertile. For some inexplicable reason, however, Philippe very much liked those hips.

Then the girl, feeling the knight's eyes thoroughly explore her body, turned and looked at him with her emerald green eyes and gave him a broad smile, showing with her bright white teeth. Straight away Philippe felt a cold sweat come over him. He had never experienced anything like this in his life before but now, without knowing why, he could not take his eyes off the girl, feeling an irresistible attraction towards her.

The exquisite creature, continuing to smile at Philippe, began to walk towards the Knights Templar. When she reached the table, she said in a playful, velvet voice:

"Good evening. What can we offer you?"

Francois, seeing that Philippe remained silent, asked the girl:

"Is there some speciality of the house? We haven't been here before and we would gladly try it if there were one."

"Then try the pork with oregano, that's our speciality. My aunt, the cook, has no rival when it comes to making that!"

"Agreed then!" said Francois. "And two glasses of wine." Then the girl, instead of leaving, and blushing slightly, asked Philippe:

"You, sir, would you like anything else?"

"I…well…no" Philippe stammered, and then, suddenly regaining his composure, asked the girl, looking her boldly in the eye:

"But I would like you to tell me your name."

The girl twirled her right braid in her fingers and said, somewhat self-consciously:

"Of course. My name is Giselle."

"Nice name. I am Brother Philippe and this is Brother Francois," said Philippe, having now completely recovered.

"Judging by your clothing you are Knights Templar, aren't you?" asked Giselle in her turn, appearing to be quite at ease now.

"Knights Templar, at your service miss," replied Francois, bowing, after standing up briefly.

"Well...nice to meet you. See you later. I'll get your order now," said the girl, and, without giving them time to answer, disappeared into the kitchen straight away.

Francois smiled slyly, giving Philippe a nudge with his elbow.

"I see you liked the little one. Go on then!"

"I will not deny it. To be honest it is the first time I have felt like that about a woman. But don't forget our vows. Supposedly, we, as members of Fede Santa, are supposed to be able to control our desires."

"How boring you can be!"

Francois's voice sounded full of disapproval and his eyebrows came together in a grimace.

"Listen my friend," he continued. "All these things belong to the past and are related to another life. Here there are no sieges and no Infidels, only services and gentle walks. That's what I thought in the beginning, but you will get bored doing the same things over and over again."

Philippe rolled his eyes in surprise:

"So, you mean that you…"

"Yes. I was also led astray twice before you came. And many of our Brothers too. I didn't tell you. Alright, I am not proud of it, it just happened. But if it's love then things are different. Since when is it right to control such a beautiful feeling? Love is not a sin, isn't that what the Ancient Greeks said? You two, judging from the way you look at each other, seem to have mutual feelings, and it is a pity not to experience them if you can. No one will know anyway, except us three."

"And what should I do, marry her?" said Philippe somewhat ironically. "You know that that would be impossible!"

Francois made a gesture of disapproval with his hand:

"Don't be irrational. She knows very well that that is out of the question and she will not ask anything like that of you. She saw that you are a knight. She just liked you. That's what I think.. I wish something similar had happened to me too!"

He fixed his eyes on the table and continued to talk in a low voice:

"With women of the streets there is no love, only lust and that is definitely something that is not good for someone who possesses self-awareness. And that is exactly why I would not want to be carried away into something like that again…"

Then he leaned backwards and stretched up his arms because they had become numb. He had time to say nothing more as the girl put a plate of sizzling meat and two cups of wine in front of them. Philippe looked at her long, slender fingers as she put the plates on the table and, now persuaded by what his friend had said, felt his last doubts go away. He made the girl a bold suggestion, barely recognising himself:

"Would you like to join with us for a while?"

The girl seemed happy briefly, but then grew a little hesitant.

"I would really like that. But, as you can see yourselves, there is a lot of work and my sister, who usually helps too, is not here today. However, tomorrow, she will be here, so I will be able to sit with you for a little if there isn't much work to do. Will you be able to come back tomorrow?" she asked, looking at Philippe somewhat imploringly with her large emerald eyes.

"Definitely. Alright then, tomorrow," said Philippe, and Giselle, after saying goodbye to them, went back work.

However, all night she exchanged secret looks and smiles with Philippe, making him burn with desire and leave Francois with most of the delicious pork they had been served.

25

Poitiers, December 28, 1306

lement stood up from the red, velvet armchair in the papal palace and drew the heavy curtains with a deep sigh to look out at the white landscape. Thick snowflakes had been falling since the night before in Poitiers and the white veil that had covered everything made a sharp contrast with the dark blackness he felt in his soul at that time.

The old Pontiff, with his crooked nose and weak constitution, had been racking his brain for some days now with everything that Philippe had told him in the letters he had recently sent him concerning the famous order of the Knights Templar.

Philippe had talked to him plainly of a host of suspicions held against the order and accusations openly made against it of heretical practices and immorality. He had also provided him with the names of witnesses that he claimed to be reliable, and that would bear out these accusations.

Clement let the curtain drop softly and headed towards the table where a cup full of wine had been left, with slow, heavy steps. He brought the cup to his wrinkled lips and felt a little better when he felt the drink wash against his palate.

"No, I do not believe these accusations," he said aloud, bringing his hands down onto the table.

Then, burying his face in his calloused palms, he continued to talk to himself, shaking his head:

"Of course I do not believe the accusations Philippe and his lawyers have made up with their sick minds. It can't be that those who so faithfully served Christ all these years and gave their lives fighting for Him are heretics."

A gentle knock on the door interrupted this monologue and the Pope raised his head up at once and shouted:

"Yes?"

The door opened and Clement's young secretary appeared in the doorway:

"He is here, your Holiness," said the young man, looking intently towards him.

The old man seemed a little upset when he heard the news.

"Alright. Wait five minutes and then show him in. I will be ready."

The secretary bowed and disappeared at once, pulling the door shut softly behind him. The Pontiff began to pace nervously up and down in the big room, returning to his thoughts of before. So De Molay was here.

The Pope himself had called the Grand Masters of the Hospitaller and Knights Templar to come and meet him in Poitiers so that they could talk about the future of the orders now that Outremer was permanently lost, and also of their possible merger. Foulques de Villaret, however, the Grand Master of the Hospitaller Knights, had not been able to come until then. The siege of Rhodes by the Hospitallers was in progress, and its outcome still uncertain.

The Greeks of Rhodes had fought back bravely against the Hospitaller fleet, who had managed to take, only after treachery, the fortress of Filermou, while the siege for the occupation of the main city of Rhodes was continuing unabated, making Foulques's absence from the battlefield impossible at that time. The Grand Master had said this himself to Clement in his letter in response to the papal invitation, ending ended his letter with a promise that he would try to visit the Pope the following year.

Clement was now anxious to meet De Molay, who had managed to come in person, and judge for himself the man about whom he had heard so much that was contradictory.

In the long years that Jacques had been the Grand Master of the order he had come to be liked by some kings of Europe on the one hand, but on the other hand many others drew attention to the intellectual poverty of the leader of an order with such a great history and contribution to Christianity, as well as his lack of imagination and flexibility.

"Let's see what I can do to help him, particularly to protect him from the rapacious appetite of the king of France," thought Clement as he made himself comfortable in his cosy armchair, his curiosity peaking.

"A merger might solve the problem in the end. As long as Molay himself also works in that direction."

There was another knock on the door and, after the Pope had replied in the affirmative, it opened and a tall man with a beard, haughty appearance and arrogant expression entered the room. He was wearing the formal cloak of the Knights Templar on top of his tunic with an embroidered red cross, and wore a sword on the belt around his waist. In his early fifties, his beard was white, making a sharp contrast with his pitch-black, vivid eyes.

"Whatever he might be like as a character, he certainly carries himself in accordance with his office," Clement thought before he addressed Jacques, who had knelt in front of him and kissed the top of his hand as a sign of respect.

"Welcome, my son. I wish you a pleasant stay in Poitiers with all my heart. Did you have any time to rest after the long journey?"

The Grand Master stood up in front of the Pope and, in his deep voice, replied to Clement:

"No, I came straight to you, Holy Father. Rest can wait. Anyway, Paris, from where

I came, is not that far away."

"So let's get straight to the point. I imagine you know the reason I called you here, you and your counterpart in the Hospitallers."

"Yes, Holy Father. I am aware of the difficult situation my order is in, but also that of the Hospitallers. I would like to inform you that, for the time being at least, I have made the decision that our base will remain in Paris."

Clement frowned and looked at Jacques disapprovingly. "He can't be so stupid," he thought. "Doesn't he realise he is in the hornets' nest? Maybe I should tell him about the charges Philippe has made. Carefully though, so I don't expose the king." Then he said to the Grand Master:

"Maybe it would be wiser, my son, to find an island to use as a base, just as the Hospitallers have done, for your campaigns against the Infidel? I believe that they will take over Rhodes soon. You could make Cyprus your base. I'm afraid Paris is a little far from the fields of battle. Not to mention that l hear that it is a place where your men are corrupted, since they are made idle against their will, having no armed action to undertake."

De Molay looked at the Pope, surprised.

"What do you mean when you say they are corrupted, your Holiness?"

Clement folded his arms, leant his elbows on the arms of the chair and looked at the person he was addressing intently:

"There are some suspicions, my son, concerning your order. Some rumours, which I do not know if they are true, talk about sodomy in the ranks of your order and blasphemy against the name of our Lord Jesus Christ. I would like to hear from your lips, my son, the truth and nothing but the truth, as far as those horrible rumours are concerned." Jacques gave out a cry of indignation and made a grimace that showed his disgust at what he was hearing:

"Father! How can you believe these baseless rumours, which are nothing but vile lies, which our enemies, who are envious of us, spread? You know very well what my order has contributed in the struggle against the Infidels all these years. My men are monk-warriors who honour our Lord and serve Him with all their heart! Hundreds of them were beheaded by the Infidel while in captivity because they refused to renounce Jesus! You cannot, therefore, be telling me now that, after all this, they have been committing such outrages!"

"He is right and the strength of his indignation certainly shows, as I believed, that Nogaret's allegations are unfounded," thought the Pope before he replied to De Molay, somewhat uncertainly:

"I know all this, my son, and I believe you. But today's political climate, and only that, is responsible for the accusations which are being made against you, since people see you wandering around aimlessly and covet your wealth, so much so that they are willing to accuse you of anything. So why don't you go back to Cyprus to resume attacks against the Infidel and silence those who make accusations against you?"

Jacques shook his head.

"I am afraid anything like that would be impossible, Holy Father. We weren't able to impose our our authority over the inhabitants of the island. The Greeks there hated us and during the time we were on the island they constantly created problems for us."

The Pope snorted in disappointment before he went on:

"Now let's talk about the merger of your order with the Knights Hospitaller. It is the only way for your order to continue to make a constructive contribution to Christendom. Foulques de Villaret, your counterpart, my son, in the order of Hospitallers, has promised to come here next year so that we can see how this merger can take place."

"On this subject, I have prepared a memorandum to submit to you, in which I give the reasons why this merger cannot take place."

Unable to believe his ears, Clement clenched the arms of his chair so hard that his calloused hands turned white. He at once asked the Grand Master, who seemed unaware of the fact that the Pope was furious, to give him the memorandum.

Jacques then took some pieces of paper out of his robe and gave them to Clement, who immediately began to read through some parts quickly, very curious to see what De Molay's arguments against the merger were:

"... The plan to merge two orders so old, debases them and eliminates the competition necessary for the continuous self-improvement of the Brothers... the Hospitallers are mainly involved in works of charity, whereas our order is dedicated to military campaigns so both orders exist to serve very different purposes........... the two orders possess property in unequal amounts so sharing them would be unfair.. the Rule governing the way of life followed by each orders is different, so it would be very difficult for those Brothers forced to abandon their own, whether Knights Templar or Knights Hospitaller, to change their habits... there is, therefore, an urgent need for a large-scale campaign to be organised against the Infidel to which all the kings of Christendom will contribute.."

The Pope dropped the papers into his lap and, once more, put his face into his hands, sighing desperately. No, he could not bear any longer , at least at this moment, to continue reading such lame arguments. He raised his head and looked in bewilderment at the man sitting opposite him. Lost for words, he continued to wonder how the Knights Templar could have elected such a foolish man to be their Grand Master, his intellectual poverty was evident in the nonsense he spouted in his memorandum.

"Maybe this man is afraid to give up his place to Foulques de Villaret. He is simply vain. He is, however, putting his order in danger this way..." thought Clement and put his face in his hands again. Jacques continued to look at him, wearing the wondering expression of a small child. Clement then said, his voice fading:

"My son... you can go... I shall read your memorandum carefully and we will talk again... I wish you a pleasant stay in Poitiers..."

The Grand Master, not in the least bit aware of the consternation he had caused the Pope, bowed in respect and kissed his hand once more.

"My compliments, Holy Father. May God grant you long life."As De Molay went through the door one thought kept coming to his mind:

"Might it be possible that the existence of Fede Santa has been leaked? Only that could explain the wording of such accusations against my order, as rites such as ours can easily be misunderstood or misrepresented. But, no, no way. It must be just silly rumours spread by our enemies."

Back in the room, the Pope, his face still in his hands, well aware that the meeting with De Molay had proved a miserable failure, said to himself bitterly:

"What am I going to do, my God, with those Knights Templar and the greedy king? Thy will be done…"

26

Paris, February 18, 1307

 y dear Brother Philippe,

I hope you are well and have adapted to your new life in Paris. Forgive me for these many months of silence but I have only now found the time to write to you. I have greatly missed your company, our walks and conversations! The only thing I have not missed are our sword-fights and that's because I am involved in their like on an almost daily basis!

I am writing to you now from the fortress of Filermos in Rhodes, which we took in November. We are laying heavy siege against the stubborn Greeks so that we may take the city itself with the help of the Venetian pirate Vigniolo de Vignioli. We have also taken the surrounding islands, which he will keep, while we will have control of the island of Rhodes, which is the largest.

The siege is quite difficult, but, as we have a significant number of ships, I want to be optimistic and believe that my order will soon enter the gates of the city, which will become the base for our attacks against the Infidel. Fortunately, up until now, losses among my men have been tolerable.

This island is ideal for our naval base. It is on the trade routes, in the centre of the Aegean and from it we will be able to control almost all of mare nostrum.[101] I hope that your order also finds a place for its base as ideal as this one so that we can continue the battle against the Infidel together.

I must go now, my fraternal friend, because many tasks await me. I wish you continued good health and hope to see you soon. If everything goes well, I will come to Poitiers next year to meet with the Holy Father and your Lord Master. May our Lord Jesus Christ grant you health and long life.

Your eternal friend,
Foulques de Villaret,
Grand Master of the Knights of St John..

***

Philippe folded the letter carefully and pushed it into a fold in his shirt. Then, after he had blown out the candle which stood beside his bed, he lay just as he was on his straw mattress, keeping his eyes open. He put his hands behind his head and pulled the woollen blanket over him. Then he began to listen to the rhythmic breathing of his Brothers, who were sleeping, breaking the silence of that freezing night in February.

Foulques… How much he had missed him! Having just read his letter and vivid memories of him coming to mind, Philippe wondered: "What would his friend have to say about Fede Santa?" He had often asked himself that question in the past during his meetings with the Hospitaller in Cyprus, and before that in Outremer. He had always come to the conclusion that it would be unwise to say anything to him about the organization, although he had no doubts about entrusting his friend with a confidence, as the two of them always shared their innermost thoughts. However, he believed, deep down, that Foulques, having stronger opinions in these matters, would react negatively to such beliefs. Anyway, he didn't want to expose the organization, since he had promised never to talk about it to someone who was not a member. This was the only important part of his life that Philippe had kept secret from his fraternal friend.

Now there was also Giselle in his life and she was an important part of it too, so inevitably, Philippe asked himself another question: "What would his friend have to say about his relationship with Giselle?" The knight was certain that his friend would strongly disapprove of the, illicit from every point of view, relationship he had entered into with the girl for about a month now.

The cherry taste of her velvet lips and soft skin came flooding into the knight's mind and he immediately felt his member stir with passion and his mind fill with guilt.

"I am a monk… my God, forgive me!" he murmured, but calling on God could not take Giselle from his mind.

In the end, after going with Francois to "Belle Nuit" to eat, and getting to know the girl better, Philippe had decided, with Francois's encouragement, to allow himself to be pierced by Cupid's arrows. When the two lovers were together, they felt that the whole world belonged to them, they forgot about rules and restrictions and would lose themselves in each other's arms.

Yes, their meetings were absolutely illicit and they both knew it. Philippe, however, was not a man who could easily subdue his feelings to cold logic, however much remorse tortured him about the violation of the vows he had taken as a monk. The attraction he felt towards the girl was irresistible and, by mischievous coincidence, mutual.

Giselle, beautiful, sweet and very understanding, was the bright sunbeam in his, otherwise monotonous, life. The twenty-three-year old girl had lost both her parents at a very young age. She and her sister Irina been raised by mother's sister, whose husband was now the owner of the inn, where they now worked for a small allowance. Indeed, the two girls, since they lived in the inn, ate there and had no living expenses, were saving this money for any difficult times that might lie ahead.

Giselle's uncle and aunt had two daughters, who had married at a very young age and were now helping their husbands work. They were in no hurry for their two nieces to marry because they needed their help in the inn. Isabelle, Giselle's aunt had certainly realised that something was going on between the mature Knight Templar and her niece, but she turned a blind eye.

"Our relationship probably suits them," Giselle had once told Philippe, "because it wouldn't suit them if I got married and left the inn. Then who would they have to help them for so little money? They know that you can't marry me so they can rest easy. And I much more prefer to lie with you, even if we are not man and wife in the eyes of the Church, than be forced to be with some fat peasant all my life!" And then Giselle would smother Philippe in kisses, making all of his reservations disappear.

Philippe smiled faintly in the twilight as he brought his beloved to mind. All said and done, it was nice here in Paris. And it wasn't only because of Giselle that Philippe was having fun here. It was because of Francois, Fede Santa, but also because of the relaxed mood that now prevailed in the Temple. Philippe felt at home in this city, which was, in any case, a part of where he had grown up, his homeland.

He could not get to sleep because he was simply not feeling tired. The unexpected meeting he had outside "Belle Nuit" some days ago with a person he never expected to see again, Gilles Aicelin, came to mind. This was the man Philippe had saved from robbers when he was still young, before he had gone to the Holy Lands.

Gilles was now quite old. However, he still had his place in the palace as Keeper of the Royal Seal, having succeeded his father many years before now. His appearance had changed a great deal, just as Philippe's had.

It was he who had finally spoken first when the two had come across each other outside the door of the inn. Philippe was going in, Gilles was going out. The two men had looked at each other for some time before Gilles had decided to speak first:

"I know you from somewhere... My old mind is having difficulty remembering but I am certain... Philippe!" the old man said after a while. "It's you, my saviour!"

For a moment Philippe thought that the old man had taken him for someone else. However, he had then remembered the incident with the robbers in the woods and had shouted out:

"Gilles! I truly never expected to see you again!'

The two men had so many things to say that Gilles had gone into the tavern again and had drunk a little more wine with Philippe. Gilles had spoken to him about the grandchildren he now had from his daughter and about many other things that were happening in Paris. Philippe, on his part, had spoken to him about the Holy Lands and his experiences there, which had sounded very interesting to the elderly man, who was clearly touched by their meeting, as his bleary, wet eyes had shown. The two men had chatted for a long time, as if they were going out together every day, making Giselle look at Philippe impatiently after the tavern had emptied, wondering who the elderly man that the centre of all her beloved's attention that night was.

Gilles had seen the looks exchanged by the couple and Philippe had been forced to admit their relationship to the astute old man, who had given him a paternal pat on the back, and said:

"It doesn't matter Philippe, you have done so many good deeds in your life… Always for others and your order. Do something for yourself for once. Listen to me, true sins are other things!"

With this advice, Gilles had unwittingly reminded Philippe of his father, Jocelyn, and that is why he had felt, for a moment, a brief sting in his heart on remembering him. In the end, Gilles had said goodbye to him, late at night, with these words:

"I was very happy to see you and I believe we are going to see each other here again. Don't forget that I owe you a favour. So if you ever need anything, don't hesitate! You should know I regard you as a son and I will never forget the good you did for me!"

At some point Philippe's mind grew tired recalling the events of recent days and the knight began to yawn. At last he was sleepy. So he brought his love back to mind once more, laid his remorse aside, and sleep generously brought her to him in his dreams.

27

Poitiers, September 14, 1307

his is a disgrace! I will not tolerate any other such rumours about my order! I demand that you conduct a thorough investigation into the matter!"

The enraged voice belonged to Jacques de Molay who, some days before, had returned to Poitiers for a new audience with the Pope. In the intervening months he had convened a secret meeting in Paris, in July, with a view to fighting the slander that was being spread about his order. He had sent out a circular, after decisions had been made at the meeting, to all the Knights Templar houses reminding them that the Rule prohibited discussion of the order's secrets with those outside it.

De Molay had done this mainly with the members of Fede Santa and their heretical, for the time, beliefs in mind. He thought that the rumours concerning the order were based on precisely such leaks of information about that particular organization. Now, the last thing that was left for him to do to scotch these rumours was, in his opinion, to demand that the Pope investigate the case himself.

Clement put both his hands up reassuringly and calmly replied to the Grand Master of the Knights Templar:

"Calm down, my child. I agree that, since these rumours, which are so embarrassing for your order, have not come to an end, a full investigation should be conducted into the matter. I shall write to the king of France and inform him that you have requested that the matter be looked into."

The Grand Master's voice now sounded somewhat calmer:

"Thank you, Holy Father, and forgive me for my agitation but it is not possible that…"

A gentle knock at the door silenced Jacques, and made him turn towards the door, now opening wide. A Hospitaller of about fifty years in age now made his appearance. It was Foulques de Villaret, who had managed to keep his promise and finally visit the Pope, after first sending him written notification of his forthcoming visit.

Always maintaining his dignity, Foulques allowed his black robe with its white embroidered cross to gently touch the floor as he respectfully bent down to kiss the hand of the Holy Father, who showed his pleasure with a smile and then indicated that he could get up. The two Grand Masters looked at each other carefully for a seemingly endless moment and eventually greeted each other with a nod of the head.

"Welcome, my son. I am very happy you have managed to come, albeit after some delay. What about the siege of Rhodes? Are the schismatic Greeks still giving you a hard time?"

Foulques cleared his throat a little before he spoke:

"As you can see me in front of you, Holy Father, that means that the siege has finally ended successfully. On the day that our Church celebrates the Assumption of the Mother of God the city opened its gates to us. It must have been a gift from Our Lady to her children, who were in difficulty.[102]"

"Undoubtedly," replied Clement with a smile. "And how do you intend now to put your acquisition to use?"

"I think you know, your Holiness, that our order has, I would like to believe, a substantial, strong fleet. We shall therefore conduct raids against all the coastal cities of the Infidel or against their ships, which very often sail in south of mare nostrum. Also, it goes without saying that, if all the crowns of Europe decide to mount an armed campaign against the Muslims, we shall be the first to participate."

"I am very happy that you continue to actively offer your services to Christianity," Clement said and then cast Jacques a withering glance:

"I would like to be able to say the same about your order, my child."

De Molay ignored the Pope's disapproving look and said boldly:

"We do not have such a large fleet since Paris, which is our base, does not have access to the sea. However we will take part with all our forces if such an action is decided. This an opportunity for me to express my opinion on this matter." Jacques cleared his throat and began to make expansive gestures to add emphasis to what he was saying.

"I am in favour of a passagium generale, which is a large scale campaign, and not a passagium particulare, which more limited, as I often hear some put forward"

"Your opinion is undoubtedly correct, Brother Jacques," as always with great presence of mind, Foulques broke in. "However, I don't believe a passagium generale could be put into effect at this time. No king can afford to raise an army large enough to meet the needs of such a campaign."

Annoyed, Jacques looked at Foulques and replied:

"I am not talking about an immediate military campaign, dear Brother. The goals I set are long term ones."

"And until this passagium generale takes place, my son, what are you and your knights going to do exactly? Because you need to do something to stop the spread of the malicious rumours about your order!" the Pope asked De Molay, with palpable irony.

"Unfortunately we can do nothing but wait. What is needed to completely crush the infidels is, if anything, a full scale, well-orchestrated operation." Jacques replied somewhat sadly, apparently not having discerned the irony in Clement's voice.

The elderly man exchanged a look full of disappointment with Foulques and decided to change the subject and talk about what interested him most, now that the two Grand Masters were present:

"As for the subject of the merging of your orders, dear Jacques, I read the memorandum you submitted to me on the matter last and I would like to stress to you, my child, that I do not find any of the reasons you have given me important enough for it not to take place."

"No, your Holiness," Jacques disagreed. "During my stay in Paris in the summer I discussed the matter with many of the Brothers and we all agreed that, at this moment, anything like this is out of the question."

Scowling, the Pope turned to Foulques.

"What do you have to say on the matter, my child?"

Foulques, prepared for a question such as this, replied confidently.

"For the time being I would not leave the island I took with so much difficulty for another base, for the sake of a merger between our orders, unless, of course, our Brothers, the Knights Templar agree that we should keep Rhodes as our larger, and main, base from now on."

"What I understand is that neither of you wants to lose his office," thought Clement, resting his elbows on the arms of his chair, before he finally said, somewhat abruptly, snorting disappointedly:

"Then go in peace both of you and act as you believe. However, I think that it would be in everyone's interest if you agreed to this plan. Reconsider. May the Holy Spirit grant you divine guidance".

The two Grand Masters realised that the audience had now come to an end and, after bowing in front of the Pope, they both headed out.

They were both happy about the conversation that had taken place. Especially Jacques, who walked proudly, with his white robe flapping in the autumn breeze, casting the occasional contemptuous glance towards Foulques, who, of course, did not waste the opportunity to reply in kind.

The Grand Master of the Knights Templar could never have imagined that the request he had made for papal investigation into the slander that had been spreading about his order would be precisely the reason Pandora's Box opened faster.

28

Paris, October 11, 1307

o I am listening gentlemen," said the king in a voice that betrayed his curiosity, to Guillaume de Nogaret and Guillaume de Plaisians, who had just entered the throne room and were standing opposite him with a smiles of satisfaction glued to their faces.

"I believe that our efforts have now begun to pay off," said Nogaret smiling malevolently and, after he had gone up to the king, gave him a letter that he was holding to read.

Philippe read the letter quickly. When he had finished, he looked up at his two lawyers, who were anxiously waiting for him to finish reading, and said:

"So things are happening as we expected. And exactly at the right moment, so that our actions will justified. That dolt, De Molay, has ordered a papal investigation to scotch the rumours that are tarnishing his order and Clement is asking for our help in carrying it out successfully."

"Which we will offer to do for him with great pleasure, won't we your majesty?" Nogaret said to the king, giving him a knowing look.

"Of course. Anyway we are ready," he replied. "About a month has passed since we sent our sealed orders to our bailiffs and seneschals throughout the realm, asking them to make discreet preparations for the arrest of all the Templars in France. Just remind me, my dears, what exactly the charges made in the warrant are."

De Plaisians spoke now:

"The warrant accuses the order of crimes against God, Christ, the Church, the western kingdoms and public decency. Also of involvement in witchcraft, heresy, sodomy and treason.

Philippe smiled:

"I see you included everything."

"That's the right way to do it, your majesty," Nogaret broke in

"Do you think anyone suspects?" the king asked anxiously.

"Out of the question," Nogaret replied in a way that brooked no objection. It's been over a year since we expelled all the Jews from your realm[103]. The matter has now been forgotten and no connection will be made between the two events. If, however, you agree, there is something more we can do to keep our plans hidden even further."

"What?"

"Tomorrow is the funeral of your sister-in-law, Catherine de Courtenay, the wife of your brother Charles de Valois. So I suggest that you let De Molay, who will be present at the ceremony, hold the pall covering the coffin, as if he were also a close relative of yours. You will honour him in this way as if he belonged to your family and no one will think, not even the man himself of course, that you are to arrest him the next day. What do you think?"

"By Our Lady! That's a wonderful idea my dear!" cried out the king, unable to hide his enthusiasm. "So be it. This is a wonderful opportunity that should not be missed!"

"So the only thing left that now remains," de Plaisians spoke now, his face somewhat overcast, "is to notify the Grand Chancellor and Keeper of the Royal Seal Gilles Aicelin of our intentions."

"Correct. A man with such important duties must be told about something so important. His seal is needed for the final arrest warrant the day after tomorrow," the king agreed.

"What if he doesn't agree?" de Plaisians wondered anxiously. "Gilles' reaction to these things has always been unpredictable. He didn't seem very happy about the arrest of the Jews."

"Don't worry," Nogaret broke in. "Anyway, even if he disagrees, he can't go against the king's will."

"Exactly. I shall, therefore, call him straight away, now that you are present, so that we can get it over with."

Philippe rang a bell that was placed on the table next to his throne. The door opened straight away and the old valet who entered the room bowed before the king.

"Tell Master Aicelin to come here straight away."

The valet nodded and ran to do what the king had ordered and, in less than fifteen minutes, Gilles was standing next to Philippe's lawyers, eager to hear the reason why the king had summoned him so suddenly.

"My dear Gilles, I called you to inform you about the actions we intend to take in the coming days that concern the order of the Knights Templar."

Gilles, his wrinkled eyes open wide in surprise, nodded. The king indicated to Nogaret that he should go on.

"Dear Gilles, as you must also have heard, rumours have recently been circulating about the order of the Knights Templar recently that are by no means flattering. They talk of heresy, blasphemy and sexual perversion, to make matters brief."

"I am aware of these rumours, but I am also certain that they are have no foundation whatsoever." He then turned to the king, gesturing emphatically. "Please don't tell me your majesty that you believe these slanders about the Knights Templar! The order is above all suspicion." Philippe did not reply and Nogaret, annoyed at the interruption, glared at Gilles said:

"Allow me to disagree, Gilles."

Nogaret took the papal letter that the king had left on the table next to him and gave it to Gilles.

"If the rumours were completely unfounded, Clement himself would not have ordered a papal investigation into the matter." Aicelin, his hands trembling, took the letter from Nogaret's hands and began to read it, unable to believe his eyes, as the others watched, satisfaction on their faces. He gave the letter back without saying a word, but glared at Nogaret. Although the letter was real, he remained unconvinced. He knew Nogaret and the trumped-up charges he made too well. The king took advantage of Aicelin's silence and said:

"So we ask of you, Gilles, as the Great Chancellor of France and Keeper of the Royal Seal, to approve the arrest of all of the Knights Templar in the kingdom of France, to answer these charges, the day after tomorrow, October 13th 1307, and to place the seal on the final order concerned, which will be filed in the royal archive."

Gilles then raised his hands and shouted as loudly as his old lungs would allow him to::

"No! I refuse to endorse a complete fabrication such as this, the motives for which I am very much aware. Last year I had the blood of innocent Jews on my hands after I signed the order. I will not do the same again, and have innocent people thrown into your dungeons!"

The king's face hardened after his initial surprise. The truth was that, neither he nor his lawyers, who looked aghast at the brave old man, had expected such an outburst from Gilles.

"Be careful Gilles, showing such disobedience towards your king may take a heavy toll on you and your beautiful family..."Philippe said in a voice that could barely be heard.

Gilles swallowed hard. He soon, however, regained his composure. He quickly took the great golden signet ring off the middle finger of his right hand and flung it hard down at the king's feet, shouting:

"If that's the case, your Majesty, I resign! You can appoint someone who is willing to put your wicked plans to effect in my place!"

Then, glancing towards Nogaret, he turned and headed out, adding:

"Although I think you have already found my replacement!"

Before the elderly man left the room, Philippe addressed him in a harsh, threatening voice:

"If the slightest information about these plans leaks out I shall hold you responsible Gilles! And then, believe me, you and your whole family will never see the light of day again!"

Aicelin slammed the door behind him, showing, at first sight, that he was unconcerned by the king's threat. Inside, however, he knew that the hard-hearted monarch would not hesitate to carry it out.

As he left the palace, he put his hands over his face in desperation and, paying no attention to the guards at the entrance who were looking at him with puzzled expressions on their faces, let out a doleful cry:

"Why God?"

How could he live for as long as God had decided with such a weight on his conscience? That he had known about the impending tragedy and had done nothing to prevent it? Then the image of his daughter, his wife and his grandsons in the hands of Philippe's guards came into his mind and he shuddered. No, his hands were tied. Unfortunately there was nothing he could do. Then he remembered the Knight Templar, young at the time, who had once saved his life from robbers.

"He must be saved! I owe him this! Anyway, won't some of them manage to run away?" he thought and at once started walking home, trying to think of a way to warn Philippe alone of the mortal danger he was in.

"I shall hide him in my house at first," the benevolent former Chancellor thought," and then we shall see what to do."

Back the throne room, the three men went on talking angrily:

"The idiot!" the king said angrily. "Who does he think he is and dares to doubt my decisions?"

He rose to his feet and snatched the ring up from the floor. He sat back on his throne and played with the piece of gold jewellery in his hand a little, looking at it thoughtfully. Then he stood up again and went up to Nogaret, who was standing opposite him, took his right hand in his own and placed the ring on Nogaret's middle finger, saying:

"Guillaume de Nogaret, from this moment forth I appoint you Grand Chancellor of France and Keeper of the Royal Seals. Do you accept this honour?"

"It would be a great honour, your Majesty," Nogaret answered dutifully. "I hope I prove worthy of the trust you have placed in me."

The king patted Nogaret on the shoulder and sat back in his throne, rubbing his hands:

"All right then, if everything goes well, soon our vaults will be filled with the Knights Templars' fortune." He then indicated to the two men that the audience had come to an end.

Philippe's two lawyers smiled at the king knowingly and headed, in turn, towards the door after bowing low.

***

It was cloudy at dawn on October 12th, as befitted the funeral of the young Catherine De Courtenay. The weather had continued to wear its sad face even as darkness had begun to fall and the ceremony was about to end.

The death of the unfortunate woman had been the result of heavy bleeding following the birth of her first child. The newborn baby had survived and was now safe in the arms of her carer back in the palace. The broken-hearted husband, Charles de Valois, walked ahead of the funeral procession next to his brother, the king, and the queen.

The procession had started from the Cathedral of Notre Dame and was now heading towards the cemetery. Behind the royal family came Catherine's coffin. The body could not be seen in the coffin as it was covered by a red pall. Its edges were held by distant members of the royal family, or people favoured by the king and appointed by him, as a sign of his absolute trust in them..

One of them, as had been decided the previous day, was Jacques de Molay. He was holding one of the edges of the red pall, walking proudly with his white robe waving in the breeze, his face with its trimmed beard shone with joy despite the sadness of the occasion at which he was present. Such was the honour the king had granted him.

The procession was making its way through the dense crowd of Parisians that had gathered there for the occasion, as they would do on every public occasion, providing them with a distraction from their hard and monotonous daily existence. They had all come to see the royal family at close hand and wonder at the luxury of the king's clothes, or were there simply out of curiosity. They were certainly not there out of grief at the death of a woman they had never seen and who had lived her life in luxury, unlike the Parisians themselves, most of whom lived in abject poverty.

Many Knights Templar and knights from other orders were also watching the funeral procession, including Philippe and Francois. The day's event meant that the knights in the Temple of Paris all had leave that evening after the funeral.

As soon as the procession had passed the spot where the two knights were standing, Philippe turned towards his friend and said to him, smiling:

"I'm going to Giselle now. Our obligations are over. We have admired our Lord Master and mourned for Catherine, haven't we?"

Francois smiled in turn, and indicated that they should make their way out of the dense crowd.

"So we have. Shall we to dine together first? I think that they will have a lot of work in the tavern today and it will take them sometime to shut up shop."

"Good idea! Let's go then!"

The knights headed towards the tavern "Belle Nuit" at once. Giselle was taking an order from a table by the door and Philippe almost knocked her over as he opened it. As Francois had predicted, the tavern was very busy. Philippe was very happy to have his friend there to keep him company as the night wore on and his sweetheart could not leave as her sister would have been unable to both take orders and serve on her own.

When all the tables had emptied, the hour for dinner[104]. Giselle and her sister were cleaning the tables when Francois stood up and said goodbye to Philippe.

"Goodbye my friend! I'm going back to the Temple!" Then he added laughing slyly:

"Someone must cover your absence, mustn't he?"

He patted him on the shoulder amicably and disappeared at once before Philippe had time to reply. Almost at that same moment Giselle gave him a secret nod that indicated that he should come up to her room.

Philippe left two coins on the table and quickly climbed the stairs that lead to the second floor, to Giselle's room. He took his clothes off straight away and lay under the blankets to wait for his beloved.

Not more than ten minutes could have passed before the door opened and the young woman appeared in the doorway, sweetly smiling at Philippe. She was wearing the green dress she wore at work again, the one that brought out her emerald coloured eyes so well. As soon as she saw Philippe under the blankets she began to unbutton her dress, without talking, with crafty, cat-like movements, her back turned to the knight who had sat up on the bed and could not get enough of watching her.

The young woman was taking off her corset when she turned to him, looking at him naughtily. She let the corset fall softly to her feet, left it on the floor and headed towards the bed with slow sensual movements, enjoying her nakedness and throwing the Knight Templar mincing looks. She sat on Philippe's thighs, wrapped her knees around the knight's waist and her arms around his neck.

"I've missed you!" she whispered adoringly and straight away her rosy lips immediately found his. After a passionate wet kiss, Philippe gently moved her face away from his and looked at her tenderly, stroking her cheek with the index finger of right hand:

"I've missed you too!" he said, his voice hoarse with passion. "More than you can imagine!"

His hand went straight to Giselle's breast, stroked it for a second and went towards her moist sex. Giselle began to moan with pleasure and put her head back. Philippe held her tightly and gently entered her with his, for some time now erect, member, making Giselle moan even louder with pleasure. Their intercourse was short, but intense and passionate.

After the two lovers had climaxed at the same time, experiencing supreme pleasure, Giselle laid her head on Philippe's chest and they stayed this way for some time, without talking, while he stroked her hair gently and tenderly. In the end, after the two had burrowed under the warm sheets, still in each other's arms, Philippe said to Giselle:

"I feel so complete when I am near you! I wonder if such was the passion Tristan and Isolde felt for each other."

"What memories you bring back to me now!" the girl said wistfully. "I very vaguely remember my mother telling me their story shortly before she died!"

"My mother also told me such stories. Tristan and Isolde, Arthur and Guinevere, Siegfried and Krimhild[105].

Giselle ran her fingers through his hair.

"Which of these characters do you feel you can identify with most?"

Philippe thought a little.

"Mmm... probably with the passionate Tristan. I feel such an attraction for you, that it is truly as if I have drunk a love potion!"

Giselle's expression became sad for a moment:

"I hope, however, that our story does not end in the same way..."

As if to confirm Giselle's words and before Philippe had time to answer, the shadow of an owl appeared at the window of the room and immediately began to hoot in its monotone. Giselle jumped up from the bed, breathless:

"There! See? An owl is a bad omen! Something bad is going to happen!"

The Knight Templar, who did not share her concern, sat up and hugged her tenderly:

"Don't worry; I will not let anything bad happen! Our future is in our hands – we will not to end up like Tristan and Isolde[106]"

"I am afraid no one can escape their destiny..." Giselle said melancholically.

"Nonsense! Man makes his own destiny. Let's get some sleep now, it's late," said Philippe, his eyelids heavy with sleep.

They lay under the warm blankets again and Morpheus quickly took the carefree Philippe into his arms, as the knight lay in his lover's arms. Giselle, however, lay awake for a long time, looking at the bird's shadow on the window of her room. Dark thoughts went through her mind, as if she was certain something bad would happen to them, something that that nightmarish night owl was, undoubtedly, foreshadowing.

She eventually managed to fall into a troubled sleep, full of nightmares, trembling now and then in her sweetheart's arms, when the first rays of light began to slowly penetrate the dark veil of night. It was dawn on October 13th, 1307.

29

Paris, October 13, 1307

he service of the first hour had just ended and Jacques de Molay was in his office. He was busy checking some financial documents which concerned the Temple's income and expenses.

"We are doing well, very well," he thought happily, looking at his papers.

There had been no decrease in the Temple's income, despite the fact that the order was no longer receiving generous grants and all kinds of donations as it had in the past. This was not only because the order drew income from its estates and the various items of agricultural produce it sold, but also because it continued to enjoy exemption from tax. What's more, there were no longer the castles in Outremer to maintain, something that had swallowed up the order's income at one time.

"When the passagium generale that we so desire takes place, we will be able to contribute," thought De Molay and rose from his chair.

He put his cloak on and left his office, heading towards the stables. He asked the groom to bring his jet-black stallion to the entrance because he wanted to inspect the order's vineyards as the harvest had just ended.

The guard at the entrance, a young red haired sergeant, bowed respectfully when he saw the Grand Master and De Molay prepared to mount his horse, which his groom had just brought to him.

Jacques had just taken hold of the reins when the sound of clanging swords drew his attention and he turned towards the guard at the entrance. What he saw made him let out a loud cry of surprise and terror.

About two hundred soldiers with the King of France's emblem on their shields appeared out of nowhere and began to enter the Templar's grounds. De Molay looked at the guard, who the soldiers had disarmed and immobilized, in terror.

Jacques let go of the horse's reins and ran towards them:

"What is the meaning of this?" he asked, furious.

"It means that all you Knights Templar are under arrest from this moment on in the name of the King of France," a large man with rugged features, who seemed to be the commander judging by his insignia, answered him bluntly.

Before De Molay had time to reply, two soldiers took hold of him and tied his arms behind his back despite his fiery protestations.

"You have no right! My order is only accountable only to the Pope!"

"The Pope himself has ordered an investigation into the crimes of which your order is accused and our king has simply offered to help him," the commander said coldly, then at once called to his men:

"Don't let anyone get away!"

Meanwhile, with all the commotion, many Knights Templar, sergeants and also people working in the grounds of the Temple had come to the entrance to see what was going on. Very few of them had weapons in their hands and so were unable to resist the king's soldiers. Those who did, seeing their Grand Master in danger, were quickly subdued by the king's superior forces.

Francois was one of those who came out armed to see what was happening. He put up a brave fight, but did not manage avoid capture in the end. Even the Temple workers and grooms were arrested.

De Molay was still unable to believe that Philippe, who had honoured him with his trust only the previous day before, had behaved with such insincerity towards his order. At the same time as the sad procession of the one hundred and thirty eight Knights Templar who had been arrested was about to set off on its way towards the dark royal prison in the palace, he asked the commander:

"May I at least know on what charges we are being arrested?"

The commander replied curtly as he put his sword back in its scabbard, without even bothering to look at his prisoner.

"These are details Master Nogaret knows. I am just doing my duty. I imagine that when the time comes, he will see to it that you are properly informed."

The knights taken prisoner began to make their way through the streets of a city that had just started to stir from its night time torpor, causing its astonished inhabitants to comment on the arrest of the once mighty knights that had taken place so quickly and so suddenly.

Some of those in the crowd were glad because they disliked these arrogant and money loving knights, others however believed from the beginning that the knights were completely innocent and the victims of a conspiracy. Nevertheless, the impression this event made on the people of the time, no matter how they regarded the arrest of the Knights Templar, is very neatly captured in the words of an unknown poet of the time:

In the year one thousand three hundred and seven, and mark it well

The time they arrested the mighty Knights Templar

Those who once were of the bravest were ill-used

I believe it was definitely the work of the Infidels

The year I said before

The fearless Knights Templar were arrested

By the king of France.

I do not know if it was fair or unfair.

In October, one dawn,

It was Friday...[107]

As arrests continued throughout Philippe the Fair's kingdom, Giselle opened her eyes, finding herself in Philippe's arms after an uneasy sleep. She could hear a commotion in the streets, something unusual for that particular time of the day..

Still troubled by the previous night's sense of foreboding, she turned and looked at the man she loved, still sound asleep. For a moment she was reassured by his presence beside her. She hugged him so tight that in his sweet sleep he let a sigh of pleasure leave his lips. She stayed that way, awake and curled up in his arms, for some time.

At the same time, on the ground floor of the tavern, a servant sent by Gilles was knocking hard on the door.

Late the night before Gilles had summoned Claude, his most loyal servant, and he had given him the task of bringing the Knight Templar Brother Philippe to his house in secret. Gilles had told the servant everything – the good deed the knight had done for him, Nogaret and the king's evil plans, his resignation - and had asked him not only to swear not to breathe a word of this, but also to make sure he brought the knight to his home so that he could be rescued.

In the thick of the night, Claude had run to the Temple and had asked the guard at the entrance to tell Brother Philippe to come down without fail, at Gilles's request. The guard, however, had returned empty-handed and told Claude that Brother Philippe was not in his dormitory. It was against the rules for him to be outside the Temple so it was best if he searched for him no further, in case others became aware of his absence.

Claude had then run back to his master, who was bitterly disappointed by the failure of Claude's mission at first, as he wanted to keep him out of Philippe's clutches by any means. In a flash of inspiration, however, his elderly mind had turned to his encounter with the knight at "Belle Nuit", and his illicit affair with Giselle. So he had sent, dawn having broken in the meantime, his servant to the tavern, begging God with all his heart that Philippe would be there.

"If he has gone back to the Temple then he is done for," thought Gilles, pacing up and down in his living room, knowing that the king would have had his people remain in all the Knights Templar Houses in France, at least for the first twenty four hours after the arrests.

Giselle's uncle and aunt, who had just woken up, opened the door, terrified at the sight of the unexpected visitor who had come so early in the morning. He had a small pouch with him.

"My good people, please tell me if you know of a Knight Templar in your inn?" Claude said quickly, unable to hide his obvious agitation.

The couple looked at each other, taken aback. It was, of course, a common secret that the Knight Templar slept with their niece now and then. They had seen him the night before when he stayed with her, but why was this mysterious man asking? They neither knew if his intentions were good nor did they by any means wish their niece's promiscuous behaviour to bring shame on them. So they remained silent, not knowing how to answer their unexpected visitor.

Claude could see what they were thinking and was quick to clarify the situation:

"I intend no harm, my good people, rather, this is a matter of life and death. You'll soon see why I am asking you."

Finally the man said to Claude firmly:

"There is a Knight Templar upstairs, on the second floor. I'll allow you to go up but I'll have no scandal or mischief on my premises."

"Don't worry, nothing like that is going to happen," replied Claude, and without wasting any more time, he headed inside towards the stairs that led to the floors above, leaving the couple dumbfounded at the door.

He was soon outside the only door that was closed on the second floor and knocked hard on it three times with the palm of his hand.

Inside Philippe woke up from his sleep, jumped up, surprised and found Giselle next to him, half-naked, looking at him in both fear and bewilderment.

"Who is it?" Philippe asked boldly without getting up, remembering what had gone on the night before. He was almost certain that it would be Giselle's sister or her aunt or uncle and that they would want to give her some task or other, as they had done before in the past.

"I am looking for the Knight Templar Brother Philippe," the mysterious voice replied behind the closed door.

"Don't open Philippe! I'm afraid! Who could it be at this time of day?" Giselle said, distress obvious in her voice.

Without answering Giselle, Philippe was out of bed in a flash and, in his breeches and shirt."That's me. Who is asking for me please?"

"My name is Claude and I am a servant of Gilles Aicelin. I bring you a very important message on his behalf. Please let me in! It's for your own safety!"

Philippe motioned to Giselle to get up and get dressed a little further off, which she did straight away while he was unlocking the door.

Claude burst in at once and said to Philippe:

"Brother Philippe, my master has sent me to take you to his house in all secrecy. You are obviously unaware of this but at dawn all the Knights Templar in the lands of Philippe the Fair were arrested on his orders! Put on the clothes I give you and come with me right away if you want to live!"

Philippe, surprised and not believing a word he had heard, replied, somewhat angrily:

"Are you in your right mind man? What's all this rubbish you are telling me? Our order arrested? And how do I know you are telling me the truth?"

A sigh left Claude's lips and at once he wearily took out a folded piece of paper from a fold in his clothes and gave it to Philippe, saying:

"Fortunately my master foresaw your reaction and gave me this letter. Read it please."

Philippe took the paper, unfolded it, and began to read carefully:

Dear Philippe,

I know that you will find it difficult to believe my servant, but for your own safety you must come with him. Up until the day before yesterday I was the Keeper of the Royal Seals and that is why I am in a position to know that the members of your order will suffer grievous harm in the months to come. I owe you my life so, by saving yours now, I hope to repay the favour. I'll tell you the rest in person.

Always yours,

Gilles Aicelin

Philippe looked up from the paper at Claude, who was now giving him a bundle containing the poor, dirty clothes of a tanner that Gilles had sent for him to wear as a disguise. He was standing speechless, unable to decide what to do, when a loud disturbance from the street below made Giselle run to the window to see what was going on. Philippe followed her.

The procession of captured Knights Templar had reached the tavern and a crowd was watching with a mixture of fear and amazement. None of them knew why the knights had been arrested and they stood aside, muttering in bewilderment, for the soldiers to pass. To his horror, Philippe saw Jacques de Molay at the head of the procession, his hands tied behind his back and surrounded by a number of the king's soldiers.

"I knew that something bad was going to happen!" Giselle exclaimed, and held onto Philippe tightly, terrified. Also frightened, Philippe turned to Claude, who said, a hint of triumph in his voice:

"I believe you are convinced now! So be quick!"

"Yes. If he is to hide you, go with him! I don't want anything to happen to you!" said Giselle, looking into her beloved's eyes."

"Nothing is going to happen to him since he will be with my master. Rest assured," Claude said, while Philippe, now entirely convinced by what the servant had said, quickly changed clothes. When Philippe was ready Claude opened the door and indicated to him that he should hurry.

"Just a second!" shouted Philippe. "Maybe we should wait a little for the soldiers to leave first?"

Claude smiled:

"On the contrary, it is now that we can leave safely. Under the wolf's nose... the best cover, so that no one suspects you are hiding. The way you are dressed, you have nothing to fear! You look as if you are someone I am taking to my master to be given some work to do."

Then, as if something had crossed his mind for a second, he turned to Giselle:

"Unless the people downstairs, who know there is a Knight Templar in the building, give us away!"

"Out of the question!" Giselle replied, somewhat annoyed. "They would never give someone who has not harmed them away to the soldiers! Anyway, Philippe was a regular!"

The knight went to Giselle and pressed his lips softly and somewhat hastily against hers. He felt bad wearing the clothes he was wearing. They gave off a revolting smell of skinned animal and this made him feel uncomfortable, which was why he didn't hug her. He only said, in a voice that showed absolute certainty, despite the uncertainty of what he had to say:

"I don't know when and how I'll manage it but I am sure I will see you again. I will not leave you this like this. All I need know is that you'll be waiting for me and I can take courage."

She held his face in her hands and replied tenderly:

"I love you and I will wait for you for as long as I need to, I promise. But write to me, so I know you are well."

Their lips met once more in a final farewell, and Philippe quickly went down the stairs, following Claude. When he got to the first floor he turned and saw his loved one waving to him, tears in her eyes. Then, after saying goodbye to Giselle's astonished aunt and uncle, he went out into the street with Claude.

30

Paris, November 24, 1307

rancois opened his eyes. Completely naked, he saw his torturers and realised, to his horror, that he was still alive.

He had just suffered the strappado, a notorious method of torture. They had used a rope to tie his hands behind his back , and passed it over a beam on the ceiling. Weights had been hung onto his legs and testicles to increase the pain. He had then been hoisted up and quickly dropped, only for his fall to be checked centimetres before he touched the ground. The sudden jerk had left Francois with both arms broken. Even now he could feel the pain from his arms and his legs, dislocated by the weights, while blood continued to flow from his torn tentacles.

Until now he had managed, despite the intolerable pain, not to admit to any of the horrible crimes they were unjustly accusing his order of.

His suffering was not, however, over. His torturers looked at each other conspiratorially and immediately tied a thick rope around Francois' now broken body while his inquisitor began to put tallow on his feet.

Francois, realising what was to follow, began to shout desperately:

"No, not that! Please!"

His torturers though, were deaf to his desperate calls. They grabbed him and held the feet of the unfortunate Knight Templar above the flames in the hearth for a few ghastly moments. Francois began to scream as if possessed, unable to stand the pain, while in his mind he pleaded with God to release him from his suffering as soon as possible

"So, talk," he heard the inquisitor, who was looking in horror at Francois's scorched feet, say. "Admit that you spat on the cross and denied our Lord Jesus Christ."

Before Francois had time to answer, his torturers lifted him again and held him above the flames once more.

"Yes! Yes! I did!" said Francois while his torturers laid him down on a table again.

"I admit everything! I have sinned! Enough! Mercy!"

He looked at his bleeding feet. The skin was completely gone and the bones of his feet could almost be seen.

Francois knew he would never be able to walk again.

"So you admit it you heretic worm! Do you also admit that as part of the ceremony when you were initiated into the order you kissed your Grand Master at the time on the navel, penis, at the base of the spine and on the buttocks?"

"Yes. I admit it," Francois replied weakly.

"Do you also admit that in your Temple you worshipped an idol, a head, which your other Brothers told us you called Baphomet?"

Francois thought for a minute:

"What are they talking about? Forgive me God for admitting to such sacrilege, but I can't take any more!", and then he said out loud:

"Yes, I admit it."

"Very well! That's more than enough! Take the heretic back to his cell!"

As he was dragged to his cell, Francois bit his lips until they bled as he tried to bear the pain that ran throughout his body. When the door closed behind him and the knight was left in total darkness, he tried to crawl to the dirty bowl that held the little water they had left him. This, however, proved impossible. With dislocated legs and scorched, bleeding feet and broken arms, movement was impossible, not to mention the blood flowing from his genitals, yet to stop. Many other Brothers had endured the same tortures. Some had confessed immediately and others had held out for a while, like Francois. Very few had denied all charges. Who would not admit to whatever was asked of them under such torture?"

"For the obstinate heretics, there are special means of making them confess." That was what one of Francois' torturers had said to him, three days before, when they had gone to get him and torture him for the first time. Before that, he had spent over a month in this horrible cell, completely alone, in total darkness and eating only pieces of dry food, hearing the desperate screams of his Brothers as confessions were forced out of them

He closed his eyes and tried to think of something to take his mind off the pain that was pounding through his head as he lay on the ice-cold floor. The bleeding had drained the life from him and he knew that the end was near.

His mind went to his youth when as a young knight he had made the journey with Philippe, to Outremer full of dreams and hopes. With these pleasant memories, the pain, strangely enough, g faded away and his soul, light as a feather, left his body and passed into the incorporeal world of spirits.

The next morning, the torturers at the prison would realise that another Knight Templar had died, helpless in his cell, because of the inhuman tortures they had suffered. They would not, however, feel any sadness at this, as Francois had confessed his sins, and had saved his soul from the eternal fires of hell.

***

Philippe was pacing up and down agitatedly in the sitting room in Gilles's house, while the elderly man, from an armchair, watched him out of the corner of his eye. The knight was like a caged animal..

Since the day Claude had brought him to his house, saving his life, Philippe had been languishing away, growing worse by the day, something Gilles felt was absolutely understandable. Philippe might have been saved, but he had to come to terms with the idea that most of his Brothers would be tortured to death, something that would make him feel guilty that he had survived. What's more, it had been nearly two months since he had been out of the house. Gilles thought that he should remain in hiding to stay safe.

All this time Gilles had been hearing the news that was going around concerning the destruction of the order and the fate of its members, which had shocked the whole of Paris. Only twenty five people had managed to escape Philippe the Fair. Among them, besides Philippe, were the Grand Preceptor of France, Gerard de Villiers and Humbert Blanc, Grand Preceptor of Auvergne, who had managed, no one knew how, to get away.

Gerard de Villiers, a prominent member of Fede Santa, had managed to save most of the Acre's manuscripts from Acre, thus rescuing ancient knowledge. However, no one ever found out where Gerard went or what became of the legendary "Treasure of the Knights Templar".

Some said afterwards that Gerard went to Scotland and others, in more imaginative version of events, that Gerard sailed to America in one of the Knights Templar' galleys, one and a half century before Columbus, but not before the Vikings, who had discovered it first in the 10th century. Everything, however, remained in the realm of speculation, as not even the Knights Templar who survived, and certainly not the members of the secret organization, like Philippe, ever found out what happened to the precious manuscripts.

As for the knights that had not been as lucky as Gerard and Philippe, in the two months that had followed the arrests, everyone, without exception, had been tortured and almost all had confessed to the charges brought against them. Much to everyone's surprise, De Molay himself had confessed to prominent lawyers, only ten days after his arrest, in a public place, at a meeting that took place in the University of Paris. Only four had categorically denied the charges, Jean de Chateauvillars, Henri de Hercigny, Jean de Paris and Lambert de Toysi.

Contrary to Philippe's expectations, the Pope had complained about the usurpation of his rights by the king in ecclesiastical matters and about the haste he had shown in this particular case.

Given the limitations placed on Clement's actions, since he was in Philippe's territory, he did as the king requested and he issued the bull Pastorali praeeminentie, which instructed all the kings of England, Ireland, Portugal, Castille, Aragon, Cyprus, Germany and Italy to arrest all the Knights Templar that were in their lands and seize their assets in the name of the Pope , but he also demanded that Philippe send the prisoners to the ecclesiastical courts.

In practice it was a very long time before this came about. Philippe was extremely unhappy, since this intervention by Clement was spoiling his plans and was going to delay proceedings for many more years. At least that was what Gilles believed would happen, while the king wanted to get the knights' confessions over with within only a few weeks so that he could make use of the huge fortune of the Knights Templar quickly. It was thus, after the intervention of the Pope, that everyone was waiting anxiously to see how the drama would unfold.

Philippe had now stopped walking around the room and was gazing out of the window. Gilles got up and put his hands on his shoulders sympathetically.

"I cannot watch you languish like this any more, my son," he said to him.

Philippe's thoughts were on Francois and he replied without turning around:

"You are right; it's just that I still can't believe what has happened! I think that everything is a nightmare and I shall soon wake up!"

Gilles looked serious and thought that it was now time to talk openly with the knight who had now turned around, and was looking at him with an expression of intense sorrow.

"Philippe, listen to me. I completely understand the difficult emotional situation you are in and, believe me, it is completely normal, considering everything that has happened to your Brothers. You must, however, in some way, leave France. You are not safe here any more and all this might go on for years. You can't stay locked up in here all that time! Not to mention that if one of all those who are coming in and out of here suspects you and betrays you to the king, you will suffer the consequences. I also have many enemies that are looking for an opportunity to hurt me. Anyway, your Brothers who managed to get away from Philippe and Nogaret are all outside France now."

Philippe nodded:

"You are right Gilles. I've thought about this too and, to be frank, I know a place where I will be safe, if, of course, they'll have me there and I can manage to get there."

"I'm all ears," the elderly man replied, interested.

"That place is Rhodes"

"Rhodes?" Gilles said, puzzled.

"Yes. You maybe know that the island was recently occupied by the Hospitallers."

"I know that, but I don't see what that might have to do with you."

"I have a very close friendship with their current Lord Master, Foulques de Villaret. We fought together in Outremer and I saved his life twice. I'd like to believe that he will not leave me helpless at this difficult time."

"Then what are you waiting for? Write to him straight away so we can see if he can have you there," said Gilles, sitting back down into the armchair again, somewhat relieved that a solution had been found.

"I believe he will not object to this."

"Right then. To work!" Gilles said happily and at once clapped his hands twice loudly. Claude appeared right away and the elderly man asked him for pen and paper. When the servant brought them, Gilles stood up and left the room, leaving Philippe alone so that he could take his time over writing the letter. Philippe walked around the room once more and looked at the paper left on Gilles's desk. Once more Giselle came to mind and a deep sigh left his lips. He finally pulled up the chair, sat and began to write, muttering under his breath:

"I'm doing this for you my love… So that we can be together again when the storm passes."

31

Rhodes, February 28, 1308

It was a sunny morning, heralding the arrival of spring and Foulques was sitting at his desk in the new palace of the Hospitaller knights in the city of Rhodes, which had been completed not more than a week previously and had been built solely to house the Grand Master. In his hands he was holding, with great pleasure, the copy of a papal bull that Clement had issued on December 21st the previous year concerning his order.

Alarmed by the recent events that concerned the Knights Templar, Foulques had asked that the Pope validate their position and their new headquarters in the city of Rhodes, and Clement had ordered, in the bull, that the Hospitaller Knights be protected.

Foulques was enormously relieved. What had happened to the Templars had terrified the Hospitallers, and they were certain, once that order had been destroyed, that they would be next.

Fortunately their deployment on the island was going extremely well. It meant that they could play the role of the warriors against "the Infidel" once again, and forestall anyone who might have his eye on the order's fortune. The locals, however, did dislike them, but that was only to be expected of Greek "heretics", and none of the knights were much concerned about them.

His thoughts were interrupted by a discreet knock on the door. It was Nicolas.

"My Lord Grand Master, you have a letter. It came this morning on our ship that arrived from Marseilles."

"Thank you, Brother," replied Foulques while taking the letter from the seneschal's hands and nodding to him to leave. When he read the name of the sender on the envelope, he froze:

"Philippe?" he whispered, unable to believe his eyes. "So you're alive?"

He was at once filled with indescribable joy. After all he heard about the arrests of Knights Templar in France, he had been certain that his fraternal friend was dead. He tore the envelope open hurriedly, eager to read its content.

My Dear Brother Grand Master,

I hope my letter finds you well and settled in your new headquarters in Rhodes. Needless to say I have very much missed your company. I often look back on the times we have spent together. In the name of that old friendship I would like to ask for your help, of which I am now in dire need.

You must have heard about the unjust arrests the king of France had in store for our unfortunate order and the confiscation of its property. It was by through sheer good luck that I managed to get away, thanks to the help of a friend at the right moment. It's Gilles Aicelin, former Keeper of the Royal Seals, who has been hiding me for some time now in his house, right opposite the entrance to the university of Paris.

This, however. is becoming very dangerous, both for him and for me, since the issue that has arisen for our order has yet to be resolved and might go on for years. I must, therefore, find another place of refuge, not only for my own safety, but also for that of the person who saved me. Would you possibly be able to take me in in Rhodes? I am certain that there I could escape the wrath of the king and his lawyers. In return, I shall try to prove useful to you in any way I can.

I anxiously await your reply.
Your always fraternal friend,
Philippe de Ridefort

Foulques let the paper fall onto the desk and stared at the wall opposite him, thinking. He had to help Philippe. He was his best friend and, besides, no one had believed that the Knights Templar were heretics. The question was how he could help him in the most effective way. If he wrote him a reply, his letter would take at least one and a half months to get to Paris. If it did actually get there and nothing went wrong, would the Knight Templar be able to get to Rhodes safe and sound?

Finally, after he thought he had found the best solution, he shouted loudly so that he could be heard behind the closed door:

"Sergeant! Tell the seneschal and mareschal to come to my office immediately!"

"Right away, my Lord," the sergeant replied at once.

It wasn't long until a muffled knock on the door was heard. As soon as Foulques answered in the affirmative, Thomas and Nicolas appeared in the doorway.

"Did you call for us, my Lord?"

"Yes. Sit down."

"I would like your help in a matter of the utmost secrecy. You are not to talk to anyone else about this. Have I made myself clear?"

"You can be certain of this, my Lord," said Thomas, and Nicolas also nodded in agreement

"I don't know if you remember it from the old days, but maybe you know that I have a close friend who is a member of the order of the Knights Templar."

"'Was you mean to say. Yes, I remember," said Thomas.

"That friend of mine," continued Foulques," has managed to avoid arrest and is now asking for my help to stay alive. I want him to come here." The two men nodded and the Grand Master went on:

"He saved my life twice in the past in Outremer and I am in his debt. The question is how I can help him escape here and keep it as well-hidden as possible."

"Have you anything particular in mind?" asked Nicolas.

"Yes. I believe that the best thing would be for one of you to go to Paris and bring him here, disguised as a Hospitaller knight. What do you think?"

"I would go with pleasure, my Lord," said Thomas, agreeing with the Grand Master. I think that, at this stage, Nicolas, as seneschal, is needed here more."

"Thomas is right, I think," said Nicolas. "For the time being, no military conflict requiring the presence of the mareschal on the island appears imminent."

"Alright then. Leave right away on our ship that is shortly leaving for Marseilles. Take a uniform of a knight of our order with you so that Philippe can disguise himself and no-one with bad intentions recognises him. Go to Gilles Aicelin's house. It is right opposite the Sorbonne so you will have no difficulty at all in finding it. Tell Philippe that I have sent you to get him. No letter will be necessary. As soon as he sees a Hospitaller knight, I am certain he will understand. Have I made myself clear?"

"Yes, my Lord. Gilles Aicelin you said?"

"Yes. Anything else?"

The knight shook his head.

"All right then. Thank you very much in advance. Run and get ready and bring him here as fast as you can," said Foulques, leaning back in his chair to show that the conversation was over.

"We should be back in less than three months. Goodbye," said Thomas and left the room.

"So what have you finally heard from Cyprus, Brother Nicolas?" asked the Grand Master when Thomas left, changing the subject.

"About the Knights Templar?"

"Yes."

"Nothing. Amalric has not followed the Pope's order yet. No Knight Templar has been arrested for the moment."

"So Amalric didn't believe the story about heresy either. And in England? Did you find out what Edward did in the end?"

"Edward delayed issuing the arrest warrant on purpose. So many knights escaped. But even those who decided to stay, were simply confined to their headquarters and have even kept, I was told, their weapons," replied Nicolas, stroking his beard.

"I see. Neither in Aragon, nor in Italy, from what I also heard, did calls from the Pope produce any result. Only in Germany did they arrest the Knights Templar with the same zeal as in France."

"We are lucky to have been spared. A plot like that…" said the knight, shaking his head .

"Yes… Let's go now," said Foulques and stood up suddenly, hearing the bell summoning them to the service for the sixth hour.

Nicolas did the same thing at once and the two men left the office. Foulques' mind was on Philippe. He hoped with all his heart that Thomas would manage to successfully complete the mission he had given him.

Rhodes, December 28, 1314

ad! Dad! Come on, it's time to go to work! You promised me that today you would take me with you to the castle too! Come on! Wake up!"

Philippe, lying on the soft straw mattress, opened his eyes slowly and saw his seven-year-old son pushing him hard on the shoulder, his clothes already on.

He turned to the other side right away and looked at Giselle, who had woken up and was smiling at him, lying down as she listened to little Jocelyn wake up his father.

"Alright! I'm getting up!" Philippe said grumpily, smiling faintly, and sat up on the bed rubbing his eyes.

"Shall we go Dad?" little Jocelyn asked, looking at his father with his green eyes and pulling his hand hard.

The boy was the spitting image of Giselle, but with more masculine features, but he was more like Philippe in terms of character.

Philippe got up, put his woollen shirt on, kissed Giselle, still lying in bed and, lifting Jocelyn high, after he had first stroked his hair, put him on his shoulders.

Straight away they set off for the Grand Master's castle in which Philippe worked as a groom for Foulques.

The little boy was talking to himself, pretending to be a knight, while using his right hand to pretend he was stabbing imaginary enemies. Philippe, unable to see him, listened to him and smiled.

"Take it easy! Don't make sudden movements or you will fall!" he said when he saw that the child was becoming a little too lively.

Although it was winter, it was a sunny day and Philippe was walking slowly with the child on his shoulders, enjoying the walk to the castle. Winter here was much milder compared to Paris and he could not get enough of walks on the island throughout the year.

Without noticing it, his mind turned to the past. Giselle's arrival on the island came to mind. It had been almost a year since, to his surprise, she had appeared in front of him, not alone, but with a child in her arms, his son!

He remembered how surprised he had been when Giselle had revealed to him that she had become pregnant before they parted because of the tragic events of 1307 and had come to realise it later. He also remembered how guilty he had felt and how much he had felt for her when Giselle had told him that she had given birth with difficulty under the judgemental eye of her aunt, and her own relief when she received his letter, telling her to come to him.

She had named the child Jocelyn, after Philippe's father about whom the Knight Templar had told her so much, and she had hoped that the child would one day see his father, who instinct told her was still alive and had not forgotten her. And that is what had happened.

Giselle had made the long trip all alone with the child, using the money she had been saving all those years. The money had also helped her avoid many problems, paying off those of her fellow travellers who had approached her with ill intent.

Their marriage, which had taken place a little after Giselle's arrival on the island, in the cathedral of the Grand Master's palace, and was simply the happy end to their beautiful love story.

As for her aunt and uncle, they had been very pleased that their niece had finally left for Rhodes, since the girl now had an illegitimate child, and this brought great shame on the family.

Philippe's mind, however, was now more on the day of his arrival on the island, six and a half years ago, and on his meeting with his fraternal friend, Foulques.

Thomas had brought him to the island successfully, after a relatively quiet and uneventful trip. When the two friends had seen each other, after so many years spent away from each other, they had embraced each other warmly.

Then they had spent the whole of the day on which the Templar had arrived in Foulques' office and had talked about everything, until late. Philippe had thanked Foulques profusely for saving him, but had become dejected and rather morose when he had heard everything about his brother Templars.

He had spent the years until 1313 as a Hospitaller, now, knight, beside Foulques, remembering the woman he loved and anxious about what was to happen to his Brothers in a story of suspense and horror that went on and on.

As soon as De Molay had found himself before the papal commission, after Clement's intervention, he had revoked his confession. Knights Templar had gradually begun to do the same, saying that their confessions should not be taken into consideration because they had been extracted from them under torture.

Brothers like Ponsard de Gizy and Pierre De Bologna had declared their innocence outright and had provided the committee with a list of those who had accused the order, all of them Brothers who had been expelled from the order for their immoral behaviour. Pierre had openly accused the king and Nogaret of making a blatant attack on his order and reminded everyone of the two centuries of service the Knights Templar had given to Christianity.

By March 1310 five hundred and forty six Knights Templar had recanted, proclaiming their innocence, and it all seemed as if everything would end well, and no blood would be shed. Philippe, however, decided that under no circumstances would he allow anything of the sort to happen. So, on May 11th, the Archbishop of Sens,

Philippe de Marigny, on the king's orders, found fifty-four Knights Templar who had recanted their confessions guilty of being relapsed heretics, and condemned them to death by burning at the stake.

In the face of this brutality, the rest of those defending the Knight Templar lost heart and reacted in the way the king wanted, by keeping their mouths closed, for fear of meeting the same fate themselves. Meanwhile, in convoking the Assembly of the Estates in 1308, the king had made sure to turn public opinion against the Knights Templar.

Finally, on March 22nd, 1312, Clement had issued the bull Vox in excelso, in which he permanently dissolved the order of the Knights Templar, although he did not condemn it as heretical, due to lack of convincing evidence. He judged, however, that the legal process had so discredited the order that there was no other solution.

Their fortune, on the other hand, after so many years of scandal and uncertainty for the order, had, to a great extent, been lost. Philippe managed to reap very few profits in the end and the Hospitaller knights received even less when the papal bull Ad providam was issued by Clement ten years later.

As for the leaders of the order, on May 6th, 1312 Clement issued the bull entitled Considerantes dudum, which said that their fate would be decided by the Pope himself.

Thus, most Brothers who survived finally received good treatment in the end since they willingly, of course, submitted to the authority of the Church and were permitted to stay in their former commanderies, and even get pensions in some cases. In any case, judges in all the trials of Knights Templar that took place outside France and Germany decided that the order was innocent, so Brothers were spared.

The last act of the drama was played out on a small island in the Seine. It had filled Philippe and the entire Christian world with sadness. There in March 1314, Jacques de Molay and Geoffroy de Charney, the last prisoners, who were also members of Fede Santa, having proclaimed their innocence and refusing to submit to the authority of the Church, were burnt at the stake as heretics so that, the prosecution maintained, their heretic souls could be purified.

As the flames consumed De Molay, it is said that he called his accusers to answer to God within a year for their shameful actions and defamation of the order.

Indeed, eight days later Nogaret died, Clement passed away a month later and the king had an accident while hunting, in November of the same year, which, in the end, proved fatal. Those, however, who were present at the death of the last Knights Templar, collected their ashes and saved them as a relic, now convinced of the order's innocence.

After the Knights Templar' Grand Master had been burnt at the stake, Philippe decided that the bonds that tied him to the order were now completely broken. He was no longer a Knight Templar, but neither was he happy as a Hospitaller. His old order, and with it Fede Santa, had now died, at least for him and most people. He had, therefore, made up his mind. He still remembered, word for word, the heated argument he had had with Foulques, in April of that year when he had decided to divulge his thoughts, that morning, in his office:

"Brother, I am not happy."

That was how Philippe had started their discussion.

"I can see that and I understand why, Brother. Believe in time. It will slowly heal all the wounds of the past," Foulques had replied to him comfortingly.

"That is not my problem. I'm tired of being a knight. I want a change in my life. I am tired, brother. Very tired." Foulques eyes had grown wide when he heard this and he had tried to lift Philippe's spirits:

"Perhaps we have all grown tired, but our service to God never ends. There will always be reasons for us to fight, Brother. Don't give up…"

"Brother… there is something I haven't told you…" Philippe had said contritely, lowering his eyes and fixing them to the ground.

"While I was in Paris, I met a woman."

Foulques had almost had a stroke and had said to Philippe, severely:

"A woman? You didn't break our vows!"

"I did!" Philippe had replied quietly, taking his eyes off the ground, aware that an outburst was about to follow:

"How? Have you no principles? How could you have done such a thing! Brother, I am so disappointed in you! You know how how strongly I feel about such matters!"

Philippe had then got up and taken Foulques, who had turned his back to him, by the shoulders and said to him firmly:

"Brother, I am not like you. I never was. You know that well, all the years you have known me. I am no longer not cut out to be a knight, or a monk. I am tired. And it's not only that. All these years I have tried so hard to forget her, but I can't. I feel incomplete without her! The only thing I ask of you is that you accept my resignation from the order and allow me to work, simply and humbly, as your groom so that I can write to her and, if she hasn't forgotten me either, she can come here and we can get married! Please! This is all I need be happy!"

He had paused briefly, looking his friend in the eye, and gone on to say:

"And if she hasn't forgotten me either, then I believe that it is God's will that we should be together!"

"From knight to servant groom?" Foulques had replied, furious. "Brother, what are you saying? You, who have fought the Infidels in so many battles? How could that ever happen?"

Yet, in the end, Foulques had given in. In fact he could do no otherwise, as much as he disagreed with Philippe and as much as what he wanted seemed unthinkable to him. He loved Philippe and deep down he wanted him to be happy. So, in the end, he made him a groom and let him write to Giselle. Philippe was now a happy man.

"I want to come down, dad!" the little boy's voice suddenly roused Philippe from his thoughts as they had reached the entrance of the castle and the guard nodded him in, recognising him as one of the many servants who worked at the castle every day.

The little boy ran into the yard and headed towards the stables. He bumped into Foulques, who was coming out at the same time. The Grand Master lifted Jocelyn up in the air and smiling broadly, said:

"Welcome! Good Morning! So, child, how many of your enemies did you kill to-day?"

"One hundred!" the little one shouted excitedly and went on happily:

"When I grow up, uncle Foulques, I will become a knight like you! Won't I?"

"Yes, my boy, like me and your father!"

"So my father was also a knight?" the child asked puzzled.

"Of course! He often won at sword-play too!" Foulques replied, laughing and giv-ing Philippe a knowing look. Philippe, took the little boy by the shoulders and gently raised him up a little, saying to him calmly

"We shall see when you grow up. Now go and play." Foulques put the little boy onto the ground and he at once disappeared into the stables to see the horses. Then Foulques' eyes met those of Philippe. He smiled at him and said to him:

"Groom, don't think you've got out of it! I will be expecting you at noon for a re-turn bout at sword-play."

"It would be a great honour, my Lord Grand Master! I am looking forward to it!"

Then the former Knight Templar entered the stables. His eyes fell on little Jocelyn, who was playing a little further off with two small foals, and a tender smile at once crossed his face. He took a brush and at once began to stroke Foulques' horse.

Behind him, in the open door, he sensed someone looking at him. He turned his head, without stopping work, and saw Foulques smiling at him. He nodded and then smiled, still stroking the horse. Foulques walked away, raising his hand in salute.

Historical notes

As a lover of history and historical truth, I would like to draw, for anyone interested, the fine line between fact and fiction, which always exists in a historical novel.

Philippe de Ridefort is an imaginary person, so is Jocelyn de Ridefort and, of course, Francois and Giselle. The supposed distant uncle, Gerard de Ridefort actually was a Grand Master of the Knights Templar from 1185 to 1189.

Foulques de Villaret and his uncle Guillaume de Villaret are also real historical figures, who served as Grand Masters for the order of the Hospitaller knights from 1305 to 1319 and from 1296 to 1305 respectively.

The names of the Grand Masters of the Knights Templar order referred to in the text, as well as the years during which they served as Grand Masters, are also real. The names of the simple knights who appear in the novel are fictional, except for the names of the four Knights Templar who denied, when the order was prosecuted, all the charges that had been made against them and the two knights that supported the order after that.

All the information and the dates given about the battles between Crusaders and Muslims, the sieges of cities and crusades are real. Wherever there is anachronism for the sake of the narration it is stated in a footnote.

I have also tried to describe, as best as possible, life in Outremer, the knights' castles and the living conditions at that time. In my efforts to do this I found the wonderful work in three volumes "A History of the Crusades" by Steven Runciman valuable. Other very useful tools were the book "The Crusades through Arab Eyes" by Amin Maalouf and "The Epic of the Crusades" by Rene Grousset.

As for the initiation ceremony into the Order of Knights Templar, it is absolutely factual. The Grand Master's funeral and the election of a new person for an office, as I have described them, concern the order of the Knights Templar, but in the text they are presented as those of to the Knights Hospitaller, to serve the narrative. The two orders, in any case, followed similar procedures.

Gilles Aicelin, who served as a royal Keeper of the Royal Seal was also a real person- although his meeting with Philippe was, of course, imaginary. His resignation from that specific office actually took place, as described in the text. The whole story of the arrest of the Knights Templar with the involvement of Pope Clement and Philippe the Fair is completely true, as are the events concerning the Order of the Knights Hospitaller after the Fall of Acre.

As for the information about the orders, the story of the events after the Fall of Acre and the events, step by step, which led to the Knights Templars' arrest, the following books were very helpful: ""La vie quotidienne des templiers au XIIIe siecle" by Georges Bordonove , "The Templars and the Assassins: the Militia of Heaven " by James Wasserman, "Το Τάγμα των Τευτόνων, Η δράση των βορείων σταυροφόρων στους Αγίους τόπους και στη Βαλτική θάλασσα" Ector-Evangelos Charatsis, "Τα ιπποτικά τάγματα" Georgios Cladakis, and "The Templars" by Piers Paul Read. A great deal of of information about the descriptions of places was also taken from the encyclopedia "Papyrus Larousse Britannica".

As for the secret organization Fede Santa, it is generally accepted today by most scholars that there actually was an offshoot within the Templar's order with "heretical", for their time, beliefs. These beliefs were the result of seminal contact on the part of some knights with the mysticism of the East and Ancient Greek philosophy, as passed on by Arab scholars. The initiated Templars were a minority in the order and, of course, did not all hold such, unconventional, for the time, beliefs.

The ideas of the members of this secret organization could just as well be those developed in the historical essay of philosophy and classic civilization byTimothy Freke and Peter Gandy "The Jesus Mysteries", where conclusions are drawn and evidence is presented about Christianity's relationship with the pagan world, which remain, to a great extent, unknown to the general public.

Finally, matters such as what the legendary "treasure" of the Templars finally was, and what happened to it in the end , as well as the supposed survival of certain Templars or their heterodox views within Rosicrucian or Masonic groups, are still unsolved mysteries of history, at least for the time being. While, therefore, it has been shown that some Templars held unorthodox, for their time, beliefs, there is no evidence as to what exactly they were. What's more, the fact that the "treasure" of the Templar's was precious manuscripts is simply my opinion, held on the basis of what I feel is most likely to be true. From there on anyone can let their imagination run free and draw their own conclusions, until, and, of course if, some irrefutable evidence comes to light about all this.

ENDNOTES

1 The Mamluks were slaves in the service of the Ayyubid Sultanate in Egypt and Syria. In 1250 they managed to gain power. The word "mamluk" means slave in Arabic. Baybars the First was the founder of the dynasty of the same name.

2 This was established by St. Bernard of Klervo (1090-1153) and regulated all the aspects of the knights' lives. The practice of shaving the head was adopted by military orders for purposes of hygiene.

3 At that time the Grand Master was called "Lord" and not "Grand", as we call him today.

4 This refers to the events of 1187 and the Battle of Hattin, with sad consequences for the Christians, which will be considered much later.

5 An expression used during the initiation ceremony of a new member of the order.

6 Sergeants were warriors in the order, or grooms, lower in rank than knights and not of noble birth.

7 This is a kiss that someone inferior gives to his master and is part of feudal ritual. The oath of fidelity (Hommage) was made by all the knights to their noble masters and by nobles to the king. Thus this is something related solely to the order and has no homosexual connotation.

8 The order had two categories of groom: firstly, the grooms that were proper members of the order and served as inferior sergeants who specialized in horses, and secondly grooms that served the order as employees, were paid for their services and, of course, did not live in the order's accommodation.

9 Six o'clock in the morning.

10 9am, 12 noon and 3 pm respectively.

11 This was the name given to the Frankish possessions in the Middle East.

12 The orders of the Templar and the Hospitaller knights were divided into languages depending on their nationality, for example, the language of Provence, the language of Aragon etc.

13 After Cyprus was taken from the Byzantine Empire in 1191 during the Third Crusade by Richard the Lionheart, many Kings of Acre chose to reside there, rather than Acre, where they appointed a bailli, or commander.

14 The simple punishment meant that the person punished would have to do chores that were considered demeaning - for example cleaning garlic and garlic

grass, lighting the fire, loading the cart etc. More severe punishments included flogging, a temporary removal of the habit for a year and becoming a member of the class of servants. The harshest punishment was expulsion from the order while the lightest one included only prayers and prostrations.

15 An area of north Italy.

16 Otherwise known as the Nizari. An offshoot of Shia Muslims created in 1095. It was a sect dedicated to Hassan based at Alamut Castle in today's Iran. They became known for the politically motivated murders they carried out and, despite the fact that their victims were not as many as believed, the word "assassination", meaning political murder, has passed into the English language. The origin of the word is not clear. It is believed, however, to originate either from the Arabic word "assassin", which means guards, or from their founder, Hassan, the word "hashashins" meaning Hassan's followers". According to another theory, the word comes from hasish, which the sect used extensively.

17 The so-called "Old Man of the Mountain" (1162-1192). He was one of the most important Sevener Shias, who was accepted by the whole Muslim world. He was the leader of the assassins of Syria, highly educated and many attributed magical powers to him.

18 "Every perfect gift"

19 "The Year of Our Lord"

20 According to the Byzantines, who placed the beginning of the world in 5508 BC. Later the Irishman James Ussher(1581-1656), Archbishop of Armagh, North Ireland placed the beginning of the world on the 23rd of October, 4404 BC, Sunday at 9 am.

21 A seaside town near Gaza in today's Israel.

22 There is doubt today about whether this episode actually took place, as it is only described by William, Bishop of Tyre, who is always hostile towards the Knights Templar. It might also be a distortion on the part of the other Latin leaders of the siege who came in for criticism "because they had not followed the Knights Templar on their raid". Whatever the case, the slur spread widely in the West and tarnished the order's reputation.

23 "Holy faith", a branch of the order of the Templar order believed to have preserved and protected secret ancient knowledge, evolving into the Rosicrucians in the 17th century.

24 This was a common accusation the Muslims made towards the Christians at the time. They meant that Christians were in reality polytheists because of the concept of the Triune God, a concept which they never managed to reconcile with the Oneness of Allah.

25 The Krak's Arabic name.

26 There is no other God but Allah and Muhammed is his prophet.

27 See below for this battle.

28 This was the ninth crusade of 1271-2. The term crusade had not yet been created. However, the cross as a symbol was established by Pope Eugene III during his second crusade in 1147. We come across the use of the word crusade in a English

literary text by William Shenstone in 1757.

29 We praise you.

30 Emir of the Syrian troops since Baybars was Sultan. He became Sultan in 1279, dethroning the legitimate successors of the latter. He rallied the Muslims in his effort to drive the Crusaders from the Middle East, until his sudden death in 1290.

31 This refers to the Fall of Jerusalem in 1099, with which Crusade I (1096-1099) ended. During this the crusaders had indiscriminately slaughtered Muslims and Jews, even women and children, that had taken refuge in mosques or synagogues respectively.

32 This refers to the taking of Baghdad in February 1258 by the Mongolian army of Hulagu where, within forty days, its inhabitants, numbering approximately eighty thousand, wre slaughtered.

33 This took place on 4th July 1187 and led to the loss of Jerusalem on the part of the Crusaders.

34 He was born in 1137/38 in Takrit, Mesopotamia and died in Damascus in 1193. He was a Sultan of Egypt, Syria, Yemen and Palestine from 1174. He was the founder of the dynasty of the Ayyubids, later succeeded by the Mamluks .

35 Louis IX, King of France (1215-1270), son of Blanche of Castile and King Louis VIII the Lion. He became King in 1226. He declared the seventh and eighth crusade in 1249 and 1270 respectively. He was particularly pious and dear to the people and merciless towards the Cathar heretics in the South of France. In 1297 he was de-clared a saint by Pope Boniface VIII.

36 This refers to the seventh crusade of 1248-1250.

37 The Knights of St John traditionally maintained relationships of trust with the Genoese, while the same was true of the Templars with the Venetians.

38 This was common practice amongst the nobility of the time, who hoped for the salvation of their souls through donations to orders or monasteries.

39 Rulers with Greek culture who reigned in the 4th and 3rd century BC, during the Hellenistic years

40 This refers to the earthquake of 1274. In the beginning of the 14th century another earthquake took place and, from that time, the building was probably de-stroyed since it is not mentioned by chroniclers or, those that do, refer to it as in ruins.

41 Namely Judaism, Christianity and Islam.

42 King of the Hellenistic Ptolemaic dynasty of Egypt ,who ruled from 246 to 222 BC.

43 The only part of the Serapium that still remains standing today.

44 Roman Emperor who lived from 284 until 305 AD.

45 King of the Hellenistic dynasty of the Ptolemies of Egypt who ruled from 328 to 285 BC.

46 In 48 BC, when Caesar's fleet was torched in the harbour of the city by Ptolemy XIII's general Achillas, and the fire spread to land and to the library.

47 Roman Emperor from 211 to 217 AD

48 In 391 AD.

49 In 641 AD.

50 Belief in the union of the Christ's divine and human natures into one single nature. This was first put forward by Eutyches of Constantinople. It was rejected by the Synod of 448 in Constantinople and by the Fourth Ecumenical Council of Chalcedon in 451. However, this belief continued to be held by some communities in the Middle East.

51 A pejorative term used for western Catholics by the Greeks, which originated in former's use of unleavened bread in Holy Communion. Mutual hostility between Catholics and Orthodox reached its peak after the schism of 1054 and the sacking of Constantinople in 1204 by the Crusaders

52 Contrary to the mistaken belief, probably arising from historical epic movies like Ben-Hur, the use of slaves in galleys began in the Middle Ages and not in Ancient Greek or Roman times. In ancient times those rowing in galleys did usually come from the lowest classes, but were normally paid.

53 A term that refers to the countries of North Africa, that is Algeria, Morocco, Libya and Egypt, where many Saracen, and later Turkish , pirates - a veritable scourge for the people of the Mediterranean, had their bases.

54 An area in South-Eastern Italy.

55 This is an actual amulet from the 3rd century AD, when paganism had not yet been eradicated completely. It was in the Museum of Berlin up until the Second World War, when it disappeared.

56 Grand Master of the Knights Templar, 1156-1169

57 Grand Master of the Knights Templar, 1149-1152

58 A dictum of Monoimos, handed down to us by Hippolytus.

59 These are the so-called Gnostic Gospels which were almost unknown to researchers until their accidental discovery in 1945 by an Egyptian peasant in Nag Hammadi. Until then researchers' knowledge of the Gnostics had been limited to what their opponents, the scholastics, have passed down to us.

60 The first were followers of a religious movement in the 6th century BC who were linked to the Thracian Orpheus, and the second were followers and successors of Pythagoras (around 580-500 BC) who formed a separate school which acted as a catalyst in the development of Western philosophy, mathematics and mysticism.

61 Neoplatonist philosopher from Syria who lived in the 3rd century BC.

62 A philosophical school that developed chiefly during the Hellenistic period. Its followers professed that man should live in harmony with nature, dedicated to the state. They placed emphasis on Man's essential value, moral values and spiritual tranquillity.

63 Lucius Seneca Annaios (4-65 AC) was a Roman Stoic philosopher, politician, orator, playwriter and poet. Hewas Nero's teacher, on whose orders he committed suicide.

64 Lived around c.455 to c.360 BC.

65 Ancient Greek city in Sicily

66 The only Jewish historian that refers to Jesus is Flavius Josephus (around 37-100 AD), but those extracts that make such references are held to be forgeries by all

serious scholars of today , as they are not in his style of writing. They were probably been added around the 4th century AD by the great propagandist of the Roman Church Bishop Eusebius, to whom many forgeries and conversions of texts of the early years of Christianity have been attributed

67 Contemporary scholars have detected such additions and have also proved that the epistles of Peter, James and John are forgeries. Moreover, from the thirteen epistles of Paul, only seven are thought to be authentic. Those thought mainly to be responsible for these forgeries are tEusebius, Irenaeus, Hippolytus and Tertullian.

68 Apart from "cleaning up " the Gospels in the 5th century AD, Pope Leo the Great ordered texts that referring to mythical feats of Thomas, Andrew, Peter and Paul, that is other Acts of the Apostles, to be burnt as heretical.

69 A dualist Christian movement that developed mainly in southern France and owes its origins to the early years of Christianity. They rejected certain sacraments, such as Baptism and the Eucharist, and would not venerate the cross. Those who received the "sacrament" of consolamentum became perfecti, meaning they had reached the highest level. They lived in great simplicity as vegetarians and avoided procreation. They were also known as Albigensians, and Patarini in France.

70 This is known as the Albigensian Crusade. It was declared by Pope Innocent III 1198-1216) in 1209, with Simon de Montfort at its head. Battles took place for about forty years during which southern France was laid waste and thousands of "heretics" were massacred. In the city of Béziers only, 15000 people were slaughtered en masse. The last Albigensian castle to surrender was Montségur which fell in 1244. However, what Saint Bernard of Clairvaux, a man who enjoyed considerable prestige amongst orthodox Christians of his time, has to say about the Cathars is worthy of note: "No sermons are more Christian than theirs, and their morals are pure."

71 An area corresponding to parts of Poland and Lithuania today

72 We cannot be certain who did this - Embriaco or the Venetians

73 Commander

74 It is true that this particular Grand Master was known for his machinations on other occasions. As for this particular incident, however, which sources tell us actually took place, no one could accuse the Grand Master of the Knights Templar of intrigue, as proved later.

75 Excerpt from the apocryphal "Acts of John", which describes the initiation ceremony into the Mysteries performed by Christ and his student- helpers.

76 Excerpt from the text referred to above.

77 As above.

78 He is referring to the so-called Sicilian Vespers, the rebellion of the Sicilians, probably at the instigation of the Byzantine emperor Michael Palaeologos VIII on 30th March 1282, against the people of Anzou, who had violently conquered the island led by Charles d' Anzou. They were so named because the slaughter of the French by the Sicilians began in Palermo at the time when the bells were ringing for Vespers.

79 He is referring to the Byzantine emperor Andronikos I Palaeologos (1282-1328) and the Holy Roman Emperor Rudolf I, the first king of Germany from the

Habsburg dynasty (reigning 1239-1291).

80 Common to all crusaders' accounts are constant accusations levelled at the Greeks for their treachery during the crusades. It is true that the Byzantines often became allies with the Muslims, but this had been part of an established tactic used by the Byzantines to maintain the balance of power in the East for many years before the Crusaders came, something that the latter could never understand. As for the maritime republics, they often put profit above their political interests, and whenever they helped the crusaders, it always brought them some important benefit in trade.

81 This is the unsuccessful, as we shall see later , tenth crusade of 1290-1291.

82 He means the Byzantine Empire. The term "Byzantine" was introduced by Hieronymus Wolf, who used it in 1562 for the first time. It was established the next century by Philippe Labe.

83 Living in the 7th century AD

84 The guard's reaction should not be considered extreme, particularly in a city that was expecting to be besieged by the Muslims. Spies from both sides were something very common on both sides and there were no few cities in the Middle ages that fell because of treachery.

85 This was a sortie that actually took place on this particular date, and there were many Christian casualties, coming about , unbelievably, for the very reason described.

86 The sources tell us that this particular episode, the unfortunate proposal of surrender made to the Sultan by the Christians, really took place. However, it is still unknownwho launched the boulder onto Al-Ashraf's tent at the time the negotiations were taking place . The explanation offered later is fictional.

87 For reasons of humility, the Grand Master wore no badge or different clothing that would make them stand out from the rest of their Brother knights , except maybe for some item of jewellery in times of peace.

88 The Hospitaller knights originally wore black robes with a white cross (the Teutonic knights wore a white robe with a black cross embroidered on it throughout their existence). From 1259 only sergeants wore a black robe and the knights adopted the red robe with a white cross, for which they became known later on in the sieges of Rhodes and Malta. However, since robes of two different colours caused confusion in battle, from1278 knights and sergeants wore the red robe in battle and everyone wore the black robe in times of peace in their monasteries

89 Born 1232 in Majorca, stoned to death in North Africa in 1315.

90 Taking place in 1274.

91 The Byzantine Emperor Avdronikos II Paleologos, who ruled from 1282 to 1328.

92 The Hospitallers, unlike the Knights Templar, who never had a particularly large fleet, had turned to the sea very early on. After settling on Rhodes and then on Malta, the order would mainly engage in operations of piracy in its battle against Islam, operations that would reach their peak after Constantinople fell into Ottoman hands in 1453.

93 Today the Palais de Justice in Paris.

94 Sources tell us that Esquieu's audience with Philippe probably took place in 1305, but an anachronism is used to serve narrative.

95 The canonisation of Louis IX took placeon August 11th, 1297, during Philippe the Fair's reign within the context of the long-standing dispute between Pope Boniface VIII and Philippe. The canonisation, which took place at Philippe's insistence, was a concession made on the part of the Pope to bring this long dispute, relating to financial matters but also matters of power, between the two men to an end.

96 Philippe was facing severe financial problems, firstly because of the war with England, and secondly because of the debt he had inherited from his father, since the latter had long been at war with Aragon, financially exhausting the kingdom. The debt was around 1.5 million old French coins. So between 1295 and 1306 the currency was devalued by 200%. When Philippe decided that the country would go backt o the old currency, it lost two thirds of its value and the people rebelled, forcing the king to take refuge in the Temple of Paris. The riot in fact occurred in June 1306, but the anachronism serves the narrative.

97 Clement V had been elected Pope the year before with clear support from Philippe and was considered by all his contemporaries a puppet of the king. The former bishop of Bordeaux, with the secular name Bertrand de Got, lived up to expectations and brought in the so-called "Babylonian Captivity" of the Papacy in 1308, with Popes residing in Lyon until 1378. Clement V himself never set foot in Rome as a Pope.

98 Les Halles was the central market of Paris from 1183 to 1969.

99 The famous Louvre Museum of today would later be built on the same spot after many additions and renovations had been made to the original building.

100 The University of Paris, one of the oldest in the world, was established around 1200. In 1257 Robert de Sorbon founded the Sorbonne college, with which the University was later identified.

101 The Latin name for the Mediterranean Sea used by the Romans, which continued to be in use in the Middle Ages.

102 The Knights Hospitaller knights in fact entered Rhodes after the exhausted inhabitants surrendered on that same day, but a year later. This is another anachronism introduced for the sake of the narrative.

103 He is referring to the arrest of all the Jews in France by Philippe in July 1306. It was a means of adding large amounts of money in confiscated funds to the empty royal treasury and wrote off many debts the king owed to many Jewish lenders.

104 Around 9 pm.

105 Common popular fiction in the Middle Ages. They were adapted versions of ancient Celtic myths that had already been standardized in the versions we know today from the 11th-13th century. Much later they became the material for new poems, theatrical plays or even operas, in the form of different versions (Tennyson, Wagner etc.)

106 According to the original story in its most complete German version (by Gottfried von Strassburg c.1200), the two young people drank a magic potion that

gave them undying passion for one another. The story, however, has a tragic ending, since Tristan is fatally wounded by a poisoned arrow and dies in the arms of Isolde, who subsequently also dies.

107 The work of an unknown poet cited in "La vie quotidienne des templiers au XIIIe siecle" by Georges Bordonove